THE HAMMER FALLS

To Richard,
Thank you so much for helping make this happen.
You rock.

THE HAMMER FALLS

BY

TRAVIS HEERMANN

BEAR PAW PUBLISHING
DENVER

Cover Designer: Dean Samed

TRADE PAPERBACK EDITION

ISBN 978-1-62225-429-3

Bear Paw Publishing
Denver, Colorado, USA
www.bearpawpublishing.com

Acknowledgements and Thanks

The author would like to thank everyone who had a hand in helping The Hammer come to life: the strange toads of the Odyssey 2009 when the "The Hammer" was just a little scrub short story: Kaalii Cargill, Arthur "Buck" Dorrance, Jason Heller, Brad Hafford, Kevin Jewell, Corry Lee, Karen McKenzie (who doubled-down with critiquing an early novel draft), Kelli Meyer, Lisa Poh, Jenny Rappaport, Mary Rodgers, Peter Simonson, Meagan Spooner, Sharon Sun, Alex Wolfe, along with the indomitable Jeanne Cavelos and the discriminating Susan Sielinski. Helping The Hammer charge more fully into the world were Quincy J. Allen, Lou Berger, Gene Bild, Amanda Ferrell, Chanel Heermann, Peter J. Mancini, Aaron Michael Ritchey, Holly Roberds, and Gina Marie Vick. Thanks also to John Helfers and Colleen Kuehne for the final cuts and polish.

Dedication

To Chanel,
whose tireless support,
in spite of crazy schedules
and endless uncertainty,
makes this amazing ride possible

WARM-UP

CHAPTER ONE

Horace "The Hammer" Harkness stared the Fight Doctor in the face. "What the hell are you talking about? I've died twenty-seven times."

"I'm sorry to be the bearer of bad news, Hammer."

Horace sat up on the exam table and rested his forehead in his hands. If he wasn't feeling like he'd just had his guts strewn in ribbons across the floor, he might have put this little man through the nearest cinder-block wall. The shadows under the overhead light bank were stark. The incomprehensible EKG line scrawled across the med-scanner. The air in the exam room was thick with the smells of sweat and muscle ointment, styptic powder and blood.

The Fight Doctor peeled the scanner leads away from Horace's flesh, little stings of pain. "You're the only pit fighter ever to survive to fifty." The round-faced, round-bodied man cleared his throat and wiped sweat from his forehead. "Truth is you've spent too many years in the minor franchises, and regenites can only repair so much of that kind of damage."

"Why now?" The door of the small room was closed. No one outside would hear, but someone could certainly be listening—the sponsors, the promoter. Too much money on the line for surprises like this.

"Frankly, because you have the pain tolerance of a mammoth, and that should indicate to you how bad it is. I'm surprised you haven't keeled over permanently before now. I'm afraid you're off the card."

"Whatever happened to 'the show must go on'?"

The Fight Doctor sniffed. "Nobody wants to see a sick old man die, Hammer."

Horace slammed his chitin-hardened fist into the exam table. The biometric readouts flickered with the force of his blow. "What the fuck am I supposed to do? Do you know how many favors I had to cash in just to be here tonight? Do you have any idea how much all those treatments cost me?" Not to mention how much money he'd had to borrow for them.

The Fight Doctor was right about too many years in the minor franchises. In the minors where sponsorship was as thin as a pimp's word, even the bonuses from victories and lethalities often didn't cover the cost of regeneration. Healing too many wounds naturally had taken its toll.

"Sorry, Hammer. I don't make the rules." Clutching his clip-pad like a shield to his chest, the Fight Doctor edged back.

"The fuck you don't!" Horace's spiked boot sent the medical monitor spinning away to crash into the wall.

"Hammer, please, calm down. If you die—"

"What's one more time? After fifteen years, I'm the Main Fucking Event!"

Twenty-seven times the world had gone black. Sometimes it was slow, like going to sleep, other times in an explosion of pain. And never a white light to be seen.

The Fight Doctor rubbed sweat off his bald pate. "Look, I know it means a lot to you—"

"It means a lot to the thousands out there who remember, who came to see *me*! Me and a few guys like me built this fucking sport! Do you want to go out there and tell them they can't see The Hammer's comeback just because he had a dizzy spell during warm-up?"

"I'd hardly call it a dizzy spell. And this time could be for good—"

"What's that?" Horace cupped a hand behind his ear.

"—known each other a long time—"

"I can't understand you."

"—But—"

"You got Regenecorp's cock in your mouth. I'm surprised you don't have lockjaw by now." With a swat of his paw, Horace cleared a tray of instruments and bottles. He would never, ever admit to Ferris Wilton, MD—a.k.a. the Fight Doctor, complete with action figure, trading card, and interactive animated comic book—that moving his left elbow just right sent pain up his arm that would incapacitate lesser men. Back in '62, at Trauma in Tokyo XIV, Andre the Titan had thought it should bend just as far in the wrong direction.

"You can't intimidate me into letting you fight tonight," the Fight Doctor said, "not this time." But the quaver in his voice said precisely the opposite.

If Horace didn't fight tonight, his life might just as well be over anyway.

He stood to his full height, his head brushing the underside of the light fixture in the center of the room. "Then let me put it to you this way. I'll sign whatever the fuck you want me to sign. In blood if you want. When I'm dead, there isn't a soul on this fucking planet gonna give a shit about who's liable. But I gotta fight The Freak tonight."

The Fight Doctor sighed a little too deeply. "I'll see what I can do, Horace."

"You do that."

The doctor trundled out.

The pain in Horace's chest and left shoulder returned, a deep, throbbing ache. He rubbed his chest as he sat on the table again, reached for his duffel bag, and fished out his netlink. The icons on the screen were too small for his meaty fingers, but he managed to snag the one he wanted—a picture of Lilly and him, silken cheek to tattooed jowl, both smiling under a rain of sparkling light and neon. He had never seen eyes so big and brown before, the kind of eyes that could make a man forget his pain.

If only they didn't have walls behind them.

He felt a stab not unlike a blade punching through his sternum. He thumbed the *Call* icon. The netlink pinged. Pinged again.

The connection clicked, and a man's voice said, "Titty Twister."

"Hey, Max. This is Hammer."

"Hammer! My man! How's it hangin'!" The beat of background music pulsed behind Max's voice.

"To the knee, brother. Listen, I need to talk to Lilly."

"She ain't here. Ain't seen her since last week."

"Last week?" Horace rubbed the old, deep scar on his forehead, where Gaston "The Freak" Rousseau's kukri had nearly taken the top of his skull clean off almost twenty years ago. That had been death number fourteen. Lost a few childhood memories from that one, too.

Max said, "Yeah, don't know what to tell you. Hey, I tried to get tickets for tonight, man, but no dice. We're gonna have the pay-per-view up on the big screen though."

"It'll be a hell of a show. Listen, if you hear from her, tell her to call me. It's important."

"You got it. She have your number?"

"Yeah, she's got my number all right." Another stab.

"Kick Freak's ass, man!"

"You got it, brother." Horace disconnected and tossed the netlink into his bag.

The doctor came back with a netpad. "Do you want to review the terms?"

"Give me the fucking thing."

The doctor handed him the tablet with a trembling hand, and Horace pressed his thumb across the screen to sign his consent.

The thunder of the seventy thousand fans filtered through several meters of concrete into his dressing room, and the heavy beat of the music pounded on his skull like a fist. He hadn't fought in front of a crowd this large in over a decade. It had been a decline by centimeters over the years; the attendance at his bouts dwindling from tens of thousands in coliseums like this to a few thousand in the B-list stables to a few hundred at venues like the Rumble in Rockport, where there weren't even bonuses for getting a clean, resurrectable kill, or worse, they prohibited kills, which never brought in the same kind of crowds. Sometimes the purse didn't even pay the rent. In the big venues, there was always someone new on the rise, the hungry young ones clawing for the spotlight. The trouble with up-and-comers was they created just as many down-and-outers.

The screen on the wall came alive with the start of the broadcast.

"Live from Caesar's Coliseum in Las Vegas, Death Match Unlimited presents Fury Dome XXIV!"

The camera swept over the fighting pit in the center of the coliseum up toward the rows of cheering fans.

"Ten spectacular bouts! Twenty bloodthirsty warriors! And the rematch twenty years in the making between two of the greatest pit fighters in history!"

Las Vegas was one of the places where money gathered like iron filings to a magnet. The scent of hotdogs and burgers filtered on the breeze through the tunnels, all of them sold at sky-high prices, even though they probably weren't even real meat. Anyone who could afford a ticket to this event could afford those prices. Around the city, labor-class bars hosted pay-per-view events where the ragged-hemmed attendees would be lucky to get a cupful of popcorn.

His netlink chimed at him. Lilly's face leaped into mind, but as he fished the netlink out, he saw that the incoming address was blocked.

He answered it. "Yeah, who is this?"

"Hammer. Dmitri."

"You're calling me now?"

The voice was thick with a Russian accent mixed with snake oil. "A reminder from Papa—"

"Listen, asshole. I told you, I'll have your money tonight."

"I know you're good for it, Hammer. It's just that Papa, he gets nervous, you know? Too many guys smarter than you have tried to fuck him. Papa fucks back a whole lot harder. We'll have car waiting outside. Get 'lost,' and there aren't many places Hammer Harkness can hide, you know?"

"I'll be out back, the guy with blood all over him."

"Watch your mouth, smartass. Regenites can't put your head back on. How's that stripper you go to see so often? What's her name, Daisy? Do you know where she is right now? I do."

Horace bit back a threat, then disconnected and tossed the netlink into his bag again. The Russians owned Vegas. Loansharking, protection rackets, skimming the gambling profits, all of it. The word was that the Russian syndicate was not to be trifled with, but there had been nowhere else for him to go. Such gangster connections were part and parcel of any prominent fighter's life as the odds-makers crawled out from the cracks in the mortar and asked for a few "favors" here and there. But

Horace had been around enough to know the score, to watch his back. And if making a deal with Dmitri Mogilevich was the only way for him to have one last shot at the big time, it was a gamble he willingly made.

If he won tonight, the purse would be enough to pay off the Russians and grow himself a new heart. If he lost, he would still be able to pay off the Russians, with maybe enough money left for cab fare home, but the residuals would keep him afloat for the next couple of months. In an event as big as this one, Regenecorp, Death Match Unlimited's chief sponsor, furnished the regenerations for winner and loser.

His ravaged knees creaked like dry steel knuckles as he stepped into the hallway. His stomach still felt queasy.

A lanky, buck-toothed, teenage kid squeezed against the wall to let him by in the narrow concrete tunnel. The kid's eyes glowed with reverence. "Go get him, Hammer. Hammer Time!" He clutched his fists together above his head into the Thunder Hammer.

"Thanks, brother." He stopped and extended his hand to the young man.

A grin spread like sunrise across the kid's face as he shook. "Can I have your autograph?"

Horace's hand engulfed his. "Sure."

"Awesome! My dad always talks about seeing you and The Freak in L.A."

"Which time?"

"I don't remember, but you lost that one. He was rooting for you, though." The kid pulled a Death Match Unlimited rag-mag out of his back pocket, this week's issue with a montage of twenty-year-old animated holos depicting the last time The Hammer and The Freak faced each other. The caption read "DEATH MATCH OF THE CENTURY PART II." The kid said, "Sign it to Larry. That's my dad."

"You tell your old man to keep raising you right." Horace scribbled his signature on the cover with the gel-tip from his pocket.

"Thanks, Hammer! He'll be so stoked!"

"No problem, brother." They shook hands again. He had to be careful with the strength of his grip; he could crush a normal human's hand into crunchy red paste.

"Hammer Time!"

"Hammer Time," Horace said.

The teenager practically floated away.

Horace's netlink pinged. The screen showed an incoming address he didn't recognize. He answered.

"Hey, Hammer, what's up?" Lilly's voice, neutral, polite, without video.

His heart skipped a beat.

She sniffed. "I heard you were trying to reach me." There was an unfamiliar tremor in her voice.

"Well, I—you crying or something?"

"You said it was important."

"It's just—where are you anyway? You okay? Are you safe? You don't sound like you."

"I'm fine. What's up?"

"Well, tonight's the big fight, me and Gaston. You know, the Coliseum, biggest in a long time, maybe ever, and I thought you might be able to come. I know it's been a while. I got a couple seats reserved, see, and—"

"Oh, Hammer, I told you—"

"Listen. I know. I get it. I, uh..." He leaned against the wall. "It would mean a lot if you was here tonight." A wave of dizziness washed over him. His heart rattled and strained against the inside of his ribcage, and something was cinching his lungs closed. He covered the netlink with his hand and gritted his teeth.

She sighed. "Hammer, I would like to come, it's sweet of you to ask, but I can't. Look, I gotta—"

"Just this one time."

The words seemed to hover on her lips for several seconds. "How do I find you?"

"I'll leave word with the guards at the back entrance to bring you to the locker room."

"No guarantees, Hammer. I'm kind of in the middle of something now."

"I get it."

"Bye, Hammer." The connection went dead.

"You ready to do this thing, stumpy?" Horace said, crossing Gaston's dressing room in three great strides.

"Fuck you and your 'stumpy,' eh?" Gaston The Freak Rousseau's voice sounded like he gargled with molten glass.

They clasped their leathered, meaty hands in a powerful grip. Then Gaston feinted a punch toward Horace's stomach, and Horace's combat instincts slapped it away before it registered in his mind.

"Oh ho! I didn't know fossils could move." Gaston only came up to Horace's sternum, but the fifteen-centimeter flaming-orange Mohawk made up some of the difference. The David-and-Goliath aspect of their comparative statures was one reason their matches had been so popular back in the day.

"You just keep right on thinking that," Horace said.

"By the way, my offer is still open. Come and help me groom young nipple-suckers for the pit."

"Thanks all the same, but I still don't speak Pussy."

"But it is the language of love! Speak *Français* and pussy rains from the heavens." Gaston made an expansive gesture toward the dull, concrete ceiling. "You've met my wife."

Horace rubbed his jaw with a grin. "Maybe there is something to that...."

The air smelled of rubbing alcohol, ointment, and petroleum jelly, and his head again brushed the bank of light fixtures above, making their shadows sway. The cinder-block walls were painted white, but somehow started to gray. The light dimmed.

Gaston's voice sounded like it was coming through a steel culvert. "You okay, Hark?"

CHAPTER TWO

A voice floated into his consciousness that he hadn't heard in far too long. "What is your malfunction, pansy ass? Lying down on the job?"

His labored heartbeat thundered so loud in his ears he could barely hear her voice. "Naw, Amanda darlin', I'm just resting."

"Get up, Horace."

"Not just yet. Need to rest a minute." His voice sounded farther away than hers.

An image of the most beautiful face he had ever seen swam through the gray fog. Long, sweeping, dark curls, eyes like propane flames, and that silly golden tiara with the red star in the center.

He said, "Where you been all this time, darlin'?"

A warm, callused hand soft on his face. "You need to get up, baby. Right now."

"Just lay here a little longer."

"Now, fuck face."

"No need to get all hostile, darlin'. God, I missed you."

She swallowed hard, hovering over him. Had a tear just brushed his cheek? "Me, too."

"You never told me his name..."

Another voice intruded, male, familiar, nearer. "Hark, you need a doctor?"

"I know, baby," she said. "I couldn't."

"That was kinda mean, you know?"

"I'm sorry." Her voice receded as if through a thickening fog. Then she was gone.

"Hark, let me help you up, eh."

Horace felt himself lifted to his feet as if he was a doll.

Gaston's gravelly voice was clear. "There you go. Upright."

Horace rubbed his eyes and tried to clear his vision. The blood-thunder in his ears subsided to a distant storm. Another man was there. Horace managed to focus. "Why, Johnny Valentine, when did you get here?"

The massive shaven-headed warrior helped Gaston ease Horace against the prep table. "Freak here called me in. Y'all all right?"

"Just a little under the weather is all. Thanks, Johnny."

"Anything for you, Hammer."

"Listen, Johnny," Horace said, "your slot must be coming up soon. Me and The Freak here gotta go over the spots."

Johnny released Horace's right arm. "Yeah, number five on the card. Anything y'all need, just holler." He picked up his ceramic vibro-axe and headed for the door.

"Kick some ass, kid," Horace called after him.

The enormous axe man opened the door, then stood back as the familiar rattle and squeak of gurney and medical equipment whisked a fallen fighter to the infirmary. Through the open door, the smells of blood and viscera wafted into the room, mixing with the aromas of alcohol, oiled steel, and leather.

Valentine squeezed through the doorway and disappeared.

Gaston gripped Horace's shoulder. "That a drug reaction? Who were you talking to?"

Horace chose the easier question to answer. "Amanda Reckinwith. Her parents had a sick sense of humor. She tried to kill me once."

"Name's familiar...."

"Chromosome Clash III." The ladies had their own pit fighting circuits, with stars just as big as Horace and Gaston had been. "Amazing" Grace Benedict with her mug like a shaved gorilla; like Horace, she'd been one of the early adopters of gene-modding in the build and strength department. Then there were the tech-babes like Cassia "The Enlightened" Evajea, the sparkling assassin with coruscating lights embedded in her flesh.

Gaston's eyes brightened. "Yeah, she dressed up as a superhero."

Amanda had even licensed the tiara and lasso from the media company, except the tiara was titanium and the lasso was bioengineered spider silk laced with micro-razors. She'd nearly severed his left forearm with that lasso, and he'd taken her down by getting close enough to shatter her molded ceramic breastplate—and her ribcage—with a one-handed Thunder Hammer. Afterward, as they lay in the infirmary, waiting for their bodies to regenerate from the ghastly wounds they had given each other, they had shared a glance, then later a shower, then a solid month in Caesar's Palace StarTower, drunk on Dom Perignon, during which time she'd done her damnedest to wear him down to a nub. He'd had a hundred (and twelve?) groupies and pit girls—plus a few Fortune 500 CEOs and even a Siamese princess—in the fifteen years since then, but she had been the real deal. Tastes of strawberry lip gloss and the saltiness of her throat floated out of the dark.

Horace said, "She started hating me when she found out she was pregnant."

Gaston ran kielbasa-like fingers through the thick orange braids of his beard. "Always wondered why she quit. She was on top."

"I suggested an abortion if she was so sore about being disqualified, but..." He shrugged. Something in her had shifted, something biological, instinctive. "I wanted her to have the kid, you know? But she had to get away from the life. I couldn't quit back then any more than I can quit now." Horace took a deep breath and started circling the room, feeling his bearings return, thinking about all the messages and phone calls that had gone unanswered. "Back in '68, I got an envelope with a Singapore postmark but no return address."

"Back in '68," Gaston blew out his breath and shook his head.

"The only thing inside was a photo of a ten-year-old boy." He pointed to his chin. "No mistaking this jaw, or the eyes."

"Were they still in Singapore during the bombing?"

"I don't know."

"You look through the databases?"

"I searched for six months, hired P.I.s, even went to Singapore. Spent most everything I had. You saw the news feeds. All that was left was radioactive glass and a big empty crater. When I came back, I'd been gone just a little too long."

"*Oui*, Eric 'The Slaughterer' had all the top billing by then."

"I was old meat."

"That kid was a punk."

"Naw, he was a good kid."

"He was doping."

"So was I. So were you."

"*Oui*, but our shit wasn't as good as his shit, eh?"

They laughed together, then Gaston gave him a hard, hard stare. "So why you doing this, man? I appreciate being here again, after all these years, eh? Feels like old times. But you can't fight me, the shape you're in."

Horace sighed and looked at his iron-hard hands and thick, chitinous forearms with the wraps of gray barbed-wire tattoos that went all the way up and across his shoulders and chest.

"When I was a kid, my dear old granddad told me about his pro wrestling days. There was this guy, Lex Luger, used to say that if you could walk to the ring, you could wrestle." He looked Gaston in the eye, and Gaston nodded. "This is what I do." And because his only friends in the world were people who had tried to kill him. Some of them had even succeeded. How sad was that? "Listen, brother, don't tell anyone about this, all right? By horn-time, I'll be ready to eat your heart."

Gaston's eyes narrowed. "Whatever you say."

The frenzied sound of the roaring crowd and the pulsing thunder of the bass beat filtered down into the room. The announcer thundered to the masses: "Resurrection Watch is now underway for Randy 'The Wrecker' Washington. The Samurai's katana really did some damage."

Horace's gaze flicked to one of the ubiquitous screens where a replay showed Wrecker Washington's spectacular evisceration in enhanced 3-D. That had been a helluva cut, Hammer mused, right in the crease below the breastplate.

The announcer went on, "Regenecorp technicians are even now struggling to restore The Wrecker's life."

The video feed cut to the infirmary where the Fight Doctor and a bevy of medical techs huddled around the fighter's ensanguined corpse. Flashing lights and readouts blazed self-importantly, and nests of tubes pierced the fighter's flesh at various points. Montage of concerned faces in the crowd, kids and women looking pensive over the fate of the downed fighter.

A caption box appeared at the bottom of the screen, flashing:

RESURRECTION WATCH: ODDS OF SUCCESSFUL RESURRECTION 1:3 AGAINST.
PLACE YOUR BETS NOW IN ACCOUNT DM55588767. BETTING WINDOW CLOSES IN 1:37.

The timer counted down the seconds.

The video feed cut back to the octagonal enclosure in the center of the stadium, and the timer retreated to an upper corner. Giant searchlights speared the black Las Vegas sky and spotlights swept silver discs across the multicolored tapestry of fans.

Gaston said to the screen, "Pull it through, kid."

Horace took a deep breath. "How about we go through the spots?" The outcome of the vast majority of bouts was left up to the skills of the fighters, but the sponsors often required each match to include certain moves or events—or spots, as they were called—usually because they wanted to highlight the performance of their newest weapon or armor tech. Sometimes they just wanted their logo highlighted at a crucial moment. They wanted stuff that looked fabulous in the after clips. Sometimes, the outcome was determined before the fighters ever set foot in the pit, either by Death Match Unlimited or by one of the chief sponsors. Those matches came with a hefty bonus and comprised a significant portion of Horace's losses.

Gaston perked up. "Sure. I've got the two kukris, of course. You been using spiked baseball bats lately, eh?"

"Yeah, but those won't stand up when they drop in the bucklers for Round Two. After the No-Weapons Round, I'm going with this new vibro-cleaver."

"The NorseX one? How is it?"

"It'll split a charging buffalo from nose to asshole."

"*Magnifique*. How about surprises?"

"Retractable punch dagger in my left bracer. You?"

Gaston smiled and lifted his chin and raised his thick orange beard, revealing a small sheath woven into the braids. "Electro-fiber dagger. The manufacturer is classified, but they're humping bunnies to get this stuff on the market." He pulled out a strip of gray cloth hanging from a narrow plastic grip.

"Nice!" Horace breathed.

Gaston thumbed the switch, and the micro-battery sent a current through the memory fibers, snapping them straight and rigid. From a supple strap of cloth to deadly weapon in less than a millisecond. "I'll bet that cost you."

"Endorsement deal from the manufacturer. It's a sample."

"Sharp?"

"You can shave with it, if you're careful. Care to try it on your balls?"

"I'll pass. Still using 'em."

"I'll make 'em look good."

"You always do."

Gaston's white teeth grinned between flaming orange beard and mustache. "Good to be working with you again, *mon ami.*"

Horace clapped him on the shoulder. "Let's give 'em their money's worth."

Back in his own dressing room, Horace clomped the massive aluminum case up on the prep table, unsnapped the heavy latches, and opened the clamshell. His signature body armor with its yellow-orange flames, scored and repaired and re-stitched, waited inside to offer whatever meager protection it could from weapons designed, at least in part, to penetrate it. Just like his body, every scar told a story. The fresh, new sponsorship logos covered some of the old scarring—NorseX, EnerGen, PeaceTech. Plastered right over his heart, Regenecorp's logo was the largest, mandatory for any match sanctioned for regenite tech.

Sponsorship wasn't what it used to be, a pittance now. With even half of the sponsorship dollars he used to receive, he would never have needed to talk to Dmitri.

He typically needed about ten minutes to strap on the lightweight ceramic plates embedded in carbon-nanofiber-impregnated leather, but tonight his hands kept fumbling over the buckles and snaps. It didn't fit right, wasn't falling into place like it always did.

Gripping the edges of the table to steady himself, he wished the eels in his head would quit squirming. He had to get his shit together. He extracted a hypodermic from his case, pulled out a little bottle of his Go Juice, a potent cocktail of steroids, amino acids, enzymes, hormones, and god knew what else. It was too soon before the fight, but it had enough adrenaline that it might keep his heart going for a little while longer. *Standard dose plus fifty percent oughta do it.* Strange how the prick of a needle could be so exquisite compared to the sheer volume of physical torture he had endured, but nevertheless it was a rush when it went up into the vein.

Sheer power and ferocity surged like lightning up his arm and spread crackling through his left shoulder into his chest. His heart kicked, then roared like an antique V-8. The struggle in its rhythm disappeared, all cylinders firing in perfect powerful rhythm like a turbo-charger dumping fuel and air by the bucket into every chamber. He squeezed his fist and savored the familiar rush.

Starting with his arm, the grayish tattoos across his body began to glimmer with a blue-green light as the enzymes in the Go Juice energized the bioluminescent ink. Now he glowed in the dark, just like his action figure, complete with Thunder Hammer action and removable entrails. Too bad the action figure had been discontinued ten years ago. Maybe after tonight they'd make an updated version.

He took a deep breath, let it out. He was almost starting to feel like himself. All he had to do was beat Gaston tonight and his worries were over. New heart, clean slate.

The intercom dinged with a guard's voice. "Hammer to the rear entrance. Hammer to the rear entrance."

Two security guards stood at the rear entrance to the coliseum. Above the sparkle and gleam of the Strip, searchlights and lasers painted the sky with clashing pit fighters a hundred meters tall. The Golden Spike Tower formed a gleaming, gilded needle over a kilometer high, right next to the Caesar's Palace StarTower, as if racing each other toward the stratosphere. The air still smelled of desert and the crackling ozone of hover drives. The limousines of VIPs filled the small parking lot like carefully stacked dominoes, their hover drives quiescent. Horace scanned the limousines for anything that smacked of danger, but all was quiet compared to the roar seeping over the coliseum wall.

He hardly recognized her. She wore sandals, faded jeans, and an off-the-shoulder t-shirt from some musical he'd barely heard of, quite unlike the skimpy straps, lace, and high heels he knew so well. Her hair, pulled into a stubby ponytail, was back to brown, one of the many colors he'd seen, but those big, brown eyes were still Lilly, and the square of her shoulders and curve of her neck were so like Amanda they could be two halves of the same person. But the wind brought him her scent, the delicate combination of jasmine and vanilla and *Lilly* he'd experienced so often at close range.

He cracked a grin. "You look shorter."

She smiled back, feebly, tucking a lock of hair behind her ear. Dark circles ringed her eyes, and she thrust both hands into her pockets. She cocked a foot. "No heels." Even without heels, she was tall, over 180 centimeters, willowy. "I've never seen you glowing like that before. Kind of creepy."

How many times had he imagined the inner glow pulsing out of her as she danced? He extended his hand. "Come on, I got a VIP box."

She swallowed hard. "I can't. The sight of blood makes me sick. I just... I just came because I needed some air. And it's only a ten-minute walk."

"From where?"

She shrugged off the question. "How soon before you go on?"

"Maybe an hour. Why don't you come inside?" He scanned the parking lot again. How could he tell her that she might be in danger because of him?

Her eyes glistened. "Even if I could—"

"No bullshit tonight. What's going on? I haven't seen you in weeks. I stopped down there once to give you a ticket."

Her voice cracked. "It's my son. He's in the hospital. He's sleeping now, so I had to get out of there for a while and—"

"You have a son?"

"Yeah. I have a son. A daughter, too."

"Wow."

"Look, it's not something you tell customers, you know? But I'm not at work now and—"

"No, it's not that." His chest felt like Gaston had just punched him again. He hoped she didn't hear the weakness in his voice. "How old is he?"

She hesitated.

"Come on, tell me about him."

"He's thirteen. And he's the most awesome kid, and...I don't know, I...I've been there with him for four days solid, and I'm just so tired and...Cassie is staying with my mom, but...I'm just so tired. And I'm scared. And you don't want to hear this shit from me and—"

"Lilly."

"—got your big comeback and—"

"Lilly. What's his name?"

"His name? His name is James. Jimmy."

"What's the problem with him?"

"I...I can't even say it. Something with his bones. He got in a fight at school, and some kid broke his arm in three places, and they found something with his bones. It's like they're soft or something, not enough calcium. Before he was born I couldn't afford the gene tests and—"

"He's gonna be okay though, right?" Through the silence for five labored heartbeats, ten, her face slowly collapsed, eyes squeezing shut. "Aw, darlin'." He sighed and reached out to put his arm around her.

She sniffled it away. "I gotta go. I'm sorry. You take care of yourself." She spun and walked off across the concrete.

"Hey, wait! Listen!"

She kept going, shaking her head.

He scanned the limousines again, half-expecting a Russian to jump out and nab her. Picking her up and carrying her inside for her own safety wouldn't work. Eventually she disappeared around the corner of the coliseum.

CHAPTER THREE

Heading down the hallway toward his dressing room, clenching his fists, he stomped hard enough to crack floor tiles. He rounded a corner as the Fight Doctor came out of Gaston's dressing room. The Fight Doctor looked like a cat caught with a paw in the birdcage.

Horace flipped him the bird.

The Fight Doctor spun and hurried away.

Horace stopped and watched him go. What the hell was that all about? It was well past time for the pre-fight checks.

The intercom dinged and called out the fighters for the sixth bout.

Fuck, he still had to finish prepping, so he hurried to his dressing room. Standing at the mirror in his dressing room, he was shaving the last of the salt-and-pepper stubble from his skull when the screen announced that The Wrecker had successfully resurrected.

"Good boy."

The camera flicked around to happy faces everywhere, and applause rippled through the crowd, except those who had bet against it.

Horace stretched and paced and swung his arms. They felt so heavy, and not just from the thick slabs of muscle he'd spent decades and hundreds of thousands of dollars building. The minutes ticked by. He watched bits of the matches. The fighters ground through battle after battle.

"No, kid, you're telegraphing the spot," he said. "You gotta make it look natural."

"Are you gonna fall for that head-fake *again*?"

Pummeling, slashing, gouging, hacking, roaring their gore-spattered triumphs and screaming their agonies to the chorused thunder of the crowd.

"Oooo, didn't see that razor-whip coming."

"Watch the upper cut with that spiked gauntlet."

His advice fell only upon the deaf ears of the 3-D screen.

Maybe Gaston had the right idea. Maybe Horace would take him up on his offer—if he survived tonight. He could teach the next generation about not only how to kill and not be killed, but also how to feed the crowd what they wanted and let the crowd feed it back.

It was a skill the great ones had. A great fighter could walk out there and suck up the vibration of the crowd like a man thirsting in the desert, take that energy, manipulate it, make the crowd feel it, take them up, take them up still further into a frenzy of roaring bloodlust. It was how stars were made.

The dressing room PA dinged, followed by the pit captain's voice, *"Hammer to Tunnel One. Freak to Tunnel Two."*

Horace took a deep breath and let it out. He pulled out his net-link again and thumbed an icon. Jack McTierney's face appeared on the screen. He hoped Jack was home watching the show, not drunk in a strip club somewhere. Private investigator friends could be useful in a lot of ways. It was time to call in one last favor.

All that remained of his life now was one last supercharge of Go Juice and the tunnel walk.

The Hammer walked alone down the concrete tunnel toward the rising wall of sound. He stopped behind the black-and-crimson curtain emblazoned with the Death Match Unlimited logo, and he heard it begin. His theme song. He breathed deep and let it wash through him.

The opening guitar riff of "Thunderstruck" tore through the Coliseum. He liked the old AC/DC version better, but the bigwigs had commissioned the cover by Death Tread. Rock n' roll wasn't just great-grandpa's music anymore.

The crowd came alive.

He counted the seconds, waiting for his moment.

The music rose, then exploded. "THUN-DER!"

He charged through the curtain.

The crowd went wild.

He threw his arms high as he strode down the long ramp toward the pit.

"THUN-DER!"

A forest of hands reached toward him and he touched every single one, smiling, shaking, meeting their eyes as if they were long-lost friends. A lump formed in his throat.

"THUN-DER!"

There was no drug, no sex, no experience that compared to the juice generated by seventy-thousand fans screaming his name.

"THUN-DER!"

The energy of the crowd washed over him, and every pain and sorrow he had ever felt in his life disappeared in the tumult. His knees were made of steel, his back rod-straight, his shoulders well-oiled pistons. His tattoos burned blue.

"THUN-DER!"

The drums sounded like twin cannons. On the screens, his face blazed forty feet high.

"THUN-DER!"

Fans chanted "Hammer Time!" and raised their hands into the Thunder Hammer. Two young women flashed their breasts as he passed. Three boys nearby saw this, cheered, and flashed theirs too.

"THUN-DER!"

Pyrotechnics blazed and crackled in time with the music, in time with his footsteps, in time with his heartbeat.

"THUN-DER!"

He strode through the gate into the pit, returning the Thunder Hammer to the crowd. Regenecorp and other sponsorship logos stippled the blood-stained floor of black chain-link octagon.

"THUN-DER!"

He threw back his head and roared into the searchlight-dappled sky. Shotgun microphones caught his voice and amplified it to the voice of a god. Throughout the multitudes, netshades fixed on him, drank in the image of him, catching stills and short clips, and enhancing the real events with data and stories from his past, fight records, trivia. The social media networks, he knew, were gushing with images of him.

"THUN-DER!"

The announcer's deep tones bellowed over the noise of the crowd. "And now, our main event of the evening. In the red corner, hailing from the independent city of Las Vegas, weighing in at 168.7 kilos, standing 210.4 centimeters, with a record of 287 victories, 192 confirmed kills, 78 losses, and 27 resurrections, Hooorrrr-uuuus THE HAM-MER HAAAARK-NEEEESSSSS!"

As the stadium exploded into frenzy around him, he knelt, humbly, in the center of the pit, and let it fill him. He took a long deep breath, then another. The floor here was pale, dry clay, soaked and splattered with the blood and fluids of eighteen other men. He ran his fingers through the coarse powder. The air smelled of earth and ozone, blood and sweat, a touch of urine from the evacuated bladders of slain fighters.

He wondered if Amanda would be waiting for him, assuming there was actually a fucking white light to be found at the end of all this bullshit, along with the son he had never met. He thought about Lilly and the dozens of times she'd writhed naked in his lap under neon bar lights, never once exposing herself.

He knelt there until Gaston's thick-laced, black boots kicked up puffs of dust in his field of vision.

While the announcer called out Gaston's statistics, Gaston paid his homage to the fans with his Freak Dance, which looked like nothing Horace had seen anywhere else: part rooster, part gorilla, part Shaolin monk.

When it was over, Horace met Gaston's gaze. The friendly camaraderie was gone; now there was only ferocity and determination. There was a lot of money at stake.

Horace smiled grimly. "Let's get it on, stubby."

"Bring it, cupcake," Gaston said, but before they turned away, Horace caught a strange look in his eye.

The pit gate swung closed, and a horn blared through the stadium at 180 decibels, initiating Round One.

The two fighters lunged at each other. Without weapons, Horace had the advantage of longer reach and fists augmented with hardened plates, the perfect biological hammers, but Gaston was too smart to come into range of those weapons. The Freak's style was to bounce and dart and roll, always striking from surprise and misdirection. Horace had a few tricks of his own, but his style was to charge in headlong, absorb what damage he needed to until he pummeled his opponents into paste.

They feinted and struck, lunged and blocked. Two minutes in, Horace's breath was growing ragged, and he could feel his heart laboring even through the veil of Go Juice. Round One was just for feeling the opponent out, wearing him down. They were both heavily armored, and besides, it was bad form for the main event to end too quickly. Neither of them was even close to done with this crowd.

His lungs began to burn, and he started counting the seconds to the end of the round. Gaston was giving him no quarter. The Freak had thirty years of pit experience, too, plus a healthy ticker. Fists and spiked boots came at him, but Horace gave it back. Twice his fists fell like piledrivers, smashing Gaston to the earth, and only Gaston's nimbleness kept him out of Horace's deadly grasp.

Finally the horn sounded, and Horace staggered to his corner, gasping, spasms of pain shooting through his left shoulder. A trainer swabbed the blood from his face, applied styptics to the cuts, and poured water and electrolytes into his mouth. A bevy of pit girls carried the next round's weapons into the ring and presented them: Horace's vibro-cleaver and Gaston's kukri. Another brought out the platter-sized bucklers painted with each fighter's personal logo.

Horace took the electrolyte bottle from the trainer's hand and guzzled it. The next horn was going to come far too soon. The strength began to drain out of his knees.

"You okay, Hammer?" the trainer asked blithely.

"Peachy."

The horn sounded.

Horace picked up the buckler in his left hand and the vibro-cleaver in his right. He snapped the cleaver's switch. The ultrasonic vibrations would have turned any dog within a hundred meters into a whimpering wreck, but Horace just felt a faint buzz. The weapon's edge was now a molecular-scale electric carving knife, capable, with sufficient effort, of splitting ceramic armor, to say nothing of going through flesh and bone like cotton candy.

Horace met the coiled knot of straining muscle in the middle of the pit, swinging, blocking, dodging, hacking. The crowd surged and cheered with each blow. The clang of metal echoed with the fans. Gaston's kukri licked and slashed. Horace swung the cleaver, but each blow went further and further astray. He met Gaston's gaze, and the ferocity in The Freak's eyes softened.

Horace swore something vile at him and redoubled his attack, but it was no good. He missed, badly, and flung himself off balance.

This was it. Against an opponent like Gaston, this was an ender.

Gaston's boot glanced off the back of Horace's head. Horace sprawled onto his face, his vision going dark. He blindly swung the edge of his buckler behind him and followed with the cleaver, but Gaston was not there. Horace's vision returned just in time for what felt like a hairy tree trunk to encircle his neck from behind.

His hand weapons skittered onto the clay as he grabbed Gaston's chokehold with both fists to prevent Gaston from snapping his neck. Attacking the chokehold with the vibro-cleaver put him in peril of slicing half his own face off.

A sputtering surge of strength, and he was able to face his opponent. They went down onto the earth, straining, grunting, gasping. The reversal had been too easy.

Then he was able to get the fingers of his left hand into the crease at the top of Gaston's breastplate.

Horace's right-hand squeezed Gaston's carotid artery, and Gaston's fingers dug into Horace's trachea.

Their eyes met.

Gaston nodded almost imperceptibly, his face turning purple. He knew about the blade in Horace's bracer. As this sank into Horace's addled brain, his grip must have slackened, giving Gaston an opening to punch him in the ear, hard. Adrenaline surged.

They clinched again, straining.

Horace touched a pad on his left bracer. The punch-dagger sprang out and speared up into Gaston's throat, through his tongue and palate and up into his medulla oblongata. His eyes spasmed in different directions, and his body went as limp as a chunk of sirloin.

A lump of sadness choked off the rest of Horace's breath and he collapsed onto the pit floor on top of his friend. It was never easy. Never.

The crowd went berserk in a tumult of noise.

The Fight Judge came into the ring to help Horace to his feet, and the medical techs whisked in to cart Gaston away for Resurrection Watch. Horace sagged against the Fight Judge, raising his good arm to the crowd, basking in the chant of "Ham-mer! Ham-mer!"

By god, he was going to walk out of here.

The announcer's booming voice proclaimed him the victor, but he could hardly hear it through the roaring in his ears.

He collapsed halfway to the dressing room.

Horace awoke slowly to the sounds he knew so well. Biometrics, respirators, all beeping and whooshing and cold. He pulled aside the oxygen mask and looked around. Gaston lay on a bed nearby.

He was breathing.

A sigh of relief washed out of Horace's chest, and he wiped his face with a heavy hand. The contusions Gaston had given him had healed. He stood up, testing his own weight. The clock on the wall told him he'd been unconscious for about an hour. After this length of time, the regenites had already repaired Gaston's nervous system. The bone would take longer. He would be on soft food for a few days.

Horace stood over him, laying a hand on his chest. An oxygen mask covered Gaston's face, and all the tubes from the treatment were still attached like octopus tentacles.

A flood of anger washed through him. Anger and shame. After all he'd done, all the training, all the doping, all the hardship and discipline, all the money he had borrowed from the wrong people—for which he must soon answer—Gaston had beaten him. Hands down. They both knew it. And they always would.

And worse, Gaston had given Horace the victory. In all his years, he had never taken charity from anyone. He was the fucking Hammer. The Hammer did for himself. He didn't need anyone.

What gave Gaston the right to just *do that*?

How the hell could The Hammer stage a Big Comeback and have it just handed to him? He hadn't earned it.

And now he knew the truth: he really, truly did not have the juice anymore.

Gaston's eyes fluttered open. A gravelly ghost of a voice, thick from the injuries to his mouth, said, "Now there's...the ugliest motherfucker..."

"Why'd you do it?"

"Talked to Fight Doctor... Told me...about your heart."

"You got kids for Chrissakes!"

"Can't work for me...if you're fucking dead, eh, dumbass...."

Horace cracked a half smile, but it felt false. "Like I would work for a stubby fucker like you."

But Gaston had faded away again.

Horace wobbled back to his dressing room, his stomach a sick morass that had nothing to do with injuries. He had won. He was a rich man. But he had to find Dmitri. Back in his dressing room, he gathered up his equipment.

His netlink pinged a waiting message from Jack: **FOUND THE KID. WASNT TO HARD. THEY GOIN 2 DSCHRGE HIM 2MRW WITH NO TREATMENT.** At the end of the message was a large dollar figure, almost as much as what Horace had earned tonight.

"Fuck!" His heart fell to somewhere near his feet. He sat down on the prep table and rested his forehead in his hands. "Fuck."

A long black limousine hovered near the rear entrance. He walked up to it, each step feeling like he had just run ten miles. The weight of what he had just done dragged at his feet as if he were walking to the gallows.

There would be no coming back this time.

A man got out of the limousine, an ex-pit fighter almost as big as Horace.

Horace said, "Hey, you Joey Luca?"

The man nodded grimly and shoved Horace up against the car, frisking him for weapons.

"What, you don't trust me?"

When Luca was satisfied, the door opened and Dmitri's voice wafted out with a cloud of marijuana smoke. "Get in."

Horace squeezed in and sat across from him and two of the pit girls from the show.

One of them had her hand in Dmitri's unbuttoned pants. "Hey, Hammer," she purred.

Luca shouldered in beside him, a hulking mass like a planetoid, complete with its own gravitational field.

"Hell of a fight, Hammer," Dmitri said, blowing another lungful of smoke. "Didn't think you'd show."

"Told you I would." Horace's brain whirled, spun, cranked, tightened like a spring waiting to explode.

"Maybe now we don't have to put pieces of you and Daisy in a barrel under the new stadium. Business is so much easier when everyone does what they're supposed to."

"I've never been much for 'supposed to.' Wouldn't be here if I had."

Dmitri smiled like a crocodile and shifted in his seat while the pit girl's hand shifted in his crotch. He cried out in sudden pain and backhanded her across the nose. She cried out and cowered away from him. "Stupid sow! Trim your fucking nails!" Blubbering sobs muffled her reply as she dabbed at a spot of blood under one nostril.

The flare of rage in Dmitri's eyes cooled almost instantaneously as he returned his attention to Horace. "You're a rich man now. Plenty left to have a good time. Hell, maybe we all go party. You can have this stupid cunt." He thumbed carelessly toward the girl he had struck. "After you pay me." At the last utterance, his eyes went cold and reptilian.

"Some things are worth more than a good time." A little kid's life, maybe, a kid who didn't deserve the shitty hand he had been dealt.

"What are you talking about?"

"I'm talking about you kissing my ass."

It took a couple of moments for the words to register in Dmitri's fogged brain. Then he sat up straight. "What?"

"I said, kiss my white pimply ass."

Rage flared in Dmitri's eyes.

"The money's gone," Horace said.

Luca reached into his jacket.

Horace threw himself into Luca, pinning his elbow and his pistol against his torso. The girls screamed. The electro-fiber dagger made a little snap sound as Horace pressed the switch while holding the soft strip of cloth against Luca's chest. The dagger stiffened instantaneously, and the monofilament edge snicked out and cut through Luca's sternum, two ribs, aorta, and half a lung. The massive slug-thrower in Luca's hand tumbled onto the seat, and the bodyguard's chin sagged to his chest.

Horace lunged across the back of the limousine onto Dmitri. The girls screamed again and flung themselves away.

The Russian was well-built, strong, stoned, and didn't have a prayer. Ring-encrusted fingers clawed weakly at Horace's face, effectual as a toddler's, as Horace held him down, ears filled with panicked shrieking.

It didn't take long for Horace to finish cutting.

He left Dmitri's head propped between his legs, then got out and stood at the curb, wiping blood from his face, spitting out the taste of it. He had never killed anyone outside of the ring before. It had been so much easier, and yet somehow terrifying.

The Russian syndicate would be on him like a bloodstain, but would they involve the police or handle everything with a silenced bullet and a body bag?

He did know one thing. A little boy now had his medical expenses paid. Little Jimmy was going to grow up healthy. And this used-up old fighter was going to do what used-up old fighters did—keep fighting until he couldn't anymore.

He waved goodbye as the hover's drive whined up and it sped away. If they hurried, Joey Luca could resurrect. Dmitri was history.

Now, he had to get the hell out of town. A quick stop at his rathole apartment to grab a few things, and then the bus station. If the mob knew about Lilly, they certainly knew where he lived. But first, a hose to wash off all the blood.

ROUND 1

CHAPTER FOUR

Intermittent splashes of streetlight washed the heads of the bus passengers. Immense expanses of darkness lurked beyond the veil of highway streetlights. Last he knew, the bus had been passing through Illinois. The rumbling whine of its power plant and the deep buzz of its tires on the road soothed him. He dozed.

In the foggy wasteland between memory and dream, Horace took his favorite table at the Titty Twister and ordered the usual, Bombay Sapphire and tonic. Bathed in shadows and coruscating patterns of laser light, he waited for her. The familiar faces were here: Max the bouncer, Ed and Sheila the bartenders, the girls he knew by stage name who greeted him with varying flavors of "Hey, Hammer!" On the chrome-and-mirror stage, Starchild writhed and spun, a swirl of glitter, silver eyeshadow, and pearlescent lipstick. But despite her exquisitely sculpted body, his attention lay elsewhere to the one called Velvet, who had just led a drunken businessman into one of the shadowed grottoes at the rear of the place. It didn't matter who she was with or what she was doing, onstage or off, he couldn't take his eyes off her. He'd seen thousands of stunning bodies and beautiful faces come and go, but Velvet had something in the eyes, big, brown pools of mystery and intrigue.

The Titty Twister was one of his favorite haunts whenever he was in Vegas. The bartenders mixed the drinks to his taste and the stable of dancers offered the kind of variety he liked. Max the bouncer was a decent sort. He was a pit fighting fan and didn't mistreat the women. Horace's first appearance had thrown Max into a spasm of fanboyish euphoria.

And then this new dancer had started about six months ago. Velvet.

He had visited several times just to see her, catch her eye, exchange a handful of words, even when his finances were overstretched. She called him by name now like they were old friends, and he'd been in enough strip clubs to recognize when friendliness was genuine. She was a little older than the other dancers, but it was difficult to tell how much. She was one of those women whose age could fall within a twenty-year window. It was the maturity in her eyes that intrigued him, a certain world-weariness that spoke to him, and she held his gaze longer than any woman since...her.

On this particular night, she returned from the dark recesses of a private dance and spotted him across the bar. The smile bloomed on her face and warmed him in a way he didn't want to think about, however much he had come here for just that.

He stood to greet her, and she hugged him with the kind of shallow, carefully guarded touch that conveyed familiarity but not too much.

"You clean up nice!" she said with real surprise and appreciation, stroking the lapel of his suit, brushing her fingers down the length of his necktie. "Where's the t-shirt and sweatpants?"

"Dumpster. Tonight, I'm celebrating." He pulled out a chair for her. "And I want you to join me."

She raised her eyebrows. "And what are we celebrating?"

"I just came from a meeting. Let me buy you a drink."

"Sure, but I can't stay too long. I gotta work the floor—"

He withdrew a stack of cash from his breast pocket and placed it on the table. Her eyes bulged. "How would you feel about me buying your time for the rest of your shift?"

Discomfort tightened her shoulders. "Look, Hammer, I'm flattered, but I don't do that kind of thing."

"That's not what I'm saying. I'm saying I got something worth celebrating and got to tell somebody. Doesn't look like my buddy Jack is going to show, so I can't tell him about it. A few drinks, and that's all. I'll make it worth your time."

She eyed the money, then him. "Okay. Deal. But I still have to go on stage."

He shrugged.

"So what are we celebrating?" she asked.

"A deal to put me back in the big time."

"A big fight?"

"The biggest. An epic rematch between the legendary Hammer Harkness and Gaston The Freak Rousseau."

She smiled. "Legendary, eh?"

"Maybe you're too young to remember."

"My folks never let me watch that stuff, but I remember you from then. It was everywhere. Hell, you still look the same!"

"Thanks."

"So when is this epic event going to happen?"

"Too early to say. Maybe six months. Gaston has to agree, and we have to book a venue. But tonight, we party. Tomorrow, I train."

A waitress brought them cocktails, plus shots of Irish whiskey. He raised his shot glass and looked into her eyes. "To second chances."

At those words, she held his gaze for a long moment, and he would have sworn he saw her eyes get misty for a split second.

Then she clinked his glass, and they downed the shots.

Then a presence loomed over them. "Sorry I'm late, amigo," said a man's voice. "I was on a stakeout. Had to wait for the money shot."

Horace stood and clasped hands with the newcomer. "About goddamn time. I thought you were dead."

Jack McTierney ran veined, leathery fingers through a slick, salt-and-pepper pompadour. About half Horace's mass, Jack moved with controlled, wiry strength. "After videoing a three-hundred-fifty-pound bank executive slip a Mickey to his secretary in a bar and rape her in a two-bit motel, I kinda wish I was dead. But the client's going to get a hefty divorce settlement and the exec will *really* want to keep that video off the net."

"He raped her?" Velvet said, her face registering less horror and surprise than it should have.

"It was pretty clear she was barely conscious. A bank like that has the money, though, to spin the media like a gyroscope. I doubt the police'll touch him."

"Lady Velvet," Horace said, "Allow me to introduce Jack McTierney, private dick."

As Jack kissed her fingers with Old World gentility, his eyes appraised her with a nod of appreciation apparently at Horace's good taste. His Arkansas twang rang like a slide guitar. "I prefer the term 'old-time gumshoe.' Dick should be kept private. Pleased to meet you, little lady." Then a raised eyebrow to Horace, "So?"

"They're going to float the idea to Gaston."

"Soo-perlative," Jack said. "A hootenanny is indeed in order."

As the night went on, the conversation went from raucous to raunchy, hilarious to flying high, thoughtful to almost existential. Velvet touched Horace many times, her hand warm and gentle. On stage, she was as stunningly beautiful as ever. At the table, she was surprisingly witty, with more game than he had encountered in years. He had had glimpses of this in their past interactions as the layers of defenses slowly peeled away, but experiencing it here in full flourish was not only a hell of a lot of fun but a clear reason for her success in a business that used and discarded women like condoms.

Fortunately, he was on his game that night, too.

"What's your real name?" he said.

"It's not a good idea for me to tell customers that."

"I promise I won't tell anyone."

"That's what my last stalker said."

"Do I look like I need to stalk anyone?"

"He said that, too."

"I'm not the kind of guy who gives up."

She nodded appreciatively. "I can see that."

"Hey, if you don't want to tell me, that's cool, but you can ask any girl in here if I've ever caused trouble."

"I already did. They said you're a stand-up guy."

"Cost me a lot of money in bribes."

"All for me?"

He winked at her. "Yeah, all for you."

But she still didn't tell him her name.

The weeks melted away as they laughed and drank. Some nights he paid her to dance for him, some nights he didn't. Some nights more girls joined their little party, contributed some fun and titillation, and then floated away. Some nights Jack joined them and contributed his unique brand of patter, dark and rich and potent, like a good bourbon. And when Jack departed, he kissed every dancer in the place good night, paused in the exit, and gave a bow with panache and aplomb.

Memories of her floated one into the other, building blocks of trust and appreciation accumulating between them, all of her smiles, the sound of her deep-throated laughter, floating in his head. Across those interactions, she started gravitating closer to him, and when they talked he was conscious of her proximity warming his arm, his leg, but didn't dare ascribe any importance to it. For enough cash, he could take her into the back room and have her grind on him all night long. But that would be a business transaction. This felt different somehow.

"I'm thinking about quitting," she announced one night.

"Why?" The sip of coffee sent a jolt across his palate and into his brain.

"I'm too old."

"Bullshit."

"Customers like the young ones." She leaned back in the diner booth, and her gaze traveled around the room.

"Not everybody."

"Don't lie to me. I've seen you."

"I've been a dirty old man for a solid decade. I figure I get better with age."

Her expression turned bitter. "Women just get old. Until we become invisible." Her voice softened. "Some kid the other day called me grandma. I punched him. Almost got fired." She sipped at her cocktail to help swallow something else.

"You might as well tell me your name. If you quit, I won't know what else to call you." He said it jokingly, but she still crossed her arms.

After a pause, she said, "Why me?"

"'Why you' what?"

"What are you doing here? With me?"

"I thought it was because we were getting better acquainted. You and ol' Jack are the closest things I got to friends in this town."

"You think I'm going to fuck you?"

He leaned back in his chair and looked at her, let the question hang between them. "That's a mighty hostile way to ask if I'm hitting on you."

"Are you?"

"When I do, you'll know."

The following day, he had received a single line of text message, forwarded through the cobwebs and tumbleweeds of his public fan mail interchange.

My name is Lilly.

The day Horace and Gaston signed the contract to fight in the Coliseum preceded the night Lilly sent him into a tailspin.

Swathed in silk suits instead of armor, Horace and Gaston met in the holo-plastered hallways of Death Match Unlimited. Surrounded by 3-D holograms of pit fighting legends, they stalked toward one another.

"Now there is the ugliest motherfucker I ever seen, eh?" Gaston called.

Horace said, "My god, you look like the inside of an elephant's ass."

Gaston's hairy paw clasped Horace's like a vise. "You smell like one, eh?"

"Must be your breath." They embraced, laughing. "You are still the hairiest sumbitch I ever seen. Now you're all old and wrinkled, you're starting to look like a scrotum."

Gaston punched him in the breadbasket, a blow that would have likely ruptured the spleen of a normal human. "Fuck you, eh? As long as I don't look like *your* scrotum. I come out of retirement for this?"

Horace's stomach surged and roiled, and a throbbing ache spread through his left shoulder. He forced a smile. "You can't get this kind of abuse anywhere else. Fucking good to see you, man. How's Montreal?"

"Much safer than the Business."

"Still running that gym?"

"Ah, *oui*. I stay in shape, don't have to get killed, and the little ones think I am God. It is a good life."

"Hell, I heard they actually allowed you to procreate."

"Yah, boy and a girl now, six and eight."

Horace scratched his head. "Holy shit, where does the time go?"

"Into life, *mon ami*. After all this, you should come to Montreal, see my gym. We teach the young ones together, eh?"

"Sorry, I don't speak Pussy."

"Yah, you The Hammer. The man who never stay dead, eh? Twenty-seven?"

"Twenty-seven."

"And five of those belong to me."

"Fuck you, I still have you by two."

"Maybe not after this, eh?"

"Yeah, after this I'll have you by three."

While the ink dried on the contracts, Death Match Unlimited booked the swankiest suite in Caesar's Grand Palace, brought in a fortune in drugs and liquor. Promoters were there. Executives from Death Match Unlimited were there. Marketing people from Regenecorp were there. Local fighters were there. Hookers were there. The hotel supplied a case of Dom Perignon. It was all just like he remembered it. It was like he had never been gone. The hotel suite thrummed with the likes of people with whom he hadn't rubbed elbows in over a decade.

Funded by a massive promotional expense account courtesy of Regenecorp, Horace hired Lilly and three other girls from the Titty Twister to perform, along with two male strippers for the high-powered female executives from Regenecorp. Jack and Gaston were hitting it off at the bar while Max made sure none of the drunken businessmen overstepped with the dancers or mistook them for hookers. Cash flowed and spirits rose and the party roared deep into the night like a freight train of drunken debauchery, the kind of party attendees would still be talking about in their old age.

When she was not dancing, Lilly hovered near Horace and allowed him to introduce her to everyone. Throughout that night, a tension between them, like a rubber band, drew them closer. When other men attempted to snare her attention, she simply looked at Horace and gave him a silent smile.

The whiskey flowed, and finally her slight frame overcame her practiced tolerance for liquor. By this time, the guests had dispersed. Max snored on the couch. Gaston and his bikini-model wife had claimed one of the bedrooms for a "night of wild time away from the kids, eh!" Jack was chatting up one of the female Regenecorp executives, who leaned into him enough to make it clear they were minutes from closing a very carnal deal.

And then a song came over the sound system, an old country song about love's impossible timing. "Omigoddancewithme!" Lilly said.

He took her in his arms right there. Unsteady as he was, he had to support them both. They danced the final half of the song with her cheek against his breast. He couldn't be sure if she were trembling or if it was just the liquor. When the third verse came, so steeped in yearning for someone far, far away that his own heart began to ache, she said something he couldn't hear.

"What?" he said.

Her enormous brown eyes turned up into his. "We should stop pretending." Her gaze flicked toward his lips. And there she was, in this perfect moment, the moment he had been dreaming about, the moment he had wanted from the moment he first saw her.

"You're the only man who's ever been this strong for me," she said, but her words were so slurred together he needed a moment to process them, and in his own addled mind they didn't entirely make sense.

"Being strong is what I do," he said. "But I don't kiss anybody who's not gonna remember it the next day."

"Wh-whut?" Her breath came confused, blinking as if she couldn't parse what she had heard. Her eyes glazed, and she fell against him.

"Whoa, there. Let's get you to bed." He swept her up in his arms, a fraction of the weight of the barbells he had been pumping, and carried her into the unoccupied bedroom, where he laid her on the bed, took off her shoes, and returned to the bar. Jack had just launched a tongue-wrestling match with the Death Match executive.

Horace sighed, poured himself another finger of scotch, and went out to the balcony overlooking the jeweled beauty of Las Vegas, breathed deep of the cold desert air and this life he had missed for so long. The Hammer was *back*.

A few minutes later, the sound of vomiting came from the master bathroom. He found Lilly there, hunched and spasming over the toilet bowl. When it subsided, he brought her a glass of water and a towel. She thanked him sheepishly and allowed him to help her back to the bed, where she passed out within moments.

He covered her up and returned to the balcony, where he slept in a chaise lounge until the sun drove railroad spikes into his eyes. In the harsh light of morning, she was gone.

In the days and weeks that followed, a wall came down in front of Lilly's eyes the likes of which he hadn't encountered since Amanda had told him she was pregnant. He tried to visit Lilly at the club, but she was "too busy" to do more than exchange shallow greetings and spent most of his visits hiding in the dressing room. The light in her eyes disappeared as if a lid had been thrown over the spark.

One night, he took her by the elbow.

She jerked her arm away. "What? What do you want?"

"I want you to tell me what's different now! What happened?"

"What are you talking about?"

"You telling me you don't remember?"

"Remember what?" Her eyes flared with challenge, with desperation that he not put anything into words that she would have to deny, even though she knew every word of it would be true.

"Nothing," was all he could say.

Horace woke to a sound that blared a warning through his half-conscious mind. The whining rumble of the bus' power plant, the hum of the road, the chill of the window against the side of his head remained, but those were not what had awakened him from his haunted doze. The murmur of quiet conversations between seatmates was not what had slapped him from sleep.

Here in the rear of the bus, the noise of the power plant was greater. Snatches of sound filtered rearward along the window glass: snoring, words, faint strains of music from earphones.

And there it was.

Someone toward the front was speaking Russian, quietly.

CHAPTER FIVE

Horace sat up straighter and peeked across the tops of the seats. Right behind the driver, a man sat alone, talking to someone. He tried to remember what the man looked like but couldn't bring him to mind. All he could see now was a brown-fringed bald spot, nodding. Then the man's head straightened, and the Russian fell into silence.

Horace's hand slipped into the pocket of his leather jacket and found the slim grip of the electro-fiber dagger, the blade safely retracted.

The only question now was whether the Russian was a hitter, a tail, or just some poor unrelated slob. How could they have found him so quickly? The world was full of surveillance cameras tied to biometric recognition systems, but he was counting on being a needle in a haystack. Granted, he was an overlarge needle, but if they really had tracked him down already, their reach was far greater than he had anticipated.

A hitter wouldn't take the shot on the bus; cross-country buses like this one dripped with surveillance, and the corps that owned the bus lines would come down like an anvil on anybody jeopardizing their business. When Horace was a kid, law enforcement was left to police; nowadays it fell just as often to corp security forces. In some areas of North America, where megacorp power was most concentrated, police forces were little more than a sham. Corp security forces each had their own brand of justice. No, if this guy was a hitter, he would wait for a rest stop, where a getaway car would be waiting. Or maybe he had a buddy waiting at the next rest stop with a nice, quiet rail rifle. Mono-fiber *shuriken*—little spinning razor-blades invented centuries ago by ninjas and modernized with twenty-first century technology, propelled at Mach 15 by silent bursts of electromagnetic flux—would cut through Horace like he wasn't even there, even if he wore his armor. The mob had taken to using them for prominent hits when they wanted to make a point.

If the man was just a tail, Horace could not exactly stealth his way out of sight. At 210 centimeters and 170 kilos of pure muscle, he stood out like a mammoth among sheep. But then, he might keel over while trotting across a parking lot. His borrowed time was ticking away, but he would be damned if some Russian punk punched his time card.

The bus hummed along. Patches of light slid by, small towns disappearing into the sea of time behind him, fading into the past. An old woman tottered back to the toilet a couple of meters from where Horace sat. He tried to catch her eye, but she wouldn't look at him. A waft of cloying chemical deodorant burst out as she opened the toilet door and closed it quickly behind her. He was used to her reaction. Just like sheep didn't care to socialize with wolves, most normal people instinctively gave him a wide berth. Not that most normal people had anything to fear from him. He did all his killing in the pit. Except for Dmitri. What a can of hellworms he had opened up.

Gaston had told him once, after the last time Gaston had killed him, "*Mon ami*, we were born in the wrong fucking century, eh? We should have come out of mama's womb with axe and shield in hand."

Horace had said, "Who says I didn't?"

But even a vibro-axe wasn't something to bring to a gunfight, and the dagger in his pocket was for up-close-and-personal only. He knew the basics of firearms—at least enough to know which end to point at the other guy—but in many ways they had grown so advanced and arcane they required special training to pull the trigger.

The driver spoke over the PA system, "Happy three a.m., everyone. We'll be pulling into a rest stop shortly. This will be your last chance to stretch your legs before Toledo."

Horace sat up straighter and rubbed his eyes, then his face. He was doubtless quite a sight by this point. Yeah, he had "nice, non-threatening guy" written all over him. Then again, the woman was probably only ten or fifteen years older than he was, and here he was, thinking of her as an old lady.

When had he gotten so goddamn old?

The bus slowed and eased toward the right onto the offramp, pulling into a sprawling parking lot with a brightly lit fueling station at the center. Fast-food neon splattered the night above an accretion of buildings and brands, all under the Fusion Corp logo. Vehicles and transports came and went. The bus pulled into the rainbow glow of the central building.

"We'll be pulling out again in about thirty minutes, folks," the driver said, opening the door and shutting down the power plant.

Passengers stood and stretched, yawning, scratching, funneling toward the open door. The man up front did not move. Horace waited until all the other passengers disembarked, but still the man stayed put, just a bald spot visible above the seat.

Time to find out. Horace stood, having to stoop under the low ceiling, pulled his duffel bag and aluminum equipment case down from the rack, and moved toward the front of the bus. Letting the man believe Horace was getting off here would force his hand. Horace threaded his way between the seats and then pretended to snag his equipment case on something beside the man, giving him a look at the guy.

Completely nondescript, thirties, thin, dressed in bulky peacoat. He could be carrying an arsenal under there. His gaze darted toward Horace's luggage, but otherwise remained downcast. Horace slid by him.

The driver peeked out of his enclosure. "You getting off, sir?"

Horace said, "Gotta make a call."

"We're leaving in thirty minutes."

"Got it."

A cool night breeze carried the smells of oil and rubber. When he was a boy, it would have been diesel exhaust, but not anymore. Even at three a.m., this place bustled with activity, mainly truckers coming and going. A broad line of transport rigs were lined up in the far side of the parking lot.

Near them, a garishly painted road train stood parked like a line of six old rail cars. The doors hung open. The train's engine resembled the bus behind him, a twenty-year-old hauler. On the side of it was painted "*Norman Trask Promotions*" in gaudy flames and holographic sparkles.

Why did the name Norman Trask ring a bell?

Might as well go take a piss before the Russians shoot me, Horace thought. Shoehorning his bulk into the bus toilet was more trouble than it was worth most of the time. He carried his two bags with him into the rest-stop toilet, keeping the electro-fiber dagger palmed in his right hand. People either stared at him as he passed or their eyes avoided him like he was a rust blight leper.

In the toilet, he clumped his luggage down on either side of him and stepped up to the urinal. Advertisements for farm implements, penis enhancements, and strip clubs filled his vision.

The strip club advertisements brought Lilly to mind, but she'd made it clear there was nothing between them. Besides, him being anywhere near her put her and her kids in danger.

One of the toilet stalls opened and a man came out. The man paused. "Holy shit!"

Horace glanced over his shoulder.

"Holy shit, it *is* you. Hammer Harkness!"

Standing perhaps a hand shorter than Horace but just as broad, the man beamed with a crooked, gap-toothed grin, crinkling the leathered maze of wrinkles and scars that made his face.

Horace grinned back. "Why, Sam Striker. I'd shake your hand, but I got a cock in mine."

Striker laughed. "Nice timing, as always."

Horace shook, zipped, and turned.

"Small world, huh?" Striker said.

"Why, the last time I saw you was what, Rio in '64?" Horace said.

Striker shuffled his feet. "Yeah, met a nice gal, got married. She didn't take kindly to me getting killed all the time."

A weight settled on Horace's already unsteady heart. "Good for you, brother."

"You're still at it. Damn, I watched you and The Freak the other night on pay-per-view. What a trip that was! Just like the old days. Ol' Freak recovered okay?"

"Yeah, resurrected fine, no permanent damage, they said."

"Ah, that's good, that's good. Yeah, me and the wife are on the way to Buffalo for a recruiting convention. Plus signing autographs and such. A little extra dough, but I got a good day job."

"Yeah?"

"Consulting for Death Match Extreme. Screening new fighters and such. It's a good gig, and I still get to watch the Business, you know? It's not easy putting godhood aside."

"You said it, brother."

"So where you headed?" Sam said.

"Montreal." This surprised him. Until that moment, he hadn't thought about where he was going, except away from Las Vegas. "Gaston offered me a job in his training camp."

"You retiring?"

"I wouldn't go that far."

"Well, the fresh meat could do a whole lot worse than learning from Hammer Harkness."

"Then when they come crawling to your doorstep they'll be the biggest badasses you've ever seen." Horace cracked a grin.

"They'll never be the badasses we were."

"Fuckin'-A."

"Let me buy you a cup of coffee."

Horace considered for a moment. "I'm not gonna say no."

Out in the shop next to the coffee machine, they got cups of cheap roadside coffee, just the kind Horace liked. When he was a kid, they called places like this "truck stops." Nowadays, they were "comfort opportunity pavilions." He scanned the shop's patrons over the racks and rows but did not see the Russian. Holographic animals danced above snack racks and drink dispensers—pink sloths, blue elephants, a drug-addled raccoon. Buxom females and bulging males posed and flexed and beckoned toward profusions of hyper-specialized widgets and useless trinkets. The air itself sparkled so thoroughly it was like being inside a fireworks display. It all gave him a headache.

They sat in a plastic booth at a plastic table near the window. The stubby hairs on the back of Horace's neck would not lie down as the vast light-smeared blackness outside yawned at him. An army of Russian hitters could be watching him from the darkness right now.

"So did you get a load of that road train out there?" Sam said.

"You don't see the traveling circus leagues much anymore."

"You ever hear of Norman Trask?"

It came to Horace then. "Yeah, I met Trask way back in the day. Threw him a bone once."

"Now that you're back in the Big Time," Sam said, "you gonna miss the minors?"

How many times had he asked himself the same question, especially on those nights when he wanted to quit but couldn't bring himself to do it? The minors, of which that road train outside was no doubt a part, had kept him going, kept him fed, and in an array of ironies, kept him alive.

That stab of failure came again. He was washed up. There would never be another score like his fight with Gaston, ever again. Until he got a new heart, he wouldn't be able to go toe-to-toe with a high school wrestler. The Hammer's run was over, once and for all. Never again would he charge into the pit with his theme music thundering through a coliseum crammed with a hundred thousand fans screaming his name.

What would he do when that yearning returned, the one that drove him into the gym, into working promo events, angling for another chance to put his life and the life of another fighter on the line, in a VFW somewhere for seventy people? Events like that could not afford a full suite of regeneration for the loser, and all the winner got was a month's rent with two months of healing to do.

Across the parking lot, people were gathering around the road train doors. The headlights came on.

"Hey, hot stuff," came a female voice from over Horace's shoulder. "Who's your—why I'll be damned. Hammer Harkness!"

"And you must be Mrs. Striker." Horace offered his hand to the woman standing by the table.

"Thea," she said, shaking his hand. She tossed long silver hair over her shoulder and grinned a brilliant smile. Her denim-and-leather swathed body was taut as a twenty-year-old's. Sharp eyes glittered behind violet glasses. "And you won't remember me. I was one of the pit girls you didn't sleep with."

"I don't know that I'd remember you if I had. What were you doing, Sam, picking up girls in grade school? Trolling maternity wards?"

Thea laughed and slid into the booth beside her husband, snuggling up to his bulk with a slim shoulder. "You're still so full of shit, but I always liked your brand of it."

"What made you hook up with this lummox?" Horace thumbed toward Sam.

She looked at her husband, and her black eyes sparkled like onyx. "It certainly wasn't his manners."

"It was all about dentition," Sam said with a grin missing a couple of teeth. "And muscles. She likes really big...muscles."

She punched him in the arm. "How's life for you, Hammer?" she said. "You got a good woman to keep you between the ditches?"

"Uh, no." Suddenly the conversation was making him as uncomfortable as sitting beside this big window. Why hadn't he cracked smart-ass right there? "I guess I'm too attached to weeds in the grill."

They laughed, and then he spotted the Russian walking across the parking lot.

Horace tried to gauge him, but the man was so utterly nondescript that he couldn't get any kind of read. The man didn't move like a fighter: in shape perhaps, but not a trained martial artist. Those guys moved like oil. That made him a shooter, and the peacoat was too bulky to discern if he was carrying weapons. Horace's eyes followed him into the building, past the counter until he disappeared into the toilet. Horace shifted his body so that watching the toilet was less blatant and sipped his coffee.

"What the hell is this old lady doing?" Sam pointed out the window as the woman from the bus toilet stepped right up to the other side.

The next thing Horace saw was the barrel of a pistol yawning at his face like a cavern.

"Look out!" Thea screamed.

Horace threw himself sideways. A hail of slugs exploded the glass inward, tore chunks out of the tabletop. Something tugged at his jacket and shoulder. He snatched up a napkin holder and flung it backhanded at the old woman's face. As she dodged the missile, he lunged out of the booth and seized the edge of the table with both hands.

Thea was screaming, sprawled on the floor with Sam on top of her.

Horace heaved up the tabletop, tearing it away from the wall with a crunch, and flipped it vertical, filling the window. Screams filled the store. An alarm blared.

Horace grabbed both Sam and Thea by the collars and charged toward the rear of the shop, dragging them behind.

The Russian man from the bus came out of the toilet, black metal in both hands. Automatic pistols came up, tracking laser dots.

Horace dropped Sam and Thea and dived behind a rack of snacks. Almonds and shrapnel sprayed above him. Sparks and soda fountained over him from behind. The air was muffled, as if cotton filled his ears. More screaming. He snatched up an entire meter-high rack of donuts and flung it toward the gunman. A crash and a curse. The whine of a hover drive blasted grit through the shattered front window.

Thea was crying.

His heart pounded like a broken trip-hammer in his chest, out of rhythm, out of time. Cold sweat flooded his skin.

He charged over the shattered snack rack toward the gunman, roaring like a bull. If Horace could get close, the Russian would be pasted bone and gristle. But he wasn't going to make it.

The autopistol barrels swung toward him like lethal black eyes.

Sam Striker righted himself with long-practiced ease and charged toward the gunman. The gunman managed to half-turn, but Striker swept the man's legs. The Russian went down hard on his back, and the autopistols blasted holes in the ceiling.

There was blood on Sam's hand as it came down like a knife on the Russian's throat. The crack of cartilage sounded somehow louder than the gunshots. Horace grabbed the smoking-hot gun barrels in his hands, yanked the pistols out of the man's grip, and then stomped a massive boot down with all his remaining strength on the man's chest.

The man lay there, choking out his life, eyes crazed but ferocious. Horace flipped the autopistols properly in his grip and cast about for the old woman. Beyond the vertical tabletop, a glimpse of a gleaming black hover car slid away from the front of the store.

Shredded napkins and foil packaging fluttered to the floor like confetti. Smoke dissipated. Heads poked up over the racks of junk food, peering through incorporeal, holographic buttocks. "Somebody call the cops!" a voice said.

"And an ambulance!" Sam said, turning back toward Thea, who lay sobbing and gasping under a pile of pretzel bags. He reached out and clutched her hand. "You're gonna be okay, baby! You're gonna be okay."

"Where's she hit?" Horace said.

"Looks like through the ribs," Sam said. "Missed her heart." He pulled the netlink out and his thumb did a quick dance. "Don't worry, baby. Ambulance is on the way."

Horace experienced a pang of envy that the Strikers could afford full medical. Without it, no private ambulance service would bother, and never mind any hope of regeneration.

"Oh...it hurts," she gasped.

"I know, baby. It always hurts." He slid beside her and laid both hands over the wounds, one entry, one exit. The exit wound under her arm was bad, the size of her fist, pouring blood through Sam's fingers.

Horace tucked one autopistol under his arm, grabbed a fistful of paper napkins, and handed them to Sam, who wadded them up to put pressure on the wounds. "You'll be okay. People come back from way worse than this."

The Russian choked and clutched at everything within reach for two endless minutes before his eyes glazed, with Horace standing over him, both hands full of autopistol.

Everyone else had fled outside. The alarm finally silenced.

"They were after you," Sam said to Horace, with Thea nestled in his lap, pale as death.

Horace nodded. "Certain people are unhappy that I won that last fight." It was close enough to the truth for now. Sam knew full well. Being in the Business for any length of time inevitably led to contact with the mob. Extortion to throw fights and peddle influence were something every fighter had to deal with at some point.

Horace put down one of the pistols and rifled through the Russian's pockets. He found a shiny new netlink and a wallet bulging with cash. He took both.

"What are you doing?" Sam said.

"If I'm going to see my next birthday, I need to know who's after me."

A sudden, bizarre stench filled the air. Horace had only looked away from the Russian for a few seconds, but already the corpse looked a month dead, flesh bloating and then sloughing away before their very eyes.

Both men swore and scrambled away, Sam dragging Thea with him.

The flesh dissolved, and moments later, even the skull and bones were dark sludge. Even the clothing was fading in color, starting to fray and disintegrate.

"What the fuck is that?" Sam said.

"No idea, brother."

A voice came over the PA system. "This is the Fusion Corp police. Drop all weapons and come out with your hands up!"

"I'll go first," Horace told Sam, then he roared toward the window. "We need paramedics in here!"

CHAPTER SIX

Horace bid Sam and Thea goodbye, then the ambulance doors closed. She was already swathed in the familiar tubes of a regenite infusion. Four corp security cruisers, a fire truck, and a forensics transport created a blinding cacophony of light in front of the shop. One of the cruisers followed the ambulance toward the expressway, having to pause at the exit gate to let the two-meter concrete barrier retract into the ground. Another such barrier blocked the entrance.

It wasn't until the police pointed out the blood on his hand that Horace realized he had been shot. Two bullets had given him their little kisses, one through the meat of his shoulder, the other creasing the back of his forearm. The chitin plating of his forearms had turned the shot aside, but the inside of his jacket sleeve was wet with blood.

The paramedic wanted to take him to the hospital.

"Nah, just stitch it up right here," he said.

"I'm not allowed—"

"I don't care about what you're allowed," Horace interrupted. "I don't have the money for a hospital trip. I'll give you a thousand dollars to stitch it up right here. I know damn well you got the know-how."

The paramedic shrugged. "If you say so."

A security officer questioned him while the paramedic stitched. The wounds would hurt a lot more after the adrenaline wore off, but Horace and pain had been fuck-buddies for years. The guys who couldn't take pain didn't finish the second day of pit fighter training camp. Besides, his left shoulder hurt worse. Fortunately, that pain had faded. He didn't want to think about what it had been.

Horace gave his account of what happened, playing up the story that he hadn't been expected to win the fight with Gaston. His victory had pissed off the wrong people.

"What the hell happened to the corpse?" Horace asked. "I've never seen anything like that before."

The cop pulled his wrist away from interfacing his netlink, and his eyes focused on Horace. "Hyper-germ implants. Megacorp black ops have been using them for years, but now the mob has picked them up. A capsule in the chest cavity. The heart stops, the capsule releases flesh-eating superbacteria. Five minutes later, nothing left but toxic goop. It's a damn efficient way to do away with fingerprints, retinal records, even dental records, minus fillings. And the goop is deadly as hell for several hours until the bacteria eat everything and die off. We're going to have to shut down this whole place for at least twelve hours."

Horace whistled. Somehow he couldn't muster much sympathy for the loss of corporate profits.

"Before we let you go," the officer said, "there's just one last thing."

"What's that?"

The officer smirked, "Your autograph, Hammer?"

Horace smiled. "Sure."

"For my kid, you know." The officer held out his notepad and pen, and Horace signed it. "Thanks!"

A short man with a shiny dome and a comb-over approached, a cigar clamped in his teeth poking through a walrus mustache. Beady eyes glanced between Horace and the officer. "Hey, flatfoot! I gotta get on the road! How long before we can get out of here? "

The officer's eyes narrowed. "When we're damn good and ready. Sir."

"Sorry about the flatfoot crack, officer. I'm a businessman. Gotta roll, you know. Anything I can do to help?"

"No. Sir."

"I guess we got off on the wrong foot. Norman Trask." The man offered the officer his hand.

The officer hesitated before shaking it.

"When I say help, what I mean is, anything I can do to hurry things along?" He reached conspicuously into his pocket.

"No. Sir."

"And when I say hurry, I mean like in the next half hour."

The officer's frown deepened. "If you don't shut the fuck up—right now, sir—I will personally guarantee you are stuck here until next month. After all, this is a murder scene. A *massive* investigation."

"Fine, fine, officer, whatever you say. Anything I can do to help our boys in...well, brown, I guess. That hat looks like a million bucks on you."

The officer walked away with a look of careful restraint on his face.

Trask looked up at Horace. "And what's your story, Tiny? You look a little worse for wear."

"It's been a while, Trask." Horace offered his hand to a man he hadn't seen in twenty-five years. With the memory came curiosity, and he searched his recollections. Trask had had more hair back then, but the same low, sturdy frame. "Sorry to hear about Rush. He was a hell of a fighter."

Trask averted his eyes. "Yeah, a big, beautiful bunch of bad luck. Poor bastard. If only."

"'If only' is right. That guy was going straight to the top." Horace's details on Trask's career were a little fuzzy after two and half decades, but he still remembered Trask's fighter, Sirius "The Demolisher" Rush, and the beatdown Rush had given him. And it had all been a favor.

A cocky, up-and-coming Hammer Harkness, approached by an unknown promoter named Norman Trask in a parking lot after a fight, saying this amazing young fighter might be able to give The Hammer's rising star a challenge in the pit. And if Hammer gave The Demolisher a chance, Trask would owe him a huge favor.

Back then the pit fighting scene was a new, booming industry, a new Wild West where anything was fair game. Deals were being made—and broken. Careers were being made—and broken. And this fast-talking young promoter named Trask said he had an eye for fighter flesh, and Sirius Rush was going to make a name for both of them. If only they could break in with a big bout against an established name. A few years into his career, The Hammer was already a rising star. There were those who had given Horace his breaks, and it stoked his ego to think he could do it for somebody else.

So he'd fought Sirius Rush in one of the most spectacularly bloody matches of those early years, before the weapons got so wild and advanced—and Sirius Rush had handed The Hammer his ass on a platter.

Horace had licked his wounds and then used the beating to mature and grow as a fighter.

Rush had been launched into the stratosphere of wealth and celebrity. Endorsement deals. Massive contracts that brought more mainstream sponsors into the fold, helping this ultraviolent sport into the mainstream. Rush had it all. Fighting ability, presence and charisma, dashing good looks, a bevy of Hollywood starlets for girlfriends.

For about eight months.

Until a stim-addled trucker hauling a load of rebar had turned Rush and his hover cycle into a smear of hamburger and lubricant.

When Rush died, all those contracts and residuals had died with him, leaving Norman Trask to disappear like a UFO off a radar screen.

"So what are you doing here?" Trask said. "Of all the places on the continent, we run into each other at a piss-ass rest stop."

"I was just having a cup of coffee. That your rig over there?" Horace gestured with his head toward the road train.

"Yeah, Norman Trask Promotions, that's me. Don't think I didn't recognize Hammer Harkness across the parking lot."

The paramedic gave Horace's shoulder one last swab with antiseptic, then slapped a broad swath of gauze across the wound. "You're all set, sir. But take it easy. You tear those sutures, you'll regret it."

"Thank you, ma'am. You do good work." Horace pulled his cash out of his pocket, thumbed off a sufficient sheaf of bills, and handed them to her. "I know good stitches when I see 'em."

The paramedic flushed slightly, took the bills, buckled up her kit, and retreated to the other ambulance.

"C'mon," Trask said. "I got a Glenfiddich 40 burning a hole in the bottle."

Horace followed Trask toward the road train, scrutinizing the fighters standing beside the open doors who were, in turn, scrutinizing him right back.

The sides of the cars were opened up like boxcars, with pneumatic steps descending to the pavement. Horace carried his duffel and equipment case.

The promoter walked with a slight limp, his barrel-shaped body trundling along, trailing a curl of cigar smoke—at least it was a good cigar. Leather loafers that were expensive ten years ago, now scuffed and worn; rumpled trousers; a sport jacket that didn't lie well over his slight paunch.

Horace glanced back toward his bus. Across fifty yards of parking lot, Horace's bus driver, leaning against the side of the bus smoking a cigarillo, watched him go. Nowadays, as AIs had taken over most driving tasks, calling him a bus driver was an anachronism. He was more a security guard and tour guide these days, depending on the sophistication of the vehicle's controlling intelligence. His presence on the bus had probably deterred the two shooters until they reached the truck stop.

The Russian hit team knew where he was, knew which bus he was on, probably would expect him to get back on it. Which meant that they might be waiting for the bus at the next stop. But how had they found him so quickly? He couldn't remember when the two assassins had boarded the bus, but they hadn't gotten on in Vegas. How far would they chase him?

As he drew nearer to the road train, expressions of recognition bloomed on several hard faces. A tall, lithe woman looked him up and down, her face all sharp angles and flat planes and pale, flinty eyes.

Grunting at each step, Trask climbed into the fluorescent cavern of the front car. Horace followed him into the comfortably appointed space. Playbills and autographed holos plastered the walls. The great ones, Gunnar Jackson, Blade Rodriguez, El Toro, from the early days of the neo-gladiators. Even a couple of faded, yellow photos of pro wrestlers from when Horace's granddaddy was a kid—Hulk Hogan, Andre the Giant. There was even a photo of Thundertron, champion of the United Cyber-Fighting Federation, the cyborg fighters.

"Have a seat," Trask said as he rummaged around under a counter, gesturing toward a couch of plush, scarlet velour.

Horace set down his things and eased himself onto the couch, which he wasn't certain would support his weight. A puff of dust and the waft of stale cigar smoke surrounded him.

Trask drew out a nearly empty bottle of scotch and displayed it with a cigar-clamped grin. "For special occasions."

"What's the occasion?"

"That remains to be seen." He set a glass onto the counter and poured a finger. Seeing there was only a dribble left in the bottle, he emptied it into the glass, hesitated a moment as if thinking he might keep it for himself, then offered it to Horace.

Horace took it. "Thanks, brother." He held up the glass of whiskey that likely cost about a month's rent. "You got good taste." He hadn't been able to afford a drink like this in years.

Trask grunted and poured himself a glass from another bottle, the kind of stuff available on any liquor store shelf. "Not many special occasions lately. Times are hard."

Horace listened for bitterness in Trask's voice. How must a guy like that feel, someone who had once stood to become filthy rich, only to watch it evaporate in a split second of bad luck? But he heard nothing except a jaded matter-of-factness. "But I don't need to tell you how hard things are, do I?"

"No, you sure as hell don't." Horace took a sip and savored the smoky honey-burn. "I worked the minors a long time."

Trask pulled up a chair and looked at him with the kind of no-bullshit expression of a shrewd used-car salesman reaching for a stack of cash. "But you just had an enormous score, massive pay-per-view contract, and you even got the win. You should be in Rio, swimming in pussy, champagne, and residuals. But you're on a piece-of-shit bus to Nowhere. Let's just say something's wrong with this picture."

The scotch in Horace's beveled glass caught the light.

Trask continued, "Hell of an event, you and The Freak." He rolled the cigar between his thumb and two fingers. "So why'd he throw the fight?"

Horace tried to play dumb. "What're you talking about?"

"Don't insult me. You don't work fighters as long as I have and not see when a fighter throws a bout. You might as well have painted it on your forehead. He held back the kill shot three times."

"I don't know what the fuck you're talking about. You'll have to take that up with him." Horace's heart tripped over a rib. Anger roiled inside him.

"Yeah, whatever. Look, it's not my business. But we both know you got a problem needs solving."

If Trask knew, others with similar skills would have seen it. Nothing would ever be said publicly, but the insiders would know.

"And I do owe you a favor," Trask said. "Don't think I forgot."

"That favor didn't pan out for you so good."

"Doesn't matter. I don't like owing people. It's one I've had on the books for a long time, and I'd like to clear it," Trask said.

"I hear you talking." Horace took another sip.

"I don't know if you've seen the news feeds or rag-mags, but you are on fire right now, my friend. You ought to be riding that wave, get what you can for as long as you can."

"That'd be the smart thing to do," Horace said. But ultimately the wave would subside and slide back into the ocean. Horace had not been following the news feeds after the fight. He had pulled the battery from his netlink, leaving it dead in his pocket so he couldn't be tracked. "Trouble is, the smart thing hasn't always been my thing."

Trask laughed with a tinge of something that was not mirth. "I'd say that's true of most people. Where you headed?"

"Montreal. I'm going to see about retirement." There it was again.

"Doing what, polishing up your French?"

"Gaston Rousseau's got a training camp and gym, wants to hire me."

"That sounds very...stable." The inflection on the last word was not a positive one. "That what you want?"

I want a new fucking heart! "We'll see. I think I need to rest for a while." Lay low.

Trask eyed him for a long moment over the rim of his glass. "That wasn't just a robbery or some shit back there."

Horace took a long drink.

"Who'd you piss off?"

"Russians."

Trask rubbed his stubbled cheek with a meaty hand, calculations flickering behind his eyes. "How much heat you got coming down?"

"That I don't know." The attempted hit at the rest stop was brazen. Dmitri's father, Yvgeny, was no doubt monumentally miffed about

Dmitri coming back without his head. Neither could Horace let Trask know just how much boiling oil he was swimming in. "But I need a ride. I need to disappear until the heat fades." He looked Trask squarely in the eye.

Trask nodded as if he had been waiting for Horace to say it. "Trouble is, I'd rather be a live asshole than a dead one."

Horace took another sip, feeling the burn down his throat, the cascade of subtle flavors of honey and oak and lost dreams crossing his tongue, filling his nose as the burn faded. Would Trask turn him over to the Russians? How much would they be willing to pay? What was Trask's price?

"Those guys on top," Trask said, "like we were once, can fall a long goddamn way. For all I know, you're strung out on HypEx and Russian whores. Promoters like me can have a reputation too, but it generally involves things like greed and who fucked who over. If you're really into it with the Russians, you might be wondering, 'How much will this guy sell me to them for?'"

Horace nodded.

"The Russians don't play nice. I try to make a deal with them, they're more likely to kill me, then you, and then everybody on this fucking train, just to make a point. So let's not tell them you're here."

Horace nodded again.

Trask said, "If they slice the parking lot video of you getting on this train, you might have already fucked me over before we even pull out."

Horace leaned forward, elbows on his knees. "I don't want anybody to get hurt on account of me. I just need to get off this immediate spot before the next hitter shows up. The next rest stop, I don't care."

Trask's eyes narrowed, calculating, chewing on his cigar. "A couple of things are working in your favor here. One, this whole train is full of trained badass killers, in case you forgot. Granted, they ain't much with guns, but don't get within reach. Two, I got other defenses that shall remain mum's the fucking word. You don't run this kind of operation as long as I have without making a few mortal enemies."

"I don't have any money to give you. I can't afford any public appearances or fights. At least until I get this cleared up. But I'm willing to make it up you in any way I can. I'll owe *you* a huge favor. Name it."

"Teach my fighters."

Fear around his ticker made Horace hesitate. "I can't train them either."

"Like I said, I got me a whole trainload of badass larvae. They're fighters, every one of them, but none of them are great like you, like The Freak."

"I can't train them." He rubbed his chest.

"I got a trainer. I want you to *teach* them. Help them over that next step. Make them *stars*." Trask's eyes twinkled with ambition. "I want every arena these boys walk into to go rabid-berserk-screaming-insane. I want their faces on the cover of every rag-mag from here to Buenos Aires. *You* can teach them how to do that."

Trask downed his whiskey with finality. "You ride with us to Albany. I got an empty berth. Had a fatality last month, poor bastard. Albany's a skip and skedaddle from Montreal. You ride with us that far. You do your best to teach my boys. In Albany, we re-evaluate. What do you say? You're talking so fast I can't get a fucking word in."

Relief flooded Horace in a warm gush. He raised his glass. "I say I'd be much obliged."

CHAPTER SEVEN

Trask led Horace onto the pavement toward the rear of the road train, passing a couple of knots of fighters who all eyed him with mixtures of surprise and awe. He nodded to them as he passed. All of them were at least twenty years his junior. Young, hungry, desperate to build a record and stay alive long enough for a shot at the big time, but already showing the scars of natural healing that regenites would have simply erased.

"Hammer, the Crew," Trask said. "Crew, The Hammer."

As they walked toward the rear car and passed out of the other fighters' earshot, Horace said, "All these guys know me. How long before they start spreading the word to their networks?"

Trask said, "I'll take care of that. I run on what you might call a supervised public relations system. Nobody on this train spreads anything on the net without my stamp of approval."

"How do you manage that with wireless everywhere?"

Trask tapped his temple with a finger. "Best not to ask too many questions."

The rear car looked like something out of an old film, a train car repurposed for highway travel, complete with sleeping berths with Murphy beds and a hallway so low and narrow Horace had to stoop and walk sideways. At least he got a berth to himself.

Trask opened a door and gestured Horace into one of the sleeper berths. "An elephant could fill this up with a good dump, but it's what we got."

"I've had worse."

A couple of heads poked out of other berths, one a young woman.

Trask said, "You look like you need some Z's. Make sure you powder your nose. And, oh yeah, any of my boys gives you any shit, feel free to put them in their place, but don't injure them. Keeping them alive already costs me a fortune. Tina, what the fuck, you never seen a legend before?"

A woman in her midtwenties with hair a rainbow of pink, purple, blue, and orange, stood in the doorway of the berth next to Horace's. "I see you every day, Mr. Trask."

"Suck-up. This here is one of the great ones. Meet Horace The Hammer Harkness. They call him—"

"The Man Who Won't Stay Dead," she said. "Twenty-seven resurrections, 287 victories—sorry, 288—plus 192 confirmed kills. Last weigh-in, 168.7 kilos, 210.4 centimeters." As she reeled off these statistics, she looked him up and down. Dressed in white tights with red and black polka-dots, a faded red tank top, both arms fully sleeved in tattoos of Chinese dragons and characters, cherry blossoms, and *geisha*, she came to about his solar plexus, all round-faced, brown-eyed, sweet and adorable beyond comprehension.

Horace hated her already.

"Hammer, Tina. She runs the spit bucket and writes story copy."

Horace cracked a grin. "Since when do they let junior high kids manage blood-swabs?"

Tina's face darkened, a plump lip stuck out, and she stalked toward him with a pointed finger. "Since I'm the best there is, spit wad." Then she glanced sheepishly at Trask. "I mean—er, Hammer, sir."

Horace laughed at the conflict in her expression.

"You two play nice," Trask said. "I'm going to bed."

After Trask disappeared, Horace stowed his duffel and equipment case in his berth.

Tina leaned against the doorjamb, crossing her arms. "What the hell is a fucking legend doing *here*?"

"Needed a ride. What the hell is a snot-nosed kid doing with these yay-hoos?"

"Eat shit, Methuselah! I can handle myself."

"Is there a shower in this place?"

"You do smell like rancid road-ass. Shower's right in the back, but there's no hot water."

"I've smelled worse." Horace dragged a towel out of his duffel. "And you're not allowed to check me out when I'm coming out of the shower, kid. I'm old enough to be your father."

"Grandfather."

He could stand up straight in the berth, just barely, and faced her in the doorway. "Father."

"Whatever you say, Moses."

Horace shut the door to the cramped shower compartment and thumbed the switch on his netlink. He may as well turn it on for a few moments before the road train departed. The Russians already knew where he was, at least for the time being.

The first thing he saw was a long string of requests for interviews and media appearances. He could milk those for some cash—if he lived long enough.

The second thing was a voice message from a blocked source, two days ago. A thick Russian accent, coarse and throaty. "You the deadest motherfucker ever to get dead!" A deluge of garbled Russian followed until the message ended with a click.

"People threaten my life every day, you pud-knocker," Horace grumbled.

A voice message from Lilly, so choked with emotion she could barely get the words out. "Hammer, I don't know what you did or how you did it, but...thank you so much! The doctors say Jimmy is going to be okay." Her voice, weeping and half hysterical with joy, made his heart flutter. He closed his eyes and took a deep, slow breath. "Hammer, I wasn't very nice the last time I saw you, and I'm sorry. Call me."

A warm shiver raced up his spine and across his skull, and he almost choked with a sudden surge of emotion. His thumb hovered over the *Call* button, but he paused. He didn't dare talk to her right now. What had he wanted her to do anyway, after his grand gesture? Come over and do him right then and there? Believe the look in his eyes that said he wanted more from her than just the pink parts?

"Goddammit," he muttered.

Instead of calling her, he thumbed in a message:

I CAN'T CALL NOW. THERE ARE REALLY BAD PEOPLE AFTER ME. THEY MIGHT COME AFTER MY FRIENDS TO GET TO ME. TAKE A VACATION. AND STAY OFF THE NET. I'LL CALL WHEN I CAN.

But what if they already had her? He should have warned her sooner, told the cops or something. He was short on friends as it was without putting her in danger.

There was one more friend, however, who might be willing to help him.

He thumbed Jack's icon. Two rings, and a tinny Arkansas twang with a four-pack-a-day habit buzzed into his ear. "Hammer, you're alive, you crazy bastard!"

"Yeah, brother, still upright and ambulatory, at least until the Russians catch me."

"Word on the street is you kicked the fucking hornet's nest."

"Stomped on it a couple of times."

"What'd you—scratch that, I don't wanna know."

"Smart man. I need a favor—"

"You want me to look after Lilly for you." The grin in Jack's voice came through loud and clear, along with the hint that this would not be an unpleasant task.

"You'll have to put this favor on credit. I'm tapped. Take her somewhere safe."

"What if she ain't inclined to go?"

"Convince her. She's got two kids."

"Look, amigo, I made the funds transfer for you, but that boy's gonna be in the hospital for a few more days. They were talking about DNA reconfiguration, gene therapy, plus regeneration."

The boy would be a target for as long as he was in the hospital. The thought of that old hit-woman waltzing into the boy's hospital room and delivering a double-tap made Horace's teeth grind. "Fuck."

"Fuck is right. What you gonna do?"

"Destroy the entire Russian syndicate if I got to."

"I might could keep an eye on her."

"Thanks, brother." Horace swallowed hard. Another debt he would never be able to pay. "You're not going to be able to reach me. I'll call you when I can."

"Keep it tight, amigo."

Horace thumbed off the netlink, closed his fist around it, and pressed his forehead against the fiberglass bulkhead.

The blood ran cold down the drain of the tiny shower stall. The inside sleeve of his leather jacket would be stiff with dried blood by morning. Even tepid water felt good after two days on the road. Waves of exhaustion stole the strength from his limbs until his hands felt too weak to grip a weapon. He let the shower massage the back of his neck until his muscles began to uncoil. Had he really been so tense for so long? The gunshot wounds would ache like hell in the morning, and worse the day after.

Would he have done anything differently over the last twenty years if he'd known that he would end up like this, a broken-down, old warrior with a bad ticker? After twenty-seven resurrections, some of the damage to his heart was permanent. There was no fixing this one. It was a new heart or a new urn. His winnings would have paid for a shiny, new heart, but there was an innocent kid and a desperate mama who needed the money more.

What about cybernetics? There was a whole league of cyborg gladiators now, doing much the same thing as he had been doing for decades, but flashier now, taking even less of the edge off of death. But those guys had high-powered corporate sponsors, the military-industrial kind that banked on prosthetics and enhancements that exceeded anything biology could do, and a ruling body Horace wanted to be nowhere near. The microprint on those contracts had to stretch into the thousands of pages. He'd heard some of those guys were working under repossession clauses: break the contract and they come and repo your limbs and organs. Corporations had turned government into an afterthought, running roughshod over the entire human race.

Running roughshod over an aging stripper and her son with a rare bone disease. The only way he could protect Lilly from the Russians now was to get as far away from her as possible and hope they didn't go after her anyway. A sigh leaked out of him at the possibility that she might be dead already. He could just hear Dmitri's voice, "Come and get your little titty-flasher, Hammer. Papa is unhappy with you."

By now, Dmitri's head and body had been joyfully reunited in a nice urn on Daddy's mantelpiece.

There was no way the old man would let Dmitri's death go unavenged. The Russians were worse than the Italians for their vendettas. They would hound Horace into an excruciating demise. And with his heart like this, that kind of relentless stress would take a toll very soon. For all he knew, he could die on the crapper during a strenuous dump.

He snorted at the idea of such a fool's death. A nobody's death.

How many more scars would he need to add to the road map on his body before he got somewhere he wanted to stay for a while? Every scar was a story, some of them triumphs, some of them defeats, some of them screaming clusterfucks. Most had been inflicted since the glory days of his early career. Way back then, the resurrections and regenerations all came on someone else's dime, Regenecorp showcasing their world-changing technology. Nowadays, it was a whole different world, one he was barely a part of anymore.

How far would he have to go to evade the Russians' reach? Maybe he would never go far enough. Maybe he just wanted the wild ride. Maybe what he told Thea was true: he loved the ditches.

A knock on the metal door. Tina's voice came through. "You about done in there? You need a wheelchair?"

"I got your wheelchair right here, kid." Wow, what a lame comeback. Why couldn't he ever think of the snappy ones until hours later?

She snorted. "We're pulling out, and Bunny drives like a fiend. You might want to hold onto your walker."

The hiss of releasing air brakes echoed through the floor.

He shut off the water and toweled dry, babying his wounded arm, and stepped out into the hallway naked, concealing the goodies with a dangling towel.

Tina stepped backward with a strange grace. "Well aren't you a sight."

He paused at the door of his own berth. "I told you, you're not allowed to check me out."

"Just seeing if you needed a wheelchair, Grandpa." She crossed her arms. "Do you automatically assume every woman you meet wants to sleep with you?"

"Are you telling me they don't?"

"So is every woman a sexual object for you?"

"I prefer the term potential partner. It takes two to tango."

She rolled her eyes with an exaggerated sigh. "And sexist pigs *still* exist."

"Hey, there's no need to insult me. I love women." And he had once killed the great love of his life.

Tina sighed and rolled her eyes. "Look if you must, but if you try to put the moves on me, I'll end you."

Another head poked out of a berth further forward, the mature woman with the angular face he had seen outside, perhaps ten years older than Tina. The older woman spied Horace and smiled.

Horace winked at Tina. "See?" Then he slipped into his berth, slid the door shut, yanked the Murphy bed out of the wall, and collapsed into it.

Before sleep claimed him, the room around him filled his mind with its own stories, echoes of a life now absent. A poster-size holograph of a beautiful woman taped to the ceiling. Stuck in the mirror over the minuscule bureau, a photograph of the same woman embracing a young fighter. A young, dead fighter.

Through his memory flashed a parade of faces, opponents who had not come back from death. Poor bastards. Well, most of them. Angus "The Highlander" MacLish had been an evil prick, someone who reveled in the killing itself, an abusive sadist who also liked to beat on pit girls and groupies. Crushing the Highlander's skull with a Thunder Hammer, knowing MacLish's entire brain would be rendered into crunchy blood-paste, knowing such a traumatic brain injury was irreparable, even by regenites, had been Horace's gift to the world. MacLish's ex-wife had sent Horace flowers. The rag-mags had put the blow on every cover for a month and had made Hammer Harkness a name to be feared in the pit.

The aches seeped out of Horace's body into the bed. Streetlights shining through the window angled out of sight. The bed lurched once and began to vibrate with the feel of the road.

Horace jerked awake at a knock on the door. He lay naked on the bed, heedless of the cool air sifting through the cracked window.

"Who is it?" he croaked.

The door slid open to reveal the hard-angled face of the woman. "Let's just say I'm a fan." She smiled, apparently unfazed by the naked, hairy mound of muscle and scars in front of her.

"You getting a good enough look there?"

She opened the door just wide enough to admit her lithe form. She wore a black, silk robe that clung to her like synth-skin, embroidered in gold and scarlet with dragons and roses. "Not quite. I'm Jocie."

"Well, Jocie, I'm kinda tired. How about you hold that thought till tomorrow?"

She had a dancer's body, coal-black hair pulled into a tight bun behind her head, eyes roaming across his flesh with increasing hunger. "What thought is that?"

He elbowed himself up into a sitting position. "Lady, looks to me like you got a mind to fuck my brains out."

"Is that so? Aren't you a little full of yourself?" A small mouth quirked a half grin.

"Introductions aren't usually made in the buff."

"I'm not in the buff." She sat down on the bed with the strong, smooth grace possessed only by bodies honed for decades. A swath of silky thigh lay revealed all the way to the crease of her hip. Her face was a little too angular to be beautiful, her eyes a little too sharp to be warm, but there was no question about the temperature of other parts.

"You sure as hell are buff under there," he said.

"Well, we're used to our bodies on display, aren't we, people like us. Our bodies are our livelihood, aren't they? Meat for the masses." The lean of her shoulder accentuated one flawless breast and mostly exposed the other one. "And some of us have more to offer than others."

He hadn't gotten laid in months, training hard for his bout with Gaston. There just hadn't been time. Not that he hadn't tried to coax Lilly into the sack, but that had gone strangely awry. Now, this Jocie, he couldn't take his eyes off her, and neither could his dick. It started to thicken against his leg. He sat up and threw his feet over the side of the bed.

"Look—" he began.

Then a knock came at the door. "Hey, *Jocasta*, you in there?" Tina's voice, strangely emphasizing the name.

Jocie's eyes narrowed. "What do *you* want?"

"I heard Lex is looking for you."

Jocie called back, "Tell him to keep fucking looking and mind your own business!"

The door cracked open and Tina's face appeared. "Wow, you work fast. Come to think of it, *Jocasta*, we just passed a dumpster that would be perfect for you to suck cock behind."

Jocie jumped to her feet, pulling her robe tighter around her. "You are such a fucking...urchin! I'll bet you know all the dumpsters!"

Horace watched this interplay with growing amusement.

"Besides," Tina said, "you don't wanna fuck this guy. He's so old, his heart's liable to explode." She made an explosive gesture with her fingers. "*Coitus interruptus.*" She faced out into the hallway. "Oh, I think I hear Lex coming now."

Without ruffling another feather, Jocie turned to Horace. "Perhaps we can have a *private* conversation sometime soon."

Tina slid the door open for her. Jocie breezed from the room without another look at Tina. Tina slid into the room, closed the door behind her, and faced Horace squarely. The beginnings of his hard-on melted away, and he picked up his towel and wrapped himself in it.

"What, are you suddenly shy now?" she said. "Old school coming out?"

"You're starting to piss me off, little girl."

Her brow furrowed. "Fuck you, Humbert. You don't want any piece of that." She thumbed over her shoulder. "I was just saving you more drama than you need."

"Who's Lex?"

"The sawmill sound down the hall. Her husband. He's been Trask's number one for the last six months, and he flaunts it around this place like he's the Second Coming. I call her Octopussy. She doesn't have nearly as many orifices as she wants."

"And how does Lex feel about this?"

"He likes having the hottest woman on the train, but he's too dense to realize he's in what you might call an open relationship. Plus he's mean and thinks he's on the way up. Challenging Hammer Harkness might be just the ticket he's looking for."

Horace nodded, but Jocie was hardly the hottest woman on this train. And something had felt nonkosher for a reason. "Thanks for the heads-up, kid. I appreciate it. But don't ever just walk into my room again. For your own safety."

"You're welcome. But don't ever call me kid again. For your own safety."

"Deal."

"Deal."

CHAPTER EIGHT

Horace slept the sleep of someone six-months-in-the-ground. If he hadn't been in a locked room, he might have had to fight off buzzards trying to eat his liver.

The road train lay quiet, stationary, the power plant spooled down. Traffic noises and sunlight filtered through the blinds he didn't remember closing.

His shoulder seethed with a burning ache. In retrospect, having the paramedic stitch him up might not have been the wisest course of action. If any bits of clothing remained inside the wound, he was in for a screaming infection and might end up in the hospital anyway.

He pulled out his other set of clothes and got dressed. The sleeve of his leather jacket was, as predicted, stiff with dried blood, so he left it off. Sighing at the loss, he looked at himself in the mirror and considered raking a razor across his skull, then decided it would be best to let his hair and beard grow out and obscure his tattoos.

Midmorning sunlight painted rails on the bed. Through the open window wafted the smell of...breakfast. Bacon, eggs, toast, sausage, a glorious explosion of smoked meat and grease. What an incredible luxury, that much real meat. Just what his heart needed. He peeked outside.

A brown field stretched into the distance, a failed crop of something that had withered to ankle-high. A huge billboard beside the field read "*PROPERTY OF AGRIMAX.*"

Around the road train at this roadside picnic stop, a smattering of other vehicles, mainly transports, lay quiescent. Across the field on a gravel road, a horse trotted along ahead of an Amish carriage.

The train's second car opened into a broad awning sheltering several retractable picnic tables where a couple dozen people sat at breakfast. A broad grill belched swirls of steam and smoke, with a short, stocky brunette working it like an Olympic short-order cook.

When Horace approached the tables, heads turned. "Morning," he said.

Some of them returned the gesture, others simply nodded. Seated beside a man almost as large as Horace, Jocie's flinty eyes slithered up and down his body as she smiled at him. The man beside her let the surprise on his face hang out like a flasher's genitalia. He leaned over and said to her, "What the fuck is Hammer Harkness doing here?"

Jocie whispered back, "He got on board last night, sweetie. Now don't be rude."

Trask stood up and gestured Horace over. Horace joined him.

Trask said to the woman doing the cooking, "Bunny, a plate for our new guest."

The woman turned around, drank Horace in with one glance, and grinned. Black jack-ins embedded behind each ear peeked through shoulder-cut, mousy brown hair. She had the middle-aged-spinster-cat-lady-next-door look, but a kind smile and eyes that glinted with strange lights.

She scooped a huge mound of scrambled eggs out of an enormous, cast-iron skillet, loaded him up with at least ten slices of thick-cut bacon that smelled maple-cured, and four pieces of thick, multi-grain toast slathered in butter. "I'm Bunny," she said. "A pleasure to meet you, Mr. Harkness."

"Horace. My friends call me Hark." He offered his free hand, and she shook it.

"My god," she said, marveling at Horace's hands and forearms. "Are those real?"

"They're not cybernetics, if that's what you're asking," Horace said. He knocked on his forearm with an equally hard knuckle. "Gene mods."

She blinked once, eyes going blank for a split second, then focused on him again. "Ah, Horace *The Hammer* Harkness."

"One and the same."

"I get it now. The Thunder Hammer."

"My signature move."

"You'll have to forgive my momentary ignorance," she said. "I just drive the train."

She had strong hands, firm hands, tattoos across her knuckles, and she held onto his just a little too long. He winked at her. She blushed and turned back toward the grill, giving him a better look at the hardware behind her ears.

Trask wiped his mouth with a linen napkin. "Bunny's what you might call our engineer."

Bunny's eyes flickered as if reading something only she could see, and her ears flushed pink. "Impressive record, Mr. Harkness. And that *Maximus* photo spread. Ooo la la."

For a moment Horace wondered how she suddenly knew about the twenty-year-old promo spread of him flexing with and without a Speedo... "Ah, implants," he said, a smile of understanding spreading across his face. "At least you picked the good ones."

"The net never forgets," she said with a sly little smile.

Horace sat down at the table with Trask and happened to catch Tina's eye at the corner of the far table, chomping on a piece of bacon like she had a tapeworm.

"Whuh?" she said with her mouth full.

Trask sipped steaming coffee from a cracked porcelain cup.

Horace took it all in, and it all felt familiar, comfortable. Like hanging out with a large extended family, complete with internecine dramas, friendships, stories, passions, and even, he suspected, enemies. "You've got a good operation here, Mr. Trask."

Bunny brought him a cup and offered to pour. He accepted it with thanks.

A pair of hot eyes awled into him, and he caught Jocie's husband staring at him. Horace eased back, narrowed his eyes, and held the gaze, for several seconds, for half a minute, for a minute, each passing second stoking the fire of challenge in the other man's gaze. Finally Horace winked at him, and the man looked away with a scowl.

Horace stood up and addressed the tables. "Time to cut through a little bullshit before it gets too deep. You all know who I am. Mr. Trask here was nice enough to let me travel with you for a while. But I don't have any plans to get back in the pit anytime soon. I'm not after anyone's bunk." Several of the other fighters relaxed a bit at this. "I've worked the minors and outfits like this one for years. Anybody looking for a light sparring partner, you just got to ask."

"Mighty big of you," Jocie's husband grumbled.

"Lex!" Trask said, "Show a little respect."

Lex stood, fists on the tabletop. "To what? A half-eaten piece of meat?" He stepped away from the table, snatched Jocie's arm, and dragged her after him. She stumbled and protested, trying to pry his fingers loose, but had no choice but to follow.

"Who shit on his toothbrush?" someone mumbled after Lex and Jocie had gone. Laughter rippled around the tables.

Trask put his hands on his hips and surveyed his fighters. "You all know The Hammer here. And you all got a lot of potential. You are all supreme badasses in training. But they call our outfit the minors for a reason. Hammer here, he's going to show you how to make the big time. You gotta learn to work the crowd. You gotta learn showmanship. Be the difference between a neighborhood butcher and an all-star chef with his own show."

Horace said, "I'm here to help you fellas out."

Several of the fighters nodded with appreciation.

Trask said, "Right, then. First class starts in the gym in two hours."

Horace's eyes bulged.

An endless ribbon of concrete spooled out behind the road train. Even though it was designed to travel long distances without a break, the next few days were slated to be one stop after another. Half a day in each of several cities, Toledo, Cleveland, Buffalo, and finally Albany, where a full card of matches was scheduled in a local arena, Trask's fighters versus another stable calling themselves the Death Dealers.

This East Coast circuit was unfamiliar to Horace. He had spent most of his career in the west and bouncing around the Pacific Rim, so he didn't recognize any of the names from either of these stables. Such was the minors.

He lay in his berth thinking about what he could possibly teach these guys. He racked his brain, but exhaustion lay over him like a lead apron. In his early years, a number of mentors had dealt out their wisdom from the ranks of pro wrestling and MMA leagues. Pit fighting had been a unique fusion of those sports with the advent of regeneration technology. They had all made it up as they went, the fighters, the promoters.

Horace listened to his heart beating, wondering when it might run down like an antique grandfather clock. A little catch in the gears and he would just...stop. He had stopped before, twenty-seven times—from blades, axes, trauma, blood loss—like going to sleep, but there wasn't any dreaming. And the waking up was like being dragged out of a box full of nails scraping across his mind, harsh and cold and then there he was, back among the living, with billions of programmed molecular-scale protein machines teeming through his body, rebuilding him with flawless precision, better than his body could rebuild itself.

But after last night, it was like he had fallen into a deep, black funk that could not be assuaged. The sound of Thea Striker's wounded screams echoed in the coliseum tunnels of his memory. A sense of lonesomeness washed over him, like a man stuck in the middle of a freezing river with a mile to either bank, adrift in a current he could not see. His whole life, he'd been a man who clutched his destiny in both fists, but this sense of being not only adrift, but relying on the help of others, and moreover, putting those others in jeopardy, scared him more than any pit fighter with a vibro-axe. With the price on his head, he felt like a grenade ready to go off in somebody else's lap.

When moods hit him like this, his first impulse was usually to go find the closest strip club. And that was where he'd met Lilly, her enormous brown eyes like those of a doe. Her smell, the feel of her skin, her high, firm breasts like half grapefruits, her ass grinding on him and the hot crucible nestled between taut buttocks, and then that one flabbergasting night that had set him all but off the rails. The aching almostness of it. His list of sexual notches was high-powered and well into the triple digits, but he had never made a serious run at a stripper. Jack had once warned him from his own experience: *You think after spending hours having to give a bunch of yay-hoos their little thrills, she's gonna want to come home and do anything for* you, *amigo?*

But he hadn't felt that kind of *real spark* since Amanda. She had disappeared so completely that her absence left an echo shaped like her in his life, an echo so profound her name felt hallowed. Only two women had ever truly touched him. One was alive—as far as he knew—and the other was dead—as far as he knew.

Maybe he just needed to get laid. In the light of day and the knowledge of her entanglements, putting Jocie's ankles up around his ears didn't seem like nearly as attractive a diversion as it had last night. Lex was a killer, no question—not that Horace feared him even a little—but a guy like that was prone to rampage, and when a guy like that lost control, even bystanders got hurt.

In light of that, along with the fact that Horace's impulse to bed every buxom female in sight had diminished somewhat by the time the Big Five-O arrived, he thought it best to keep it in his pants when she was around.

He climbed out of bed with a snort of profanity.

Out in the hallway, he passed Tina's open door, where she sat in her berth with her sneakers up against the window, reading an old-fashioned paper book. Today, she looked like a polka-dot rainbow had exploded, complete with glittering holograms of shifting star fields on her clothes that moved as her body shifted.

Without turning, she said "Ready for your seminar, Spartacus?"

"Going stir crazy thinking about it. Needed to stretch my legs." Then he saw the old holo-poster on Tina's wall. His woman of wonder, in three dimensions and bigger than life, fist raised, blue eyes burning into him, titanium tiara glinting, and those lips he had never forgotten smiling fiercely. Words stumbled in his throat.

She caught the direction of his gaze. "You a fan, too?"

He coughed before his eyes could tear up. "Yeah. She was a goddess. Tried to kill me once."

"My dad was a huge fan. He met her once at a promo event when I was in diapers. I was maybe ten when he told me about it, but even then I could see he was smitten."

Horace couldn't tear his gaze away. "She had that effect."

"We watched a few of her old fights together. She used that lasso like no one I've ever heard of." She shrugged. "Anyway, tough-babe role models are hard to come by."

"You could do worse than learning from a woman like Amanda."

"You sound like you knew her."

"Like I said, she tried to kill me once."

Tina looked at him a long time, searching, reading him.

Horace scratched his stubble and peeled his eyes away from the poster. There was that old ache again.

She returned her attention to her book. "The gym is two cars up."

Pumping iron was almost as effective as sex for relieving pent-up angst. Maybe he could occupy himself with that. He thanked her and went forward.

At the front of the car was a sliding door leading to the next car. Like a passenger train, a rubberized canvas boot enclosed the gap between cars. The next car resembled the last, a long row of berths. The next car opened into a gym, complete with weight machines, cardio trainers, a heavy bag, speed bag, and black, polymer striking dummies. The impulse to work up a good sweat, something that often helped lube his thinking process, jumped to mind, but then his heart seemed to sidestep, and he thought it best to take things easy for now.

Two fighters were taking turns on the bench press, pumping great stacks of iron plates. The air smelled of sweat, vinyl, metal, and muscle ointment.

The fighters' expressions burned with fierce determination and the concentration required to squeeze every last gram of strength-building from their workouts. Not the time for chitchat. He simply nodded to them and passed by. What the hell could he possibly have to teach them? He was The Hammer, and that was all.

The next car forward was another set of sleeping berths. The one ahead of that housed enormous industrial refrigerators, interspersed with a fully functional galley, everything looking as if it was fashioned from great blocks of stainless steel and chrome. A dishwasher large enough for him to sleep in churned and rumbled as he passed.

Beyond the galley lay an infirmary, complete with examination table and medical equipment that was new about the time fuzz had first appeared around his willie.

Passing through the lounge car, complete with 3-D screen, couches, and bar, he finally reached the front car. Below his feet, the massive power plant rumbled and whined, pulsing power back into each car's drive wheels. From the doorway he found himself in a narrow hallway that apparently stretched to the driver's compartment, snaking behind Trask's compartment. Snoring reverberated from behind an opaque window that read "*Norman Trask, Promoter.*"

His mind wandered to unfamiliar sorts of tactical thinking. Intimately familiar with how to fight one-on-one in the pit, how to use the open space, how to crowd the fence, how to give himself more options while limiting his opponents', he now found himself gauging the possibility of combat in the cramped spaces of this enormous vehicle, what corners would be most advantageous to fight around when Russian thugs stormed the train. Jesus and Thor, he was getting jumpy. All this elaborate planning meant nothing if the Russians simply taped a few blocks of Nitrex to the hull and keyed the detonator from a distance.

The hallway ended in the plastic door to what had to be the driver's compartment. He knocked.

"It's open!" came Bunny's voice.

He pushed it open and suddenly felt like he'd stepped into a box of Valentine candy. It was a small cabin, with a bunk bed draped in pink and crimson sheets, a pink leather chair, photographs of a much younger Bunny and a couple of little girls. Pink and crimson carpet slathered the textured floor. The front of the compartment was all windshield and control panel with a chair for the driver, which now sat empty. The road train's AI was in control, but it would be Bunny's job to oversee it. At the sight of him, Bunny jumped so high she almost bumped her head on the ceiling. The air in her cabin smelled of cinnamon and cardamom.

"Why, Mr. Harkness," she said, "what are you doing here?" Her gaze scrambled around the room like a startled house cat. She snatched up some scattered laundry, empty coffee mugs, and a half-empty bag of pork rinds and tossed them into the front seat.

"I got lost."

"What can I do for you, Mr. Harkness?" Her cheeks flushed like polished apples.

"Call me Hark." He felt suddenly at a loss as to why he was there at all. Yearning for human contact? Maybe the lonesomeness had overtaken him. He normally had no problem ingratiating himself among other fighters. They all spoke the same language, one of physical prowess, of spots, of choreography, of weapons, of ways to work the crowds that went beyond simple blood sport.

But something was different now. Something had shifted, as if he were no longer one of them, when even three days ago he had been in his element. Then again, maybe they were all as green and stupid and clueless as he used to be. All of them were full of spunk and fire to be sure, but did they really have what it took to do anything but die a fool's death?

"A seat maybe?" Bunny said. Something in her eyes made him sit down in the pink vinyl kitchen chair she offered. She was perhaps a couple of years younger than him, with a look in her eyes that bespoke volumes of checkered history, the same kind of world-weariness that he felt in his bones made her look older than she was.

"So what's a nice girl like you doing in a place like this?" he said.

She chuckled. "Want some tea?"

He chuckled himself. "Guys like me don't drink *tea*."

"Who says?"

"I got an image to maintain."

"Well, I don't have any blood to drink."

"Beer?"

"Don't drink."

"What do you do to relax?"

She flushed again. "I can't tell you."

"Why not?"

"It's a secret."

"You on the lam?"

She rubbed the tattoos on her knuckles, nervously scratched around the implants behind her ears. "Are *you*?"

"Sounds like a story."

"Aren't they all. Everybody's got them. Sordid, tragic, lonely stories. Exciting, exultant, romantic stories. All depends on what you like. So, are you?"

He ignored her question a second time. "You don't look like the kind of person who drives a school bus."

"We all have surprises, don't we? You seem to want to talk, but you're not saying much of anything." There was nothing accusatory in her voice, only openness, a bit of warmth and curiosity, but also guardedness.

Horace clasped his hands between his knees, leaned on his elbows. "You're right. Maybe next time." He stood up and departed, feeling like a complete fool.

Horace prowled the narrow halls of the road train, trying to grasp niggling threads of something he could show these fighters. The reverence in the eyes of some of them this morning said they would listen to him. Others were just curious. All of them would likely do just about anything to walk his path, even if it meant crashing back into the minors as he had done. Some fighters went out on top, retired at the top of their game. He was not one of those.

When Trask's voice came over the PA system, directing everyone to gather in the gym, he retreated to his berth, where the pressure of doing something he had never done before weighed on him with more force than Andre the Titan's boot. He had his own prestige to uphold. He owed these people something for taking him in, even if they didn't know it.

Tina finally came to retrieve him. "They're waiting for you, O Great Sage on the Mountain."

He took a deep breath and stood, then froze.

She turned to go, then saw he wasn't following. "What is it?"

"I have no idea what the hell I'm going to say."

"Since when does Hammer Harkness get stage fright?"

"Since I've never done anything like this before."

Tina rolled her eyes. "Look, none of these Neanderthals are expecting you to dispense wisdom from on high. Considering they aren't great philosophers and deep thinkers, they wouldn't respond to that anyway."

"Hey, those are my people you're running down."

"I didn't say they're stupid. I'm saying they're instinctual. They don't think. They just do. Sound like anyone you know?"

He cracked a half-smile. "Maybe."

"Don't tell me I don't know my shit or these fighters. Just go talk to them. Answer questions. Lecture them and they'll fall asleep."

He thought about this for a moment, then said, "Right. Just gonna talk. Let's go." His voice was firm, but flop sweat soaked his armpits.

In the gym, twenty steely-eyed badasses, lounging on benches, leaning on equipment, fixed their collective gaze upon him. Lex sat on a weight bench on the opposite side of the car. Jocie stood behind him, kneading his meaty shoulders, but her eyes were fixed on Horace, simmering with dangerous wanton heat.

"First of all," he said, "I got no idea what to say to you guys. I'm a fighter, not a teacher. But first I got to thank you all and Mr. Trask for letting me ride along. This is all I got right now to repay you, so here we are." He started pacing back and forth, his brain beginning to click. "I look at all of you and I see myself and those Badass Mother Fuckers—" he enunciated each word, "—I knew when I was your age. Gaston Rousseau. Sirius Rush. Ted Zombie. The Hangman. The Highlander. Andre the Titan. Those guys were hungry. Deadly. There were also a dozen other guys you probably haven't heard of because they died early and didn't resurrect. Hell, even the women were stone killers. Titania. Gladiatrix Jones." He paused and then chuckled ruefully. "Then again, maybe you don't want me to start talking too much. I'll start reminiscing like some old geezer, and we'll be here all day."

Laughter rippled around the group.

Jocie's smoldering gaze was hot on his skin. If Lex happened to catch sight of it, the rest of this little meeting would not go well. That woman was napalm.

"I'm just going to start spouting what I know," he said. "There's no particular rhyme or reason to it. It's just shit I know in my bones.

"Rule one: don't be a dick. To anybody. Well, except your mortal enemies. That always makes good drama *if* you do it where there are cameras to see. Even if you're building a Villain persona, you treat your fans like they're gold, because without them, you're nothing. Plain and simple. If the fans don't scrape the bottoms of their pockets for every thin dollar to come and see you fight, no promoter in his right mind will keep you on board. You might as well be picking fights on street corners."

Trask leaned against the far wall, chewing an unlit cigar. "Amen to that!"

"Maybe I can put Rule One a different way," Horace said. "Remember the crowd. The crowd is your ticket. You win the crowd—learn how to work them, give them what they want—and they're yours, whether you're a Hero or Villain."

"But how do we do that?" one of the fighters said.

"First, you have to be a great fighter. Mr. Trask here has that covered. He's a damn good judge of fighters, always has been. So he sees something in you, even if you haven't hit the big time yet." These men had the physiques, hard muscles, a variety of weight classes, and they had the looks. Not all of them were chiseled Adonises, but any one of them had the potential to break out, hit the big time if they could win bouts and keep coming back.

"You got to have your own techniques, your own shtick. Use that to make your persona. It all goes back to Rule One: remember the crowd. Whatever you're going to do, do it with flair. Do it with drama. In the early days, we were trying to figure this shit out, asking fans what they wanted to see. Most of them just said, 'Fights I enjoy,' or 'If the crowd was into it, it was a good match.' What do they enjoy? They honestly don't know. But here's what we figured out they were saying. They want a story. They want to see a real-life epic battle acted out before their eyes. They want to see gods butt heads. And the stories have to be simple. The pit is not the place to act out plays of moral ambiguity."

"Oh, the irony!" Tina said from behind him, where she stood with her arms crossed.

Everyone laughed at that.

"She's right," Horace said, "but it's true. The world is an overactive bowel where people most often have to choose what flavor of shit sandwich they prefer to eat. Watching us kill each other lets them think the universe makes sense. The Hero wins, they get to cheer for the triumph of Good over Evil. The Villain wins, they get to hate that motherfucker, and then pay to see him get his ass kicked next time. And if the Hero doesn't resurrect, they get to hate that Villain all the more."

Around the group, he saw lights of recognition flickering in their eyes.

"The thing with storytellers is they got to have charm, charisma. Even Villains got charisma. Unfortunately, that's not something you can teach. You either got some, or you don't. On the other hand, if you got some, and I can see by looking around that Mr. Trask is a good judge of that, too, you can learn a few things that will give you a popularity boost. I see a lot of raw potential in this room."

Horace heard something from Lex's side of the room that sounded like a scoffing, "Fuck you."

Trask jumped forward. "You stow that shit, Lex. This man has more experience in his fucking pinky toe than you'll have in ten years. *If* you survive that long."

Horace ignored Lex's sneer as much he ignored Jocie licking her lips and looking at Horace's crotch.

And then something clicked in Horace's brain. He stood taller, ceased pacing, and squared to face them. "How many of you have died?"

Silence fell.

"Even once?"

No one answered, and the silence hung over them all like a shroud of uncertainty.

"That's what I thought," he said. "'How do I become one of the great ones?' is this huge complicated question. Charisma, character, fighting ability. All that. But here's something me and a few other guys figured out early on, and most of us went on and had great careers. The ones who never figured it out, didn't." He let this hang over them for a moment and smiled as he realized he was working them like a crowd.

"Fear of death," he said.

He paused again, surveying their faces, all focused on him. "Human beings, I don't care how badass you think you are, are afraid of dying. Self-preservation trumps all. It makes you flinch. It makes you hesitate. It makes you scared. It makes you *not* charge in when there's a chance that ender will put you in mortal danger. Nobody likes a draw.

"When me and those early fighters took death by the nut sack, we could accomplish anything, come back from anything. We might die, sure, but we were going to *come back*. That's a threshold a lot of new guys don't see until it's too late and their careers are already over. So we got this regeneration technology, right, but you gotta trust it completely. Knowing in your brain that it's there is not enough. You gotta trust in your gut that it's gonna work. That is what a lot of guys don't get. Most of them have to die a few times to figure that out. If you don't trust it completely, the fear will get you.

"Regenites have been around for forty years. Hell, the wounds they can regenerate have gotten way more serious than when we first started out. Still can't fix a decapitation or catastrophic brain trauma, but who wants to be a vegetable anyway?

"Hell, dying sucks, but sometimes it's easier than living. You embrace the dying part, and you'll get that ender shot the other guy was too scared to take. Do it *now,* while everybody else is still worrying about how to use a vibro-axe without slicing off their own face. You'll be way ahead of everybody else at this level."

Around the group, gazes turned inward and thoughtful. He was making sense to them, and Trask was standing in the back, nodding with appreciation.

Trask started to applaud.

One by one, the other fighters joined in, smiles and earnestness spreading around the room.

Except for Lex, who stood with his arms crossed. He happened to glance at Jocie and the lust-filled gaze she was showering upon Horace. Lex seized her arm and growled something Horace couldn't hear. Jocie gasped in pain, and her expression turned to fear like a dash of ice water. But just as quickly she composed herself, stroked Lex's face with a sensuous touch, and purred reassurance at him.

As the other fighters were coming forward to shake Horace's hand and introduce themselves, Lex shouldered past Trask out of the car, dragging Jocie behind him.

CHAPTER NINE

When they pulled into Toledo, Trask's showmanship opened up like a music box, and so did the road train. It made a half-moon in the middle of an old parking lot, where tufts of grass poked through the pavement like the claws of Mother Nature trying to prise a hole.

The roofs of the cars raised into great, garishly painted signs and flashing lights of muscled heroes, larger than life, determined in the midst of battle or exultant in victory. Panels on the sides retracted and red-and-white striped awnings extended. Holo-posters gleamed and moved in the kind of 3-D realism that would have been unbelievable when Horace was a kid.

This parking lot lay next to a shopping mall just as run-down as the rest of the town. The mall itself was a blockish, beige behemoth, uninteresting in every possible way. The store signs were stained with dark gray streaks from decades of pollution and acid rain. The immense parking lot consisted of tracts of weathered, cracked concrete patched by random scabs of black asphalt. The afternoon sun screamed down at them, and any hint of a breeze faded like a smoker's last gasp.

Above the distant dozen or so buildings that comprised Toledo's skyline, specks of aircraft floated and arced. They were too distant for Horace to discern if they were police or media, manned or drones. But he had to make sure to stay out of their sight. The last thing he needed was for his face to appear on some local news feed.

The crowds came, and Trask kicked off the event with a blast from a miniature Civil War replica cannon. The strange, random novelty of it delighted the crowds. When was the last time anyone had seen a 200-year-old cannon fired?

Horace hid in his berth, wishing he was out there, shaking hands and signing autographs for beaming faces. The parking lot filled with scooters and bicycles, even a few small cars.

He had started out in a stable much like Trask's, one that had hit it big in that inexplicable way some small-timers suddenly stumble into. The Oakland Buccaneers eventually became the multinational, billion-dollar corporation Death Match Unlimited, complete with its own space-plane courtesy of Virgin Galactic and a playground in a Dubai strato-scraper. As regenite technology grew more widespread, enterprising fight promoters found ways to push the envelope of what was possible. The chances of successful resurrection steadily increased. And with the sanction of the government and full support of the government's corporate sponsors, Death Match Unlimited had become a worldwide sensation, with Hammer Harkness and others like him forming the groundswell of a new sport.

He had never been one to hog the limelight—there was enough for everyone—but *god*, it was better than sex sometimes. That pulsing sensation of being the It Man, the all-there-is, the pinnacle. But his pinnacle had come about fifteen years ago, and it was a long way down. Has-beens tended to burn up on re-entry.

So he sat on a fold-out stool in his darkening berth, listening to the chatter of the crowd outside as the setting sun splashed him with horizontal lines, the laughter of happy people.

"We are the gods among men," he said to no one in particular.

"Waxing philosophical now, Socrates?"

He started, almost falling off his chair.

Tina laughed from the doorway, arms crossed, dark hair in a bun with a couple of lacquered sticks like knitting needles. "Got to be careful. I'm a ninja."

"You're a pain in the glutes is what you are."

"Aw, don't be sore. Want a beer?"

"Are you even old enough to drink?"

"Fuck you, Moses. Is that a yes?"

"Have a seat."

She dragged a chair around from her room with a six-pack of brown bottles, sat down, and put her black jackboots up on the bed. "So, seriously, I am, in fact, a ninja."

"Get outta here."

"Spar with me sometime, you'll see."

"Honey, I get hold of you just once, I could tear your arms off like chicken wings."

"Good luck with that."

"I haven't fought someone your size since grade school, aside from a different kinda wrestling, that is." He sighed quietly. Christ, looking at her, he yearned to be fifteen years younger, even ten. Practically dripping nubile vivacity, her face was achingly pretty, with huge brown eyes, button nose, and all the soft, rounded parts in the places that would have turned his much younger brain into Puree of Mooning Idiot.

She was giving him a long look, and then she moved with effortless speed. Something *thunked* into the seat of his stool, right between his thighs, a finger's breadth from his scrotum.

His eyebrows went up as he looked down. One of her black lacquered hair needles was sticking in the stool like a ten-centimeter javelin.

She crossed her arms, having spilled not a drop of her beer.

He wet his dry lips and tongue. "Uh, so where'd you learn ninja-fu?"

"It's *ninjutsu*, O Multicultural One. And there are schools. My dad was a mixed martial arts instructor who was trained in *ninjutsu*." She took a drink to swallow something besides beer.

He watched the carefully concealed grief behind her eyes, a scar she couldn't hide all the time. "What happened to your dad?"

"Convenience store robbery. Some gang-bangers strung out on Krok started shooting up the place. He took out all seven of them before the last one got off a lucky shot."

"Sorry, kid."

"I'm not a kid! He saved the lives of six other people in there. I wondered what the hell was taking him so long.... Anyway. No money, no medical plan. He died right there. No resurrection for him." Bitterness tightened her voice.

"Your mom?"

"Never met her. All I know is that she was Filipina, and dad really loved her. He would never tell me any more than that."

"So how often do you have to beat these yay-hoos away with a ninja stick?" He thumbed over his shoulder toward the fighters outside.

"Pretty much every day until they get the idea."

"What idea is that?"

"Muscle-bound meatheads aren't my type."

"What type is that?"

"The nerdy poetic type. Write me a sonnet and I'll cream my shorts."

"You're too young to talk like that."

"Fuck you, Gandalf. You don't think women are sexual beings with as much right to it as you have?"

"I know damn good and well they are." A great many purely sexual beings had crossed his path.

"Are you threatened by a woman who knows exactly what she wants, can defend that position, and doesn't need a man to make her a whole person?"

He considered this. "Threatened, no." Intrigued, yes. Feeling like a dirty old man, yes. Even in this day and age, what she described wasn't exactly typical. Women's rights had cycled through numerous fits and starts in the last two hundred years as the never-ending wheel of change ground through the road gravel of religion and ingrained beliefs. Over a hundred fifty years after women won the right to vote, in some of the country's religious or otherwise backward enclaves, women were still treated almost as brood mares, property.

She waited for him to add more, then shrugged and took another drink. "You gonna give me that back?" She pointed at the needle still between his legs.

"I'm not sure you should be allowed around sharp objects."

She snorted, stepped forward, and snatched it.

As she tucked it back into her hair, he asked, "You ever have a boyfriend?"

"Jesus Christ! Intrude much?"

"I can imagine a whole parade of nerdy, poetic types following you around like puppies."

The way she hesitated told him there had been precisely one.

"What happened?" he said.

"Same thing that always happens when you're young and stupid and drunk on hormones. It ends badly, with a bang and a whimper."

His imagination exploded with scenarios. He opened his mouth ask about them, when he noticed the tenor of the gathering outside had changed. The sounds of fun and excitement were now drowned in an obnoxious, angry chant. He peeked through the blinds.

A battered, rusty school bus with a huge, black crucifix painted on the side now sat parked about fifty meters away. Thirty-odd protesters lofted signs and chanted something Horace couldn't quite understand. The signs contained things like:

LIVE BY THE SWORD, PERISH BY THE SWORD!
BLOODY KILLERZ GO HOME!
DO YOU KILL BABIES TO?
THOU SHALT NOT KILL!
GET A BRANE MORANS!
SCRIPTURE NOT SWORDS!
THIS IS A PUBIC SPACE, NOT A BUCHER SHOP!

"Looks like we got some admirers outside," Horace said.

"Again? Is there a bus with a huge cross on it?"

"How did you guess?"

"They show up all the time. They've apparently decided we're the soulless spawn of Lucifer himself. Five-to-one the cops show up in the next ten minutes."

"Sounds like I'd be stupid to take that bet."

"Trask lets them do their thing for a while. As far as he's concerned, any publicity is good publicity."

"I see it does scare some of the fans away."

A handful of people who had been standing in line slunk away like frightened dogs.

"Yeah, but our media spike doubles or triples every time they show up, so we don't care about losing a handful of autographs."

He turned away and took a swig of the beer, some local brew he had never heard of. "Idiots like this are nothing new. They were around even in the early days, especially then." Then his netlink, lying on the bed, caught the light just right. "Miss Ninja. How evil are you?"

"You say that like mischief is afoot."

The darkness deepened around the parking lot. The protesters chanted and jeered, and just like clockwork, the police showed up and set out a cordon to keep them at a more easily ignorable distance away from the "lawful promotional event."

Horace tried to catch a glimpse of Tina on her mission, but there was no sign of her for perhaps ten minutes until she reappeared in the hallway behind him.

"Is it done?" he said.

"It's done." She plopped down into her chair with a self-satisfied grin and swigged her beer. With her spectrum of hair tied into a tight ponytail in the neutral gray sweatshirt hood and sweatpants replacing her rainbow polka-dot explosion, she looked completely nondescript.

"Aren't you going to ask me why I had you plant my netlink on their bus?" he said.

"Against the ninja code. Of course, I'm curious, but it is not the *shinobi*'s place to ask why, only the completion of the assigned mission. So why'd you have me plant your netlink on their bus?"

"There are people looking for me. This will keep them off my trail for a while."

"Kinda figured that out for myself. Was it about what happened back at the rest stop?"

He sat down and picked up his beer again, nodding.

"So now that you've made me your accomplice," she said, "I have you wrapped around my finger."

There was something in her voice that made him question whether she was joking. He regarded her for a long moment, and she took another long, slow drink of beer, utterly inscrutable. He wanted to laugh it off, but...

"Oh, don't be silly," she said with a wink.

He relaxed slightly.

But not completely, as he considered all the ways this woman could now screw him over.

"Remind me never to play poker with you," he said.

"Everybody else around here figured that out a while ago."

That night, after the crowds had dispersed and the protesters had driven away in their bus, Horace sat in his berth, familiarizing himself with Trask's stable of fighters by reading the program for the upcoming event in Albany. The main event was Lex Lethal versus The Dark Horseman.

Trask's stable had a good mix of finesse fighters, weapon specialists, mixed martial artists, and outright brutes. Lex Lethal was one of the latter. According to Lex's profile, he favored bludgeoning weapons such as maces, *tetsubo*, spiked gauntlets and clubs, with an aggressive, charging-bull fighting style. Definitely not a finesse man.

Movement in the doorway door caught Horace's attention. Bunny stood there, giving him a look or wonderment and awed fear.

"I can't believe you," she said. When his confusion prevented him from answering, she came in and sat on the bed, her hands trembling. "I haven't seen a sweep net like this in a long time."

"You going to have to tell me what you're talking about," he said.

"You have some scary flipping people after you." She swallowed hard, and her eyes were flicking back and forth at lightning speed from him to some internal data feed, multi-tasking little bits of meaning from several directions at once. When she finally spoke, her voice took on a strange arrhythmic cadence. "During the promo event, at this one moment, there was this enormous spike of net activity. It was like someone turned a homing beacon on, right in this vicinity. Are you going to pretend you have no idea what I'm talking about?"

"No. What happened?"

"It was like someone called *sooie!* to a bunch of starving hogs, or laid out a fresh carcass for the vultures. Spybots started circling, converging from all over the net. The hard and soft networks in this area went crazy. So when the spybots got a lock on that signal—your netlink signal—they got close enough for me to check them out."

"You don't just have implants. You're a slicer!"

"Rehabilitated." She held up the prison tattoos on her knuckles. "Anyway, the higher-level code was something I hadn't seen before, so I corralled one of the bots and de-compiled it. It was written in Cyrillic characters. Russian."

Horace nodded slowly.

"But it's not smooth like government surveillance stuff. It's rough, back-alley, brute-force kind of stuff. Nothing elegant about it." Her expression twisted with distaste. "I'm still trying to track it, but they're good at covering their tracks, as good as the black mercenary agencies."

"Would it scare you worse if I told you I already knew most of that?"

"No, because I haven't gotten to the worst part." She swallowed hard. "No one in the world has this kind of slicing expertise except major governments, the Chinese Triads, the Indian Tigers, and the Russian Mafiya. Heck, the Russian FSB steals their slicing tricks from the mafiya. Trackers, feeler-bots, contact-sifters, the whole shebang. I would be completely unsurprised if everyone you had ever contacted from that netlink now had taps on their voice and data accounts. You're in some deep poopy, my friend. And so is everyone you know."

A Lilly-scented chill went up his spine. "Don't I know it, sister."

"Turning that thing on was a death sentence."

"I know. That's why I don't have it anymore."

She deflated with relief. Her gaze flickered again for several seconds. "Yes, it's gone."

"Are we pulling out soon?"

Even as she nodded, the awnings and signs whined and clunked as they retracted. The hum of the power plant grew.

"If they get a fix on me again somehow," Horace said, "can you block their slicers?"

"Block them, yes. Fight back, no. I'm prohibited from doing anything invasive or destructive. I have a lock on my software as part of my parole. The spybot I tore apart was already highly illegal, so I could have my way with it. Care to tell me who it is?"

"The Russian mob."

"Does Trask know?"

"He knows."

"What did you do?"

"Do you really want to know?"

"Yes."

"I cut off Dmitri Mogilevich's head and left it in his lap in the back of a limousine."

"Why?"

"He threatened someone I care about."

"But now his organization is threatening everyone you care about."

"Looks that way."

"What are you going to do about it?"

"Kill them all."

"I doubt that's a feasible plan."

"It's all I got."

"How are you going to manage that?"

"Working on that part. Then again, if they catch me, problem solved."

"But not a solution that looks good for you."

"I've had my life."

"That's a pretty fatalistic attitude."

"Realistic. I got no regrets. Well, maybe one or two. But going down fighting sounds better than being the meanest geezer in the Old Fighters' Home. And now they've been thrown off the trail."

"The only question is how long before they figure it out. If they interrogate any of those people, they may well put two and two together about how the netlink got on their bus."

Horace had nothing to say to that. He hoped that he hadn't just called down a drone strike on a bus full of ignorant Bible-thumpers; however misguided they might be, they didn't deserve extermination.

"You are a pack of trouble, Mr. Harkness."

"Call me Hark."

"To be honest, I'm not sure I want to be your friend." She stood.

"Wait a second." He reached into the pocket of his bloodied jacket and withdrew the netlink of the Russian assassin from the truck stop. "Can you slice this?" He held it out to her.

"Let me guess, it belongs to the bad guys."

Horace nodded. "I'm looking for numbers. Evidence. Physical addresses. If I have to, I'll start paying personal visits."

Bunny stared at it for almost a minute before she took it from him.

She held the netlink in trembling hands, but it wasn't just fear in her eye. A hint of challenge gleamed deep from behind some internal firewall.

CHAPTER TEN

Early the next morning, Horace stood in the door to Bunny's cabin. She tossed something at him, small and shiny, and he caught it against his chest. The Russian netlink.

"It's clean," she said. "Don't thank me now, but I poked into it. That *was* one very dirty device. Right before it sensed me poking around and wiped itself. *But* I was able to retrieve all of your data from your old one during the night before it went offline."

"Good morning, Miss Bunny," Horace said, nonplussed at being summoned to her cabin at the crack of dawn.

Her face was pinched. "Did you catch what I said?"

"My old netlink went offline?"

"Someone either turned it off, or it was put out of commission." She let that hang in the air a moment before continuing, "And about the dirtiness of that little toy. It was running on a pirated piggyback signal. Encrypted. Untrackable. I changed the code on the piggyback signal so that it's now unique. I even scanned it for any add-on homing signals. It's still untrackable, but now it's yours."

Horace stared at the piece of plastic, glass, and microcircuitry. "Miss Bunny, I don't know how to thank you."

"Thank me by not dying, and by not getting me killed along with you. There's something you obviously haven't registered yet. If *I* could slice your old netlink and matrix all your data, contacts, messages, and stuff, so could someone else."

At that, a chill went down his spine.

"The password is 'Bunny Rules,'" she said and went back inside.

The ring chime for Lilly's netlink dinged for thirty seconds, then the system asked if he would like to leave a voice message. He didn't. He tried two more times, without result, the sense of dread in his belly deepening with every passing chime.

"Dammit." Then again, in her line of work, for safety's sake she probably wouldn't answer an unknown caller.

He called Jack, who picked up on the second chime. "McTierney Investigations."

"Jack, it's me."

"Hammer? Sweet titties, amigo, I've been trying to get ahold of you!"

"Here I am. What's the skinny on Lilly?"

"She's gone, man. Can't find her. Or her kids. She hasn't been to work, checked her boy out of the hospital early. I went to her place, but there's two goons watching it."

"Goddammit. You sure it was her who checked the boy out?"

"I couldn't get anyone to tell me it wasn't. I ran a trace on her netlink, but it's offline, just like yours has been."

"I'm calling from a friend's."

"There's something else. I might have to go underground myself for a while. My car was busted into and ransacked last night. My office and apartment might be next. I don't plan on being here when they are."

"I'm sorry about all this, brother. I gotta find a way to make it go away without giving them my head and nuts on a plate. When I got a plan, I'll let you know."

"You could go to the cops, the FBI."

"And go to jail for Murder One, right before the Russians shoot me in my cell and ass-fuck my corpse? You know there's plenty of cops on the mob's payroll."

"Witness protection?"

"I got a slicer here tells me that their netbots are on par with the Feds. They want to find me, they'll find me. For all I know, they've sliced your netlink."

"Jesus, man, you're getting paranoid."

"No, it's probably *worse* than I think. This needs to go away. *I* have to make this go away. If you hear anything about Lilly, let me know, right? For all I know, she took my advice and went on vacation."

"Sure thing," Jack said, and they disconnected.

Maybe if he left some sort of text message that only she would understand, she would figure it out. After a moment, he thumbed in:

> **HEY THIS IS MAX FROM WORK. GOT A NEW LINK. YOU BETTER CALL ME. THE BOSS IS PISSED.**

At least that would get her attention. And so the waiting game began.

That afternoon brought another town, another promotional stop, this one piggybacking onto an event between two other stables. Trask's road train parked in a field outside of Cleveland. Another road train and two caravans of buses arrived in the field, the two pit fighter stables set to compete on tonight's card. Due to a city ordinance prohibiting gladiatorial events, this event was to be held outside the city limits. Over the course of the afternoon, an enormous tent pavilion went up like a circus big top, transports full of plastic and aluminum bleachers pulled in, disgorged their contents, and moved on while teamsters stacked and assembled everything. Within hours, the field went from grass and weeds to sparkling neon circus. Oversized holograms of the fighters populated the area like giants, posing, striking, hamming it up for the holos.

Music rose from well-hidden speakers, a rotation of heavy steel and ragged electronica, the theme songs of the various fighters echoing across the grassy, windswept plain. Rope fences went up as if by magic, so that when the cars and transit buses began to arrive, people with lighted batons were able to funnel them into some semblance of order. The smell of popcorn, funnel cakes, roasted nuts, and grilling pseudo-meat filled the air. A clown on stilts drifted through the crowds, dancing, cavorting, pantomiming for teenagers too cynical to be amused. A trailer of four rotating searchlights punched holes in the empty dusk sky. Spectators crossed the field on foot.

It was a perfect, late summer night, steeped in carnival atmosphere and soon-to-be-spraying blood. Four contract ambulances and a Regenecorp medical transport were parked behind the pavilion. The transport would carry a full suite of regeneration equipment.

Regenecorp sponsorship had made the neo-gladiators a viable

sport, complete with heroes, villains, and drama. Even in the early days of Death Match Unlimited, the money circulating around the league, the stables, the stars, and Regenecorp had been firehoses fed by millions of rabid fans. To be sanctioned by Regenecorp meant your stable could be viable—if they played the right game. Failing to scratch the right backs, shake the right hands, or bring in big enough crowds meant a stable's promoter would see his fighters forced to fight less lucrative, nonlethal bouts, forced into low-level hospitalization for purely natural healing—if they weren't killed outright. Without potentially lethal bouts, the crowds stayed home and watched the killer stars and bloodthirsty gods on pay-per-view.

Now, for the first time since he was a teenager, Horace stood on the outside. It felt strange not to be gearing- and psyching-up for a match.

Trask's stable was not here to compete, only to promote the upcoming spectacle in Albany and help build drama and storylines for the minor league rag-mags. Throughout the afternoon, most of the fighters were shooting challenge spots, wherein they talked smack to the opposing fighters, building drama into their pit fighter personas, establishing who the Good Guys were, who the Bad Guys were, and who was gunning for whom.

Every stable had an array of not only fighting styles, but also personalities, character archetypes that matched well and built compelling stories with other archetypes of other stables. The Clean Cut All-American versus the Dastardly Foreigner of Most-Hated Nationality Du Jour. The High-Class Man versus The Ignorant Hick. The Lumbering Behemoth versus the Bouncing Battler—a pairing that had made Horace and Gaston famous. These archetypes worked almost as well for the female stables, although they had some of their own, such as The Sultry Vixen and the Buxom Badass Girl Next Door.

The rag-mags filled neighborhood supermarket magazine stands and flew across electronic media worldwide, a frenzy of photos, vids, stories, and drama. Fans counted the days when the pit fighters came to town and gave them spectacle.

City ordinances be damned, the people of Cleveland were no different than anyone else. They wanted to see two powerful men face each other with weapon and armor and shield like the warriors of old, in a battle where only one would leave the arena the victor. They wanted to see stories unfold, vendettas waged—however contrived and fictitious—wrongs righted at the point of a vibro-sword. They wanted to see the drama of mortal combat, and in the end, they wanted blood.

Horace was tired of being in his berth. He wanted to feel the crowd, smell the sweat, and taste the action.

He put on a pair of sunglasses, borrowed a surgical mask from the infirmary and a featureless black hoodie from Trask's workout gear, and slipped into the crowds.

Part of him knew how stupid it was to appear in public. Letting his beard and hair grow out for a couple of weeks might obscure some of the tattoos on his head, but it wasn't there yet, and there was media everywhere. All it would take was a networked camera to sweep across him just once, and all this running would be for naught.

With a fistful of corn dogs, he wandered toward the media tent. No one challenged him, taking him for just another one of the fighters going incognito. Flash bulbs and floodlights filled the interior of the red-and-white striped tent. Along the far side, Lex Lethal was posing for stills, dressed in his black armor plating, crudely stenciled skulls spray-painted on each breast. He was all corded arms and curled hair, an ill-tempered Adonis wearing his fiercest expressions.

Horace hung to the rear of the crowd of rag-mag reporters and photographers. Trask stood just close enough to Lex to make his proud, cigar-chomping presence prevalent in the photographs. Video cameras pushed forward, and someone passed Lex a microphone.

A reporter called out, "So what do you have to say to the Dark Horseman? He says he's ready to ride you hard and put you away bloody."

Lex stabbed a thick finger at the camera, veins on his neck standing out like ropes. "The Dark Horseman better ride his ass out of town, because I'm coming for him. I'm gonna make him into a gelding! I'm gonna beat him like a rented mule!"

Lightning quick, he tossed a little plastic skull into the air and reached for a scabbard at his belt. The snap-hum of a vibro-blade filled the tent, Lex slashed up with a gladius-style short sword, and the skull fell in two vertically divided pieces. The cut was as smooth as if the plastic had been molded that way.

Lex pointed the still-humming gladius at the camera. "That's right,

Dark Horseman, I'm coming for *you*. When I'm done, you're dog food!" The whites of his eyes blazed with ferocity.

Having seen enough minor league fighters come and go, Horace had to admit Lex Lethal possessed the ferocity and camera presence to be a star, a memorable Villain. Getting noticed by the right sponsor or the right recruiter could launch him into the big leagues.

"Thanks, got it," the camera man said.

Lex deactivated his blade and relaxed.

Trask stepped forward. "All right, that's it, everyone. Thank you for coming! I'd say it's time to get ready for the show tonight, huh? Am I right?" He grinned.

As the reporters gathered up their equipment, Trask whispered something to Lex, to which Lex simply listened impassively, nodding slightly.

When they had all gone, Trask spotted Horace standing at the back. "What the hell are you doing here, Tiny? Are you *trying* to get made?"

"Going stir crazy." He took off the sunglasses, pulled the mask down, and addressed Lex. "That was a good spot, brother. Good technique on the sword. Nice show."

Lex snorted. "What the hell do you know, you fucking fossil?"

Horace stiffened. "I know good technique when I see it, I know presence and potential when I see it, and I also know a wet-behind-the-ears, no-respect dipshit when I see one."

Lex lunged forward, but Trask jumped between them. Lex's chest plate knocked Trask's cigar loose. "Hold it, fuck head!"

"I'll eat your fucking heart!" Lex snarled.

Horace said, "It's all gristle and you haven't grown out your big-boy teeth. Sorry, I was wrong, you'll never amount to anything." He turned away. "Fire him now, Mr. Trask. Or just let him die when the time comes. All you got there is a killer. He's no pit fighter."

"We'll see, you tottering old fuck!" Lex yelled at Horace's back. "We're gonna throw down!"

"Bring it on, dipshit." Horace walked away, flexing his fists, knowing he'd just painted another target on his back.

CHAPTER ELEVEN

The crowd pouring into the giant pavilion resembled most crowds elsewhere, with the exception that people looked more run-down here. These people walked with the shuffling step and threadbare clothing of those accustomed to soup lines, never having recovered from the Greater Depression.

At least Cleveland still managed to cling to some kind of existence, unlike Detroit, which had degenerated into a crumbling ghost town buried in rust and tenements, much of which had been reclaimed by nature and scavenger gangs. But these people had come in their overalls, dungarees, t-shirts, and cracked plastic shoes to see a show, and damned if they weren't going to see a show.

Trask and the other two stable bosses were doubtless meeting behind closed doors now, drinking scotch and making deals. The business end of the Business was as much about who one knew as it was about skill or heart. Knowing the right people made its own luck. Horace's involvement with his first stable had raised him to stardom. A rising tide lifts all boats. He'd been lucky there.

There were too many eyes, too much media attention around for him to step into the pavilion, even with his disguise. Too much could go wrong, so he retreated to the train, chafing at the sense of imprisonment, angered at being chased out of his own home, as it were—the fights themselves.

Inside the train, he found Tina and three of the other fighters in the lounge car, gathered around the screen, which was playing the prematch commentary by local sportscasters, along with slow-motion, blood-spray-enhanced clips of previous bouts by these fighters.

"Pull up a wheelchair, Hammer," Tina said.

"Don't mind if I do," he said.

The other three fighters introduced themselves as "Mad Killer" Kevin Michael, Jax "To The Max" Gavillion, and "Skullcrusher" Camden James. They shook hands with mixtures of politeness and reverence.

Kevin Michael said, "That was some good stuff you told us, Hammer. I don't know if it'll help, but I'll be thinking about it until we get to Albany." His eyes glinted with light that said they were cybernetic.

"Man," Gavillion said, "I grew up watching you. We couldn't get the pay-per-views in my 'hood, so I used to sneak out and go to a bar outside the Poor Zone just to watch you. Loved The Freak, too, and that enormous motherfucker, like eight feet tall."

Horace smiled. "Andre the Titan."

"Yeah, Jesus Christ, that guy was a monster."

Horace held up his arm. "Yeah, he tried to make my elbow go both ways once. Still kills me sometimes."

"An honor, Hammer," Gavillion said.

Horace shrugged. "Thanks, but we're all just doing our jobs, right?"

Tina took a drink of beer. "You guys should all hug and shit now. Or make out or something."

"Yeah, you'd like that, wouldn't you," Kevin Michael said.

They all laughed, and Horace sat down in one of the chairs upholstered in the cracked-orange-vinyl style, the purchaser of which had to have been colorblind.

"For a couple hundred smackers," James said, "I'll make out with whoever you want."

"So, 'Skullcrusher,' how's that movie deal coming along?" Kevin Michael said.

"My agent's still working on the terms," James said.

Tina cranked her head toward Horace. "Skullcrusher here got a gig in a porn vid."

"This body's gotta pay for itself every way it can," James said, kissing his massive biceps. "And it ain't hard-core porn. It's erotica."

"So does that mean you have to just pretend to fuck?" Michael said. "All limp dick and strategic camera angles?"

"I don't know."

"No money shot?" Gavillion said. "If I was gonna be in a porno, I better be doing some fuckin'."

"I don't know!" James' face turned red. "Now leave me alone, you fuckers."

Gavillion and Michael slapped him on the back, laughing.

The night's first fighters charged onto the screen. The rumble and thud of the intro music pounded from the screen and through the walls of the train from outside, rattling the windows with its power. The roar of the crowd followed close behind like the sound of a rising wind.

The camera panned around the audience of perhaps three thousand, many of whom were standing in the peanut gallery around the raised platform where the cage stood, with its two-meter chain-link walls. Sponsorship banners hung in brilliant multitudes from on high—Monsanto, Regenecorp, World MegaBank, Magic Marijuana.

Elevated above the cage were six VIP booths, populated by men in silk suits—Horace recognized a pro rugby player from the Cleveland Clubbers among them—and women sparkling with diamonds and the most intense beauty money could buy. Spotlights swept the crowd. Even on a scale like this, so much smaller than the event with Gaston, the pageantry and larger-than-life spectacle were as important as the fights themselves.

Horace leaned back in the chair and watched as the fights began. His attention drifted from evaluating the combatants' technique to their stage presence, to listening to the fighters banter. Tina's attention was fixed on the screen, and Horace could see from her gaze and subtle reactions that she was responding to the same things he was in the matches. Moments of triumph, the skills pitted against each other, failures of courage or will. Weapons flailed and bashed. Screams of rage and pain were drowned in the surge of the crowd. Blood and meat splattered the clay surface. Epic battles between would-be gods.

"Whoa, there went his arm!" Michael said. A severed forearm tumbled free and landed in the dirt, titanium buckler falling loose. The maimed fighter succumbed to shock and blood loss moments later and passed out. While the other fighter roared his victory, Regenecorp medtechs rushed out with a gurney, scooped up the fighter and the arm, and whisked them away for resection.

After a brief on-camera interview with the victor, who graciously praised his opponent's skill and courage, the master of ceremonies came into the cage with a microphone. "And now, let's thank our generous sponsors with a big round of applause!" The audience obeyed. "Another round of applause for our Regenecorp medtechs, how about that!" More applause. "And now, one lucky audience member will receive a great prize, courtesy of Regenecorp!"

The camera cut around the audience to men and women looking hopeful, some of them taking out their tickets, clutching them.

"And the winner of Regenecorp's Good Neighbor Prize is... Jonathan Cavallo! You are the winner of a full year of individual medical coverage, courtesy of Regenecorp!"

The camera cut to the bleachers, to a man steeped in hard work. A moment of joy beamed on his face until he looked at his pregnant wife, who hugged him with all the joy she could muster, and his joy crumbled. With tears glistening in his eyes, he faced the cameras, raised his hands and clapped, hard and slow. Beside him, his wife wiped tears steeped in a new kind of sadness and worry. As it was an individual policy, she and her pregnancy would not be covered. She was still on her own when the baby came, and so would the baby be.

The next fighters on the card exploded into the pavilion amid fresh fanfare.

Something about the look on the wife's face stabbed Horace in the belly. "I gotta get some air."

He pulled up his hood, replaced the sunglasses and mask, and stepped outside. He wanted to punch something. He wanted to apply a Thunder Hammer to the skull of someone who deserved it, like the Regenecorp exec who thought up that promotion. It was a common thing, especially in the minor leagues where most of the fans were too poor to afford medical. The medical costs of that baby's birth—exempt from the father's "individual coverage"—would put the family in the poorhouse for decades, unless she gave birth at home in the bathtub.

In a world of twelve billion people, the most effective way to control population growth was with carefully restricted medical coverage. The cost of simply going to the doctor was beyond the reach of the labor class unless a person's employer had a doctor on the payroll, in which case the worker started tallying up debts to the company. Anything more complicated than a runny nose incurred major expenses. The twenty-first century version of the company store. Those without medical paid cash. No cash, no medical. With enough cybernetic, genetic, and regenite intervention, the wealthy could easily live to a hundred and thirty. Horace had only a couple more years to go before he crossed the life-expectancy finish line of the labor class. But the megacorp party line simply crowed about how they had successfully leveled off the world's population growth. A few well-placed wars in hand-picked locales also helped burn off the rest of the human chaff.

With nowhere for his ire to go, he thrust his fists into his pockets and slid into one of the fighter entrances. The security guard looked him up and down and admitted him with a nod. The next fighters from this stable were too busy warming up, psyching themselves up, to pay him any attention. Horace found a spot inside the pavilion where he could watch the cage through a gap in the bleachers. The atmosphere in the tent pulsed with an energy no 3-D screen could recreate.

Horace had grown up watching mixed martial arts and professional wrestling on television, and it was a kickboxing exhibition in a little arena in Nebraska that had seized the imagination of a small-town boy far too big for his age. The exhibition had been a mix of amateurs from the local gyms and a handful of touring professionals.

In one bout, a fighter had landed the most perfect kick he had ever seen, a snap kick straight to his opponent's abdomen, right in the liver. The solid, meaty thud had echoed through the arena like a side of beef dropped from three meters. An instant of silence descended. The audience gave a low, awe-stricken *Ooooooo*. The victim sank to his knees, clutching his belly. The referee jumped in, waving away the next kick that would have been to the man's face, and it was over. The man fell sideways. The crowd exploded. And little Horace MacElroy was hooked.

The air in the tent smelled of blood, sweat, and beer. A margarita vendor circulated through the stands, a ten-gallon plastic tank on his back with a hose and dispensing gun in hand, and twin holsters full of plastic cups on his hips. As the bouts passed, one by one, the crowd grew ever more raucous.

In the interval before the main event, a scuffle broke out in one of the opposite bleachers. Harsh words and shoving became clutching hands and torn collars, until finally two burly men were whaling on each other, scattering the people around them. Security rushed to the scene, tased them both, and dragged them outside.

The main event featured two heavyweights, and they started with long weapons: one a spear, and the other a trident. The trident man's face was drawn from a horror novel. Gleaming titanium tusks, ten centimeters long, had been implanted in his jaw, with matching horns jutting from his brutish forehead. His face had been painted or tattooed scarlet, and the only thing that would have further completed the look was a forked tail. He wielded his trident with a vicious stabbing style that looked more dangerous than it actually was. The other fighter was one of the Good Guys, blond and wholesome, with gleaming breastplate and a smile like a toothpaste model. But he moved like a pit fighter, bore the determination of a pit fighter, and the way he handled his spear bore the marks of training in Japanese spear technique. A Knight and a Demon. Good versus Evil. A story to be told.

They thrust and swung and strained, batting away each other's attacks, the Demon trying to snare his opponent's weapon with the trident, the Knight swinging his bladed spear like an extra-long sword, slashing at the Demon's face.

Cheers rose and fell. The trident pierced a calf. The spear slashed off two of the Demon's gauntleted fingers. Blood flowed. Cheers exploded in a frenzy as the fighters attacked, straining at each other, muscle to muscle. Then Round One ended, and trainers rushed in to slap synthskin bandages over gaping wounds, staunch blood flow, give the fighters a quick drink, and retrieve the Demon's fingers.

The Demon snorted and spat blood. The Knight sweated and gritted his teeth.

When the horn sounded again, they launched themselves at each other with fresh ferocity. Another round of all-out slashing, straining, screaming mayhem drove the crowd to even greater heights of frenzy, shrieking themselves hoarse.

Horace felt it rising, that exquisite, juicy pulse, and yearned for it to be pouring into him.

When the second round ended, blood poured from between the

Knight's breastplate and backplate. The trident thrust had been too quick to see how deeply the point had gone, but the display screens replayed it over and over again between rounds. The Demon had gained advantage, but his strength had been spent. He could barely lift his weapon.

Pit girls circled inside the cage with their Round Three placards, wearing nothing but glitter and G-strings. The tumult of the crowd did not subside this time but continued to build with anticipation of the final round. The bleachers rocked with stomping feet. Three thousand fans sounded like ten thousand.

When the fighters went at each other again, the crowd thundered like crashing surf.

The Knight charged, using the spear shaft like a quarterstaff. Then suddenly he pulled the spear shaft apart, revealing a blade hidden in a secret sheath. The Knight stabbed the blade down into the Demon's neck, just above the breastplate. The Demon roared and blood spurted. Then the Demon head-butted the Knight with his fearsome horns and tore a gruesome gash in the Knight's face, from the bridge of his nose to the bottom of his jaw.

The two staggered away from each other. Blood-smeared teeth gleamed through the gash in the Knight's cheek.

The crowd descended into screaming madness.

The Demon swung weakly at the Knight, but the Knight staggered back out of range. The Demon sank to his knees, blood pouring from his mouth. The Knight charged forward, and with a kick to the Demon's chest, laid him flat on his back on the blood-spattered clay. Another kick sent the trident spinning away.

The Knight staggered, struggled to stay straight, but raised his arms to the crowd. In that moment of triumph, Horace saw something else in the Knight's eyes: the hunger.

The Demon's hands went limp.

Screaming with triumph, the Knight reached down and grabbed one of the Demon's horns in one hand, clutching his spear in the other. He raised the spear, preparing to stab again, and turned to the crowd.

The crowd was chanting: *"KILL! KILL! KILL! KILL! KILL!"* Beer flew from outflung cups. In a crowd like this, comprised of mostly poor people, human life meant nothing because they viewed their own lives as worthless: a dollar a dozen, bought and paid for by the gross, by corporations whose sole purpose was the exploitation of resources. With their worthlessness proven to them over and over again, they believed it in their bones with the certainty of gravity. Watching enough blood spilled, they could begin to forget their cruel lot, the hand they were forced to play by circumstance of birth or the whims of luck. Being forced into indentured servitude in company towns across the Old Rust Belt was preferable to an axe in the guts—at least most days. What did that mean, then, for the fighters who gave them the blood they wanted?

The Knight milked the crowd for almost a minute, egging them on to greater frenzy, pantomiming a death thrust, taunting his barely conscious opponent.

In the wild light of the Knight's eyes, Horace sensed the madness creeping from the crowd, seeping into what had been, up to now, a hard-fought, professional bout, a fair victory. In seconds, the Knight would turn from fighter into murderer, so drunk with the rush of blood and cheers and victory that he all he could think of was drinking more of the fire hose of rage and excitement, gulping it down, bathing in it.

"Don't do it, kid," Horace muttered where no one could hear but himself.

Then the Knight stabbed again into the Demon's throat, through it, into the clay below, grinding back and forth through gristle and bone, slicing and tearing through spine, muscles, arteries. When he finished, the Demon's head lay half-severed, blood fountaining out of the hideous injury.

Some people sat down, pale and sickened, while those around them continued their cheering rampage.

And then the Knight collapsed as well.

The crowd oscillated from shock and revulsion to bloodthirsty glee.

Medtechs rushed into the cage.

Horace crossed his arms and shook his head. Injuries like the Demon's were almost impossible to regenerate. No one had yet successfully reattached a severed head, and there was little holding the Demon's head to his body. It was in the minors like this that most deaths happened. Organizations like Death Match Unlimited couldn't afford for their gods to fall. What had happened just now would get the victor kicked out of the major leagues for life. But not here. And for the Knight, he had broken the spell of the story, ruined the illusion. Heroes did not kill like that.

The announcer's voice came over the speakers. "Resurrection Watch is now underway for Asmodeus! Have you ever seen an ending like that! Have you *ever* seen a finish like that! Regenecorp physicians are even now struggling to restore The Demon's life."

Above the crowd on the massive screens:

RESURRECTION WATCH: ODDS OF SUCCESSFUL RESURRECTION 1:98 AGAINST.

PLACE YOUR BETS NOW IN ACCOUNT DM99938732. BETTING WINDOW CLOSES IN 2:00.

The timer started counting down the seconds. Some of the crowd was already threading toward the exits, others madly texting into their netlinks.

With a sick taste in his mouth, Horace returned to the train.

Halfway there, his netlink buzzed in his pocket with a message from Jack, a simple news headline from the *Las Vegas Gold Standard*:

LOCAL DANCER AND TWO CHILDREN MISSING

CHAPTER TWELVE

Horace shuffled into the train in a daze, glancing over and over at the screen of his netlink. The only image in his mind was what men like the Russians would do to a woman like Lilly; the scars, both physical and mental, they would take glee in inflicting. Her two children, tossed into a shipping container and locked in the dark until they died of thirst. And all to take revenge on Horace, whom the children had never even met.

He kept muttering "sonofabitch, sonofabitch" over and over.

He entered his berth and slammed the door behind him.

What could he do? What could he do?

Call them right now?

No, not yet. He had to *know* whether the Russians had her. First he had to *know*.

A second after he slammed the door of his berth behind him, he whisked it open again and dashed out, almost tripping over Tina, who was returning to her own berth. Sensing a middle finger extend behind him, he ignored it like a charging rhinoceros.

His hand was quivering like a leaf when he knocked on Bunny's compartment door and went inside without listening for a response. She reclined in a chair, her eyes fluttering over internal readouts and menus he could not see.

After a few moments, she levered herself up on an elbow. "Who the—oh, Mr. Harkness. Am I going to have to start locking my door?"

He held up the netlink she had given him. "Is this thing untraceable? Untrackable?"

"I told you it was."

"Because I'm just about to call fucking Satan himself. If I do, can he trace it back here? Can he trace it back *here?*"

"I would say no. Well, probably not."

"Goddammit! Can he or can't he?"

"Look, Mr. Harkness, in the slicing business, there are no absolutes, or if there are, they last about a week until someone finds a workaround. It's a constant arms race, a playing field that changes from minute to minute. I cannot guarantee that Satan doesn't have some hotshot slicer who can put me to shame. But like I told you, it's running on a pirated piggyback signal, which takes world-class slicers to trace, and even then it takes time."

"How much time?"

"I could not say. A minute? Maybe two?"

"Are you willing to bet your life on that?"

She swallowed hard, took a deep breath. "Yes."

"Can you put an app on here that watchdogs spybots? Lets me know if they're getting close?"

She nodded. "It'll take me until tomorrow to put together."

"If I'm still alive in the morning, I would appreciate it, sister."

He returned to his berth, his fingers stroking the netlink's smooth contours in his pocket. Lilly's voice kept echoing through his head:

Hammer, I wasn't very nice the last time I saw you, and I'm sorry.

Call me.

We should stop pretending.

He called Dmitri's number. Dmitri was in the grave by now, but they would have held on to his netlink.

On the fifth chime, someone answered on audio only and rumbled something in guttural Russian.

Horace said, "This is Hammer. I want to speak to Yvgeny Mogilevich. Right fucking now."

The audio went muffled.

The next voice spewed Russian invective.

"Save it, fuck face," Horace said. "You're not going to scare me."

"You got a lot of fucking balls, Hammer," the voice said, but it was not a compliment.

"What do you want from me?" Horace said.

"Simple. I want your balls stuffed in your mouth and your head over my fucking fireplace. Nothing less will satisfy me. The question is not, you live or die, but how you die. And who dies with you. She is very beautiful. I see why you like her. We are not cutting yet."

"Let her go!"

The voice laughed. "Predictable. I start cutting and send you some nice video. You come to me then?"

"Let me talk to her."

"You don't give me orders. I give them to you. You come back to Vegas. You come to me. I kill you with pliers and blow torch, feed you to my dogs. But I let your whore and her kids go. You don't come, maybe I start on boy first, turn him into girl."

"Let me talk to her."

"You come back to Vegas by tomorrow night, I don't start cutting."

Horace glanced at the connection timer, which was rapidly approaching two minutes, and disconnected.

For a while he sat there drowning in helplessness and impotent rage, squeezing the netlink until the plastic started to creak. He put it down and clutched his hands.

He was not cut out for this. He was not a secret agent or an action-film hero. He was just a palooka who knew how to put on a good show. How could he hope to go into the monsters' very lair, save not only Lilly but also her kids, and kill Yvgeny Mogilevich? Then again, how could he be sure they actually had Lilly? She may have decided to disappear at Horace's advice. The Russians knew Horace cared about her. Of course they would say they had her, anything to get him to give himself over to them. How could he be sure? He couldn't, unless he saw her or heard her voice.

A string of profanity slow-dripped from his lips.

Life was so much simpler when he had nobody to worry about but himself, when he was responsible for no one but himself. But at the same time, perhaps part of him had been waiting his whole life for someone to fight for, to protect. In this case, however, she hadn't wanted his protection, hadn't wanted him to fight for her, had turned him a chilled shoulder at every turn of her high heel. Except once, that little glimmer that sat there in the corner of his head like an ember that wouldn't go out.

We should stop pretending.

Call me.

"Knock knock," came a sultry voice from the door.

He hadn't closed it.

Jocie stood in the doorway wearing a silk robe, this one so white and sheer that the dark circles of her nipples shone through, small and delicate and upright. Long, lithe legs went all the way up and disappeared just barely in time.

He stood up. "Now is not a good time."

She stepped inside and closed the door behind her. "When would be a good time?"

"How about when you don't belong to somebody else?"

"I don't belong to anybody," she said breezily.

"I think Lex would beg to differ."

She shrugged. "He's already asleep. The night is too young for some people." She had a body fit for sculpture and oil painting. Trouble was, she knew it. A long finger slid between the white silken folds, parting them ever so slightly to bare the flesh all the way to her belly button.

He was ill-prepared to guess whether there was any other scrap of garment at all under there. "So what is it, the sex or the drama that gets you off?"

She scowled and crossed her arms.

"If you weren't married to a stone-cold killer, I'd throw you down on this bed, turn your world inside out, and send you packing in the morning."

She scoffed. "You're afraid of him!"

"Not even a little bit. I've seen a hundred just like him rise and fall. Most of them got back up again. And I've seen more just like you. Here's the thing: I got my own drama to contend with. There's no pussy in the world worth the drama you're toting around."

Anger flared in her eyes, and the smooth planes of her cheeks flushed red.

He stepped toward her and started herding her toward the door. "Goodnight, Jocie."

Her anger subsided into a petulant pout, and the robe came open just enough to reveal that she was, in fact, naked underneath. But she held her ground inside his room. "Goddamn, can't a girl have any fun? You can't even give her a drink?"

"I got nothing to drink. Good night, Jocie." He took her by the shoulders, intending to gently guide her toward the door, but she stumbled somehow and fell. Her head struck the edge of the door, and she went down the rest of the way with a further cry of pain.

He reached down to help her, and she screeched, *"Don't you fucking touch me!"*

Her voice echoed down the hallway.

She elbowed herself up and felt gingerly over her head and face. "Get the fuck away from me!"

He stepped back.

Tina's voice came into the hallway, "What the hell—?"

"He tried to hurt me!" Jocie cried.

Tina knelt in the hallway and helped Jocie to her feet.

Lex's voice boomed in the hallway. "What the fuck!"

Horace turned the moment over and over in his mind. He was strong as an elephant but had long mastered the excess, especially around women a third of his mass. She had all the grace and body control of a trained dancer. There was no way she just "stumbled." But as heavy footsteps thumped down the hall, there was nothing he could say that would make any difference in what happened next.

"Baby, are you okay?" Lex growled as he looked past her at Horace.

"He tried to hurt me, baby," Jocie said.

A blip of logic never once crossed Lex's face, not a single thought about why his wife was already in Horace's room, all but naked. He charged into the room with murder in his eyes, bowling Jocie and Tina over.

Horace clenched his iron-hard fists and met him. He caught Lex's first blows on each arm, and countered with a knee to the gut that luffed Lex's sails. But Lex came back with a flurry of strikes and blocks, almost kung-fu style, driving Horace back until they crashed onto the Murphy bed. The bed had no choice but to succumb to three hundred kilos of straining muscle. Amid wood splintering and a shriek of protesting metal, it collapsed. Fists rained down onto Hammer's head. Lex had his own biological weapons, spiky bone protrusions that emerged when he clenched his fists. The spikes tore gouges in Horace's cheek and skull. Blood flowed into his ear. His mixed martial arts training took over and he heaved Lex up, sliding, writhing, and finally flinging the other man to the side in a wrestling-style reversal.

Tina was in the hallway yelling. Her jackboots retreated down the hallway.

Jocie was giggling.

Horace turned his own massive, hardened fists against Lex, hammering his skull, his back.

Using his own shoulder as a fulcrum, Lex executed a perfect *jujitsu* throw, snatching Horace's arm and levering him. Horace's feet went high and slammed into the wall in the cramped compartment, and the rest of him crashed onto his back, hard, the remains of the bed frame jamming into his spine.

Lex's hands went for Horace's throat, eyes blazing with bestial fury. Lex's spiky knuckles gouged under Horace's jaw, tearing flesh.

Men loomed over them. Strong hands snatched at Lex's arms and shoulders, dragging him off. Skullcrusher James and Kevin Michael arm-locked him, left and right, and he snarled like an animal.

Jocie was in the hallway, laughing.

Horace got to his feet, his back protesting being slammed against the edge of the bed frame. Lex lunged at him again, but the other two fighters held him fast.

"This ain't over!" Lex roared.

Horace wiped his lip, a tremulous shudder shooting out from his heart through his arms. "I don't expect so."

"I'll fucking kill you!"

Trask's voice sounded from the doorway. "Not on my train, you won't."

Jocie jumped forward. "Mr. Trask, he—"

"Shut it," Trask said.

"I ain't gonna let this go, Mr. Trask!" Lex snarled, then stuck out a finger. "You and me, Hammer. Out front."

Horace blinked. "You're saying you want a *duel*?"

Trask said, "No fucking way! I'm already two fighters down, and you got a bout in three days!"

Lex said, "The old fuck hurt Jocie! Ain't no way I can let that stand!"

There was only one way to make this end. Horace said, "Nonlethal. No weapons, no armor. Sunup." He cracked his thick knuckles.

Trask's eyes narrowed and he chewed his cigar, glancing back and forth between them. "You guys want to work it out that way, fine. But the first guy who tries to go lethal gets tased into a coma and left on the side of the road." He turned to Lex and met his gaze. *"Capisce?"*

Lex snorted, appeared to bite back a few choice words, then took Jocie by the arm and dragged her away.

"And the loser pays for this fucking bed!" Trask shouted after them.

Trask spun on Tina. "What are you looking at?"

She raised her hands. "Just a bystander, Boss!"

Trask grunted and stomped after Lex and Jocie.

When he had gone, Tina stepped into the compartment. "Jesus, I kept expecting to hear someone say, 'Pistols at dawn!'"

"Sometimes you gotta go old school." Horace wiped at the blood on his face with the back of his hand.

"And by old, you mean Cro-Magnon." She raised her hands and gaze to the sky. "Somebody tell me why I hang out with cavemen!"

Horace grinned, tasting blood in his teeth. "Because we're so charming." Then the humor evaporated as he realized he might not have until morning. There was no way he could be back in Las Vegas by tomorrow night except by plane, and he didn't have money for airfare. He had tapped out all his favors. He had to make some money by tomorrow night.

And then it came to him.

CHAPTER THIRTEEN

In another abandoned parking lot near Buffalo on the edge of a crumbling business park, bathed in the gray light of dawn, surrounded by buildings utterly lacking any architectural grandeur, far from the watchful eyes of any megacorp or law enforcement drones, in a ring of fighters both stern-eyed and jovial, Horace and Lex faced each other, naked to the waist.

Trask stood between them. "Now listen here. This is nonlethal. Hammer, I can *not* afford to lose my number one fighter, even though he's a jealous, moronic asshole. Lex, if word gets out that you dishonorably killed the legendary Hammer Harkness in a nonlethal grudge brawl, your career will be *over*. You both got me?"

They both nodded. Horace cracked his knuckles.

"And if there's any regenerating to be done, you pay for it yourselves. Got anything to say?" Trask said. "Want to kiss and make up?"

"I got something," Horace said. "A little bet. There's nothing to gain here for me. I'm here defending my good name. I didn't touch your wife until she came into my compartment last night hunting for some action—"

"Fuck you!" Lex roared.

"—and I politely turned her down. This is all a setup, and you're too fucking stupid to see it. So I propose a bet."

Trask took out his cigar. "What do you got in mind?"

"Loser pays the winner twenty thousand."

"You're on!" Lex snarled.

Trask said, "All right, then. You all heard it."

Of course, Horace didn't have twenty thousand dollars, but no one carried that much cash. He was gambling that in the heat of the moment Lex would agree to the bet and they would handle the particulars of the funds exchange afterward; and then all Horace had to do was school this moron in the finer social niceties. And if he lost, well, there wasn't much further for him to fall. The second hand on his clock of borrowed time was picking up speed.

Trask backed out of the ring of onlookers.

Lex closed the distance, and they began to circle each other, like old-time boxers checking for weakness. A night's sleep had cooled Lex's temper and let calculation and strategy into his brain.

Based on what he'd seen of Lex already, Horace had concocted his own strategy, which amounted to counterattack. Lex had the advantage of a healthy heart. As long as Horace could minimize his own exertion and let Lex wear himself down, he had a chance. Lex's martial arts training had made him deceptively fast for such a big fighter. Nevertheless, all it would take was one solid shot from Horace's iron-hard fists; he had won fights in such manner before. He did feel a little naked without his armor, and Lex's knuckles could take out an eye with a lucky shot. But Horace's fists could break ribs, crush a skull, and rupture internal organs.

Lex lunged forward swinging. Horace blocked, dodged, and jabbed a solid left into Lex's cheek, snapping his head back.

Anger flared in Lex's eyes, quickly staunched by the self-control of an experienced fighter. Horace's respect for Lex grew in that moment. The great ones knew how to harness the Beast, knew when to let it off the leash. The ones who descended into mindless animal brawling would lose more often to the careful, calculating fighter who could bide his time while the animal expended himself.

Lex went low, grabbing for Horace's legs, but last night Horace had watched enough video from the net to recognize Lex's moves. Horace countered easily and drove a hammer blow into Lex's kidney. Lex didn't flinch—any pit fighter's training inured him to pain—but Horace knew it hurt. Lex would be pissing blood later.

Horace caught Lex's head under his arm and squeezed, brought his free fist down hard onto Lex's ribcage. Lex wrenched himself free and backed off, wincing, unsteady on his feet. Horace watched Lex's eyes, guessing from hundreds of experiences in the pit, in the boxing ring, on the wrestling mat, what Lex was going to do next.

When fighters got hurt, some felt that twinge of desperation that they were not the iron-hard badasses they believed themselves to be. So to reclaim that confidence, they turned the hurt around and went on the attack, which was exactly what Lex did. Sometimes the fresh ferocity worked, sometimes it didn't.

Another whirl of flailing fists. The fists raked bloody furrows across Horace's arms, across his chest and shoulder, but he avoided the brunt of the damage and countered with a heavy boot to the inside of Lex's thigh, spinning the fighter's leg out from under him. As Lex tried to recover his balance, Horace went on the offensive, pummeling forward with punches and elbows. A bone-cracking shot to Lex's sternum knocked him onto his back.

The pain and humiliation stoked the rage in Lex's eyes into even greater heat.

Horace tried to give him an out. "Had enough?"

Lex roared and lunged to his feet, charging fists first. Horace tried to bat them away, but one of them got through to Horace's ribs. A stunning pain shot through his ribcage, drove the breath out of him. His heart stuttered. He staggered backward.

Lex lunged, and Horace caught him in a bear hug, trying to hold him long enough to catch his breath, recover his bearings. Multi-colored sparks splashed his vision. The strength drained out of his left arm. Lex squirmed free and kicked at Horace's knee. He turned his knee aside just enough to let the brunt of the blow pass without snapping his ligaments.

Horace clinched him again, trying to shake the sparks away so he could see, trying to gather his breath and let some strength return to his arms.

And then he felt the opening, the instant where Lex was just a sliver off-balance, a moment of relaxation in the right muscles. Horace spun, cranked Lex's head, and levered him over his hip. Lex's feet flew into the air as his torso slammed into the ground. Horace hammered a fist toward Lex's face. Lex saw it coming and tried to move his head, but it wasn't enough. Horace felt something crack in Lex's cheek. Lex's body jerked, stiffened, and went limp.

All went still, the onlookers holding their breath.

Lex lay motionless.

Horace wobbled to his feet. Cold sweat exploded over his body. He couldn't breathe. His left arm was a slab of tingling numbness all the way to his fingertips.

Not now... He had to hold his feet just a little longer. He had to *win.*

Jocie screamed and rushed to Lex's side.

He couldn't find the face to match Trask's voice. "That's it then."

Horace said, "I guess it is." He collapsed to one knee, then onto his side.

Rosy fingers of sunrise painted ribbons of contrails above. A sliver of moon hung overhead, so clear.

A few meters away, Jocie was crying over Lex. "Lex, wake up, you idiot! Wake up, baby!"

Lex's voice rumbled, strangely muffled. "Something broke... Hurts."

Someone rolled Horace onto his back. Faces circled his vision.

There were small, cool hands on him. "Hammer!" Tina's voice.

"I knew this would be a fucking fiasco," Trask growled. "Carry them to the infirmary."

"Go Juice..." Horace rasped.

Tina leaned so close he could smell the jasmine of her soap, the apple shampoo of her rainbow hair. "What?"

"In my equipment...with injector." It was all the breath he could muster.

Tina disappeared from his vision. His head swam, and his vision went gray.

And then it blazed to life again with Prismacolor 3-D clarity. He was sitting up, gasping for air, and a syringe was sticking out of his chest like an arrow. He touched it, stared stupidly as it twitched rhythmically with the beat of the muscle it was embedded in. *Tick-tick-tick-tick...* A freshly wound antique watch. He wrapped numb fingers around it, pulled the needle out of his heart.

Bunny said, "Mr. Trask, we need to get him to a hospital."

"Yeah. Jesus, Horus, and Thor, what a fiasco."

As the Go Juice suffused Horace's system, his tattoos blazed blue. So strange that his symbols of readiness to fight were so bright when there was no fight left in him.

He got to his feet, electricity spreading through his veins, jolting, sporadic.

Jocie and another fighter were helping Lex into the train's infirmary car. Lex was holding his cheek.

"I'm fine," Horace said.

"No, you're not," Bunny said. "I already called an ambulance."

An explosion of dizziness almost brought him to his knees again, but arms caught him. "No, I'm not."

Images and impressions wandered through the gray fastness of his perception, half-glimpsed, half-remembered. Lifted by two paramedics onto a gurney. Morning sun shining through the rear window of the ambulance, the mask over his face, the sting of the IV. The sweat sheening his body, even though he was freezing; the incessant pain in his chest, squeezing tighter with every heartbeat. Fluorescent lights sliding through his vision. The bustle of activity around him. Trask's voice talking to someone.

"Patient's name?"

"Uh, Jim. James Smith."

"What's his medical program?"

"He doesn't have a medical program."

"Then he doesn't qualify for regeneration. The best we can do is stabilize him. Does he have the money to pay?"

"How the hell should I know? Look, he's only been with us a few days."

The voices receding, people surrounding him, a cold stethoscope on his breast. The wires and sensors now attached to him. The beep of the machines.

Throughout it all, he floated in serenity. He'd trod the expanses of this vague, vast grayness so many times it was part of his reality, this netherworld between life and death, between being *on* and *off*.

The injections began, and he succumbed to unconsciousness.

The sound of a sliding curtain intruded upon the haze of sleep. A man in a white coat stood beside him, carrying a datapad. The Fight Doctor, Ferris Wilton, MD.

"What the fuck are you doing here?" Horace said.

"I'm Dr. Pentz, Mr. Smith." The doctor's voice didn't match the Fight Doctor.

"Huh?"

The Fight Doctor's face melted and became a woman's, hovering beside him. "You're still groggy."

Horace blinked and rubbed his eyes.

Dr. Pentz smiled at him, then took a stethoscope and applied it to his chest, watching the biometric monitor. She had kind, green eyes and a face lined by years of stress. She put the stethoscope away. "Do you remember anything?"

"I'm in the hospital." Each word felt like spitting out a cotton ball.

"You are indeed. And you're very lucky."

"Twenty-seven times."

"What?"

"Never mind. When can I go?"

"That is indeed the question, Mr. Smith. Your friend, Mr. Trask, tells us that you have no medical program. By law in the State of New York, we're only obligated to keep you for twelve hours."

"Peachy. Gotta go anyway."

"We've done full scans on your heart. The amount of scar tissue boggles my mind."

"I'm a pit fighter."

"So I gather." Her lips twisted into disgust. "I must say that I regard your profession—and its corporate sponsors—as utterly reprehensible. It puts the lowest possible value on human life."

"Human life has always been cheap, Doc. Just ask any king or corporation ever born. Some of us are just born to be meat for the machine, and not many of those ever see the gears."

"I prefer to be less cynical, Mr. Smith."

"So give it to me straight, Doctor. I'm guessing I don't have much time."

"I could give you the whole spiel about watching your stress level—"

Horace burst into painful laughter.

"—and watching what you eat and taking it easy before your heart explodes. But I'm not going to do that. You're right when you say you don't have much time. Could be days, could be a year. You need a new heart."

"I know."

"We could give you an artificial one, if you had a medical program."

"I looked into it. There aren't any made that fit a body this size. I'm outside specs. They can't handle the flow load for what I do. Besides, I'd rather have a new one of my own. But I don't have the money for that either."

"The scarring alone... Tell me, how have you kept yourself alive?"

"My Go Juice."

"What is in this Go Juice?"

"A bunch of stuff. I got a friend who mixes it up for me. Keeps me coming back when the ticker sticks."

"Have you any idea how dangerous—?" She stopped herself. "Never mind that."

Horace chuckled again. "Beyond a certain point, decisions get a whole lot easier." Then he took a deep, ragged breath. "Now, I'm gonna give it to you straight, Doctor. I don't have the money for a new heart. I can't stay here, and the longer I do, the more danger *you're* in. But... there are people depending on me right now, today: a woman and two kids, life or death. What kind of fix can you give me to keep this ticker going the next time it decides to crap out?"

She chewed on the end of her stylus.

"Something on a budget," he said.

She paced. "Why should I, if you put such a low value on your life?"

"Because it's your job. Just like it's mine to be an entertainer."

"A butcher, more like."

"I am one entertaining butcher. Neither of us can change the world, Doc. But like I said, there are people who might be dead if I don't help them. Help me save them."

"Who?"

"A friend and her two kids."

"What can you do?"

"I have no idea. But I have to try."

She eyed him for a long, long time, chewing on her stylus. "There is one possibility that will work strictly temporarily. It's cheaper than re-growing a new heart. We can mount an EKG monitor on you, sort of like a pacemaker, and rig it with an injector of your Go Juice. Next time you flatline, it injects you."

"Sounds great. How much?"

She gave him a scary figure.

"Shit, Doc, no problem. Just let me go rob a bank first."

"Even if we do this, it is not foolproof. There will come a time when no amount of Go Juice or anything else will restart that heart."

The thought of keeping Lilly and her kids out of the hands of the Russians meant a whole lot more to him than anything else. "Thanks for your concern, really. How soon could you rig one up?"

"First you would have to verify that you have the funds available."

"You let me worry about that."

"Next, we would have to get you out of this hospital. This is somewhat outside the system."

CHAPTER FOURTEEN

"I tried to bring you a nice Geriatri-Cal," Tina said, sitting down beside the bed, hands stuffed in her jeans pockets, "but they confiscated it at the door."

"I appreciate the thought." Horace leaned back on the bed, trying to muster a smile.

Her eyes wouldn't meet his, and there was a seriousness lurking there, like a stain behind a patch of brittle plaster. She wiped at her nose.

"So what are you doing here?" he said. "Aren't you all supposed to be back on the road by now?"

"Trask canceled a couple of the promo events, so we still have time to make Albany. Besides, they're kicking you out of here in the morning anyway, right?"

"So they tell me."

"I brought you your netlink." She offered it to him. "Thought you might like it to pass the time."

"Thanks." He took it, looked at it, thumbed the print reader.

There was a message from Jack. A twinge of fear wormed into his belly.

"What?" she said.

"Huh?"

"Your face just went from ghost to phantom."

"It's nothing." He wanted to get out of bed, put his feet on the floor, gather up his belongings, and jet back to Las Vegas. But the EKG/injector had not yet been installed. He might keel over just walking out the door. Realizing how cavalier such thoughts had been in the past, he knew that now was different. The grave beckoned him now, closer than at any point in his life, even the times he had been killed. Why was he so reluctant to die *now*, compared to all those times he had faced it in the pit? Was it because his final moment of mortality was staring into his face, so close he could smell its breath, or was it because of something else? Had it ever felt any less real? Going into every fight, he was always aware that something unexpected could happen, the kind of thing that would preclude regeneration, or worse, leave him a vegetable or an invalid. There were more than a few fighters like that; long forgotten pieces of meat kept alive by tubes and nurses.

He had also spent the last hour wondering how he could scrape up the cash to pay for the injector in the first place.

"I thought I should tell you something," Tina said, smiling crookedly. "We know you don't have the scratch, so we passed the hat. They'll be coming to put in the injector in about half an hour."

Horace's mouth fell open, and words would not come. Here he was again—the washed-up old has-been living off the charity of others. Fresh anger rose in him. "No, you can't—"

She waved him off. "Swallow your macho pride, it's already done. Besides, you got enough to worry about. I tried to ask Bunny about what's up with you, she seemed to know something. I've never seen her shut up so fast." Elbows on her knees, Tina glanced repeatedly between Horace and her clasped hands as she was talking, and cleared her throat a little. "Trask says we're pulling out in the morning...."

She kept talking, but Horace retreated into anger. Why would these people throw together their hard-earned money in times so hard for a beaten-down old man with nothing left to offer anybody?

No one wants to see a sick old man die. Was it that simple? Was that how he saw himself now? How long would he let other people help him limp along?

"How's Lex?" he said.

"Still an asshole, but a little more tolerable now that he's been put in his place. He's gonna have to win in Albany. He had to regenerate a cheekbone. On top of what he had to pay you, he's broke. No more new shoes for Jocie."

"That woman—"

"Is a fucking succubus, didn't I try to tell you?"

"Yeah, you did."

"Right now, they're back in their compartment, scheming like Machiavelli's bastard kids."

"Who?"

"Never mind. Get this, I heard them talking one night, right? Have you heard about these new cybernetic implants, you know, for the vagina?"

He chuckled, even though his throat was still dry, "The porn-star ones that pulse and vibrate?"

"Right. One night she was trying to talk Lex into buying her one of those, along with breast implants."

"Could be interesting."

"If by interesting you mean dripping with putrescent pustules. Did you see that thing when she went down? Looked like an old catcher's mitt."

He chuckled, and pain shot through him. "Don't make me laugh."

At that moment, Dr. Pentz walked in. "It's time, Mr. Smith," she said. "There's a taxi outside."

The taxi took him to a run-down building in a neighborhood abandoned by everything except stray dogs and vermin. Graffiti plastered the few walls still standing. But this building, what looked like a hundred-year-old medical clinic, had a moving van parked out front. A couple of orderlies helped him from the taxi to the front door. The moment he passed inside, the feel of the building changed. The interior was ancient but spotless. Two thin, pale-skinned people sat in the ancient waiting room, watery-eyed, beaten down, dirt-poor, but hopeful. All the fixtures and architecture were old, built before the turn of the twenty-first century, but the equipment in the operating room looked new enough to be functional. Dr. Pentz was there with two nurses.

"What is this place?" Horace said.

"It doesn't exist. Completely off the grid," Dr. Pentz said.

"But why?"

She tied a surgical mask around her face. "We have a corporate medical system that turns human life into a commodity, a profit margin. Some of us still believe medicine is more than that. We acquire equipment and supplies as best we can from bankruptcy auctions, refurbishing salons, charitable donors." She gestured him toward an upright surgical chair.

The procedure itself took remarkably little time. They placed a palm-sized box of plastic and stainless steel, about two centimeters thick, directly over his heart, and secured it to his flesh with some sort of subcutaneous molecular adhesive.

"As we discussed," Dr. Pentz said, "this device will monitor your heart. It's powered by bio-electricity and body heat. If you experience another cardiac arrest, it will inject your Go Juice, as you call it, directly into your heart via high-pressure molecular injectors. No needles, but it will sting significantly."

"That's okay, Doc. I've already had a needle in my heart today." He chuckled, but her brow remained furrowed.

"The device is fairly durable, as long as no one hits it with a weapon. If it's torn off, you'll have a square of muscle laid bare. That will also sting significantly."

Horace looked down at it, grinning in spite of her wry tone. "You're a peach, Doctor. What happens if I push this red button?"

"You give yourself a full dose. Overdo it, and your heart will probably explode anyway."

"How many doses does it hold?"

"Three."

"What if I need to refill it?"

"There's a reservoir here under this flip-up stopper. Just pour it in."

"I shoulda gotten me one of these years ago! Anything else I need to know?"

"Nothing that you'll listen to."

"I know you don't approve, Doc, but thanks."

"Be well, 'Mr. Smith.' You'll be free to go in a few hours, after the adhesion has finished setting. Meanwhile I have other patients."

After they had gone, he eased back into the chair, picked up his netlink, and looked at it. There was still that message from Jack, hovering over him like a harbinger of merciless doom. Did he really want to know? Something told him that it was bad.

Jack's message:

THIS CAME OUT AN HR AGO. POSTED ON UNDRGRND FEED. GOT UR NAME ON IT.

The message was attached to a video. He connected to the video. It opened to a happy scene of dancing teddy bears and frolicking unicorns with the caption:

A LOVE LETTER TO THE HAMMER.

The video dissolved to a dark smear of grainy, jumpy video that eventually resolved into a dim room of cinder-block walls. Two fluorescent lanterns hung from hooks in the ceiling. Standing in the center of the room was a woman, nude, bathed in pale, flickering light, with ropes knotted around her wrists, pulled tight toward opposite walls. Brown hair shadowed bruised, puffy cheeks and eyes. Blood ran from her nose. She was weeping through a filthy-looking gag. The netlink screen was too small for him to discern if she was really Lilly, but from here the tall, willowy body certainly looked like hers. He knew the curve of her breasts, the shape of her nipples, the bones of her slim hips.

Something thick and bitter welled up in his throat.

Three shadowy men occupied the shadows around her, all of them swathed in black clothing, patent leather hoods with pinholes for eyes and ragged slashes for mouths. The camera approached her, and the weeping grew louder. The dull steel of a knife blade appeared in the frame in the other hand of the camera operator. A tuneless humming started from the camera man, as if getting ready for some mundane everyday task that was not altogether unpleasant.

The camera circled her, ducking under her arm. The humming continued, and her weeping turned to whimpering. The other men remained still.

The cameraman laid the flat of the knife blade against her naked back. She flinched away from it. He stroked her with the steel, slowly and sensually, as if it were a lover's feather. The point raked a line of pink welt across her petal-soft skin. There were the two moles below Lilly's right shoulder blade. The point of the knife paused there, as if considering whether it should connect the dots.

Horace clutched a hand over his mouth. He wanted to turn it off, tear his eyes away, but he didn't dare. He had to *know*.

The knife moved out of frame, which hovered upon her shoulder blade, slid up her long shapely neck toward the side of her head.

The frame jerked slightly. She gasped, flinched, and cried out in pain.

Nausea washed through him.

The video cut to a black silhouette in a shadowy room. Jars glinted on shelves surrounding the silhouette's chair. "Sleep well, Hammer, get your rest," said Yvgeny Mogilevich's voice. "Because I'm going to fuck you. And I'm going to keep fucking you until I can't fuck anymore."

The video dissolved to the face of a brightly grinning teddy bear. The teddy bear winked.

Across the room, Tina slept in the chair.

He had kept the volume on the video low, but the sound of the woman's shocked outcry stabbed deep into his brain and writhed like a speared cobra.

Helplessness washed through him in a sick deluge like he had never experienced before. A few hours out of commission, and he had lost her. Or maybe he had lost her.

At least there was one bright side. If Lilly and her kids were already dead, suicide missions were always easier to pull off than rescues.

CHAPTER FIFTEEN

Amid the predawn mustering of light at the horizon, with a sweatshirt covering the box implanted into his chest, Horace walked out the front door of the clandestine clinic to the taxi. It drove him through empty, debris-strewn streets to where the road train waited. Alone in the taxi with no driver, the unfamiliar weight of the box hanging there in the center of his chest, gave him too much time trapped with his thoughts. Horace's battered old heart clumped along as it had for a while, but today with a more uncomfortable weight upon it—all these people he barely knew were treating him like family. They didn't have to call the ambulance. They didn't have to pay for his new injector out of their own pockets. They didn't have to wait for him, losing money with every passing minute in lost promotions and missed appearances. The thought of it brought a tightness to his chest, a thickness to his throat, neither of which came from his bum ticker.

The moment he stepped into the door of the rearmost car, the power plant began to hum with strength.

Bunny's voice came over the PA system, "All a-*board*!"

The train eased forward.

Back in his berth, Horace eased himself into the chair. He still had the bruises from Lex to contend with. At least the lacerations under his chin had been bandaged.

Unfathomable weariness suffused him. Everything hurt. His eyelids felt like sandpaper. Lead weights hung from every limb. He hadn't slept a wink while waiting for Dr. Pentz to give him the green light to leave. Every time he closed his eyes, the knife slid across the inside of his eyelids, across her naked back and the two moles he knew so well, and her gasp of shock sent another lump into his throat. Another pile of guilt, a whole goddamn smorgasbord of it. He scrubbed a hand over his stubbled face.

He took his netlink toward the front of the train and encountered one of the other fighters, Saul Shockwave, a short, spitfire of a man with his hair twisted into a pincushion of bleached spikes.

"Glad to see you up and around, Hammer," Saul said with a solemn nod.

"I'm much obliged to you. To all of you." Horace offered his hand, and they shook earnestly. His voice still sounded like he'd smoked eight cigars in a row, but at the sound of it, heads emerged from the berths.

With the lump still in his throat, he shook hands all the way to the front of the car. Jocie and Lex, on the other hand, were not to be found.

The same happened in every car moving forward, going through the gym, one fighter after another offering their hands, their respect, their admiration, anecdotes about the first time they had seen him fight. It was too much. By the time he reached the front of the train, the thought of another well-wisher made him want to flee like a wounded buffalo.

Bunny answered his knock immediately. "Come on in, Mr. Harkness."

He shut the door behind him. "You've already done plenty, Bunny, and I'm grateful for that, but...there are some things I gotta know."

She regarded him from her kitchen table, where a bowl of breakfast paste sat before her. "Are you hungry? I can offer you some of this. It's not bad if you drown it in sweetener."

"No, thanks." There wasn't a cell in his body that felt like eating after what he had seen. "There's...this video." How could he even expect her to watch such a thing? "Could it be faked?"

"What kind of video?"

He sighed. "Maybe a snuff film. I've seen blood and gore scattered from here to Timbuktu, but nothing has ever affected me like this," he said.

She flinched a little. "Do you love her?"

"It's my fault. That's their way, the Russians. Cross them and they kill your whole family. I should have known better. I was afraid they would go after her."

"There was nothing you could have done differently."

"I didn't have to cut Dmitri Mogilevich's head off and leave it in his lap, for starters."

Her lips quirked into a grim smile. "Maybe, but I've been around, too. I've been in the joint. I can say with certainty it wouldn't have mattered. They would still have gone after her or her kids. They always go after the kids..." Her voice cracked and trailed off. She clasped trembling hands across her stomach. "The only thing you could have done differently would have been never to get involved with them in the first place."

"Never been a foresight kinda guy." If he was honest with himself, he'd thought he would either be able to repay the debt or be dead anyway.

Bunny's eyes drifted to the 2-D photograph of Young Bunny with two daughters, her face tightening into a mask.

After a long moment, he said, "Are they alive?"

Her gaze never left the photo. "I'm sure they are. Somewhere. Working off mom's 'debt to society,' complete with brainwashing and full medical." Then she swallowed hard, shook herself, and straightened up. "Okay, I'll have a go at your video."

She sat back in a chair. Her eyes fluttered slightly, looking simultaneously inward and outward. "There's all kinds of chatter, it's hard to sift through. Found the video."

"Can something like this be faked?" he said.

"Maybe. Have you seen the John Wayne and Audrey Hepburn version of *Gone with the Wind*? Any visual image can be faked with enough time, equipment, and skill."

"Is it?"

"I'm not a video expert. I don't know what to look—oh, my god!"

"You're watching it now?"

Her hand clutched her mouth. She nodded, her gaze staring into the depths of the net. "Sick bastards! Pardon my language. Just FYI, the FBI is looking into it, too. They have bots that sniff out this kind of thing. The footprints of their crawlers and sniffers are everywhere around this thing."

"Maybe the FBI can find her." Federal law enforcement still existed, but had been diminished by decades of budget cuts and scandals.

She snorted. "Do you think an organization like the Russian mob can exist without the sufferance of the government? The FBI only investigates when the stink reaches heaven. I've been doing a little more sniffing of my own, by the way. This guy's name, Dmitri Mogilevich, it shows up all over the place. Front companies and dummy corporations daisy-chained all the way to the moon. They have their fingers in hundreds of pies, and I'm still counting. Trouble is, I can't *do* anything to them."

"So, do you know someone who can check out the video?"

"Already sent the message." Her eyes focused on him again. "If he's awake, he might get back to us before the water's hot. If he's not, it'll be a few hours. Want a cup of tea?"

Horace took a deep breath and rubbed a hand over his stubbled pate.

"So how do you feel?" she said.

"About which part?"

"Your heart."

He rubbed the flesh around the box embedded in his chest. "Like a shopping cart with a wobbly wheel." The urge to just leave Bunny alone roared through him—it was a dangerous thing, being his friend.

She got up, poured some water into a teapot, and put it in the thermolator to warm. "You like cardamom?"

"What's that?"

"Never mind. I'll make you some tea. You should try it. It'll help calm you down. In fact, given your condition, you should probably make that a way of life."

"I'm starting to get that." He pointed at the ear and back of his skull. "So what's it like?"

"Being a slicer? Having an AI embedded in my brain? Having a firehose to the entirety of human knowledge and folly pumping into my head? Which do you want first?"

"Your call."

She set out a cup for Horace, and with strange precision measured out some tea leaves into a ball of wire mesh. "Well, first of all, it makes me one of the most cynical people on Earth. Twelve billion people on this planet and half of them are below average intelligence—or below average ethical standards. The rampant stupidity of so many just boggles my mind, and it's all up there to pour into your head like vomit, all the time and forever. And you know, there's just as much sweet and uplifting stuff out there, people helping people, inspiring people, but it's so hard to remember any of that in this deluge of sewage that would spew directly into my brain if I'd let it.

"Back in my twenties, we did a lot of great work, dragging some of the megacorp filth into the light of day. It was a constant struggle, like watching some dinosaur eating everything in sight and then crapping all over the world because it thought it had a right to, because isn't that what capitalism is for, making money? Then there's me and other people like me trying to help clean it up. That was us, trying to clean up dinosaur crap with teaspoons." Her face was grim. "I have six hundred thousand terabytes of stolen data in a secret server only I can access, enough criminal evidence to bring down three megacorps and half the U.S. government, so much that even I don't know the extent of what's in there, except that it's damning as heck for a lot of powerful people. But I can't get to it because my AI has a lock on him for my parole."

The thermolator dinged; she took out the teapot and placed the tea ball into it.

"Your computer's a him?"

"Yeah, I programmed him to sound like Jimmy Stewart in my head. And he gets a little miffed at being called a computer. That's like calling a twentieth-century computer an abacus. He prefers to be called an artificial person."

"Okay, artificial person then."

"Growing up with my grandmother, she was a fan, so I saw a bunch of his old movies. It's just comforting hearing the voice, reminds me of my nan. But things are different now, right? From when we were kids? Back then, the civilian government at least pretended to function, instead of being a rubber stamp for the megacorps and the military. They called me the White Rabbit, because anytime anyone got close to catching me, I just threw up a cloud of trippy chaff and disappeared down the rabbit hole. But then I screwed up, just once. I got caught.

"The prison guards, such clever souls, started calling me Bunny. I did my time. And when I got out, everything was different. Nothing that I knew, nothing that my AI used to have down to a science was useful anymore. Everything I knew was caveman tech. It's taken me a long time to catch up, plus having to work around and around the locks that they put on. All these young hotshots just tear up the quantum matrices. Half the time, it's like they're speaking a different language. Then there's the whole getting-old debacle."

He laughed wryly and raised his cup. "Hear hear, sister."

"My brain used to be able to keep up with Jimmy. Now Jimmy has to wait on me most of the time. I used to be able to go days without sleep, completely immersed in whatever gallant crusade I was on. Nowadays I'm happy to be in bed at nine p.m."

"Are they ever going to take the locks off?"

She wiped a tear. "Not until I give over the data. I refused to, so they put the lock on me. It's like kneecapping a runner intentionally. Why would I give up something I worked so hard for? They won't open up the lock until I do. My case gets reviewed every two years, but it's a farce. But I haven't been the same since prison. Prison is not good for cyberpaths."

"Cyberpaths..."

"People who connect directly, wirelessly. Like telepathy, but this is real. For instance, I can sense your netlink right there, its connections to the networks around us. It's like a little rainbow dot that I can reach out and touch with my mind. Prisons shut down cyberpaths. Our AIs are nullified, our connections squelched." She swallowed a hard memory. "The only way I can describe it to you is suddenly being struck blind and deaf all at once. Or having ninety-eight percent of your memories suddenly turned off, and you're left feeling like an honest-to-Isis idiot, like most of who you are just suddenly went dark. Even though less than one percent of what comes into an uplinked brain is your own experience, it all still touches you, sits out there waiting, like a hundred billion lives you've already led, and all you have to do is reach for them."

She wiped her eyes again, poured two cups of amber-brown liquid, unleashing scents both unfamiliar and delicious, spicy and subtle. "Every day I was in there, I wished they had just killed me. It would have been more humane." She cleared her throat and swallowed again. "And then I got out." She offered him the cup.

"Thanks," he said, and took a sip. The teacup looked like a thimble in his hand. Subtleties swam over his tongue, across his palate, and when he breathed, they filled his nose as well. His hand started shaking. He put the cup down and clasped them between his knees.

Her gaze had gone distant, lost in some vast universe of memory. "And that's what it's like. It made losing my kids feel like a walk in the park." She squeezed her eyes shut. "Losing my kids was like losing all my fingernails and toenails, but losing my mind..."

"What happened to your kids?"

"The things I was doing cost those corps a *lot* of money. They indentured my kids to help pay it off, and I went to prison. I had never even heard of such a thing, but when the corps got to write their own legal codes with the rubber stamp from the Supreme Court, everything changed." Her gaze went distant again. "They're in their twenties now, got high-paying jobs with full medical, but they have to pay most of their salaries back to the company, and they're utterly brainwashed that their mom is the most heinous criminal who ever lived, since it's because of me that they live in servitude."

"So you don't see them?"

"I keep tabs sometimes, but they've made it clear that I should never contact them. Their owners told them that if they try to contact me, they'll lose their 'jobs.' They'll never be free."

They sat in silence for a while, each sipping their tea.

When the silence grew too taut, Horace said, "That's fucked up." It sounded lame even as it came out of his mouth, but it was all he could manage.

Then she blinked and said, "My friend got my message. He's going to go through the video pixel by pixel, looking for anomalies." She dabbed at her nose and her voice lost its wind, dwindling to a whisper. "Come back in an hour."

Trask slid back from his desk full of papers. "Sit down, Hammer, take a load off. You look like you need it. Whiskey?"

"The crack of eight a.m. seems like the perfect time." Horace sat across the desk from Trask's chair. The shades were open and the countryside whooshed past outside, brown fields and struggling forests. The last couple of years had seen a drought in western New York, which, with the proximity of the Great Lakes, had not seen a drought in living memory. Endless fields of AgriMax corn looked brown and curled, hypnotic rows sweeping past, cast into shadow by the low-lying sun.

While Trask poured him a finger of whiskey from a decanter, Horace said, "Mr. Trask, I'm here to thank you for what you did. You already stuck your neck out for me, just letting me get onboard. And I certainly didn't intend to get into anything with any of your boys. And I sure as hell wasn't expecting anybody to pitch in for this thing." He rapped the box on his chest with a knuckle.

"The fact you didn't expect it is exactly why everybody pitched in. It wasn't so bad when we spread out the cost a little."

"Whose idea was it?"

"Tina's."

Surprise clamped Horace into silence momentarily. Then he remembered her sleeping in the chair in his room. The wooziness of the experience had let that fact whisper past him.

"She's a good kid," Trask said. "And handy with the gauze and blood-stop."

"Where did you find her?"

"Her dad trained a lot of guys. He was good. Word gets around. I knew of him but hadn't met him. When he got killed, a lot of people in the Business mourned him. And there's this poor little sixteen-year-old girl. Too mouthy by a mile, a weird, little nerd. She disappeared for a while. God knows what she got herself into, poor kid. But we were in Little Rock and there came this kid, god knows what she was doing there, all growed up, asking me for a job. I was a little worried that a cute little thing like her might not be able to hack it among all these knuckle-draggers, but her dad was one of the best."

"She is awfully easy on the eyes."

Trask's eyes fixed and narrowed on Horace. "And fucking smart. She's read more books than both of us put together."

"How was it for her, among these cavemen?"

"Well, on the second day, we were setting up for a promo gig in Tulsa. Ricky Khan started putting the moves on her, being a little too pushy about it, and she just takes him down, right there. And all she used was his finger." Trask stuck up his index finger. "Never seen anything like it. He tried to get up again, which was his second mistake. Never was too bright, that guy. Anyway, he's dead now. Dumb son of a bitch got himself killed in a bar fight. So she's been with me four years. They still get drunk on occasion and think they can get into her pants, but she seems fine with reminding them otherwise. Gets along with most everybody."

"Except Jocie."

Trask snorted. "About the time I get ready to fire Lex just to get rid of her, he wins a big bout and makes me a stack of money, so I don't. But she's a poison pill, that one."

"Mr. Trask, when we get to the next promo stop, I'd like to sign some autographs. Whatever your standard rate is. And you and everyone who contributed get to keep all the money." He rapped the box again.

"You sure about that?"

He thought about the video. "I don't know I got any reason to hide anymore. If they find me, it might be high time to settle up with them."

Trask leaned back in his chair. "It's your skin."

Horace's netlink chime woke him from a nap in his compartment. Between Trask's whiskey and the lack of sleep the night before, he had crashed hard.

He answered it. "Yeah."

"Mr. Harkness, it's Bunny. Your video."

He tried to gauge the result from the sound of her voice, but got nothing. "I'll be right there."

"Are you all right? I've been trying to reach you for half an hour."

"Naw, I'm raring to go." At least he had woken up.

In the driver's compartment, she sat him down with another cup of tea and faced him squarely. Her face was tight and serious.

"So what's the verdict?"

"The verdict is inconclusive."

"What the hell does that mean? Is that her or isn't it?"

"It's not that simple. I'm going to let you talk to Bobcat directly.

He can explain it better than I can. Just a second while we sync." Her eyelids fluttered, her head twitched to the side, her jaw cranked open and closed. Then she straightened up and stared straight ahead.

"Sir, you can call me Bobcat." It was still her voice, but it had taken on an Australian accent.

"Pleased to meet you, Bobcat."

"So, to business, mate. Has the video been doctored or constructed in some way? Yes, it has. The images of the location and the men standing around her have been modified. Data debris everywhere. That is a very slapdash job, that is. The image of the woman as well has been altered. Her face has been shadowed, but because of the angles, the shadows, and her hair, it is impossible to discern if that is indeed her real face. There is evidence that the shadows there were deepened—"

"What about the moles on her back? Were those real? Were they painted in somehow?"

The reply came with about a one-second delay. "No, they were real. The woman in the video is not computer generated, and the moles were real."

"Fuck." Horace said it slowly, a sibilant exhalation trailing off to a painful clack of the tongue.

Again the one-second delay. "She was indeed tied up that way. I checked the data integrity of every frame. The ropes were real. She was naked."

Nausea washed through him.

Bunny's eyes watched him as if they were the only thing in her head that she controlled. The sadness and concern in her eyes did not correlate with the matter-of-fact, analytical tone of her voice.

"You said the location was modified?" Horace said.

"Yes, the dungeon-like appearance was enhanced, shall we say, although I cannot say what it may have looked like otherwise. It cannot have been too different, or the shadows would have been completely wrong, and those would have left more evidence of tampering. I'm sorry I cannot be more conclusive. I'll send a complete report to Bunny for you to read at your leisure. This has been the executive summary."

"Thanks, brother. Anything I can do to repay you?"

"An action figure. We could never get those Down Under."

"You got it."

"Relinquishing vocal control back to Bunny. Cheers, mate."

Bunny blinked twice, shuddered, and rubbed her face. "Oh, Mr. Harkness, I'm so sorry."

The nausea passed, however, replaced by the heat of anger. "They're playing games with me. It doesn't matter if that's really Lilly, the effect on me is what they want."

"What are you going to do?"

"Start playing their game myself."

ROUND 2

CHAPTER SIXTEEN

The train pulled into Buffalo, New York, barely in time for the promotional event. The grass-peppered parking lot outside Ralph Wilson Stadium was already starting to fill up with people camped out, waiting.

The ancient football stadium had seen better days. The Buffalo Blazers had played there for more than eighty years, had even gone through a couple of name changes along the way, but now it had been abandoned for a newer, bigger, flashier facility about ten years ago, a place with real-time holographic capability on the field itself. This old stadium was now being used by a conglomerate of area high schools and the State University of Buffalo.

Horace felt the old gridiron history seeping through the concrete under his feet as he stepped off the train. Gone were the days of pads and helmets from when he was a kid. Regenecorp and the availability of regeneration technology had evolved American football into a game more resembling rugby on Krok. Injuries were commonplace, including broken necks, shattered ribs, and splintered joints. What would have been career-ending injuries when he was a kid were now just another day at work for modern-day football players.

With fans already gathering here for the event, Trask and the fighters hustled through the setup process, deploying the tables and flashing lights, setting up the chairs, signing in the local models hired to be their own kind of attraction. If there was anything that went with brawny, hard-knuckled fighters in the minds of the public, it was breasts, booty, and brilliant smiles. It was not an association that Horace cared to do away with. Buffalo was a much larger market than the last promo event.

Trask was pulling out all the stops. Each fighter would have a spokesmodel beside him at the table, ushering the fans along, being generous with collagen kisses and saline squeezes.

Trask even wheeled out the half-scale replica of a Civil War-era cannon, loaded it with paper packets of black powder and blank wadding, and used it to signal the commencement of the event. A thunderclap and a cloud of blue-gray smoke, and the few hundred fans cheered. On the heels of the cannon report, music pulsed from the speakers, echoing across the expanse of parking lot.

Horace would stay out of sight until Trask's special entrance for him, planned for the height of the crowd's attendance.

In his compartment, Horace dressed himself in the only show suit he had brought with him and tried desperately to forget that every impulse told him to get to Vegas, hitchhike if he had to. But there was no way he could be there in time.

The show suit was a sequined explosion of holographic flames on black elastane. The neckline was V-cut to his sternum, meant to show off his massive pectorals; however, it would now reveal the box over his heart. The best concealment he could manage was a black t-shirt under the show suit. The t-shirt ruined some of the effect, but that was preferable to answering a thousand unpleasant questions.

Every ten minutes or so, a female voice, slick and sultry, came over the PA system outside, extolling the fans to "Stick around for a *very* special guest." The lines stretched out to scores waiting their turn for autographs and photos with the fighters and models.

About hour into the event, Tina knocked on his door. "Two minutes, Methuselah."

"Thanks," he said. He took out his injector and a bottle of Go Juice. Something in him wanted to give these people a real show, even if all he was going to do was walk down to the pavement. More than any time he could remember, this felt like it might be his last appearance ever in front of a crowd. He shot himself in the arm and sighed at the rush throbbing through him, the way his heart sped up, the way his muscles felt like electrodes in a lightning storm, the way his tattoos blazed to life.

Opening the door, he found Tina waiting in the hallway.

Her eyes bulged for a moment. "By the power of graybeards, you do clean up. When you're not mostly dead, that is."

"Glad you noticed, Short Round. Take me to your leader."

And then of course, following her, he felt like a dirty old man again as he simply could not take his eyes off the way she moved, the way her orange-and-yellow polka-dot tights hugged her legs and buttocks. She had that grace that real martial artists possessed; it was simply inherent in who she was, like a dancer's grace mixed with a restrained explosion. Her ponytail stuck out from the back of her head like the tail of a feisty young filly, erect and bushy.

She led him to the central ramp that led down among the tables. The hubbub of the throng, numbering perhaps a thousand people, came through the door: laughter, conversation. In the air above the crowd, hovering at the periphery, was a drone about the size of a trashcan lid, probably from the local media. Horace immediately ducked back, but then chided himself for foolishness. He was done hiding. In less than a minute, the entire world would know exactly where he was.

Trask's voice came over the speakers, unusually deep and resonant. "And now, the moment you've all been waiting for!"

Deep bass throbbing filled the air, building anticipation. He smiled as the pulse of "Thunderstruck" filled the air, but not the newer commissioned version—the old-school rock-n-roll version from his Grandpa's time. The change in tune caught the crowd's attention.

"Our special guest, a true legend of the pit, a fighter whose records will stand for ages to come!"

The crowd hushed, and the music intensified. They raised their faces in curiosity, smiles of wonder began to spread, expectation. *Could it really be* him*?*

"Fresh from his spectacular comeback victory in Fury Dome XXIV!"

Recognition and hope burgeoned in the sea of faces with their eyes glued on the curtain behind which Horace awaited his cue.

"Yes, that's right, you know who I'm talking about! Hor-ussss the Ham-Murrr Haaaark-ness!"

The cannon pounded the air again in synchrony with his theme song.

Horace thrust the curtain aside and stepped onto the ramp. The crowd roared in delight. Standing there overlooking them from the two-meter-high ramp, he raised his arms and shook his clenched fists to the sky. The crowd went berserk, jumping and cheering, arms raised in Thunder Hammers.

His throat clenched again and his eyes teared up. If this was to be his swan song, let it be a good one. He answered their Thunder Hammers with his own and roared at the sky with all the ferocity he could muster. Whorls of neon tattoos blazed over his arms and face.

The media drone zoomed nearer, floating eight meters over the heads of the crowd. A throng of net-shades fixed upon him, registering his identity and feeding it out into the vastness of cyberspace.

For almost a minute, he fed the crowd his ferocity and grandeur and drank their accolades by the gulp. Then he strode like a Goliath toward the pavement. He went to the barriers and touched hands with as many fans as he could manage, and the expressions of awe and excitement on the faces of even the youngest filled him with the kind of warmth he could get nowhere else. God, he loved this. When he had greeted everyone he could reach, Tina caught up with him with a stack of holo-prints, and they took up a position at the last of the line of tables.

Throughout the next hour, he signed scores of autographs but made sure to extol the virtues of the other fighters in Trask's stable. Going down the line to each of them, he posed for photos and video shots with the other fighters.

Even Lex, with the bruising on his face all but healed, grinned broadly and shook Horace's hand for the cameras. Lex's grip was too fierce, but Horace let him have this little attempt to reclaim his pride. Something told him he wouldn't have any more trouble from Lex as long as Jocie stayed the hell away from him. Together they mugged it longer than anybody, and the crowd devoured it. Lex Lethal, as the most established fighter in Trask's stable, already had a sizable contingent of his own fans.

For these minor-stable, unknown fighters, Horace's presence lent credibility and prestige, a connection with tradition and success, and as the photos circulated worldwide over the next day or two, their media and social recognition ratings would receive a substantial boost. Trask had been a genius setting this up.

He spotted a sparkling silver sports car as it slid into the parking lot, making every other vehicle in the parking lot look like an antique wreck; the newcomer was a leopard among swine. The car did not park; it simply stopped, and a man got out, smoothed his bright purple hair, straightened his silver-gray suit, adjusted his cuffs, his gleaming platinum watch. Another man got out of the car, the bodyguard, dressed in a dark suit, shades, wearing a fiercely pointed goatee.

The scent of mobster emanated from the man, wafted across the distance, but this was no hitman. Hitters were steadfastly nondescript. Here was a peacock in his prime, out to make himself seen. The crowd parted for him magically, as for a shark swimming through a school of fish.

The gangster's presence put Horace on instant alert. He started looking for directions to run—or pathways to attack.

When Trask intercepted the man with a big grin and open arms, Horace relaxed slightly. The man returned Trask's embrace with a cool smile. Trask led him through the crowd, behind the tables, and straight toward Horace.

"Vince, meet The Hammer," Trask said, "Hammer, this is Vincent."

Horace extended a hand and Vincent offered his, slim and tan and encrusted with jewels embedded into his skin glinting in the spotlights.

"A pleasure," Vincent said with a smooth nod and a New Jersey accent.

Trask turned to the crowd. "Sorry, everyone! The Hammer needs a break! But he'll be back in a just a few minutes!" He took both of them by the arm. "Let's go have a drink, boys."

In Trask's office, Horace and Vincent seated themselves comfortably while Trask poured three glasses of amber liquid from a decanter, brandy this time, into three teardrop-shaped snifters. Trask pulled his chair from behind his desk and sat with them in a loose circle, striking a posture of relaxed nonchalance. Vincent's bodyguard stood in one corner of the room like a grim, silent statue.

Trask said, "Vincent here's a fan, Hammer."

"I always like to meet my fans," Horace said, never taking his eyes off Vincent.

Vincent leaned back and sipped his brandy, a glint in his eye. "Used to watch you all the time when I was a kid."

Horace smiled. "Thanks." Hearing it over and over again was making him feel old. "I always try to put on a good show."

"You did, my friend, you did," Vincent said.

Trask jumped in. "Vincent here loves the fights. He's a...a great patron of talent."

Vincent looked at his perfectly manicured nails. "I enjoy it a lot, it's no lie. But it's the helping people I like the most, you know? I like to help fighters. I make it my business."

Horace nodded. Players like this had been around since the sport had gone national, ever since the days of nonlethal mixed martial arts, since the days of boxing, since the days of bare-knuckled backlot free-for-alls. Cultivating favors, fudging odds.

It was hardly surprising that Trask had a relationship with a guy like this. The question wasn't whether Vincent was connected, but to whom he was connected. In fact, it would be no surprise if Trask had such relationships all over the country. Horace struggled with the impulse to say, *Get me on a hyperjet to Vegas tonight and I'll do anything you want.* But some deeper instinct told him that would be an utterly futile gesture.

In the dim light, Vincent's suit sparkled with thousands of tiny, subtle lights. His gaze was a cool blue, fixed upon Horace for several long moments as he sipped his brandy. "You play poker, Hammer?"

"I have, but never made much of a study at it."

"I play quite a bit. I'm pretty good at it. To be a good poker player, you have to be good at reading people. You been around a while, Hammer. A fighter doesn't get to where you been without seeing a few things, without knowing a few people, without getting on the wrong side of the wrong kinda people, you know what I mean? Ol' Norm here, he knows I like fighters. He knows I been a fan of yours a long time. So when he invited me here to meet you, there wasn't any question. So I'm sitting here looking at this fighter, this *fucking legend*, and I'm thinking to myself, all he sees is another one of those guys he's seen a hundred times before. Hell, he's seen everything under the sun, am I right? Am I right?"

"You're not wrong," Horace said, taking a slow sip, wishing this guy would get to the point.

"I'm sitting here looking at this legend and he's fresh off a big win, but somehow that's not registering, like he's got bigger problems. It's written all over his mug, like a tattoo on his forehead. Like what the hell is he doing with Norman Trask? No offense, Norm, but you're not the major leagues."

"Don't I know it," Trask said, lighting a fat, black cigar with a little blowtorch.

Vincent went on, "I'm a guy who likes to help people. I consider it my civic duty. Sometimes, even legends need a little help. Sometimes, the legend gets a little tarnished, you know?" He breathed fog onto his brandy snifter. "Needs a little polish." He rubbed the fog off with his cuff. "Just a little polish. Just a little. So I put my ear to the grapevine just now and listen, and some wild, crazy shit comes through."

"And what have you heard?" Horace gave him a long appraisal, looking for evidence of any wetware. If he had implants, they weren't visible like Bunny's.

"That you have a strong dislike for vodka."

"Again, you're not wrong."

"See, already we got so much in common, Hammer! I hate vodka, too! But it's fucking everywhere, soaked into every goddamn thing. Most of the time, people are chugging the stuff, and they got no fucking idea. Vodka and fucking borscht everywhere. *Capisce*?"

"I'm with you, brother."

"Too much alcohol makes it hard to do business, right? Hard to do your job. It just gets in the fucking way. Drink too much and you're like the cute little girls on spring break, chugging the stuff like it's water, and it makes them do stuff that would make their mothers commit suicide. I think we need to sober up. Get straight. Make a little room for other kinds of business."

His gaze leveled into Horace's again for a long moment.

Then he smiled, "A toast, gentlemen. A toast to new friendships!"

They all leaned forward and clinked glasses, took a sip. But somehow Horace still didn't feel friendly.

Vincent said, "I'd hate to see a legend just disappear into the vodka, you know? Get pickled. That would be a shame, such a shame."

"I hear it's possible to drown in vino, too," Horace said.

Vincent chuckled. "Sure it is, but it's less harsh, you know. Wine is good for you with a nice meal. Vodka just burns and makes you stupid." He sucked something from his teeth. "How long you boys gonna be in Buffalo? We should do a night on the town! I can show you around, get us some girls lined up. It ain't Atlantic City, but Buffalo's got a lot going for it, you know?"

Trask said, "That would be a smash, Vince, but we're on the road to Albany tonight after this gig. Fight night in two days."

"Come on, Albany ain't the other end of the fucking world! You guys come with me tonight, after your thing here is all wrapped up. Have a little ziti, a steak, some vino—in moderation!—what do you say? A little hospitality never hurt anybody."

Vincent did have a certain easy charm about him. Horace had encountered mobsters at a number of levels, from dull-witted thugs to captains to the made men, but few of them possessed this guy's good looks and genuine smile. His voice carried a bit of real excitement, a real sense of wanting to show The Hammer a night on the town, not just adding a node to the network of favors and obligation that all mobsters traded in if they wanted to live to a well-seasoned age.

"By the way, Norm," Vincent said, "you still got that fine little thing working for you, that little rainbow girl?"

"Sure do," Trask said.

"I like her. Bring her along."

"Nah," Horace said, "she stays here."

Vincent's smile faltered. "And why's that?"

"I could use some action. The kid would be a total cock block."

Vincent took a slow sip. The smile didn't come back.

Horace said, "If you're trying to get in her pants, I don't blame you; but let's leave her out of the men's discussion." The Italian mob was still an Old Boys' Club. "There might be more to talk about...vodka and such."

Vincent nodded at that, bared his perfect set of teeth into that brilliant smile again. "Fair enough. You're The Hammer, after all."

Horace rejoined the festivities after Vincent's flashy departure. As soon as he set foot outside again, another wave of applause erupted from the crowd.

Demonstrations commenced. Several of the fighters showed off their deadliest weapon techniques on human-shaped dummies. Vibro-blades and spiked gauntlets ravaged the dummies, sent limbs and heads flying. The fighters even offered fans a chance to try their own hand with the pit fighters' actual weapons—for a premium fee, of course. The fighters made it look easy, and the fans made it look difficult, but they puffed up and glowed with glee at the chance to actually wield a vibro-axe. Horace was always relieved after such demonstrations when the fans thankfully failed to sever their own limbs. Vibro-weapons were some of the deadliest hand-to-hand weapons ever made, with edges that vibrated like reciprocating carving knives. They could slice to the bone with just a touch. He thought about that electro-fiber blade he'd used to kill Dmitri. Those could take the bone, too.

After an hour, another drone appeared in the air directly above, similar to the first, with the other media drones swooping and hovering.

For two hours, they all pressed the fan-flesh. They laughed and smiled and hugged and high-fived, and as the word must have gotten out about The Hammer's appearance, the size of the crowd ballooned for a while. A van from a local media hub came and interviewed Horace and Trask.

Of course, everyone wanted to know when The Hammer's next fight was, but all he could do was politely demur with vagaries and bravado, which, of course, resulted in a fresh burst of autograph signings at three hundred dollars a pop. Fistfuls of cash and coin changed hands.

It all felt like the Big Time again, the height of his career. He was The Star, however fleeting he knew it to be.

After three hours, when the last of the fans, even the latecomers, had been juiced by their contact with celebrity and sent away clutching their prizes, and the models paid and whisked away in their battered hover-limousine, the fighters stood alone amid the carpet of food wrappers and discarded flyers.

Trask approached Horace, grinning so wide his back teeth gleamed. "What a show! What a goddamn show! I think you can safely call the hospital bill square."

"I'm happy to hear it. It felt pretty goddamn good."

"Excellent!" Trask clapped him on the back.

By this time, Horace's tattoos had faded to black and the familiar fatigue had crept back in.

Trask circulated among the other fighters, clapping them on the back for a successful show.

Dressed in a corseted scarlet dress, Jocie hugged Lex's arm with big smiles and ignored Horace completely.

A cooler of beer appeared on one of the tables, and bottles spread round the group with clinks and fizzing.

Outside Trask stood up on one of the chairs, cigar in one hand, beer bottle in the other. "My beautiful, bastardly badasses! Congrats on a great pull. We're going to ride the buzz from this all the way to Albany. Once we get there, we'll have a light training day, another show like this one tomorrow evening, and then the night after this, the fight night itself. I expect every one of you will leave your opponents in a bleeding pile. Am I right?"

The fighters cheered and raised their drinks.

"So live it up tonight," Trask said. "Tomorrow is training. And I have it on good authority that some of those models are coming back later to ride with us to Albany."

Growls and laughter of lascivious anticipation sounded among the fighters.

"Mad Killer" Kevin Michael raised his bottle, "To Mr. Trask! The best boss in the fucking world!"

Hoots of agreement rose with more beer bottles.

Trask grinned and took a bow.

Horace's netlink chimed with an incoming call. Jack McTierney's leathery mug appeared on the screen. Horace's heart skipped a few beats and he headed through the door into the train, stepping out of easy earshot. He answered the call, "Jack."

"Goddamn, Hammer, you got balls like a fucking elephant," Jack said. "You're all over the net!"

"That's the plan, brother."

"Or you're crazier than a shit-house rat."

"Listen, you got anything on Lilly? That video—"

"I saw that video. Scary shit. Look, I've been doing a little scratching around in the dirt. That Russian, Dmitri. He's got—had—four different aliases. And do you really want to know where I found a couple of those other names?"

"I think you'd better tell me anyway."

"Boards of directors. I'll send you a file with the names. Six *megacorps* that I found so far. This is scary, beyond-the-law-and-common-decency stuff, amigo. These guys have their fingers in *every goddamn thing*. Maybe even Regenecorp. I'm still trying to verify that one."

Horace wasn't surprised. The Russian mob had been extorting professional athletes for a hundred years. How much extra money could they make if they could fudge the odds on some poor sod's Resurrection Watch? *Too bad, poor Johnny Pit-Fighter's resurrection didn't take.*

Jack lit a cigarette and took a drag. "A couple of these corps look like fronts for some very nasty shit. Shipments to and from the anuses of the Earth, the kind of places where the only currency is weapons, slaves, and pirated tech."

"I didn't know these Russians were that big—"

"You got no idea!" Jack's normally low, calm voice went a little shrill. "Do I gotta remind you the megacorps have their own sets of laws? We're talking asteroid mining, fissionables—"

"What's that?"

"Fissionables. Plutonium, enriched uranium. All those old nuclear missiles that rotted in the silos and had to be decommissioned. All of that decommissioning was handled by private contractors. And our boy's on the list."

"Jesus Christ."

Just down the hallway, Bunny appeared and leaned against the doorway, watching the festivities outside, arms crossed, a bemused smile on her face.

Horace said, "I suppose it's stupid to ask if any of this can be taken to the police or the FBI."

"These megacorps write the FBI's budget."

Horace rubbed his eyes and felt that despair tugging at him again.

The connection went dead.

His gaze fell upon Bunny just in time for her bemused smile to flash-evaporate into a look of confusion. She touched one implant behind her ear, shaking her head as if dazed. The lights on the train went out, casting the outside festivities into darkness.

Bunny's gaze darted toward the sky, searching.

A sudden wind whished over them, and then the sound of a turbine as a sleek dark bulk hove into view above the train, drifting ten meters overhead. An aircraft, a drone, the size of a small car.

Twin blue eyes on an underbelly turret swiveled toward them.

CHAPTER SEVENTEEN

In the swirl of dust, Trask and the fighters gazed upward.

A silent strobing burst of blinding sapphire flashes turned the dust clouds in the parking lot into a nightclub dance floor.

Except for the cries of confusion. Then pain. Jocie screamed.

Dozens of tiny flames burst into incandescence on the ground, and on the flesh of the transfixed fighters. Trask dove for cover under one of the aluminum tables. The light splashed rainbow splotches into Horace's vision.

The fighters began to topple.

The aircraft maneuvered. The turret swiveled. Another strobing burst, as brilliant as the facets of a sapphire in the sun, flashing like a sewing machine needle. Or a silent machine gun.

Gobbets of parking lot concrete glowed molten.

Bunny screamed, "Get down! Run!"

Inside the train car, Horace threw himself out of sight of the thing, crawling toward Bunny.

Sounds of pain outside, coughing, gagging. The stench of seared flesh and burning blood blasted inside the train on the jet wash of the hovering machine.

Bunny called to him. "A corp security drone! It's got a pulse laser!"

Horace peeked through a window. The robotic blue eyes swept around the scene, surveying the men squirming on the ground with smoking, sizzling pockmarks across their bodies. Some weren't moving at all.

"Where's Trask?" he said.

"I don't know!"

The bulk of the drone was just visible around the angle of the open door.

"I've already called the police!" she said. "You know what they said? That *thing* is exercising its rights! It's *legal*!"

"Can you get us out of here? Get this thing moving?"

"All the signage and tables are deployed. Some of them aren't automated."

"Undeploy them and fuck the rest. Get us out of here!"

"What about everybody outside?"

"Leave that to me!"

He lunged outside. The turret swiveled. He threw himself under an aluminum table. Another cascade of strobing brilliance left streaks in his vision and a burning sensation in his forearm. The stench of molten aluminum and burnt flesh was acrid in his nose. In his forearm was a blackened pinhole leaking blood. Having passed through the metal table, the laser beam fizzled in the flesh of his arm.

He heaved to his feet, lifting the table into a shield. With it standing upright between him and the drone, light shone through the multitude of blackened perforations across its surface. Nevertheless, it might save his life.

Clutching a support contour on the table's underside with one hand, he ran toward the nearest man on the ground, Skullcrusher James, and hooked a twitching arm, dragging the fighter behind the table, half-upright, and toward the door of the train. James staggered and coughed burnt blood. The stench of seared flesh clung to him. Horace practically threw him up into the train.

His heart pummeled against his breastbone.

He went for another.

The drone maneuvered for another shot.

Horace grabbed "Mad Killer" Michael's arm, rolled him over. The young fighter failed to respond, and two blank, cybernetic eyes stared from a face with two seared punctures.

Lex staggered to his feet, Jocie thrown over his shoulder like a limp rag, and hooked another fighter's arm, dragging him upright and stumbling for cover.

Another flashing burst punched a spread of fresh holes in Horace's shield and drew a painful furrow across his cheek. A fighter, propped up on an elbow nearby, screamed and spasmed and collapsed.

A thunderous report and a cloud of smoke erupted from Trask's miniature Civil War cannon.

Standing behind the cannon, Trask howled with pain.

The drone jerked and spun.

Horace's tattoos came to life.

He charged toward Trask, who lay on the ground beside the smoking cannon. The cannon lay on its side.

Sparks dribbled from a ragged wound squarely in the center of the drone's fuselage.

Trask rolled around, clutching his arm. Horace reached him, snatched him by the collar, and dragged him behind the upright table.

Trask's left wrist bent in a way far too rubbery to be intact. "Couldn't get the elevation. Had to hold it like a gun. The recoil..."

The power plant of the road train hummed with life. The flashing lights and signage began to retract. The horn blasted.

"Hit it again!" Trask rasped, gesturing to a nearby box filled with paper packets full of powder.

Horace snatched the cannon, then the box of ammunition, and dragged them close.

The drone's whining turbines began to labor. Then the sound of gunfire erupted from the train. A pistol barrel poked through one of the rear windows and hailed slugs at the drone. Most security drones were armored against small-arms fire, but the unseen shooter was accurate. Ricochets popped and whined. Glass shards tinkled to the pavement. A bullet took out one of the turret's sapphire eyes.

"Ten packets, then ball, and pack it good!" Trask said.

Horace grabbed a handful of powder packets, stuffed them into the barrel, reached in the box and felt around until his fingers brushed one of several lead balls about the size of a large apricot, then jammed it in too.

With a quivering hand, Trask handed him the solid brass ramrod. "Pack it all down!"

Horace took and jammed the ball as deep as it would go, then spun the muzzle toward the drone.

The drone spun its nose toward the train and slid backward, putting distance between itself and the train.

Dread sluiced ice water through Horace's veins. Under the drone's wings hung missile pods. In a flash of fire and ribbon of smoke, a missile streaked toward the train. The detonation shattered the last train car like a watermelon hit by a sledgehammer. Splinters and shrapnel spun in all directions. The shockwave blew the table over into Horace, smacking him across the skull before it flew past and away. A shard of bulkhead like a spinning guillotine whooshed overhead.

Trask was talking, but there was no sound but the ringing in Horace's ears.

He spun the cannon muzzle toward the drone, sighted down the barrel with one blurry eye, yanked the lanyard hanging from the breech. Nothing happened.

Trask slapped his leg, yelling something.

"Cap!" Trask screamed. He reached out with copper cap similar to those used by Horace's childhood pop gun, but the size of a child's fingertip. Trask stumbled forward, opened the firing mechanism, and jammed the cap onto a nipple.

At half the frequency of before, laser pulses raked the bodies on the ground again.

Trask set the cannon's hammer. "Line it up!"

Horace grabbed the tongue between the wheels and realigned the muzzle.

"Left! No! Fuck! You take the lanyard!" Trask thrust the lanyard into Horace's hand. "Fire on my ready!"

The drone hovered and ducked as sporadic fluctuations in its power unsteadied its own aim.

Trask adjusted.

Horace waited. With their shield gone, they were sitting ducks.

The turret swiveled toward them.

"Fire!"

Horace yanked.

The cannon roared and bucked, and a cloud of blue-gray smoke obscured their view of the target.

But they could hear the whine and the raking squeal of failing turbines.

The drone fell nose-down into the earth and struck with a crunch. The tail smashed down a second later. Sparks and smoke scattered from the fallen drone.

Not far away, the road train burned.

Horace staggered upright, his breath ragged. Trask clutched his shattered wrist to his chest.

"Nice shooting, Tex," Horace said.

"It's a hobby."

Horace hurried toward the bodies strewn before the road train, bleeding onto the pavement.

Ten hunks of meat pierced by needles of blue light. All dead, among them Jax "To The Max" Gavillion and "Mad Killer" Kevin Michael. And there were no Regenecorp techs anywhere nearby. No hospitals nearby. There would be no coming back for them. And there would be no police coming to help them. The drone had come from some corporation claiming to be protecting its "rights." Having had several decades to write their own rules, they could do whatever they wished.

Optics on the drone's nose cone spun toward Horace, tracking him.

"Holy shit, that thing's not dead!" Horace shouted. He dove for the door of the train again.

The laser turret on the underside struggled to rotate, but it was bound in place by the drone's weight. Horace grabbed up one of the vibro-axes that had been used for the demonstrations and charged the machine.

The axe's hum whispered up his arm, and he fell upon the drone with savage ferocity, careful to stay out of the arc of the laser turret. Even the armored hide of the drone could not withstand a full-on assault by a vibro-axe wielded with the power and fury of Hammer Harkness.

Sparks exploded around him as he smashed all the optics and sensors he could recognize, severed the control harnesses of the missile pods, chopped deeper and deeper into the fuselage until he found its quantum computer AI brain, and destroyed it with a howl of rage.

Only after all that, with his tattoos gleaming like neon lights, did the drone die.

He didn't want to look at the human arm, severed at the biceps, lying on the ground nearby, bone-spiked knuckles clenched into a loose fist.

He didn't want to think about a rainbow-haired smear of bloody paste that might be waiting for him in the wreckage.

CHAPTER EIGHTEEN

Flames licked the darkness and spat blacker smoke into the night sky. The wreckage had been blasted dozens of meters in every direction.

Horace ran for the wreckage of the last car. Where had Tina been? In the last car. She had helped him with his armor. Had it been her, Lex, or somebody else shooting from the window, creating the distraction without which he and Trask would have been cut to pieces by the pulse lasers?

"No, no, no..." kept coming from his lips as he climbed into the tangled mass of twisted metal and licking flames.

A scrap of scarlet dress fluttered in the breeze, hanging from a jagged finger of frame.

"Is anybody here?" he called. "Anybody!" He flung aside sheets of hot metal. The only thought he could muster was *More innocent blood on my hands.*

Voices called to him from the forward cars, but his ears weren't working. He squinted through the smoke.

Tina and Bunny were leaning on each other as they stepped down from the front car. Both of them bore wide-eyed expressions of pale shock and horror at the carnage laid out around the pavement, and the smell of seared flesh and blood emanating from the bodies. Tina pulled away from Bunny, jumped to the ground, and vomited. Bunny clutched her mouth and laid a gentle hand on the girl's back.

Relief so profound burst through Horace that he choked back a lump in his throat and wiped at the wetness in his eyes. Their voices sounded muffled through the ringing in his ears.

Trask stumbled toward Bunny and Tina. "You two all right?"

"Ambulance is on its way," Bunny said.

Tina straightened and wiped her mouth. "I'll get the med kit." She ran into the infirmary car.

From where he stood rooted among the wreckage, Horace could hear her through the broken windows rooting around in the infirmary. Every window in the train had been shattered by the explosion's pressure wave.

He shook himself and moved to the next forward car, peeling back sheet metal and debris for signs of dead and injured.

Trask's voice came to him. "That had to be Lex shooting. He and Jeremiah were the only guys with handguns, and Jeremiah was already cut to pieces. Poor bastard saved our bacon."

A couple of fighters had emerged from their cover under the train, clutching at their blackened pinhole wounds. Tina had the first-aid kit.

Then Bunny's voice cut through the smoke and night. "We have to go! *We have to go right now!* There's another one coming! ETA, two minutes."

Trask sat against a massive tire, cradling his arm. "How do you know?"

"I got a solid lock on that thing's transceiver signature. It was an autonomous AI, but it was also in direct contact with someone, taking orders. Right before the attack, it started jamming the area. My wireless connections all went dead. Now, I'm picking up some net chatter that looks like another one. Look, we *have to go*."

Trask yelled, "Everyone, on board! Bunny, can you slice it somehow? Buy us some time?"

"I can't! What about the bodies?" Bunny pointed at the sprawled corpses.

"We can't resurrect them. They're headed for the morgue. If that second one gets here, we're all done for. Help me up. Let's go."

Horace grabbed up the cannon tongue and wheeled it toward an open storage compartment under Trask's cabin.

A heavy clank shuddered through the train as the linkages detached between the destroyed rear cars.

"Everybody up front! Right now!" Trask said. "Bunny, we're only taking the engine!"

The engine car came free of the second car with a clank and a pneumatic hiss. Horace slammed the storage compartment shut.

The remaining fighters dragged themselves as best they were able into the engine car. The doors shut, and the wheels rolled them away from the rest of the cars; in effect the engine became a somewhat beefy bus. The vehicle circled and reeled out of the parking lot onto the street, lurching them painfully around inside.

The door between Trask's compartment and Bunny's was open. Bunny sat in the driver's seat for the first time Horace had seen.

"Go, Bunny, go!" Trask called to her from his office chair. "Get us out of here. And run dark!"

Every light in the vehicle suddenly went dark, leaving them in blackness.

"You have a stealth-mode road train?" Horace said.

"I got more than that, but nothing that can shoot down a drone," Bunny replied. "We're not the fucking military!"

"You guys did pretty well with that cannon," one of the fighters said, a man named "Cherry" Jubal Lee. Jubal sat on the floor, his breathing ragged, clutching his right breast, blood leaking between his fingers.

"We can't exactly mount it on a turret," Trask said.

"We need to get to a hospital!" Tina shrilled. "Hospitals are neutral zones!"

"Do it!" Trask called to Bunny.

"Doing it!" she called back.

"Is it following us?" somebody said.

"Can't say. No radar! But I'm listening to its comm traffic. I don't think it's made us. The nearest hospital is five klicks from here."

"We can make five klicks!" another fighter said.

"Not if there's traffic!"

"What the fuck is a klick?"

"They wouldn't attack us in traffic!"

"Don't bet your life on it!"

"What did it want? Why did it come after us?"

"It's me," Horace said. "They're after me."

Silence settled over them like a stifling blanket.

"I'm sorry," Horace said. "It's my fault. They're not going to stop. They'll never stop."

Wind whipped through the shattered windows as the bus picked up speed, sucking curtains and blinds outside. Horace cranked up one of the blinds, swept the curtains open, and stood before the window overlooking the increasing flow of traffic around them, scanning the night sky for any sign of hostile pursuit. Cars and trucks honked their horns at the massive vehicle traveling with no lights.

The drive to the hospital was among the longest twenty-minute spans of Horace's entire life. Bunny had called ahead so that, when they pulled up the drive to the Emergency Room, a line of white-sheeted gurneys spilled out to meet them. All praise to full medical.

As Trask and the wounded fighters were wheeled inside, Horace sat down beside Tina on the couch. He put his arm around her shoulders; they were shaking. "You all right, kid? You're not hurt?"

She sniffled, and he practically saw her lip stiffen. "I'm fine."

"I thought that was you shooting."

She wiped her nose. "I thought it was you. It came from your window."

"I guess we're both okay then."

"I guess so."

"I gotta get this armor off. Can't breathe." He gathered himself to stand, but in a flash found two wiry arms wrapped around his neck and a warm cheek against his, the cool kiss of a tear squeezed between them. He encircled her with his massive arms, and in them, the shudders in her body began to subside.

Then she jerked herself away and hurried down the steps into the hospital.

Horace let his breastplate hang loose. As the minutes ticked by, his tattoos dimmed. There were only two doses of Go Juice left in his injector, and his entire supply had been in his equipment box in his compartment, along with his weapons and the rest of his gear. Since it was custom-formulated for his biology, Go Juice was not something he could buy off the shelf. Only a few gray-market pharma-techs associated with the pit fighting scene dealt in such concoctions; the earliest he could get more, even if he had the money, would be probably a week.

The guilt gathered upon him, drove him deeper and deeper into the couch cushions, like a wrecking ball settling onto his lap. Dying in the pit was one thing—pit fighters made a choice to be there, to seek the limelight, to strive in the ultimate contest between two warriors—but bystanders being slaughtered as collateral damage in someone else's vendetta demanded justice, retribution, vengeance.

The weariness of running gnawed at him. Trying to shrug off the weight, he got up and paced, trying to think of ways to go on the offensive, to free Lilly, to put Yvgeny Mogilevich's head next to his son's.

Bunny came from her compartment. "The news is calling it a corporate skirmish. Law enforcement is staying out of it," she said.

"Peachy," Horace said.

"I had Jimmy do some digging."

"Do tell."

"I ran the numbers on that drone. It's a security model, the kind that patrol factory campuses in sketchy areas, registered to InVista Corporation."

"Never heard of InVista."

"Me neither, so I sent a bot to sniff out the paper trail. Turns out InVista has a factory here in Buffalo. The paperwork says they make molded plastic and ceramics for the International Hockey League. Helmets, armor, spiked gauntlets and such." A sense of intrigue and satisfaction crept into her voice. "The thing is," she said, "they've never actually had any injection molding or 3-D fabrication equipment delivered to the site. Nothing to *make* anything. I've checked the neighborhood surveillance cams, at least the ones that are working. Nuking the entire zone would be an improvement."

Horace leaned forward, elbows on his knees. Decrepit industrial zones like that peppered every city in North America, a deep, spreading rot, like necrotic tissue that could not be excised.

Bunny said, "The registration for the action of the drone tonight was filed legally. It was a 'preemptive strike to assert corporate rights.' InVista filed the registration about fifteen minutes after your appearance began. You were all over the net." She swallowed hard and teared up for a moment. "All of the guys were."

"So is there any doubt InVista is a front company for the Russian mob?" Horace said.

"You're pretty smart for a palooka."

"And you're pretty ballsy for a dame. Is anyone really surprised that some company no one has heard of is a fake? We've uncovered a paper company doing bad deeds. So what?"

"Those drones aren't cheap. Anyone with that kind of money to burn has high stakes on the line if they're exposed."

"But how do we prove it? Since the corps cover the cops' payroll, who would we tell if we *could* prove it?"

"Still working on that."

He looked her in the eye. "You're amazing."

She blushed. "Child's play. I used to do stuff like this in my sleep."

Then it came to him. "I'll tell you how we prove it."

Horace asked the attending nurse in the Emergency Room kiosk how Trask and the injured fighters were doing.

"We're assessing them all now," the nurse said. "Laser wounds are a nasty business. They're worse than knife wounds. They boil the water in the surrounding tissues, which causes them to expand and rip apart. I didn't think pit fighters used lasers."

"We got caught in some corporate crossfire."

The nurse grimaced and shook his head. "They kept that kind of thing out of this city for a long time. I guess it had to happen eventually. They're worse than scavenger gangs." With a glance at the ruler-straight blackened furrow across Horace's cheek and the bloody bandage around his forearm, the nurse said, "Come on back and we'll patch you up."

"I can't pay you."

"Screw the rules," the nurse said. "Come on."

Horace went.

After the nurse disinfected his wounds and sealed them with synth-skin, Horace relaxed in the waiting room with a cup of beautifully awful vending machine coffee and thought about his plan. He molded it into a number of different shapes and tried to look at it from different angles.

Then his netlink chimed. Lilly's face appeared on the screen. He stared at it for a moment, a shudder of mixed dread and hope shooting like an explosion of fireworks mixed with artillery. Another chime. He thumbed the biometric scanner and answered.

"Hello," he said.

"Hello? Hammer?" It was Lilly's voice.

His heart kicked his sternum and his knees turned to raw steak. "Is it really you?"

"Yeah, who else would it be?"

Relief like the touch of warm breath and jasmine perfume flooded over him. His voice caught.

"You okay, Hammer? You sound funny."

Was it possible she had no idea about what was going on? "Never mind that. Is everything okay there?"

"Yeah, I did what you said, took the kids on a road trip. We're—"

"Don't tell me where you are! Your phone is probably tapped!"

"What!"

"How's Jimmy?"

"I have to take him back to the hospital next week for another treatment. You're scaring the shit out of me! What's going on?"

"There are some very, very bad people who are very, very pissed at me. And I hate to tell you this, I feel so awful about it, but they're going after my friends."

"How bad are we talking?"

"The worst."

For several long moments, all he could hear was her breathing. When she finally spoke, her voice was hard. "The next time I see you, I'm gonna beat the shit out of you, you hear me? A stiletto heel to the sack!"

"I'm sorry, darlin'. I'm gonna make this go away, but until then you got to lay low."

"I've had stalkers before. I can take care of myself. Have you gone to the police?"

"This is bigger than the police."

"Feds?"

"Bigger than them, too."

Another long pause, then a taut sentence: "Why did you wait so long to warn me?"

"They were tracking my netlink. And, well, I've been in the hospital myself. Wasn't exactly conscious for a couple of days."

"Hospital!"

"Yeah, but don't worry about that now."

"How can you expect me to talk to you, but you won't tell me anything?"

"I...you're right. But I can't tell you over the phone. I'll tell you all about it when I see you. You'll know everything that you want to know, I promise. Deal?"

There was no reply.

"Lilly? Hello?"

Silence.

He tried to call her back. The netlink beeped that the call had been disconnected.

Tina walked up and sat down beside him, hugging her elbows.

"This is not a good time," he said.

"It never is. Bunny told me about your plan."

"She shouldn't have done that."

"Fuck you, Gilgamesh. You need somebody to watch your back. Besides, your infiltration skills rival those of a drunken water buffalo. I'm coming with you."

"I can't let you."

"Look, I lived on the street for two years after my dad died. I didn't have to, he left me a little money. I wanted to. I looked at it like the capstone project of my training. I was hungry a lot, I stank, but I learned a few things. There used to be these samurai called *ronin*. It means 'wave man,' somebody tossed on the waves of life. They were warriors without masters, cast outside the bounds of society, bandits mostly, but not always. Not always." She took a deep breath, and her face hardened.

"What the hell are you talking about?"

She sighed. "A bunch of romantic bullshit. When are you going?"

"How about now? One in the morning is the perfect time for sneaking around."

"You going to wear that?" she said. "You look like you're on fire. At least you're not glowing anymore."

"All my other clothes went boom."

"Then you're staying in the getaway bus, Geezer."

"Getaway bus. So much for any plans for stealth."

"That thing's a tank. Bunny says the only eyes in that neighborhood are surveillance cams. We'll park a few blocks away."

"You guys have done this before?" he said.

CHAPTER NINETEEN

The dark streets of the decrepit industrial park gave refuge to a darker, box-like bulk that moved with precision and relative silence. The air smelled of earth poisoned by rancid petroleum and caustic chemicals with an undercurrent of industrial lubricants and solvents. Breathing the air for any length of time would give anyone a headache.

Sitting cross-legged on the floor near Bunny, Tina said, "Running dark is a little creepy."

"Only human eyes need lights," Bunny said.

Horace had covered his armor with a black, hooded sweatshirt and sweatpants, purchased at a local all-night discount store. He no longer looked like he was on fire, but the seams of the sweat gear were stretched almost to ripping. At least now he didn't feel utterly exposed. With a vibro-axe in his hand salvaged from Trask's storage compartment, he felt almost at home. With a black silk scarf covering his face, his disguise was complete.

"You look like a Viking cosplaying a ninja," Tina said. She had attired herself in the same sort of black clothing, face and hair obscured by a bandanna and hood, soft rubber-soled shoes instead of her jackboots.

Bunny said, "I'll monitor the net chatter. Anyone showing up here at this time of night might bring some security, so get your butts moving and don't dawdle. After your little shopping trip, it'll be dawn in two hours."

They set their netlinks to intercom mode and plugged in earbuds so they could talk to each other.

With the axe in his hand, Horace stepped out into the chill autumn night. The jagged hulks of abandoned factories and half-empty warehouses were black silhouettes against the sky's glowing haze of city lights. Only directly above were a smattering of stars visible. Dark, empty streets and crumbled pavement stretched away in all four directions. An occasional streetlight flickered beside a surveillance mast with a camera mounted atop it, faint pools of luminescence swallowed by shadow.

Tina stepped out beside him and set off at a brisk trot in the direction of the InVista factory.

Horace trotted after her, feeling like a lumbering elephant behind a gazelle. As they went, he went over the map of the place again in his head. The main building was two hundred meters long, eighty meters wide. A chain link fence with one front gate, minded by a guard shack. A sprawling parking lot for employees, a holdover from the days when factory workers could afford cars. A massive central building with walls of steel and concrete, a few small windows near the roof.

The streets were little more than paved trenches between fences of chain-link, devoid of anything to mask their approach. There were no sidewalks, no cover for them to cling to. Gang symbols decorated great swaths of the pavement, which told him the security bill was not paid with any regularity in these parts. His heartbeat slowed a bit. This place was as silent as an empty desert, bereft of traffic noise or commerce, except for the wind. In the distance, one unknown factory blazed with third-shift activity, but this was not their destination.

Horace and Tina approached the InVista factory from the rear entrance near the loading docks. Fresh, shiny razor wire topped the rusty, chain-link fence surrounding the factory campus.

Tina whispered into her netlink, "Any sign of motion detectors or heat sensors?"

Bunny answered, "Nothing like that in any of the data logs. Of course I'm looking at three-year-old records. It was all I could get my hands on. But I'm keeping a close eye on the alert feeds."

Tina produced a bolt-cutter, which Horace used to make quick work of the rusty padlock on the chain. From where they stood, two surveillance masts were visible.

"There are two surveillance masts inside the fence," Tina said. "Are they active?"

If they were, Horace and Tina might already have been detected.

"They are," Bunny said, "but there's no security provider on record."

"What's that mean?" Horace said.

"It means," Bunny said, "that they haven't kept up on their security bill, or they have a security force on staff."

The ambient glow of the city lights painted the intruders black against the pale, crumbling concrete as they ran for the loading docks. A single light fixture provided the only illumination under the eaves covering the concrete docks, a meager splash of flickering grayness. More gang signs slathered the massive, corrugated garage doors. Tina pointed to the single gray fire door, just at the edge of the light.

Smudges of shadow clung like tar to the earth and frustrated him. In his mind, weaponized defense turrets, security bots, and guards with guns lurked in every pool of darkness.

"Places like this always have an alarm system," Tina whispered.

"Odds are good," Bunny said into their ears.

Tina peered up the wall at the windows five meters up. "Think you can boost me up there, Aging Hercules?"

"What do you weigh? Fifty kilos?" Horace said.

"Fifty-one."

"Maybe."

"You going to catch me if you miss?"

"I guess we'll see.

The wall between them and the window sill was rusty corrugated steel, with no finger- or toe-holds. The only possible purchase was an electrical conduit running horizontally about a meter below the window, toward the light fixture above the loading dock.

Both of them took deep breaths. Then he cupped and locked his fingers, and she put her small, soft-shod feet into his hands. He hefted her a couple of times, adjusting his angles for maximum thrust.

"Ready?" he said.

"Go."

A deep breath, a massive heave, and she was flung skyward like a doll.

But not five meters.

She scrabbled at the steel with fingers and toes, clawing for that last half-meter. Then she caught herself with her fingertips on the electrical conduit. She hung there for a moment, breath whooshing in and out of her. He waited below, arms outstretched to catch her.

"You all right?" he whispered.

She peered up at the window, gauging the distance. "I can make it."

There was no other possible purchase between her and the window. But she chinned herself up, swung up a foot to a junction box just within reach, hooked her toes there, adjusted her fingers, reached up for the window, fell short, levered her fingers higher with toes and upper body strength, and caught the lip of the window with two fingers, then four. A moment later, she had both hands on the window sill, drawing herself up, planting both feet precariously on the conduit, peering into the darkness inside.

"Don't see anybody," she said. "Looks mostly empty. There's some equipment. Place is dark."

She pulled out a small knife and started prying at a pane of glass about half a meter square. The ancient glazing gave way without breaking the glass and she eased the plate gently inside, careful to keep her fingers around the edges lest it fall in and crash to the floor, and then angled it outside where she balanced it precariously on-edge atop the junction box. The slightest gust of wind could catch it and send it crashing groundward. The empty pane was large enough for her to worm through the opening.

The last he saw of her was her feet disappearing inside.

"She's inside," Horace muttered.

"Clear so far," Bunny said.

Tina gave no reply, and Horace was forced to wait, blind and deaf to what she was doing. Seconds ticked into minutes. He clutched his vibro-axe, wrung the textured rubber grip, and waited beside the back door. The only sounds coming into his earbuds were occasional breaths of exertion or the faint click of a door latch.

"There's a keypad system, no print scanners," Tina whispered. "All the exterior doors are alarmed, and so are the offices."

"You see anything?" Bunny said.

"I can see down through the center of the plant. Nothing here. No machinery... Wait... Yeah, by the loading docks, there some equipment stored. Hang on."

Half a minute passed. "Oh, shit! There's a security drone, parked near the opposite end of the plant, just inside the main doors. It's not moving."

"Stay the hell away from it!" Horace said.

"I'm not seeing any transceiver activity," Bunny said.

More damnable, interminable silence.

Horace did his best to breathe deeply, slowly, trying to control his heart rate. The last thing he needed right now was for his heart to seize up, which would hit the Go Juice trigger, and then he would glow like a neon sign, probably even through the sweatshirt. This was no time to be flashy.

The crackle of plastic sheeting came through the earbuds. Tina's voice hissed and popped. "This equipment here, it looks like Regenecorp regenite stations."

"Take some photos," Bunny said. "Find serial and model number plates. Send them to me, and I'll start running the numbers."

Horace's netlink started to beep with incoming photographs. Checking one, he found a blurred image of a stamped serial and model number plate, illuminated by her flash that was too close.

"There are thirty-seven units," Tina said.

"Get as many numbers as you can."

Another two minutes ticked by. Breeze whispered over his cheeks.

Then something crashed to the ground next to him. His heart leaped, and it was half a second before his brain registered the sound of shattering glass. The precariously perched pane of glass had fallen. He breathed deeply, then again, and again.

"Okay," Tina said, "Got 'em. Gonna try the offices."

The moments raked across Horace's mind. His jaw ached from clenching his teeth.

Then Bunny's voice. "Heads up, Tina, you just triggered an alarm. The alert just went out. Get out of there."

Ten seconds passed.

Bunny said, "The closest manned security station is about a kilometer. Hold on.... There, I just bought you some time. I just triggered alerts all around this district. They're going to have their hands full. Move your butts."

A sound began to grow from somewhere inside. The wall started to vibrate. Something echoed within, the sound of a turbine.

"Look out!" Bunny said. "The signature for a security drone just popped up."

"It's awake!" Tina said. "Ahh!"

Horace heard a nasty crackling pop through his earbuds, corresponding with a sound inside he couldn't identify.

So much for stealth. Horace snapped on the vibro-axe and chopped into the door lock. The steel door gave way like sackcloth under the edge of the axe. Moments later he had torn through the lock and flung open the door.

In the distance, through the forest of girders, a dark, shark-like bulk was floating toward them, beacons flashing on its stubby wings. Tina huddled about thirty feet from him behind one of the plastic-swathed regeneration stations.

"It shot something at me!" she said, clutching her shoulder. A shimmering bluish laser beam flicked across the distance, held for a split second on the regeneration station, then a massive, blinding arc of electricity thundered like the arc of a welder down the rod-straight pathway of light. Sparks exploded, fountaining over Tina. The stench of ozone and burnt plastic filled the air.

Horace lunged for her. A massive chunk fell away from the station sheltering her, released by a gouge in the molten plastic. The drone was still a hundred meters away but closing quickly.

Horace snatched a handful of her sweatshirt and flung her toward the back door. She hit the ground and rolled to her feet as if she had planned it herself. Then Horace grabbed up one of the regenestations and piled it on top of another.

He heard Tina scrambling to her feet, running for the back door. "Come on!" she called.

Another blinding glare of laser, then the snapping arc of electricity down the beam blasted the regenestation he had just moved, bowling it back into him, knocking him off his feet and his vibro-axe out of his hand. His breastplate and shoulder guard caught the worst of the blow, but it took him a moment to right himself and snatch up his axe. He lunged for the door and heard the tearing whine of a minigun.

Something caught his leg in midstep and spun him around, knocking him off his feet again. Pain exploded up his thigh, but he scrambled to his feet toward the back door. Another minigun burst raked the area with hundreds of high-velocity projectiles. Spots of dim light emerged in lines and patterns on the loading dock doors and walls as the bullets perforated them.

Then he was outside, Tina was waiting for him, and they were both pelting toward the back gate. His thigh throbbed, forcing him into a limp. He tried to feel whether he was bleeding, but his fingers couldn't find any breach in the carbon-fiber armor.

The bus pulled up on the street behind the back gate.

"Move your butts!" Bunny cried over the earbuds. "Guards here in one minute!"

From the opposite end of the factory, the sound reached them of the massive main doors opening. The drone was coming out.

His legs pounded, his breath huffed, the bus started to move away without them. Tina leaped inside. He grabbed at the open door and pulled himself inside, dragging one of his feet across the gravel for several meters until he righted himself, climbed up into Trask's compartment, and collapsed on the floor.

The door closed behind him.

Bunny was already gunning the power plant, and the massive tires spun on gravel and concrete. A hard crank on the wheel rolled Horace against the wall. Everything that was not nailed down spun and rolled and tumbled to the floor. Glass shattered.

"If that drone sees us, we're fucked!" Horace called.

"I know!" Bunny yelped.

The wind whipped through the shattered windows as the bus picked up speed. In the distance, Horace caught the flashing lights of security vehicles weaving through the dark streets.

"Like I said," Bunny called back, "I gave the human guards plenty to think about. But that drone'll spot us immediately. Except for one thing..."

The bus charged through a chain-link gate and down a narrow path between towering mountains of metal and plastic.

"This junkyard right here," Bunny said.

The bus rumbled down the floor of a great canyon of civilization's cast-off detritus. Crushed cars; appliances; endless, countless, trackless mounds of manufactured garbage. The outside air wafting through the shattered windows smelled of old lubricants, chemicals, hydraulic fluid, and rust.

The bus eased into a box canyon in the garbage and stopped. The power plant spooled down.

"Hopefully, it won't spot us among all the garbage, even from above," Bunny said.

On the main path about forty meters distant sat an office shack. A light flicked on in the window.

"Uh oh," Tina said, pointing.

The front door opened and an old man tottered out of the shack, wearing nothing but striped bikini underwear and a few wisps of gray hair in unusual places, clutching a shotgun in both hands. His rheumy eyes found their way through the darkness and fixed on the bus.

Horace stepped outside, peeled back his mask, and approached the man slowly, hands in the air. "Evening!"

The old man trained the shotgun, a semi-automatic assault model, on Horace's chest. "What the fuck are you doing?"

"Uh, we don't want any trouble. We just uh..." He thumbed toward empty window bays, fluttering with curtains behind him. "We need some windows." He grinned as wide as he could.

In the distance, the whine of the drone's turbine drifted toward them on the breeze.

CHAPTER TWENTY

"Goddamn, you're a big sumbitch," the old man said. His eyes narrowed. "Don't I know you from somewhere?"

Tina stepped around him, "This here's Hammer Harkness, sir. Maybe you've heard of him?"

"Heard of him? Shee-it!" A grin tugged at the corner of a toothless mouth. The muzzle of the shotgun sagged for a moment, then snapped up again. "What the hell are you doing in my junkyard at this time of night?" He stalked closer.

"Well, you see, sir," Tina said, hands raised, edging closer to him, "there's a bunch of Russian mobsters have a base in one of these old factories, and we kind of pissed them off."

The old man spat. "I see them fuckin' limousines come and go, like they's better'n ever'body else. What'd you do to piss 'em off?"

Horace said, "Killed one of them."

"On purpose?"

Horace nodded solemnly. "I don't do that sort of thing accidentally. I'm a professional."

The old man chuckled but didn't lower the shotgun. "I was hoping The Freak would kick your ass. Had money on him, that stumpy fucker."

"Sorry to disappoint you, sir," Horace said. "Maybe next time."

Bunny's voice crackled in Horace's earbud. "Can you get the heck under cover before that drone spots your heat signatures?"

The noise of the drone's distant turbine echoed in the canyons of junk.

"Sir," Tina said. "Want to come inside? I know where the boss keeps some mighty fine scotch."

"Got anything else? Scotch tastes like puke." The old man lowered the shotgun. Then he looked down at himself, still naked but for the striped bikini briefs, glanced at Tina, then shrugged and walked toward them.

Tina and Horace did their best to hurry him into the bus. He sat down on a chair with a grunting sigh and cradled the assault shotgun over one scrawny arm like he was hunting partridge with granddad's old single-shot. Sitting in the chair with his white-fuzzed paunch hanging over his briefs and resting on spindly legs, he resembled a squatting baby bird. "Awful dark in here." He squinted toward Tina, looking her up and down.

The only light came from Trask's desk lamp. As the sound of the drone drifted in with a puff of breeze, she turned the light down further until all of them became vague silhouettes in the darkness.

"What you got there to drink, missy?" the old man said.

"Cuban rum?" Tina suggested.

"Sold."

Glasses clinked and a bottle of aged rum appeared.

The old man put a hand on his knee and looked around Trask's cabin. "Hey, weren't you all doing some sort of soiree earlier tonight? It was all over the net."

"We were," Horace said.

His eyes widened in amazement. "Is this the same goddamn vehicle? What the hell happened, did war break out while I was sleeping?"

"Something like that," Horace said.

Tina brought them glasses of rum and kept one for herself.

The old man raised his glass. "Here's to swimming with bow-legged women."

They raised their glasses and drank. The old man smacked his lips in appreciation.

Horace offered his hand to shake. "I didn't catch your name, brother."

The old man shook. "Terrence. Damn glad to meet you both. Hohlee shite, this is gonna be a story to tell my buddy Coocher. He won't never believe me."

The floor was littered with holo-prints, scattered during the fevered flight from the first drone attack. In the dimness, Horace could see well enough to pick up one of his, and he happened to have a marker still in his pocket. He autographed the holo and handed it to Terrance. "This'll help."

"Why, thank you kindly!"

Bunny's voice spoke in Horace's ear. "Ask him if he's seen anything besides limousines." The door to her compartment was closed.

"So, Terrence," Horace said. "How long you been here?"

"On this planet? Seventy-eight years. In this junkyard, twenty-two. Took it over from my brother, God rest his useless ass."

"You've seen a lot of stuff come and go."

"I see everything come and go, mostly go. Every few years some politician or CEO decides he's gonna refurbish this area. They pump a shitload of money in, try to buy out the geezers like me, bring new companies in, but it never works. When some new company they just lured in finds out how the ground is so polluted it makes all the workers sick, and the water supply in this area makes a nice oily film in your coffee cup—if you're idiot enough to drink it—well, that's pretty much the end."

"The InVista plant, you know it?"

The whine of the drone's turbine echoed a little louder in the canyons, but their irregularity made it impossible to track direction or distance.

"Go past it all the time. Hard to call it a plant. Can't say they've ever had anyone working there unless they got just a handful of employees and they all ride in limos. Seen a couple transports at the loading dock, but the transports said Regenecorp." The old man took another sip of rum and shrugged. "It's all bullshit anyway. The corps, the gub'mint, all of it. The only thing that really matters in this life is friends." He stabbed at finger at Tina. "You listen to me, little girl. Friends is everything. The people you care about is all what matters. There's your Old Fart Wisdom for the day. Come back tomorrow and I'll give you another dose."

Tina smiled. "A girl can't have too many friends."

"Oh, hell yeah, you can! Too many, and they ain't friends no more. You get you a nice tight bunch, and you cleave to 'em. The older you get, the more you need to hold on to the people from the young'un days." He squeezed his fingers into a fist and pulled it toward his chest.

A warmth of truth washed through Horace at this. And then came the accounting. He had no one like that. They were all gone.

The sound of a turbine grew suddenly louder.

Terrence glanced back and forth between them. As if coming to an abrupt decision, he downed his rum. "Well, I thank you for the hooch. But I oughta be getting back to bed."

"Sure you won't stay for one more?" Horace said.

The sound of the aircraft ebbed and diminished.

Terrence cocked an ear at the sound and said quickly, "I gotta get back to bed." He gathered himself to stand.

"Here it is straight, Terrence," Horace said. "That drone out there is not patrolling; it's hunting. You poke your ass outside that door, it's likely to get shot off. Another one just like it slaughtered at least a dozen of our buddies tonight."

Terrence sank back into a chair, eyes wide.

"And it was *legal*," Tina said.

Terrence snarled. "Fucking corps."

"You said it, brother. You're a lot safer sitting here with us until that thing leaves."

Terrence took a deep breath and let it out slowly, fingering his shotgun. Then he swallowed hard. "Maybe you're right. I'll need another jolt to get back to sleep after this anyway. This story's gonna give ol' Coocher a shit-hemorrhage."

Tina poured him another, which he took with a leathered, trembling hand.

The whine grew louder, and Horace's spine clenched tight. He stood, readying himself to act.

Bunny's voice came into his ear. "Nobody make a sound."

He put a finger to his lips for Terrence.

Terrence swallowed hard, downed his rum again, and took his shotgun in both hands.

Another puff of breeze wafted the scent of jet exhaust into the cabin. The sound rose.

And fell.

And rose.

And fell.

The sounds echoed through the junkyard canyons for interminable minutes.

The sound continued to diminish for what seemed like an hour.

Finally, Bunny said, "It's moving away. But we have to give it some time, stay out of line of sight. The targeting optics on that model can see a mouse from orbit."

With those words, Horace could breathe again. "Terrence, it's probably safe for you to go, if you keep your head down."

Terrence let out his own breath. "Gawddamn, that was just like in a movie!"

"I hate movies," Tina said.

"All right, then, I'm gonna mosey home," Terrence said. "You're welcome to stay awhile."

"Thanks, brother. And don't worry about the gate. We'll pay for that."

The old man nodded, then stood up, stretched his legs, and turned toward the door. The back of his underwear disappeared between pale, wrinkled cheeks.

Tina clutched a guffaw tight into her mouth.

Sunrise crept between the mountains of refuse, casting dark, jagged shadows over old tires, refrigerators, battered vehicles, water heaters, and countless discarded relics of use and obsolescence. Horace dozed on Trask's sofa, Tina curled up like a fetus between the arms of the office chair. Light filtered through the breeze-ruffled curtains, nudging him to wakefulness.

He elbowed himself upright with a groan, stood, and stumbled outside to relieve himself near the garbage. In the morning silence, tremendous snores echoed from Terrence's shack, and he couldn't help but smile. "Jesus, what a sight, that old coot."

There it was again, that word. *Old.*

He chided himself. No time to feel sorry for himself.

"Bunny," he said, knowing his netlink was still set to intercom mode. "Are you awake?"

"I am now."

"How soon before we can roll out of here?"

"The coast is clear now, I think. The drone has been back in the shed for about half an hour."

"Have you talked to Trask?"

"He's out. They're putting his arm back together."

"How would you feel about driving us to Vegas?"

"You're on Krok."

"I'm kidding." Half-kidding. He had to get to Las Vegas. He had to make all this stop, one way or another.

"I gave Jimmy some jobs while I took a nap," she said. "He ran the serial numbers of those regenestations. All of them have been reported stolen."

"Then why were they delivered in Regenecorp trucks?"

"See? You're not a palooka after all. And we found something else. Those machines were all used at Death Match Unlimited events, the big ones. And all of them are associated with failed resurrections. And in all of those cases, the odds said the fighters were expected to make clean recoveries."

"So they fudged the odds, killed some fighters, and made millions." His teeth clenched.

"Billions. And they ditched the evidence here. They're too expensive to be simply discarded. Better to take them out of circulation for a while, change the serial numbers, and put them back into play."

One of those regenestations, or another like it, could have been hooked up to Gaston. What if Gaston's resurrection had somehow failed? The entire pit fighting industry relied on the integrity of those machines. For his entire career, he had relied on the integrity of those machines. His insides turned to boiling water, and he swore invective that peeled the veneer from the walls. His entire grand speech to these fighters—those that were still alive—had been turned to so much bullshit.

"Somebody's going to pay," he said.

Tina sat up and rubbed her eyes.

"Good, you're awake," Horace said. "If it got out that Regenecorp rigged those machines..."

Bunny said, "They would not be able to withstand the public uproar. Their stock would crash."

"Heads would roll." Horace liked the idea of that.

"And if Death Match Unlimited found out Regenecorp was pooping around with the lives of their fighters..."

"A clusterfuck of epic proportions. The fighters would march into corporate headquarters and kill every executive they could find."

Tina cleared her throat and piped in. "Then you really would be like Spartacus. You could lead the gladiator rebellion."

That was one of her references he understood. "Except weren't they all crucified along the highway as a warning to others?" After a moment of thought, he said, "Regenecorp has no real competitor. They have the patents locked tighter than a virgin's asshole."

He could practically hear Bunny blush through the earbud. "Uh, right," she said.

Tina said, "And if we try to prove this, drag it out into the daylight, those machines will evaporate like the wisp of morning dew on the hair of Hammer's back."

"Uh, gosh, you're both so...poetic," Bunny said.

"Someone's got to give you people some culture," Tina said.

"Hang on a sec," Bunny said. After a moment, she said, "I just heard from one of the boys. Trask is awake and he wants us. Let's get back."

"You're lucky I don't fucking fire you right now, the both of you," Trask thrust a short finger at both Tina and Bunny, his eyes blazing. "Or have you arrested for grand theft. You took the last asset I fucking have, that road train engine, and you put it in shooting range of another one of those fucking drones."

He lay in his hospital bed, his arm in a cast reaching beyond his elbow. His face was haggard, his cheeks pale, his sparse hair flying in all directions, and his voice hoarse, but his eyes were bright and focused like lasers on all of them.

Bunny said, "We thought you'd want a little payback—"

"Pay those bastards back by giving them my fucking engine, too?"

Horace said, "Take it easy, Mr. Trask, they did it—"

"I know *why* they fucking did it. And don't try to tell me it was all your idea, Hammer." He glanced pointedly at Bunny.

"Why aren't you pissed at *him*?" Tina said.

"Because he doesn't work for me. And I *am* a little peeved." He turned his ire upon Horace. "If there was ever a case of someone sticking his neck out and getting the whole fucking head cut off, it's me, this bullshit, right now. And those poor fuckers we left out there on the pavement!" His voice cracked, just once, then he cleared his throat and regathered himself. "Albany is off, and I was counting on it to get through the next six months."

"At least we're alive, Boss," Tina said.

"I'm not sure that's such a—" His voice caught, then came with a heavy sigh. "Nah, that's feeling-sorry-for-myself bullshit. Of course I'm glad I'm alive. I built this stable. I've had to start over before, I can do it again. But we're up against the fence on this one. My headliner and half my fighters are dead, and the rest will be recovering for weeks. The repairs on the road train are more dough than I can scrounge and will take weeks if I can find it. If I can scavenge up some bouts for the boys that are left—someday—we'll be traveling by pack mule. Hammer, I—"

"It's not Hammer's fault, Boss," Tina said.

"I know that!" Trask snapped.

"It's like your friend Vince said," Horace said. "There's vodka in everything."

Trask's eyes narrowed. "What the hell are you talking about?"

"We found something," Tina said.

CHAPTER TWENTY-ONE

After they had shoehorned enough words between Trask's expostulations of vitriol to make a coherent account of what they had uncovered, Trask lay quiescent, his mouth working as if he were chewing on a cigar.

"Motherfuckers," Trask said. "If this gets out, it could destroy the entire sport. Every league in the world."

"And that's just the beginning," Bunny said. "How far will these people go to protect their operations? Regenecorp still has contracts with every First World and corporate military on the planet. The only other company even close to having regenite technology was a defunct Japanese company called Gen-Key."

"Never heard of them," Trask snorted.

"That's because they died under an avalanche of patent litigation and corporate sabotage ten years ago. When other possible competitors saw what happened to Gen-Key, they packed up and quietly faded into the woodwork. Regenecorp has enacted seven military actions against companies who gave the slightest whiff of getting into the regeneration business."

"Never heard of those either," Trask said.

"I hadn't heard of it either, until just now when I went digging. The news stories were all buried. The investors tried to hide those companies in places like Burma and West Africa. Hundreds of employees from those companies were killed during the actions. And you've never heard of that because events in countries like those never reach even the Top 1000 news stories here. No offense, Hammer, but the color of *your* underwear is more important to most Americans than a genocide-driven famine in Africa that costs hundreds of thousands of lives. And the megacorps who own the media companies aren't exactly interested in covering the wars they started."

"Nothing like facts to assuage my broken heart," Trask said wryly.

"The greed these gangsters slop all over this planet hurts people," Bunny said, her voice turning angrier by the word. "I fought against people like them for years, until the Feds caught me. The good that I had done was less important than making sure they silenced me, that the poopheads in charge stayed in charge, and didn't have to worry about little old me."

Horace said, "Didn't you say that you have a huge pile of data hiding somewhere? You think there's anything in there that might help us put a torch to the Mogilevich empire?"

"I'm sure there is," she said. "But I can't get to it. The passwords and encryption are coded to my DNA. I'm the only person on this planet who can access it. But I can't, because of the lock on my AI."

"So how do you get the lock taken off?"

"Bribe my parole officer." She tucked a few strands of hair behind her implant. "I'm only half-kidding. The handling of cyberpaths' AIs is strictly at the discretion of the individual parole officers. Like I told you, they're not going to release my lock without me giving up the data, and there are people with a whole lot of money who can pay to make sure he keeps me quiet. It is de facto locked, permanently."

"But do you think your parole officer would consider it?"

"I have submitted a request to him every month since I got out of the hole. He apparently has me flagged for automated form rejections."

"What about the press?" Tina said. "Can we go to them with the photos? There's gotta be a gonzo journalist out there who would love to stick it to one of the most powerful megacorps in the world."

"You said it right there," Trask said. "'The Most Powerful Megacorps In The World.' Remember what Bunny was saying about those companies in Burma and Africa? Unless said reporter has his own army to safeguard his personal well-being, you're going to have a hard time not getting the door slammed in your face."

"So then, what?" Tina said. "We're just fucked? The whole world is just fucked? Forced to let these mob cartels and their hand-fed politicians and their corporate toadies shit all over everything?"

Horace said, "They've been doing it for over a century, kid."

"Right!" she snapped back, "And because they're so huge, with all the power and all the money, the world looks more like feudalism and tyranny."

Horace said, "Democracy has been a pretense ever since I was a kid."

Trask snorted. "Listen to us, talking like we're great thinkers going to solve the world's problems."

Horace said, "I just need to find a way to get my friend Lilly out from under these people." She was fine when he spoke to her, but it could only be a matter of time before they moved on her. The doctored video sent to intimidate him showed that their data feelers went very deep.

Tina said, "So who's Lilly? Catch me up on your personal life, O Venerable One."

"A friend of mine."

"Girlfriend?"

He paused. "Not really, no."

"So you want her to be your girlfriend."

"I don't know."

"Are you sleeping with her?"

"No—"

"But you want to."

"Well, sure—"

"So you just want to bang her."

"Not exactly."

"Man, she's got you *all* twisted up! Can *you* tell if you're coming or going? I can't tell the difference between your face and your ass. Who is she?"

Bunny, having watched this entire exchange with a faint smirk, chimed in, "A dancer."

"And by dancer, do you mean stripper?" Tina said.

With every word out of Tina's mouth, Horace felt more and more foolish and defensive.

Tina rolled her eyes. "You're in love with a *stripper*? We're all dancing around in the mouth of death for a *stripper*?"

Trask said, "Judging by the look on his face, Tina, you'd be wise to shut your trap just now."

Horace looked down at the warm metal in his hands, the railing of the hospital bed. It wasn't straight anymore.

Somewhere in the room, a netlink chimed with an incoming voice call, the sound of Beethoven's Fifth Symphony. Trask said, "Where the hell is my phone?" Tina found it in his trouser pocket and handed it to him. He answered it.

After a short, terse conversation consisting mostly of grunts of acknowledgment mixed with, "Sure, sounds great," Trask hung up and looked at Horace. "Well, that was my buddy Vince. He heard all about our little altercation last night and wanted to check on our well-being."

"What a guy," Horace said. The idea of engaging with another mobster twisted his stomach into sour knots.

"Watch the sarcasm. He's as stand-up a mobster as you'll find anywhere. And he's a capo in the Magaddino family. They've been big in the Buffalo area for a hundred and fifty years. Don't forget, he's a fan. You and me are going out tonight. He's sending a car for us at seven."

"Sorry, my wardrobe's a little sparse at the moment."

"Vince is a traditional sort of guy. Show up in that and he'll be insulted. You need to go shopping."

Horace sighed. "I don't suppose I can say no. Can't we just rent a tux or something?"

Tina snickered. When she noticed everyone looking at her, she straightened her lips as best she could. "Sorry." When she failed to erase the smile completely, she said, "It's just so adorable! The Hammer in a tux. Like giving a Neanderthal a top hat and cane and teaching him to sing 'Puttin' on the Ritz.'"

Trask's glare dimmed her smirk. "You're missing the big picture here, Hammer. This guy we're hanging out with tonight." He spoke some words slowly, letting them seep in. "Vince represents an *organization*, an *organization* that might have an *interest* in making trouble for the *same* people who are making trouble for *you*. Do you follow me yet?"

"The enemy of my enemy is my friend."

"Bingo," Trask said. "Now let go of my bed."

"Dammit. Sorry."

Trask said, "Vince may have something interesting to say."

"I'm not putting any more favors on credit," Horace said.

"Look," Trask said, "I got a lot of interest in getting clear of these bastards, too. *I'm* on their radar now, because I took you in. If you get clear, so do I. So shut the fuck up, and let's see what we can do to make that happen."

"Great!" Tina said, "So when do we leave?"

Horace said, "You're not going."

"Shut up, Old Jules, I haven't had a night on the town in ages!"

"This is a guy party," Horace said.

She scowled. "Such bullshit. Next you'll be telling me I can wear pants!"

"Now, hang on a minute, little girl, it's not like—"

Her eyes blazed. "Little girl! Sorry, Grandpa, I couldn't hear you with the pigtails in my ears."

"You can wear pants all you want!" Horace said, his brain starting to spin and flounder like a wobbly tire at the force of her oncoming tirade.

"Women can wear *pants*? Oh, my god! I didn't know! Mine always caught on fire the moment they came in contact with my lady crotch! I even tried wearing boxers to trick the pants, but it's like the pants know I'm keeping a vagina in there. Poof! Burst into flames."

"That's what I'm afraid of."

"Yeah, you and every other male on this planet is afraid of a little ol' vagina—"

"Will you shut up a second and let me explain?"

"See! *Now* you're trying to silence my outrage because you know you fucked up!"

Horace sighed and walked toward the door. "You're not going."

On his way out, he thought he heard, "Like you're going to stop me."

CHAPTER TWENTY-TWO

Complete with red-and-white checked tablecloths, flowers on every table, and the smells of fresh bread, simmering marinara, and roasted garlic filling the air like an olfactory symphony, Campanello's was a classic Italian restaurant.

The district was one of old brownstones and crumbling concrete, but with a character that reached back a hundred and fifty years. Flowers bloomed in window boxes, and the street was empty of the ubiquitous, uncollected garbage endemic to so many modern cities, a symptom of the systemic indifference toward anything with "public" as part of its description. This neighborhood was clearly under someone's oversight, someone's protection.

Sicilian folk music, a harmonic sauce of *organetto* and violin, played from invisible speakers and laced every corner of the restaurant's interior, every mahogany nook, every shadowed booth. A smattering of patrons of all walks of life dove into heaping mounds of pasta and marinara. A few narrow-eyed men in slick, sparklesilk suits lounged with painted, buxom divas. In the corners, thick-shouldered, bull-necked men in less ostentatious garb picked their teeth and simply watched.

In such surroundings, Horace's patched together attire made him feel like a fool, in spite of the desperation of his situation. Bunny had found him a second- or third-hand beige sport coat, plaid trousers, and a white button-up shirt washed so many times it was practically see-through. It was all utterly hideous, a stain upon the eyes, a fashion holocaust. But still more appropriate than bloodstained black pajamas.

Bunny had found his attire in a second-hand clothing store near the hospital. All of the new clothing stores were downtown among the mazes of steel and glass, where the fancy boutiques lived, where it was fashionable to be seen, where armed security checked the credentials of every customer. Out on the fringes of town, where labor-class folks and IT drones scraped out a living with scraps from the megacorps' tables, the only clothing stores were second-hand.

"This is all I could find in Wooly Mammoth size," she said as she handed him the bag.

"Look, Bunny, you didn't have to—"

"Zip it, buster!" Bunny stuck a finger in his face, her eyes flaring with anger. "You've destroyed the livelihoods of everyone still alive, just by showing up. Did any of us ask for this? No! I didn't have to do this. And you didn't have to bring the wrath of the worst mobsters on the planet down on our heads."

"I'm sorry—"

"I gosh darn know you're sorry! Just shut up about it! We all have to get through this together now."

Her words echoed in Horace's mind as he looked down at his getup, at how ridiculous he looked. He was dressed to impress all right, but not the kind of impression he wanted to make. Nevertheless, all the wounds on his face from the many fights of the last few days made him look like a mighty rough customer.

As he passed through the restaurant with Trask and the limo driver, the men straightened their posture and narrowed their eyes, the women clutched their companion's arm or turned pale, staring.

In a private dining room upstairs with no windows, Vincent greeted them with a big grin. "Fellas! Glad you could make it!" He gave Trask a manly embrace, then turned to Horace. After a glance up and down and a suppressed smirk, Vince embraced Horace like a long-lost brother.

Vince was dressed like a fashion model ready for a magazine holo-shoot. Dark suit, pearlescent black shirt, chrome necktie, a flower in his lapel.

"If I'da known this was a dress-up affair, I wouldn't have had all my clothes blown up," Horace said.

Vince gestured for them to sit. "It's been a day, right?"

Charging to the forefront of Horace's mind was the memory of a meeting that started not unlike this one, where he had asked Dmitri Mogilevich for a massive loan, without which he could never have rebuilt himself for his big comeback. And how charming and amiable Dmitri had been, and how Horace had known it was bullshit all along, but he went forward anyway.

Dmitri had been a brutal, self-indulgent sadist, a chip off the old block. How could Horace believe that a mere difference of ethnicity would make Vincent any less so? What if Trask was just as willfully blind as Horace had been?

At that moment, a woman's silhouette emerged in the entrance and slid into the room like liquid elegance. A stunning black dress cascaded delicately over a shape made to be devoured. Her flashing eyes like deep-roasted almonds seemed to take in the room with a single glance, matched the olive-smooth skin and subtly sparkling dress. Raven hair gleamed, spilling over her toned shoulders. Within a second, she had supplanted a Bollywood starlet among the top three most beautiful women Horace had ever encountered. She moved with a grace and poise usually reserved for old black-and-white movie stars. Audrey Hepburn, Elizabeth Taylor, Catherine Zeta-Jones, and Ingrid Bergman, the goddesses who had enthralled him as a teenage boy knee-deep in his father's classic movie collection, all before him now reincarnated into one being. She made Lilly—and even Amanda—look like Nebraska farm girls.

If this goddess was one of Vincent's cheap squeezes, Horace was going to throw up on his plaid trousers.

"Meet Roxanne," Vincent said. "Roxy, this is Norman Trask, a friend and business associate."

Trask's eyes bulged like dinner plates, and his cigar dangled loosely from his lip.

She nodded with a faint, implacable smile.

Vincent said, "And this is—"

"Hammer Harkness, of course." Her voice, deep, full, and vibrant, carried an accent that sounded perhaps Eastern European.

Horace held her dark, smoky gaze and gently squeezed her offered hand. Where in the hell had someone like her come from? And what was she doing here? And why the hell did he have to meet her dressed like the village idiot?

Trask said, "Vince, where in the hell did you find her? Lady, what are you doing with this guy?"

Vincent said, "Roxy and I go back a long way. Monaco, wasn't it?"

She smiled vaguely and settled into a chair with a taut ripple of flesh. "That was the beginning."

Horace's mind buzzed. The beginning of what? Such was the power of her presence that his mind sparked with burning questions. He wanted to know everything about her. Then he chided himself for the distraction, but the way that dress clung to every succulent swell and curve of her, the fluidity of every smallest movement, the way her eyes had already sized him up as if she had known him for a thousand years, seized his attention and would not let go. His heart thumped hard several times against the box fixed to his breast. He felt like an idiot schoolkid with his first crush. Moreover, bathing him in her ageless gaze, with the state of anti-aging and aesthetic beauty technology, she could have been anywhere between twenty and sixty.

She allowed Vince to take her hand and kiss it.

Vince said, "Roxy likes the fights, thought she might like to meet you, Hammer."

Horace said, "We appreciate the invitation, Vince. A lot has happened since yesterday." The promo event felt like a lifetime ago, with worlds of pain interposed. The aches were fresh.

Trask snorted. "Worst goddamn twenty-four hours of my goddamn life. Pardon the language, madam."

She nodded.

After they ordered food—since Horace hadn't eaten a proper meal since yesterday morning, he ordered the biggest steak on the menu, with extra pasta—Vince eased back in his chair and fixed Horace with a long, searching look, steepling his fingers against his lips.

"So, Hammer," Vince said, "what on earth ever gave you a taste for vodka?"

"That's a complicated question."

"We have all night. And if you want help taking care of that problem, the particulars matter."

Horace considered for a moment, appraising Vince and wishing his eyes could feast upon Roxanne until they were full.

Trask stepped in. "Hammer here spent a lot of years in the minors. He had a shot for a comeback. Playing in the little leagues is way more dangerous than the Big Time. Practically no sponsorship. Regeneration costs in the stratosphere."

Vince said, "The guys who fight their way out of the minors are the toughest there are."

"More like the luckiest," Horace said. "For every one of them that fights his way up, there's fifty who fight their way down. They get crippled, maimed, or killed. A lot of them are just as tough or tougher than the ones who make it. The pit is an unpredictable thing."

"Okay, so you needed a little rebuilding before you got in the ring with The Freak, and that kinda reconstruction costs," Vince said. "You made a deal. So you shoulda made enough on the fight to pay them back."

"I did, except I gave most of it to save a friend's kid, to pay for fixing some genetic disease he's got."

Vince leaned forward on his elbows. "So then they came after you. Used your friend for leverage."

Horace nodded. "So I left Dmitri Mogilevich's head in his lap in the back of a limousine."

"What?" Vincent jumped out of his chair like it was red hot with an incredulous laugh bubbling out of him. He began to walk in circles, running his fingers through his hair, saying, "Oh, my god! Oh, my god!"

Roxanne's eyes widened almost imperceptibly with a faint tilt of her head.

After a few moments, Vincent's incredulity diminished, and he leaned over the back of his chair. "Holy shit, Hammer. You got any idea what you've done?"

Horace frowned and licked his lips. "Yeah, I got a pretty good idea."

"You just became a *hero!* You got *any* idea how many people wanted that fuck dead?"

"Been too busy trying to stay alive to think about that."

"That *fuck* was Yvgeny Mogilevich's only son. He was the guy gonna take over when the old man retires—or gets retired. His fingers were in a million pies."

"I'm getting a pretty good idea what kind of pies," Horace said.

Roxanne's voice slid between them like warm cream. "And Dmitri was also a sadistic bastard, just like his father. A *relentless* sadistic bastard." The lilt of her voice carried shadows of personal knowledge that would go unrevealed until such time as she chose to reveal it.

"So offing him makes me a hero," Horace said. "Are all these enthusiastic new fans going to come out of the woodwork to cover my back? Take some of the heat off me?" His voice made it clear he expected no such thing.

Vincent rubbed his chin and appeared to count squares in the tablecloth.

Roxanne leaned forward in a way that squeezed the perfect swells of her breasts between her upper arms. "What about this friend of yours? The friend they threatened."

Horace's voice turned dry and raspy. "Well, she's still alive, as far as I know. But on the run—with her kids—because of me."

"A lover?"

"Let's just say, 'we'll see.'"

At the mention of the children, Vincent's face hardened like cement. "Going after kids. That's not how to do business."

"In Prague," Roxanne said, "Yvgeny Mogilevich had an orphanage burned to the ground because he wanted the land. The doors had been chained shut. Any police who investigated were killed or bought. This is just one of his atrocities. In centuries past, such men walked in the open as heads of state. Today they use the pretense of the shadows."

Horace said to her. "I get the feeling there's more to you than eye candy."

"How direct." That tiny smile curled a corner of her mouth again.

Vincent said, "So where is this friend of yours now? Maybe we could get her under wraps."

"I don't know."

The arrival of salad, bread, cheese, and wine intervened for a while, and Vincent filled the empty air with gregarious chatter. Trask reciprocated with an account of the attack of the night before, complete with sound effects. Horace had to hand it to Vincent, he knew good food.

From the mundane patter Roxanne kept herself removed. She passed the time stroking her wine glass in silent contemplation. When Horace's eyes lingered on her too long, she would meet his gaze with an inscrutable look, neither warm nor cold, simply aware and evaluating as if a core of diamond floated somewhere deep within, unbreakable, imperturbable.

Horace couldn't help wondering what kind of life had turned her into a walking mask. At times he caught her gaze upon him without any veneer that she was not, in fact, judging, evaluating, measuring him.

Over a spectacular meal, Vincent enthused about his favorite moments from the pit fighting scene, his evaluations of fighters and techniques, which Horace had to admit were spot on. This guy knew enough that there had to be real martial training lurking behind that pretty-boy persona.

After the disappearance of the steaks that must have cost a small fortune, Vincent leaned forward on his elbows and said, "So, you need a way out from under this death sentence. And your lady friend, too. You want it all to go away."

"Got it in one, brother."

"But the Russian organization is a hydra." Vincent glanced at Roxanne. "Cut off one head, and five more grow back to take its place. They can look like they're everywhere, in everything. At least that's how it might look from the outside. But here's how it really is. They got a whole army of thugs and leg breakers. They got some captains. But the Russians are not one big hydra. They're a bunch of little hydras, with a few family ties here and there. Cut off enough heads, and the monster *forgets*, because the new heads have to deal with each other, and nobody knows who's gonna bite who. And other monsters might come along and grab what they can off the corpse, you know what I'm saying?"

Roxanne's voice was solid and forceful as a brick. "The old man is *the* head of the Mogilevich syndicate. You have already killed the man mostly likely to seek vengeance for killing Yvgeny: his son. You take him down, maybe whoever comes next will leave you alone. The contenders will have their hands full consolidating power and fighting off the other mobs."

Horace said, "But I still have to figure out how to get close enough to twist off daddy's head."

"That is the question," Roxanne said.

"To be or not to be, *that* is the question," Vincent said. "And that's really what we're talking about here—suicide. That old man has more security than the fucking president of the United States."

"There might be a way," Roxanne said. "In two days, there is a special event. Invitation only. Yvgeny Mogilevich holds this event twice a year, in Las Vegas. He brings in twenty fighters for a series of 'boxing matches'. Some of them are trained, but others are simply men who have wronged him, or found themselves in the wrong place at the wrong time. It is pure blood sport. All bouts are to the death, no weapons, no armor, no regenerations. It is a shocking spectacle, but it suits his taste for blood."

Horace had heard of such events, hosted by the planet's mega-wealthy, from a guy who had survived one; but he was on a liquid diet for the rest of his life. The atmosphere around these events made Death Match Unlimited look like a teen badminton tournament. It was the realm of sadists and those desperate enough to gamble their lives to please them. He had even heard rumors of such events being fought by slaves, almost like the Roman gladiators of old. However, at this moment he would be willing to fight in such an event, kill some poor schmo for good if it meant crushing Yvgeny Mogilevich's skull into goo. But then again, he kind of stood out in a crowd.

Roxanne continued, "I could bring you in, Mr. Harkness, as my escort, in disguise. Some hair, a new face, an extra scar or two. You would hardly stand out in a such a crowd."

Vincent said, "There'll be more guns in that room than in the police arsenal across town."

"Only for Mogilevich's men," she said. "All others are forced to relinquish their weapons at the door. Except for our Hammer here, who has them built in." She squeezed his iron-hard forearm, sending a jolt of heat straight to his crotch. "As for protection, military-grade battle armor could be hidden beneath your clothes. Most of the bodyguards will be wearing it. Again, you would hardly stand out."

The things Horace had heard about military-grade battle armor made even his carbon-fiber look like archaic boiled leather, and with a higher dollar value than the lives of most of the men who wore it.

"Who the hell are you, sister?" Horace said, narrowing his eyes.

"Have you not figured it out yet, my friend?" She raised her wine glass and briefly touched the blood-red liquid to her pillowy lips. "I am another hydra."

Talk of business was tabled for a while. Vincent wanted stories of

Horace's exploits, which Horace was happy to provide, and to which Vincent offered sincere appreciation and insightful commentary, an admirer with enough restraint to avoid the realm of incoherent fanboy.

Roxanne listened with interest, but her implacable demeanor was too rigid to reveal if she were truly interested or just listening politely. But in spite of her demeanor, a constant charm radiated from her in waves. She had a way of focusing on someone that made the object of her attention feel as if he were the most important person in the room to her. This was a woman who could indeed build an empire through charm and chutzpah alone. In the annals of Horace's memory, there was no one like her, man or woman.

After dinner, another limousine whisked them to Club Neo, a flashy nightclub that Vincent owned. The back of the limousine was palatial in its luxury, a sumptuous fortress of titanium steel, bulletproof glass, leather, and liquor. Vincent checked himself in a mirror. "You're gonna love this place! You guys are desperately in need to some R & R!"

Aside from feeling that going to a club was a tremendous waste of time and that Lilly was out there somewhere, vulnerable, Horace worried that going out in public would be a tremendously dangerous extravagance, with his face flagged in every camera and database in the Buffalo area. He mentioned as much to Vincent.

"Don't worry," Vincent said. "We're going in the back entrance."

"What about cameras inside?"

"Every camera belongs to us. Neo is a registered face club. Every frame of video and 3-D is processed. We can erase your presence like you're the Invisible Man sitting next to me. It's a service we offer to some high-end clients."

"What about netlink and net-shades signals coming out of there?"

"The whole building is a Faraday cage. No signal gets in or out of there that doesn't pass through our filtered repeaters. It's a face club, right? People make or break their celebrity careers at places like Neo. Images are broadcast out of there worldwide. But we control every single frame. For tonight, none of us will appear to be present."

Horace nodded his mollification.

Trask swirled the amber scotch in his glass. "So explain this face club thing to me."

"People build their face ratings, a number that represents their worldwide popularity. You've heard of Genevieve Montier, right?"

"Who hasn't?"

"She's not the only supermodel who got her start in the face clubs. She had one good night at a face club in Paris, met the right people, made the right moves, looked like a goddess, and she went viral. Boom. Instant modeling career. Everybody thinks they got something to show off. Beauty, dance moves, style, charm, grace. They rev themselves up on their drug of choice. They meet other facers, all looking to build their own ratings. They dance. They flirt. They make out. They fuck somebody in a private room. People log in and watch. They rate the facers in real time. Some facers have armies of fans, whole subcultures with pissing matches over who's cooler, and they've never done anything with their lives except go to a fucking club, sponsored by cosmetics and fashion companies."

Trask rolled his eyes, and Horace agreed with the sentiment.

"People wanna be famous," Vincent said. "They're willing to pay a stiff admission price and extra for drinks for the chance to do that."

Trask snorted. "Kids today."

Horace could hardly fault them for the urge to fame. Back when he was just starting out—hell, even when he was on top—he would have leaped at the chance to supercharge the upward arc of his celebrity.

The limo ducked into an underground parking garage and halted.

Vincent grinned. "We're here."

CHAPTER TWENTY-THREE

The interior of Club Neo blinded Horace for several moments. Slashing lasers and explosive strobes tore through his vision, and the subsonic pounding of the music vibrated through his bones like they were tuning forks. He hadn't seen such an overwhelming spectacle of beauty and vanity since the biggest events of his younger days, which had been steeped in Hollywood starlets and perfectly sculpted icons of physical fitness. Startling profusions of thigh and cleavage, chiseled features and physiques, sparklesilk dresses and suits, styles ranging from classically elegant to almost non-existent strips of strategically placed tape. Perfect lips, perfect teeth, perfect cheekbones, perfect eyebrows, perfect hair, perfectly cultivated smiles. And all of them mixing, chatting, laughing carefully. The sprawling dance floor boasted world-class movers mixed with local hotshots.

A thudding techno-synth pounder transitioned into an electronic retro swing number, complete with faux-vinyl scratchiness that brought a number of dancers out to Charleston and fox trot.

Vince led them through the cacophony of lights toward a pool of soft radiance in a corner booth. Two bouncers in tuxedos had already cleared the booth and awaited their arrival. The eyes of the crowd followed Horace with mostly amusement, some curiosity, as if wondering what sort of stunt he was planning in his awful getup.

The knowledge that they were effectively wiped from the lens of every camera helped unscrew the knots of tension in Horace's shoulders. An almost audible pop tingled through him as that realization took hold, and he settled back into the seat of soft, white suede, like sliding into a marshmallow.

Roxanne eased in beside him but kept a physical distance. Such was her magnetism that Horace found himself wanting her snuggled up under his arm but wondering if the costs might bury the benefits in an avalanche of danger. Vincent's gaze flickered with the notice of her positioning, but his amiable smile remained in place.

The booth was acoustically shielded somehow from the pounding music, and the space here, with the gleaming white table and softly fluorescent walls, was as quiet as their table at Campanello's. Vincent's fingers worked a little glass keyboard in the tabletop.

The club was busy, but not crowded. Crowds too thick prevented people from being *seen*; the place needed the illusion of social vibrancy, but not a sweat-soaked crush. Besides, these people were too pretty to sweat.

Fist-sized drone cams floated above the club-goers, who posed for the cameras, cavorted, flashed, mugged, rubbed velvety-smooth cheeks. Four hologram tanks were interspersed around the club, each one filled with a reproduction of one of the dancers with the best moves.

The ceiling was a dome of interconnected 3-D screens that flashed with snapshots, dance clips, breasts squeezed together and genitalia meticulously emphasized, smiles and winks and luxuriant hair-flips. One of the screens was a scoreboard filled with names and ratings. The numbers, names, and icons were in constant, dizzying flux. Another screen featured face shots of viewers at home, their expressions glazed in raptures of fascination, some of them wrapped in enthrallment verging on obsession. None of those faces were as beautiful as those that filled the club.

When their drinks arrived, Trask raised his glass. "Quite a place, Vince. My hat's off to you."

Vince nodded. "I like to hang out here once in a while just for the spectacle. The best people-watching anywhere."

Horace disagreed—these days he preferred the clientele of labor-class bars and strip clubs—but he thought it politic to say nothing. Maybe when he was twenty-five, he would have enjoyed places like this in small doses. It was certainly a target-rich environment for super-charged loins, but all the people here were flaunting themselves for a rare and specialized kind of currency. On the fringes of the throngs, liaisons formed; pairs or threesomes or foursomes slipped away into discreet back rooms. The cameras unerringly noted who left with whom.

Trask seemed to notice it at the same time as Horace. "I gotta say, giving people back rooms to get it on in is a stroke of genius. Extra charge?"

"By the minute. But still cheaper than a hotel."

"Can folks at home watch them?"

"If the participants allow it. The people who come here can customize the kind of fame they're trying to build. Their sex rating is one facet of that. You want to get into porn, you jack up your sex rating. You want to build your romance rating, maybe get a career as an actress or model, you play at some family-safe love games. Some people have a gift for drama—"

Horace laughed. "That's one way to put it."

Vincent turned his gaze on Horace, cocking his head.

"Sorry, brother, I'm not making fun. But that has to be one of the most twisted things I have ever heard. All those backstabbing, manipulative games that the worst of us played in high school. Now they're used to build fame and fortune."

"You disapprove?" Vincent said, leaning forward as if ready to engage in a spirited debate.

Horace shrugged. "How can I? I kill people for a living."

They all laughed.

Horace let a slow trickle of expensive whiskey warm his throat. He turned to Roxanne, "How about you, sister? You ever play games like this?"

She sipped another glass of red wine. "In my world, the games have much higher stakes."

He clinked her glass with his. "Here's to that. There's one thing bothering me, though." He traded his gaze pointedly between Roxanne and Vincent. "Why are you so willing to help me?" He fixed his gaze on Vincent. "I appreciate you being a fan and all, but...something else is going on here."

Since Horace had first gotten on Trask's road train, people had been sticking their necks out for him and gotten their heads blown off, people who did not deserve it. At Horace's blunt question, Trask's face darkened across the table as he chewed on his cigar—but this was different.

Vincent's eyes glittered with shrewdness so sharp it could cut a throat. "You ever wanted something, seriously wanted it more than anything, but had no idea how to take the first step toward getting it? It was so distant, so surrounded by obstacles, you couldn't imagine how you would ever get there? And then, someone shows up out of the blue with a magic secret passage, a go-to-the-head-of-the-line pass, a guided smart bullet. And you still can't believe your luck, but you still gotta have balls enough to take the shot?"

Horace said, "Sounds like the story of my life."

"So here I am with a magic smart bullet right in my lap. Trouble is, the act of shooting the bullet deforms it or shatters it. No good anymore. Can't ever be used again. So if this is a *smart* bullet, does the bullet *care* if it only gets one shot?" The gleam of hate-fueled ambition and ruthlessness seared through Vincent's affable demeanor.

Roxanne leaned onto the table, folding her hands between her elbows. "What has happened, Mr. Harkness, is that you have found yourself in a nest of vipers."

Vince raised a finger to protest. "Hey now—!"

She silenced him with a gentle hand across his, keeping her dark, bottomless gaze upon Horace. "Fortunately for you, all of them despise the man who is trying to kill you. Vincent and I are but two members of an alliance, you might say, an alliance that wants the Mogilevich consortium liquidated. For them, for me, you are the perfect weapon, an unstoppable engine of destruction—and an expendable one at that."

"You don't mince words."

"I am not so heartless that I would throw your life away callously. I would very much like to see you survive this. You are...an interesting man."

Before he could absorb the implications of her words, his netlink buzzed in his breast pocket. He pulled it out and saw Lilly's face. A spike of emotion went through him. Swallowing hard, he answered.

"Hammer?" she said. Her voice sounded a little nervous.

"Yeah, it's me. Are you okay?"

Three sets of eyes fixed on him.

"Yeah, I'm fine. Look, I need to see you."

"Well, I'd like to see you too but—"

"I'm in Buffalo," she said. "Where are you?"

Hot and cold prickles dashed up his spine. "What the hell are you doing *here?*"

"I saw you on the net. I drove half the night and all day to get here. I need to see you. Right now." She sounded tired and nervous, unsure but not afraid, and most importantly, not under duress.

He said, "You need to stay as far away from me as you can. It's too dangerous."

"Look, dickhead. I've been on the road for days. I stink. My ass is getting calluses. My kids are cranky and confused. And I came all this way to see *you*!"

Vincent leaned forward. "Is that her?"

Horace nodded. His brain reeled as he tried to work through ways to retrieve her without either of them having her speak her location over data feeds that were almost certainly monitored.

"I'll send a car for her," Vincent said.

While they waited for Lilly's arrival, Horace found his stomach doing flip-flops. What the hell does a guy say to a woman whose life he inadvertently threw into mortal danger? Her half-joking threat to put a stiletto heel through his scrotum was not to be discounted. He had once seen her eyes flash with fire at a customer who must have said something exceedingly nasty, a customer who was subsequently dragged unconscious out of the Titty Twister from a platform-heel kick to the ear.

At the same time, embers of hope bloomed in him. He at least trusted Vincent enough to offer Lilly and her children real protection, if only temporarily. The softening of that gnawing worry brought a lump to his throat. If they were safe, he could focus on what he needed to do—sift the remains of Yvgeny Mogilevich into a nice sterling silver urn next to his son.

Horace turned to Vincent. "You have to scrub her from the feeds, too."

Vincent said, "Show me a photo."

Horace produced one on the screen of his netlink.

Vincent studied it for a few moments, then said, "Done."

For forty minutes, Horace waited on pins and needles, amusing his companions as his excitement built. Then the crowd parted for an Italian rhinoceros of dark-suited muscle, and there Lilly was behind him. She had already seen Horace, and a storm of emotions cascaded through her face, a slurry of hard and soft, warm and cold.

He slid out of the booth, and she ran to him. Long legs, miniskirt, sparkling gray-blue blouse, and big brown eyes brimming with emotion.

She threw her arms around him and laid warm lips against his cheek again and again. "You big, beautiful fucking idiot. You beautiful fucking idiot."

He squeezed her slim softness against him. She almost disappeared in his massive embrace. His heart tripped and fell over itself a few times, righted itself like a boy who'd just stumbled over a crack in the sidewalk. Could this be happening, finally, after all this time?

She drew back and looked up into his face. A hasty application of makeup couldn't entirely erase the lines of fatigue and fear from her elfin features or the red from her eyes. Then her gaze fell to the center of his chest, and she touched the hard box under his clothes, ran fingers around its perimeter.

He smiled down at her and said, "You're a redhead now."

She smiled back. "Rest-stop bathroom dye job."

The pressure of curiosity was palpable from his three companions. The flavor of each was unique but bore some flavor of *So this is her.*

At her quizzical look, he said, "I'll tell you everything, but lemme introduce you to a few people."

Horace led Lilly by the hand down the long hallway of the private wing. Their room was quiet, dimly lit by warm lamps of multi-colored glass, and smelled of the cologne and perfume of the previous occupants. A luxuriant couch. A small bar. A panel for room controls, music, and video selection. He made sure the video feeds were locked out.

"A little more upscale than the private dance rooms at work." A tremor of uncertainty crept into her voice.

"It's great to see you."

She smiled at him again, and her gaze fell away and looked around the room.

The awkward tension hung between them for several long moments until he gestured toward the spacious couch. "Let's sit down."

"Yeah, sure."

He sat, and she sat away, edged closer, then halted, pulled back a centimeter, fidgeting.

"So where are your kids?" he said.

"Hopefully asleep at my aunt and uncle's house across town. My uncle used to be a marine, and he keeps half an arsenal under his bed. He can handle trouble. I used to be pretty close with them when I was a kid. It's been a long goddamn couple of days in the car, you know? Haven't showered—"

"I'm sorry!" he blurted in a choked gargle. The need for forgiveness smashed into him with physical force, straight into the box on his chest. "I never meant to get you mixed up in this. Hell, I didn't expect to be alive today."

She stiffened away from him. "I gotta say, Hammer, I was pretty fucking pissed after I got over being scared shitless. Or maybe I'm just going back and forth between those two things."

"It's gonna be okay, though. I got a plan now. And Vincent out there is going to take care of you and your kids for a little while."

"Who is he? He smells of gangster."

"You got a good nose. But I trust him enough to protect you until I can do what I gotta do."

"And what's that?"

"Better not tell you that part. But I promised to tell you what's going on."

And he told her everything, in as much detail as he could manage. For what seemed like an hour, he talked and she listened. Through long stretches of the tale, he could not look at her. For others, he could not look away.

When he told her about the snuff video starring her, she asked to see it. He pulled it up on his netlink, and then had to laugh a little. In the video, the ropes were present, hanging from invisible wrists, the shadowy onlookers were present, the knife was present, as was the sound of her gasp, but there was no image of Lilly on the screen.

At her quizzical look, he chuckled. "Vince is good to his word. You're scrubbed from every frame of video coming in or out of this place."

As she watched with a quizzical expression, her chin lifted in a moment of confusion, then recognition. She said, "A couple of years ago, this regular from the club asked me if I wanted to make a little extra money for some after-hours work. He wanted to tie me up, some roleplay. There was this cold, dark room, this creepy place. He'd been reading about this guy named Marquee de Sod, or something, I dunno. I needed the money 'cause I had to pay the hospital for having Cassie. I wanted to give a clean slate, you know? It wasn't my kinda thing, but I played along, let them tie me up, shoot some video. I was never in any danger, I took Max with me. Tell the truth, I forgot about it completely until just now. Still, the room there is all wrong, creepy fucking wrong, but the ropes look right. And there was no knife. It was a riding crop. Max would have beat the shit out of anyone with a real weapon."

He put the netlink away and resumed his narrative. When his account realigned with the present, he eased back into the couch and took a deep breath. "I'm gonna make this all right. Don't you worry, darlin'."

"You're a sweet fucking beast of a man," she said. And she leaned over and kissed him on the mouth.

Something let loose in him, a tongue of flame deep inside. He took her in his arms and pulled her to him. The kiss was long and deep, tasting of strawberry, coffee, and whiskey, and her body molded to his, the softness of her pressing against the hard, square chunk of technology fused to his chest. The tongue of flame snaked up the side of his heart and sped its rhythm. His blood heated.

She pulled away, eyes wide and dilated. "I don't know how to thank you for what you did for Jimmy. It was the most generous thing I've ever heard of."

"And he's gonna be fine, right?"

"They said so. They're reinforcing his bones and fixing his DNA."

"I'm glad to hear it."

A flutter of fear crossed her face, quickly squelched. "He's dying to meet you. When I told him I knew a real pit fighter, he almost lost his mind."

Horace said, "Got any pictures?"

With a proud mother's smile, she pulled out her netlink and showed him some photos. A swarthy, curly-haired boy and a red-haired, fair-skinned little girl, complete with beaming smiles and flashes of personality in their eyes.

"You got some good-looking kids," he said.

"Don't I know it." Her gaze lingered on the photo. "So what are you going to do next?"

"Like I said. I can't tell you that."

"Get yourself killed?"

"I've died twenty-seven times."

"Shut up. Don't remind me."

"Listen, if this all works out, we'll both be in the clear. We can put this behind us."

"And then what?"

Silence hung between them like a heavy shroud.

Finally he said, "I don't know, darlin'. We kinda have to get through all this first."

She nodded and sniffled a little. "In the meantime, though..."

Standing abruptly, she moved to the control panel on the wall, bending away from him with that familiar grace, that familiar sinuous poise, those familiar hips and taut buttocks. He drew a deep breath. The tongue of flame licked him again, hotter.

A familiar song drifted into the room, one of her favorites, a simmering, slinky blues instrumental from Darryl Ray Vaughan. Then she faced him, lifted a foot against his chest, and pushed him back against the couch.

"What the—"

"Shut up and let me do this."

Smooth guitar licked a soft, subtle undercurrent of Hammond B3 organ, with a heartbeat of bass guitar and pulses of high-hat. The music embraced them like gentle hands, the kind of music to sway to.

A soft, see-through pink thong emerged like a delicate tongue from under her miniskirt.

How many nights had she danced for him over the last several months? There had been times she was wild and acrobatic, others soft and silky, others playful and teasing. There was no part of her naked flesh that was not emblazoned in his mind with eternal clarity, no part of her he hadn't seen in exquisite detail. And just like all those other times, his heart exploded in his throat.

But something was different here. This felt like the strip club fantasy, what every man dreamed of, for such a stunning woman as this to make his every dirty dream come to life, but something about this was... off. She was performing her role more beautifully than ever, but...

The blouse went over her head and fell into a sparkling pool on the floor. A sheer lace bra the exact color of her flesh, all but invisible at first glance, filled his vision as she leaned close and breathed into his ear. The scent of her filled his nose—her delicate yet provocative perfume, the scent of her air, the musky underlying scent that could only be hers. Her hair brushed his cheek and her breath brushed his throat. The miniskirt dribbled away and there was her pink thong and meticulously trimmed pubic mound, exquisitely sculpted buttocks flexing, the delicate dimples above them as she spun and swayed for him.

He cleared his throat and blinked.

Her hands slipped up her spine and released the bra. The straps slipped oh, so slowly over her shoulders and down.

There was her rippling back, and the two little moles nestled under her right shoulder blade. A spasm of pain and sharp intake of breath shot through him as the memory of a knife blade slid across her ribs.

"What's wrong?" she said.

He blinked and tried to relax, cleared his throat again. "I—" He couldn't explain it, but something *was* wrong. This felt more like a fantasy than reality.

"Just relax, baby," she said. "Let me take care of you." Her voice was smooth as warm cream, puffing in his ear.

Her hands stroked his stubbled pate, driving shivers down the back of his neck, straying fingers down his chest, slipping under his suit jacket, tweaking his nipples, rubbing them, cupping his pectorals, sliding down over his belly, onto the tops of his thighs, warmth seeping through the textured silk into the muscles that still ached from the travails of the previous twenty-four hours. She thrust herself between his knees and knelt, her shoulders between his thighs. Her soft, silky flesh pressed against him, snaked up his belly, up his chest, her cheek soft against his, sliding up until an erect nipple brushed his cheek.

"You can touch me this time," she whispered in his ear.

His hands had been clamped onto his knees with a force that would have pulverized the patella of a lesser man. With carefully restrained strength, he touched the backs of her legs, tentatively in this new territory, slid his hands up to cup her buttocks, squeeze them, then up her hips, sides, back, until they roamed over her with increasing confidence, tweaking the bands of the thong circling her hips, stroking her soft shoulders and trailing down toward her hands.

This had never happened before, and his blood thrummed at being given free rein.

Her breathing quickened.

With each rhythmic pulse of the music, she moved against him, sliding, throwing a leg over to straddle his thigh, grinding a friction of heat against him. The intensity of the song built from a casual, almost playful feel to greater earnestness, driving the notes deeper, harder.

His erection tightened his trousers with an ache of need.

A moment later, her thong came off, spun twice around her finger, and lofted across the room.

His eyes guzzled her, feasted upon her. But her expression was one he had never seen before. Ripples of fear and uncertainty. In the club, there was never a moment where she was not in complete control, but now... And there was something else, too, something he couldn't quite identify.

And just like that, her fear and uncertainty disappeared. The wall came down behind her eyes, and he recognized it instantly.

Her warm breath seeped through the fabric covering his crotch, sending fresh, tingling heat through him. Her fingers went to his belt buckle, tugging. Glimmering doe-eyes looked up at him, but they were not warm. This was all a task she had decided was necessary.

"You don't have to do that," he said.

"Just let me." Her gaze moved to button and zipper. In her eyes now was a kind of determination, a single-mindedness that had nothing to do with him, a suppression of whatever emotions were troubling her, whatever old habits died hard.

Her warm, smooth hand slid into his underwear, cupped him, clasped him, stroked him.

A tiny part of his brain recognized what she was doing and squawked with the wrongness of it, but when she took him in her mouth, even that squawking went away.

CHAPTER TWENTY-FOUR

Horace and Lilly slid into the booth with the others. Roxanne now sat much closer to Vincent, hand on his thigh, and a slim, glamorous-looking Asian woman now leaned into the curve of Trask's arm, looking very sympathetic to the cast on his arm. Silent appraisals shot between Lilly and Roxanne, like swords clashing.

In the endorphin afterglow, mellow relaxation had loosened every muscle in Horace's tired body. Beside him, the confidence that served Lilly so well on stage had mostly returned, but now he thought he could see the tiny cracks in her armor.

Lilly said, "Spectacular place you got here, Vincent."

"Thank you for noticing," Vincent said, raising his glass. "A woman like you could be famous in a place like this. How would you feel about going under my protection until all this blows over? You and your kids."

She swallowed hard, and her hand seized Horace's. "I'd be awful grateful. Being on the run sucks."

"Hammer here feels terrible about your involvement in this," Vincent said. "I hope you understand that."

She glanced at Horace and nodded. Her chin rose higher. "I run into some pretty rough folks at my job. This palooka's one of them."

Horace looked Vincent squarely in the eye. "I don't know how I'll ever be able to thank you, Vince. But you got my gratitude all the same."

The currency still traded in the Italian mob after all these decades was gratitude and obligation, and Horace had no illusions about the depth of altruism in Vincent's heart. That awful, ruthless gleam in Vincent's eye had been the first real glimpse of ambitious gangster lurking inside his charming exterior.

In that gleam, Horace saw what would happen to Lilly if he failed. She'd have a few good years left as a dancer—protected, but indentured—in one of Vincent's clubs. Or perhaps she'd be turned out as a prostitute, her kids caught in the mob's endless vortex of obligation. All for Horace's sins.

Vincent smiled an easy smile. "I appreciate that, Horace. Like I said, I like helping the right people, you know?"

"So what now, Vincent?" Horace said.

"Where are the kids?" Vincent said.

"Asleep at my aunt and uncle's house."

"Then you and Hammer take the car and go get them. The driver will take you to a safe place."

Her eyes narrowed. "Why are you willing to go to so much trouble?"

"Call it an investment in the future. And Hammer's got pretty good taste."

She paused for a long moment, gauging, calculating. Finally she said, "So when do we go?"

When they got into the air, a prim cultured voice came from all around them. "May I have the address please?"

"Uh..." Lilly said. "You're the car?"

"I am indeed, madam. Does that make you uncomfortable?"

"Well, I've just never ridden in a robot car before. Out of my price range, you know?"

"Rest assured, madam, you are in the safest of hands, so to speak. I'm a sixth-generation autonomous vehicle with senses and reaction time far superior to any human driver."

She gave a crooked smile. "That's good to know." She gave the AI the address.

"Our ride will be about thirty minutes. Please make yourselves comfortable." The hover drive spooled up and the limo eased smoothly away from its parking place.

"That's just about right," Horace said, as he took her in his arms, pulled her close, kissed her. She resisted only for the first moment of surprise, then surrendered to his embrace.

For a moment, then she pulled away.

"What happened in there..." His voice trailed off. "I don't need a personal stripper."

She stiffened away from him, anger flaring in her face. "What the—"

"Hold on a second. I appreciate you coming all this way. I appreciate the private... I'm happy as hell to see you, to have you here after all this time. But I got a long way to go before I'm the kinda guy you might want to keep around."

He looked into her eyes for a moment. There was the wall, with an entire universe of hidden wants and dreams and loves tucked safely behind it.

"You don't have to let me in," he said, "Hell, I might not let *you* in. We're both pretty fucked up as normal people go. But I do know this: I don't want to be a customer anymore."

Then he took her face in his hand, stroked her cheek, and kissed her. With shocking suddenness, tears burst out of her and she choked back a sob.

She quickly wiped the tears, eyes gleaming. "Asshole."

Then she threw herself against him.

Within moments, kisses were not enough. Hands slid into clothing again, seeking deeper ingress, seeking warm skin. In the burgeoning fervor, two buttons popped from his threadbare shirt front. Clothing peeled away, cast off into puddles on the floor. Hot mouths devoured each other, warm flesh sliding and caressing.

"You have me at a disadvantage, sir," she said. "I have never seen *you* naked."

They laughed and wrestled, licked and squeezed, as if trying to acquaint every square centimeter of their own bodies with the other's.

Worries about his heart blinked through his mind but drowned in the rush of throbbing heat.

When she settled onto him, surprise and ecstasy burst into her face. For a long moment, they paused. Her moist heat consumed his awareness in a way that he had not experienced since...

And then they began to move, at first hesitant, out of sync, but then he took her slim hips in his massive hands and moved her.

And the cries built, and the sweat beaded, and their hearts hammered against each other, and Horace's awareness became a shining river of frenzied, inescapable rapture, and the pleasure ripped through them both until there was nothing left in them but to subside, diminish, and fall separate onto the leather seat.

Afterward, he said, "Not bad for an old man."

"Holy shit!" she gasped and kissed him again, petal soft skin sheened with sweat, aglow with subsiding heat. Then her hand examined the injector box on his chest, traced its outline, brushed its surface. "We gotta get you a new heart. Somehow. The biggest one there is."

"If I get a new ticker, prepare to have your world rocked in ways you can't imagine."

"Do you know how long it's been since I had a boyfriend?"

"Do you know how long it's been since I had a girlfriend?" He knew exactly how long it had been.

"What are we doing here?" she said.

"Let's not overthink it right now. One step at a time."

A minute of comfortable silence passed. Horace was lost in the scent and feel of her.

She broke the silence with a quiet voice, cheek against his breast. "I always wanted to be a costume designer."

"Is that like a fashion designer?"

"Sort of, but for like movies or theater and stuff."

"That sounds pretty fine."

"I love fabrics, and sewing, and creating, and making a character come alive. Did I ever tell you I made the costumes for all the girls at the club?"

He shook his head.

"They kept me pretty busy at it, with girls coming and going all the time. I got started doing it for my high school theater, and just fell in love with it. I loved acting, too, being in front of people. That's why I did the modeling for a while."

"You were a model?"

"Don't sound so surprised!" She poked him in the ribs, but there was no anger in her voice, only regret. "I was in some rag-mags. I was good at it, too. The acting helped."

"So what happened?"

She leaned back and looked into his eyes for a long moment, and it was one of the few moments since they'd met when she allowed him to look into her. "I got roofied and raped by one of the event managers. Then I was pregnant. Nobody wants a model with stretchmarks." A tear trickled down one cheek, quickly wiped away. She sniffed. "Turns out nobody wants a costume designer either unless you go to school for it."

"Was that... Jimmy's biological father?"

She nodded.

"I apologize on behalf of my kind." He had had a lot of women, but he had never forced himself on anyone. "You want me to take care of him?"

She rolled her eyes. "Typical Neanderthal reaction."

"Well...do you?"

"For a long time, I'd have jumped at your offer. Not anymore. I have Jimmy now, and he's an angel."

"And Cassie?"

"That boyfriend I mentioned. What are we, sharing our deepest, darkest secrets now?" She turned away. "Leave it to me to over-fucking-share."

"You don't have to tell me anything." He had seen in her eyes just what baring that old scar had cost her. It had cost her the indomitability of her self-built internal fortress.

He hugged her close again. "No one is ever going to hurt you again, not with me around."

She accepted the hug. Another tear cooled on his chest. "Someday, maybe I'll believe you."

Shattering the moment like a dropped Tiffany vase, the AI driver spoke over the intercom. "We'll be there in five minutes."

Fuck. "Thanks, brother!" Horace called.

They finished dressing moments before the car eased to a halt in front of an old brick apartment building. The driver's door opened and closed, followed moments later by the curbside door opening.

"Let me go first," Horace said. He slid out and surveyed the trash-strewn street.

Hover-cars like the limousine offered a much smoother ride, but this was not the natural habitat for such vehicles. This was a ragged, labor-class neighborhood, where the air smelled of kerosene, ozone, and garbage. Since none of them could afford cars, they got to their daily grinds with mass transit, usually decrepit buses, some of which still ran on biodiesel like something out of the turn of the century. Hemming in a street otherwise empty of vehicles, four-story brownstones crumbled under relentless time. An angry young man walked with hunched shoulders and shuffling gait. Pools of streetlight formed pale islands in the night, flickering. A handful of windows still glowed from within, now well past midnight.

"We'll be right back," Horace told the car.

"Take whatever time you need, sir," the car said.

Horace took Lilly by the hand and led her into the building's vestibule. Flickering fluorescents bathed the chamber in ghostly dimness. The air smelled of old dust, mold, and quiet desperation. The intercom panel hung useless in long-exposed strands of multicolored spaghetti. The latch on the inner door had been extracted long ago, leaving only an empty hole bored through the wood. In other words, it was a standard labor-class tenement.

Lilly pushed the door open and led them into the narrow stairwell leading upward. Ancient boards creaked under Horace's weight, echoing hollowly in the naked column. A time-darkened wooden banister stood smoothed by the passage of countless hands. On this floor, paint peeled from plaster walls, and the space smelled of marijuana smoke, onions, and cat shit.

She led him up to a dented steel door on the third floor. The doorframe was also steel, the lock electromagnetic, embedded in the wall itself, capable of stopping a rhino in midcharge if rhinos had still existed. There had been a common advancement in door locks over the old deadbolts and chains of Horace's childhood, at least until power distribution had gotten so sketchy in run-down neighborhoods. They came with battery backups, but sometimes even those ran down.

Lilly knocked on the door. "Uncle Stan said he was going to wait up for me."

They waited and listened. No sound came from inside.

She knocked again and clutched her elbows.

A gobbet of cold dread settled in Horace's stomach as the seconds ticked by with no response from inside.

"Uncle Stan?" she called. "Aunt Emma!" Still nothing. Her voice rose in pitch. "Jimmy! *Cassie!*" She beat the door with her fist.

"Move over," Horace said. She stepped aside, and she reached into her purse and pulled out a pink pistol the size of Horace's palm. "You know how to use that?" It was an old-style semi-automatic slug-thrower, small caliber.

"Took a class."

"Please don't shoot *me*."

He threw his entire 169 kilos against the door. A charging rhino had nothing on Horace The Hammer Harkness. The door exploded inward, tearing mag-lock and chunks of steel frame out of the wall, and crashed against the wall inside. Horace stumbled into a hallway.

Lilly called from behind, "Jimmy? Cassie, baby?"

Bright light spilled into the hallway from a room to the right, ambient light from straight ahead, and beyond a hallway where dark bedrooms lay. Horace quick-peeked into the bright room and found an empty kitchen. A half-full cup of coffee sat on the old speckled-Formica table, and the scent of coffee from a pot on the counter still filled the room.

As Horace crept forward, a foot came into view, clad in leather work boots attached to a motionless leg sitting in a battered easy chair, a thick, hairy hand sagging off the arm of the chair. The smell of blood and burned flesh clung to the back of Horace's throat.

He motioned Lilly to go back out into the hallway and call the police. Her eyes shone with terror, hand clutched over her mouth.

Across the living room was a window, the view of which was filled by another brick wall perhaps two meters from the glass. Directly facing the window, slumped in the light of the lamp, was a man slightly older than Horace, with thick, workman's arms and a middle gone to paunch. A submachine gun rested between his thighs. His face was a mask of half-cooked blood from the three blackened pinholes in his forehead. His head lay half-glued to the leather of the chair from the equally neat exit wounds in the back of his skull.

From behind him came Lilly's voice, "Oh, come on! You're the police! Answer the goddamn phone!" The police would never come to this neighborhood.

Horace crept toward the dark hallway where three dark doorways hung ajar, the silence oppressive upon his ears. His hands itched for a weapon that was not a firearm, even a simple knife or club. He had more faith in his empty chitinous hands than in those same hands with a gun in them. The hallway floorboards creaking under him like a chorus of alarms, he pushed open the nearest door and found a guest bedroom also used as an office, empty, the bedcovers undisturbed.

His heart hammered at his breastbone, harder, harder.

The final room lay in darkness too deep to discern any details until he flipped on the light.

A motionless form sprawled across the bed. A gray-haired, thin-boned woman, face frozen in a rictus of terror. The front of her robe was blackened, scorched, as was the pale flesh exposed beneath it. The scent of ozone and burned flesh lingered in the air like invisible smoke.

There were no children. He called for them, checked the closets, under the bed, checked the hallway bathroom.

Horace called out. "Lilly, don't shoot me! I'm coming out."

In the hallway, Lilly was breathlessly answering questions to someone on her netlink. Address, break-in. And she kept repeating, "I don't know! I don't know! No, I don't live here!"

Finally, she disconnected in disgust. "Maybe they'll send someone, maybe they won't. This is a Yellow Zone, low priority. Jimmy and Cassie—"

"Not here," Horace said. "And your aunt and uncle are dead."

"No. No. No, no, no, no, nononononononononono..."

He pulled her close. "We'll get 'em back. We'll get 'em back. Everything will be okay."

She shoved him away with a shriek of feral rage. "*NO!*" Her eyes blazed with a crazed glare. Her fist slammed into his chin, then the other fist into his cheek. Tears streamed down her cheeks.

"Stop," he said, grabbing both of her wrists as gently as he could. "Lilly, no." Her hands became raking talons aimed at his eyes and cheeks. Her stiletto heel stabbed into his instep, piercing his plastic loafers with perfect ease. In the shock of pain, his grip slackened enough for her to twist her hands free, and she laid a tremendous slap against his left ear that popped hard against his eardrum and disoriented him for a moment, long enough for her to spin away and run down the stairs.

He chased her, limping at first. Somewhere he heard an apartment door open, then another. Hot wetness seeped into his punctured shoe, but his tolerance for pain kicked in and he picked up speed in pursuit.

"Lilly, wait!" he called.

By the time they reached the vestibule, he was two steps behind. She was outside; he reached for her, but she stumbled on the stoop and fell. Her legs collapsed, her hand reached out to break her fall, buckled under. Her face slammed against the concrete stoop rail.

He grabbed for her again and saw the spatter of fresh crimson on the pavement. The almost invisible slits opening to drool blood from her neck, from her arms. She rolled onto her back, staring up at him with eyes wide with confusion, with fear. Scarlet poured from her nose and mouth as she tried to form words drowned in blood. He stood frozen for a heartbeat in the door of the vestibule.

Then he lunged for her, snatched a handful of her blouse, and dragged her with him against the side of the limousine. Her bare arms and legs flopped in her blood, so much of it, smearing all over him. His mouth was babbling. His hand fumbled on the rear door latch of the limousine, grabbed, fumbled, finally flung it open. He dragged her into the car.

She was gasping his name, wetly, "Hammer. Hammer..."

He slammed the door shut, encasing them in a bullet- and rail gun-proof mobile bunker.

Horace roared, "Go! Go! Go!"

But nothing happened. No reply came from the car's AI.

He slammed the door-lock button, sealing them inside, then lunged forward to the opaque panel that separated the cabin from the driver's compartment. His fist destroyed the panel in two blows and revealed an empty compartment, as he had expected, but the air in the cabin smelled of ozone and burned wires. Had they disabled the AI somehow? Some kind of electromagnetic *zot?*

Ripping and tearing into the shattered panel, he widened a gap to thrust himself into the compartment. As he wormed his massive bulk through the gap, shards of the panel ripped furrows in his suit, scratched deep into his flesh. Every precious second left more of Lilly's blood spilled on the floor behind him. He kept calling back to her, "Hang on! Hang on!" his voice crumbling.

Propped in the back seat, she sagged against the window, her breathing a wet gurgle, ensanguined hands quivering against her chest.

If he could get her to a hospital within three or four minutes, they could bring her back.

Thrashing and straining to twist his long, thick limbs around so he could right himself in the driver's seat, he felt the seconds ticking inexorably past, escaping him.

His palm slammed the hover-drive control and the limousine's engines spooled up. It eased off the ground.

A triangle of brilliant green dots angled down from above through the windshield onto his leg. Searing heat speared deep into his thigh with the hiss of burning flesh and a tongue of flame as the tri-laser set the fabric of his trousers afire. Clenching his teeth at the pain, he shoved the forward thrust lever against the stop. The car surged forward with a powerful whine. The laser beams swept away from him and burned a furrow across the plastic dashboard.

His hands were shaking as with a palsy as he fumbled his netlink of his breast pocket.

"Bunny! Bunny! Goddammit, Bunny! Are you there?" he roared.

After a moment, her voice came through, murky with sleep. "Yeah, it's me. What's up?"

"Give me the hospital closest to my location! And it's gotta have regen facilities!" Even as he punched the throttle, he cast about through the windows for signs of the attack drone. It wasn't a large drone, about the size of a trashcan lid, so he doubted it could keep up with a limo going full speed, but something had disabled the AI and that tri-laser and rail gun might still do some damage.

Right on cue, a succession of projectiles pinged against the armored skin of the limo. If they penetrated, he didn't know where. The windshield glass where the lasers has passed through had slagged into a blurred patch just outside his necessary field of vision.

After a moment, the netlink pinged in his ear. "Done," she said. "About two-and-a-half minutes from your location." The location popped up on the limo's positioning map. "Are you okay?"

His heart was pounding so loud he could barely make sense of her words, his mouth so dry he could barely speak. "It's not me, it's Lilly! She's been shot by a fucking drone! She's bleeding out! They can bring her back!"

"Hammer, wait."

"What? What?"

"They won't take you if you don't have the cash—"

"She's dying!"

"No cash, they'll lock the door. The next closest is Sisters of Mercy. They have a no-turn-away—"

"How far?"

"About six minutes from you. Need me to distract any traffic police from your path?"

The limousine picked up speed. "Do it. Can't talk, but I'm keeping you on intercom. Call Trask and tell him where I'm going."

"Also done." A guided map sprang to life on the limo's screen.

He laid the netlink beside him and took the yoke in both hands. One hundred kilometers per hour down the narrow city streets. One hundred twenty. One hundred forty. May all the gods help him if he had to make a sharp turn in this lumbering beast. Was the drone still behind him? He couldn't' see it.

"Bunny, is there a drone on my ass?" he called into his netlink.

"I'm reading a couple still in the area," Bunny answered.

The yoke flexed in his hands as the hover car zipped over medians and curbs. Fortunately, at this hour, the streets were all but empty except for a few hapless taxis sent spinning out of control in his wake.

He reached the hospital in four minutes and thirty-two seconds, charged inside, begged for help, dragged a gurney outside as if it were made of tinfoil, and flung open the back door of the limo.

Lilly's eyes stared, fixed. She was not breathing. They wheeled her inside.

Someone said, "Jesus Christ, look at 'im, he's glowing!"

A deep chill settled over him, the hard cold of Antarctic winter, the kind that freezes souls into chunks of brittle ice.

The nurse was asking him questions about what happened, and he couldn't answer for certain. "Mini rail gun maybe. Some sort of assassin drone. Didn't even see it. Didn't see a shooter. Didn't hear a thing. Never mind my goddamn leg! Bring her back! Didn't you hear me? Forget the leg!"

"She's gone, Mr. Harkness."

"Resurrect her!"

"She can't pay—"

"Fuck you, I'll pay!"

"You can't pay either, I'm afraid. I'm sorry, sir. Look, we're a charity hospital. We don't have the—"

"Save her, or you're a dead man!"

"—put me down—"

"You hear me? All of you! I'll tear this place to the ground if you don't save her!"

"Security!"

"Do it! You put her on that regenestation right there! Goddammit, do it! She's got two kuh-kids!"

"Don't move! I said, *don't move!*"

"Fuck you!"

"Tase him!"

"Fuh-fuh—"

"Hit him again!"

A bestial, tortured roar.

"Holy Christ, hit him again!"

"Again!"

"fuh...fuhk...yuh...you."

ROUND 3

CHAPTER TWENTY-FIVE

Horace awoke on a lumpy bed with harsh fluorescent lights in his eyes. The air was cold and stank of sweat and excrement. His mouth was a coarse-gritted desert. His limbs were immense trunks of flaccid meat. His heart chugged and chuffed in his breast like a decrepit steam engine. Cold gray walls, cold gray bars. Snoring from nearby. A deep cavernous space. Feet shuffled without direction or purpose. Whisperings in the distance.

The moment he tried to move, his head clanged with pain. Best to leave it alone for a while. Just lie here. Gather his thoughts, gather what was left of him. Shattered. Splintered. Left in pieces on the stoop of a beaten-down brownstone in a shitty neighborhood. The fresh wound on his thigh still ached, but his fingers found a patch of synth-skin there through the seared gash in the cheap trousers. He still wore his jacket, ripped and tattered and stiff with blood that was not his. Mostly not his.

Occasionally a garbled oath would mumble out of him as the pain in his head reached a crescendo, and all he could do was clutch his head in his hands and hope it passed soon. At some point, his brain coalesced around the idea of where he was, but it didn't matter. If a dirty cop walked in and put a bullet in his head right now, it would be a mercy.

Interminable time dragged past. Self-recriminations spun in endless circles like broken wheels stuck in a marsh. He should have stopped the bleeding. He should have called for help. He should have held her while she died. He should have gone to the first hospital, smashed down the doors, and made them fix her, profit or none. He should not have left her alone in the back, choking on her own blood, unable to reach him. He should have gone outside ahead of her.

He should have been more careful.

What was going to happen to her kids now?

Some small part of his mind, the part unoccupied with pain, recognized this place it had gone, this deadly numbness, this place of retreat and hiding, this deep, dark borehole into oblivion. He had been here before, once. The only time in his life when he had given up. When he had gone to the remains of Singapore with everything he'd had for as long as he could, and found nothing.

A warm voice rose out of his memory. "She's quite a number, fuck face. A little damaged maybe, soiled."

"Turns out I like a little soiled. Why do you only come to me when I'm mostly dead?"

"That's the only time you'll listen. So *listen*. You have to stop chasing me."

"I couldn't find you. I looked and looked, but there was nothing left."

"I didn't want you to find me."

"Why, darlin', *why*?"

"Because I couldn't do it. I loved the life as much as you did. I had to cut it off completely, cold turkey, and you were part of it."

"I didn't get to tell you—"

"I knew."

"I'd have quit for you! For him!"

"Don't lie. You think it's good for a kid to watch his daddy get killed over and over? Do you think *I* could do it?"

"I'm lost. Are you still out there? Is he? Or am I just crazy as a shithouse rat?"

"Get up, fuck face. Get up, baby. Get up right now."

"Just wanna sleep..."

"She's not dead."

"What do you mean, she's not dead?"

Those words congealed into sound coming from his throat, a ragged scrape of syllables. And he heaved himself into a sitting position.

The bleary, half-lidded eyes of other prisoners regarded him with quizzical half interest. Men talking to themselves were hardly unusual in a city lockup.

Lurching upright, he leaned against the bars to steady himself. His laser wound squealed in protest. The three other occupants of his cell, any two of which combined might have matched his mass, all edged away from him and kept their glances veiled and surreptitious. Others watched with more blatant interest from the safety of other cells.

He clutched the bars, using them to steady himself, stubbled face pressing against rock-hard hands, when all he wanted to do was collapse on the floor and die of a brain aneurysm.

More time passed. No one tried to speak to him.

"Harkness," a man's voice said. "You got a visitor."

"Who?"

"Says she's your lawyer."

He sat down in the flimsy folding chair, wondering for an instant if it would collapse like folded paper, and leaned forward over the table, over his cuffed wrists. If he kept his eyes down, the light hurt less.

"You said you were my lawyer," he said.

"I am a lawyer. Princeton, Class of '49." Roxanne said. Today she was dressed in a conservative, gray business suit, hair bound into an elaborate braid at the back of her head. Her expression was even more inscrutable by day.

"What do you want?"

"We have a date in Vegas."

He surveyed the cold, green conference room, the cameras, the one-way mirror. "So who's watching?"

"I paid extra for complete privacy. Besides, this is not a high-profile case. Assault and battery and destruction of property does not warrant pitchforks and burning at the stake."

"Is she alive?"

"They were able to resuscitate her, but the projectiles perforated her aorta, and she nearly bled out again. They stabilized her with surgery but would not regenerate her. She's alive, but comatose."

The fist clenched around his heart relaxed and he nearly collapsed onto the table. He coughed back tears.

She said, "As they are not a for-profit hospital, they were morally bound to stabilize her but not keep her indefinitely. Such organizations have very little discretionary budget. She has forty-eight hours before she's designated 'no hope of recovery' and unplugged. Unless next-of-kin can be found willing to pay for her."

He sensed the pressure behind this deadline. She knew exactly how far he would go to protect Lilly. "Why do you still want to go to Vegas?"

"Yvgeny Mogilevich has Lilly's children. He will toss them in the garbage like used tissues. And he will go on using up the world and everyone in it for his own sick amusement."

Horace squeezed his eyes shut.

"Listen to me. The only way to save them is to do something. Before he can hurt them."

"But you're just another hydra, like you said. How many bodies you got sunk to the bottom of your swimming pool?"

Her face tightened. "Irrelevant at this point. Do you want out of jail or not?"

"Okay, I'm in," he said. "But if we're successful, Lilly gets a full regeneration. Do we have a deal?"

"What about you?"

"I've been a walking dead man for years. You let me worry about me. Do we have a deal?"

"We have a deal."

"Now, how do I get out of here?"

"The charges will be dropped."

"You got that kind of pull?"

"With the appropriate dollar figure applied, yes."

"And you're just investing in the future, right?"

"More like gambling. But the stakes are too high to sit out."

Horace was barred from seeing Lilly after what had happened at Sisters of Mercy. At some point, he'd have to go there and apologize to a few people, but today was not that day.

A car took Horace to a rat-bag motel called the Starlite Kiss, where Trask had holed up himself, Tina, and Bunny under fake names. The bedspreads were of scarlet velvet, the walls of blood-red fleur-de-lis print, and the refrigerators stocked with lubricants and edible sex toys—just the kind of cheesy grandeur he'd loved once, in what now felt like an entirely different lifetime.

Fortunately the room also came stocked with a few over-the-counter painkillers. He took enough of those to subdue a killer whale, stripped off the blood-crusted clothes, and lay back on the surprisingly soft bed. With the lights down low, he closed his eyes for a few minutes and was awakened by a sharp knock on the door. He ignored it, but it came again.

"I know you're in there, Hammer." Tina's voice. "Open up."

He answered her with a couple of nonsense syllables and tried to gather himself sufficiently to speak English.

"Let me in."

"You must like seeing me naked."

"I actually got your clothes here from the other night."

He opened the door a crack, and she thrust a wadded bundle through the gap. A few seconds later, he'd stripped and dressed himself again. It felt good not to have any blood on his clothes. He swung the door open and let her in.

She thrust her hands deep into the pockets of her red-and-white polka-dot jeans. "I'm really sorry about everything that happened last night. She was a looker, even had a little class for a stripper."

"Wait a—were you there?"

"In the club, yeah."

"How the—" His memory floundered for images of people that might have been her last night, but his focus had not really been on the crowd.

"Ninja, remember? Don't hurt your brain. Look, I keep asking Trask what you all got cooked up, but he won't tell me anything. So tell me."

"Listen, kid—"

"Fuck you, Grandpa Moses! I'm neck deep in this thing! Poor Bunny is beside herself, afraid she's going to lose her parole. These motherfuckers have their fingers in everything! And it's all because of *you!*"

"Like I said, stay the hell away from me and you'll be better off."

"Too late! You're an albatross who just sank the whole fucking ship, so now here we are in the middle of the ocean, surrounded by sharks and sea monsters, and the only way any of us are going to survive is if we stick together. You, me, Bunny, even Trask. We're with you whether you want us or not. So what is your plan?"

Horace turned his full attention on this brilliant, beautiful, brassy young woman, standing there in her polka-dot jeans and crossed arms, dark eyebrows furrowed over a button nose that was too cute by far for what she was capable of. "I'm going to Vegas with Roxanne, in disguise as one of her bodyguards. There's a death-match boxing event. Mogilevich will be there. I'm going to kill him."

"That's it? Sounds like a suicide mission."

"I'll try to make sure my medical is up-to-date."

"It's always going to be life and death with you, isn't it?"

"I don't know any other way."

"You need to take me and Bunny."

"Not a chance."

"No, *you* listen now. We made a damn good team the other night. And people like this mobster have layers of invisible protection you can barely imagine. That's why we need a slicer—Bunny."

"And you've talked this over with her?"

"What do you think we've been doing all day while you were sleeping off your taser hangover?"

"So we need a slicer. You're not a slicer." And the thought of what those Russians would do to someone like Tina made his stomach turn cold and tight.

"You need *me* to watch your back while you're busy Thunder Hammering."

He sat there quiet for a long time, running his fingertips over the chitinous ridges of his knuckles. "Jesus, kid, you got more balls than most guys I ever met."

"Who needs balls? I got a vagina. Those things can take a pounding."

Horace knocked on the motel room door. After a moment, the door opened and Bunny looked up at him. Her face melted at the sight of him, but she blinked it back into composure. She cleared her throat. "Yes?"

"Uh, I just wanted to say thank you for everything you've done for me." He handed her a paper bag. "It's not much."

She accepted it and looked inside. A smile erased some of the tension on her face. "Tea!"

"It's not fancy, just the floweriest stuff I could find at the market a couple blocks over."

"You went *out*?"

"Covered my face. Only scared a couple of people."

She chuckled. "Hibiscus and rose hips are my favorite. Would you like to come in?"

He stepped inside and she shut the door.

"Look, this is a lot bigger than a few cups of tea," he said. "Tina told me you two have been talking, and I—"

"Let's play Italian Mafia Bingo!" Her voice shrilled. "I've been doing a little checking on your new benefactors. Prostitution: check! Kickbacks from construction firms: check! Racketeering: check! Black market narcotics: check! Black market tech: check! Bank fraud: check! Money laundering: check! Excise tax fraud: check! The Russians practically invented that one in the Bronx back in the 1970s. This Roxanne Sukova is wanted for human trafficking across half of Eastern Europe. If my parole officer gets even a sniff of this, I will go away *forever*! No more blue sky, no more road trips to nowhere, no more tea."

"You don't have to do this. Walk away. Right now."

"I've already crossed too many lines. The best chance I have now is to see it through. In for a penny, in for a gosh-darn metric tonne!"

She sighed and sagged down onto the bed. "Trask's operation is dead. There's nothing here for me now. He hasn't admitted it to himself yet, but I've checked his bank accounts. He could rebuild, but it will take at least two years before he makes a profit again."

"I thought you said you couldn't do anything intrusive."

"The lock doesn't stop me from watching people type in their passwords."

Horace laughed. "And here I thought you were just sweet, innocent, little Bunny."

"I haven't been innocent since I was fifteen. Nowadays it's more like Bunny Who Was Long Ago Sweet and Innocent but Was Corrupted by Invisible Wars, Destroyed by Prison, and Is Now a Revolutionary Trying Hard to Be Reformed but Can't Because She's Being Led

Astray by the Irresistible Magnetism of a Hopeless Warrior Who Will Never Be Hers."

After a long silence, he sat down beside her. "That's pretty complicated."

"The decision trees in my AI boggle the mind."

He took her hand and squeezed it. She laid her other hand atop his and clutched it.

She looked up at him, a moment of hope flickering in her eyes. "You want to stay for a while? I'll make some tea, you can turn your nose up at it..."

"I can't. We're leaving for Vegas at three a.m. I'm gonna grab what sleep I can."

"I understand."

A thousand things went through Horace's mind, things he should say, but all of them sounded unbelievably lame. So he said nothing, took his hand away, and left.

CHAPTER TWENTY-SIX

The sky outside the windows of the hyperjet were a brilliant tapestry of silver and milk. Gauzy clouds glowed below in the light of the half-moon. Moonlight gleamed on the pearly wing.

Soft techno-jazz, crystal clear and vibrant as a featherlight touch, stroked the dim pools of ambient light. The aircraft was the height of luxury, constructed to dampen the noise of the engines so completely that the cabin was as quiet as an empty coliseum. This kind of luxury was not unknown to Horace, although he'd never owned a private hyperjet.

Horace and Roxanne reclined on a luxuriant couch in the rear of the aft cabin. Her lawyerly attire was gone, replaced by a provocatively-cut dress that looked like an impressionist painting.

Roxanne's handservant, Amelie, a lovely French girl, poured drinks for both of them and then departed forward to prepare Bunny and Tina a meal, make them as comfortable as possible, and keep them entertained. Roxanne had forbidden any interruption until landing in Vegas.

She swirled her glass of pinot noir and relaxed into the couch, facing him. Her musky perfume stroked his nostrils with exotic fingers. "Millennia ago, Roman women of status and means paid handsomely to be bedded by the most powerful gladiators. Of course, the gladiators were slaves who saw none of this money."

Horace's eyes drank her in: the full lips, the bottomless eyes, the body sprung from of every heterosexual man's most fervid dreams, the glossy raven hair brushing cleavage straight from heaven, and he felt nothing but the coldness, the shell, and the murderous darkness within it.

"Can you imagine it?" she said. "Fresh from bloody victories, still stinking of sweat and triumph, these men were as gods. Women came and rutted upon them because there were no men like them in the world. Not their patrician husbands, not their nubile slave boys, but these great beasts of men whose sole purpose was to kill and die."

Horace fingered his glass of Ardbeg, the smoky flavor of the scotch on his tongue much like the sound of her voice, the smell of a nearby bonfire yet unseen. The comparison between pit fighters of today and gladiators of ancient times was a well-trodden one, often discussed in the early meetings of the marketing people as Death Match Unlimited had begun to coalesce into a wildly profitable venture. And it had been much of the Business' appeal when he was still young and full of spunk. None of his high-powered bed partners had ever paid him in currency, but in favors in other realms that could be just as lucrative.

"I signed on to be a piece of meat," he said. "Some uses for that are more fun than others."

"There are so few gods left in this world." She leaned into him, her nostrils quivering.

"Once in a while, a great while," he said, "I run across a goddess who knows what she is. Even more rare, she doesn't abuse it."

She clinked his glass, and their eyes met for long moments. On any other day, he would have been ecstatic to have a woman like Roxanne looking at him that way, leaning close enough that her musky perfume formed a trail his nose wanted to follow. It wouldn't have mattered what business she was in.

Her gaze turned away, as if she had been looking for something and not found it.

Horace eased back from her luscious scent, trying to clear his head. "So, you and Vince."

"Come now, are we back in junior high? Surely you don't think Vince and I are an item."

"I don't want to step on anybody's toes." Much less piss off yet another powerful mobster. Jealousy had ruined careers all around him. The stakes here were much higher.

"Vince is protective of me. A great many men feel such things for me. The rest hate me for being a powerful woman. Each type requires a different approach."

"I can't say you need much protecting."

"Very perceptive. Nevertheless, it is sometimes a useful role to play." Her eyes met his for a long, thoughtful moment as she swirled her wine gently in its glass. "And speaking of roles, there is much to do before the event, preparations to make."

"Give me a vibro-axe and point me in the right direction."

"I admire your enthusiasm, but even you would have zero chance of success in a direct attack. Even getting into the same building with him will require special preparations. You will need to wear a prosthetic." Producing a black, plastic packet from her briefcase, she handed it to him. "This is a fingertip, made of synth-skin. Bond it to the end of your index finger. It contains a few drops of blood and a fingerprint tied to your fake identity. Mogilevich is incredibly security-minded. Everyone's DNA will be scanned against a database."

He set it aside for later. "So who am I going to be?"

"You're Frankie Rocketfist, a former pit fighter, of course, who has joined the bodyguard trade. Hardly a person to raise an eyebrow at an event like this. Pit fighters of your size are unusual, but not unheard of. Synth-skin and battle armor will conceal your tattoos. Poor Frankie never made it out of the minor leagues. If your personal history is checked—and it will be—enough of a background identity, fabricated matches and such, has been constructed to fool a cursory inspection. We'll be meeting my surgeon in Vegas to modify your face."

"What? Surgeon? I thought you were going to use movie makeup."

"Facial recognition systems can see through external prosthetics. You would be flagged instantly. No, we're going to implant temporary bone and cartilage structures under your skin, plus a neural chip in your motor cortex that will alter your posture." She touched his face with warm, gentle fingers. "Nose, brows, cheekbones, chin, gait."

He cracked a half grin. "You don't think I got enough chin?"

"Oh, my dear Horace, you're going to look and walk like a Neanderthal brute when we're through. The uglier you are, the less anyone will look at you. And of course, the surgery will be healed and assimilated immediately with regenites. No swelling or redness. And when we are through with all of this, when this vast clusterfuck is over, the implants will be removed and you will be your old, beautiful self once again."

"Beautiful, eh?"

"Hardly in a movie star or supermodel way, but..." Her fingers stroked him again. "You are like a mountain. Timeless, capped with snow that slowly erodes you." She stroked the salt-and-pepper hair that had begun to obscure his scalp tattoos. "Standing taller than anyone around you, an Everest that lesser men die on."

"That's awful poetic, sister."

She smiled, like a peek of sun through a forest canopy. "I was a literature major before law school."

"You don't hear much poetry these days."

"And that is one of the great tragedies of the twenty-first century. The plutocrats and gangsters who run this planet, men like Mogilevich, have little use for things that don't make them money. Poetry hasn't made money for anyone since the days of Shakespeare. And that disdain trickles down to the masses, who lack enough patience and education to appreciate anything beyond limericks and marketing jingles." The more she spoke, the more her face seemed to open up, like light emerging from within a slowly opening vault. "Sublime pleasures have gone out of fashion. The world has become shallow, and our entertainments with it. Empty three-dimensional heads talking at one another or screaming."

"You sound like a professor, not a mobster."

"I considered a career in academia, but it is not a place that effects change easily. It is too cloistered, too austere. I wanted something more direct. I got into this business somewhat by accident. I simply found myself one day in a position of advantage, and in a moment of...let us call it epiphany, I seized the opportunity. I have been building upon that for almost thirty years."

"Thirty years! What, did you start in the womb?"

She smiled again, and each time the warmth grew. "You flatter me. You know as well as I that the richest women can look twenty-five well into their sixties."

"Darlin', my hat's off to your fountain of youth, because I was pretty sure last night you were about half my age."

"There were fifty-year-old women in Club Neo, still chasing their dreams of fame and celebrity because, for them, fortune is not enough."

That possibility had not occurred to him. "What would be enough for you?"

"To die knowing I had done something to stem the fatal tide of selfishness that has turned the human race into a plague of locusts, devouring the planet and each other until there is nothing left but to devour ourselves. I want to reverse some of the damage these oligarchs and plutocrats have done. I want to make a few things right."

"So said every asshole dictator in history." His voice sounded harsher than he meant it, but she did not appear to take offense.

"Well said, Horace. That very thought is something I wrestle with daily. What makes me better than Napoleon, Mao Zedong, Stalin, Hitler, Pol Pot, the entire Kim Dynasty? They were pragmatic, educated, idealistic. It is unlikely I shall ever be Queen of Planet Earth, but there are a few victories that could change the course of human history. Chief among those would be mounting the head of Yvgeny Mogilevich on a spear and feeding his corpse to sharks."

Her voice had remained measured and conversational throughout her entire speech, but at her last words, Horace glimpsed in her eyes a hatred so deep and hot and seething that a shudder went through him, as if inside the vault of her core was a blast furnace. Her hatred of Mogilevich was not vague or based on ambition or jealousy, as toward an obstacle, an irritant, or an opponent.

It was personal.

"Why do you hate him so much?" he said.

"He is my father."

Horace jumped across the cabin and faced her. "Jesus Christ!"

She took a sip of wine and remained still, regarding him.

His head spun. What had he gotten himself into? He paced back and forth, his gaze fixed upon her. His emotions blazed through jungles of anger, betrayal, fear. Her eyes followed him placidly. Mumbled oaths and curses poured out of him. For several minutes, he paced and she simply waited, unmoved, unmoving.

When his agitation subsided, she said, "If you are finished, may we continue? Please."

He hung against the bulkhead, feeling that the woman before him had just become the largest gaboon viper he had ever seen, coiled and torpid, but oh-so-deadly.

"Come now, Horace. That you now know this changes nothing."

"Oh, it doesn't?" His fists clenched.

"You knew what I am before you got onto this aircraft. All that has changed is that I let you have a glimpse of *who* I am."

"I'm in the middle of a goddamn family tiff! What, are you trying to get your inheritance early?"

"Hardly. He does not even know who I am. Perhaps if I get the opportunity to cut his throat, I will tell him as he bleeds out at my feet. My mother was one of his ravaged castoffs. There are doubtless many children in the world spawned from his foul seed. But she made sure I knew who my father was and what he had done to her." Her eyes misted for a moment, and another sip of wine went down harder than it should have. "To him, I am simply an acquaintance with whom it is profitable to do business."

"What kind of business is that?"

"You're asking a woman to divulge all of her secrets?" She laughed, and he wished that he didn't find it so goddamn appealing.

"What about the charges of human trafficking?"

Her eyebrows rose. "Oh, you've been doing your homework. It should come as no surprise to you at this point that Mogilevich owns half of the police forces across Europe and western Russia. You can call those charges sour grapes. He buys and sells women and little girls like cuts of meat. Poor women, refugees from the corporate wars, their starving children. Let us just say I commandeered a rather large shipment of women and little girls bound for the sex industry across North America and Asia. I stole them, made them disappear, and gave them new lives. Nevertheless, the whole affair was spun and twisted to look like *I* was the one doing the trafficking. None of this can be proven, of course."

"But he invites you to his parties."

"You know the old adage about keeping one's enemies closer, yes? He pretends that he does not know of my involvement. I pretend that he is not responsible for the murder and enslavement of millions. It is all a game of lies. Calculations and risk assessments. If we manage to kill Mogilevich, make no mistake—I stand to make untold sums of money by seizing as many pieces of his empire's corpse as I can. It took me years of maneuvering to be invited to this event. This is my third invitation to his blood sport. He is so secure in his power, he does not see me as a significant threat, which is exactly how I want it. To him, I am merely a beautiful upstart, a curiosity, like a supermodel who can do quantum mathematics."

"Why me? Why haven't you tried to kill him before now?"

"I have never been in the position before. Certainly I could have hired an assassin, but everything would have gone to Dmitri. But now, with Dmitri out of the picture, all bets are off, as they say."

"But why *me*?"

"You have nothing to lose and everything to gain if you succeed. *Everything*. We have not discussed this specifically, so allow me to lay it out for you. If we succeed, you will have a new heart, a real one grown from your own tissue. I will even see to the regeneration of your friend Lilly, if she lives long enough."

"That's very generous. But I want a couple more things."

A belly laugh rolled out of her. "A mafiya queen offers you the world, and you want the moon as well!"

"Not for me, you understand. Bunny. You said you have influence in certain circles. After the way you busted me out of jail, I'm guessing one of them is maybe the parole system."

She leaned closer, running fingers through her thick mane, eyes glinting.

"Bunny is a slicer with a huge chunk of data locked away somewhere she can't get to. I'm pretty sure that data would be very incriminating to certain people, but it's locked up and her parole officer is a corrupt trickle-dick. You want to change the world, you can start there."

An eyebrow went up at that. "I knew she was extraordinary. She and little Tina as well. Else I would have simply used my own people. She and I will talk. And what about your little rainbow friend? I presume you want something for her?"

He sighed a little. "I can't give her what she wants."

"And what's that?"

"Her father back." His words surprised him, not only with their abruptness, but also with their truth.

She considered this for a moment. "How ironic. I want mine atomized and all memory of him expunged from the history of humankind."

"Remind me not to get on your bad side."

"I would advise against it." She looked into him again with that unabashed discernment and intense curiosity. "I must say, Horace, very few men surprise me, but you do. I have met a few pit fighters. In a callous world, they are among the most callous. It is an effect of turning the greatest of human drama and tragedy—death—into a game. Human life has less and less value these days. But you, you care about people."

Horace sighed. "My whole life, there's been damn few for me to care about. We tend to die young. The women around the pit fighting scene tend not to be brainy types or stick-around types." He gave her a long look. "I got me a shitload of pit buddies, training buddies, and fuck buddies, but real friends are hard to come by, the kind who'd throw a death match for you, or face down a drone with you, or drive across the entire goddamn country just to see you." Surprise swept through him as his eyes teared. "Trouble is, there's just no telling who I'm going to care about."

At that moment, he noticed she was closer, almost touching him with her sleek calf. "And what if they don't care about you?"

"That's what usually happens, but it's never much mattered."

Another long moment passed as she seemed to ponder the implications of what he said. "Remind me not to get on your bad side."

He cracked a half smile. "I'd advise against it."

A tension appeared in his chest, like an invisible cord tugging him toward her. It was not something he expected, even as it took hold of him.

She looked down at his hand with an amused smile. "You resisted a remarkably long time."

"Wasn't sure I wanted to get involved with a hydra. Still not."

"Afraid I'll bite?"

"I don't mind a little biting. More like too much else on my mind."

"Your beautiful little dancer?"

He took a deep breath and let it out.

"Do you love her?"

"Too soon for that."

"You're afraid of the *L* word then."

"I'm not afraid of much."

Her voice turned playful. "There is much meaning we attach to that word. Much weight. Sometimes too much." She chuckled, a deep, genuine sound. "Who would have thought that Horace The Hammer Harkness was so sentimental?"

"Trust me, sister, it surprises me, too."

"I, on the other hand, lack sentimentality." Her fingers slipped into the collar of his brand-new silk shirt of glossy, textured black, stroked his neck. "For us, it is time to seal our bargain."

He huffed a little smile. "My word's not good enough?"

"Your word is not what I want." She slid closer and lifted a leg over him, straddling his lap.

There had been only a month of his entire life where one woman had held his undivided attention, and that was a lot of heartbreak ago. After last night with Lilly, she had been floating constantly at the verge of his thoughts, wandering into the spaces between crisis moments. As he sat there with Roxanne's warm flesh across his thighs, her heat growing against his crotch, her eyes gleamed with her unrefusable intention to take him. It was something she had decided to do. He was the gladiator, the slave; she, the noblewoman drawn to his power.

An image of Lilly, comatose in her hospital bed, flashed through his mind. Lilly stumbling on the stoop, not from poor footing but from tungsten razor blades perforating her chest cavity.

Lilly's fist slamming into his cheek.

Lilly's blood on his hands.

The sound of her voice as she cried his name, gasped his name, burbled his name.

Roxanne's hands slid up his chest, up the sides of his neck, behind his head, drawing herself closer to him, those luscious lips bending toward his.

She paused and raised his chin to look into her eyes. "Let me dispel the last of your qualms, Horace. Gods are not meant for only one lover. We pass through the world, taking what we want and, if we are benevolent, giving joy in return. There is so little joy in the world. Why deny ourselves? By this time tomorrow night, we will be either successful or dead. I do not intend to leave this world without us having fucked each other into oblivion."

He pushed her back. Horace Harkness was no one's slave. If she was going to use him, he would allow it—but on his own terms. "You're going to get me close enough to Mogilevich to stove in his fucking head."

Her eyes glittered. "Yes," she hissed.

He seized her head in both hands and kissed her, and instantaneously he felt the heat explode from her. Her firm shoulders were toned and silky. Her body was as firm and taut as any of the twenty-year-old pit girls he had bedded in decades past but steeped in the kind of experience no twenty-year-old possessed, the experience of loss and pain, great triumphs and ecstasies untold, pressing down against him as the supersonic wind whistled past outside and the universe filtered through the windows. His arms squeezed her to him, and the heat within them began to build.

A deeper, darker, colder intent germinated inside him. A woman like this would use him as long as she needed and then discard him. How many of her former lovers were now dead? She would use him to kill Yvgeny Mogilevich, and if he didn't survive the attempt, her grief would be slight. But he had a purpose, too, and he needed Roxanne Sukova to succeed. His entire life had been spent dealing in the two most primal kinds of currency—death and sex. Love was a luxury to be enjoyed when the hard shit was done.

With an uninterruptible hour and a half before landing, they took their time. Clothes peeled away, piece by languorous piece. Naked, they danced with each other to slow techno-jazz. His fingers slid across matching circular scars on her back and abdomen, three sets of them, a long scar below her left shoulder blade. In a world where scars could be erased like an errant pencil mark, she wore her wounds like badges.

Her hair gleamed in the soft light, brushed his chest and belly as she leaned against him. Her dark eyes glimmered like polished onyx. Her erect nipples caressed his belly, the soft swell of her breasts pressing against him, the downy thatch of pubic hair stroking his thigh.

As they swayed together, his penis surged and relaxed against her belly in unhurried waves. He ran his fingers through her luxuriant raven hair and felt a narrow band of stiff plastic encircling the base of her skull. What abilities lurked within the wetware buried in her brain he would guess at later.

Her hands played across him deftly, softly, like a warm breeze, squeezing his buttocks, up and down his hips, cupping his scrotum, stroking him. Conscious thoughts drowned in a cauldron of primal desire.

She gasped as he shoved her onto the couch, her expression shifting to a feral, hungry grin. When he stepped up to her, she produced a condom, put it on with her mouth, then turned away and bared her haunches for him.

That was how he took her, seizing her hips and driving into her. Fast, then slow, harder, then softer, using his decades of experience to prolong the act, squeezing every last dram of pleasure from her, into her, and she squeezed him back with her deepest core.

As their bodies succumbed to the other's want, deep shuddering breaths exploded from her but she did not cry out, as if she were bottling up that energy and applying it elsewhere.

When their bodies separated, they sagged back into the couch, sheened with sweat and each other.

In the silent, diminishing radiance, beside this spent goddess with her eyes half-lidded, lips parted, his thoughts turned unbidden toward the future.

From here on out, pleasure would be a difficult thing to come by.

CHAPTER TWENTY-SEVEN

At 6:00 a.m., the desert chilled them as they walked from the gangway of the hyperjet to the waiting limousine. The sun was an imminent emergence on the horizon, painting sky and desert with broad swaths of color.

Horace honestly had never expected to return to Vegas alive. Across town he had a ratty one-room apartment that contained the scraps of his belongings, a change of underwear, even a couple of hand weapons if the Russians hadn't tossed or torched it. He wished he hadn't lost Gaston's electro-fiber dagger in the drone attack. Might come in handy where they were going.

He hadn't owned a home for many years, not since he'd had to sell his palatial house, purchased at the high point of his career, to pay for his fruitless, globe-trotting search for Amanda and their son. Since then, he had bounced from one shabby roach motel to the next, even living for a while in an old school bus converted into a camper—a vehicle he'd had to abandon when the ancient diesel engine had thrown a piston—during a stretch of time when a particularly vicious gash on his leg needed to heal, and there had been no sponsored regeneration available, and he had had to choose between food and repairs.

He'd gotten used to leaving things—and people—behind. Might be a hard habit to break.

Tina and Bunny eyed Horace and Roxanne with the expressions of those who sensed the waves of carnal afterglow emanating from their companions—a mix of envy and embarrassment, plus a wistful sadness in Bunny's case and a touch of accusation in Tina's.

Roxanne behaved as if nothing at all had happened, as if "sealing the bargain" equated with a handshake, and that suited him just fine.

As they crossed the tarmac, he pulled out his netlink and made a call. "Pick up, Jack, goddammit."

The lack of answer was unsurprising at this hour. Jack's days tended to start around two in the afternoon. So Horace left a brief message telling Jack to call him.

When they were all in the back of the limo, Roxanne pulled out a datapad. "Bunny," she said, "You will be my driver tomorrow evening. You're well-acquainted with traffic patterns and interfacing with the limousine's control package. The one we'll be using is being fitted with an enhanced communication suite that will increase your reach and data transfer rate."

"Will it have cup holders?" Bunny said.

"Cup holders?"

"For my tea."

Roxanne laughed. "Of course. And there's one other thing. Horace asked that I look into having the lock on your AI removed."

Bunny's eyes bulged. "What, really? Just like that? You can do that?"

"Your parole officer will receive the message when he arrives at his office today. Whether he acts on this directive or ignores it like most corrupt officials playing petty power games, we do not know yet."

"Golly, thanks!"

"I want a fully functional slicer, not a crippled one," Roxanne said. "And as for you." She turned to Tina. "You and I have things to discuss as well. Your identity will have been flagged as a member of Trask's organization. You will need temporary facial reconstruction also, and a finger prosthetic like Horace's."

Tina sat up straighter. "I like my face! *And* the way I walk! I don't want some brain-slicing chip fucking up my coordination."

"I like your face, too. Very much, in fact. But it's that or they will put a bullet in it the moment you walk through the door."

"Oh."

"Besides, assuming another identity, becoming faceless, wasn't that the ancient ninja's highest aspiration? To remain unseen in plain view?"

Tina grinned a little at that.

Roxanne said, "The chip will not interfere with your coordination.

It will give you the gait and posture of a runway model. We will have to go shopping. You are going to be my date."

"Your date!" Tina sat up straight again. "I thought I was going to get to wear some cool suit and shades or something and walk around next to this bruiser." She thumbed at Horace.

"Oh, my dear, you are far too beautiful to be a simple bodyguard. You would draw more eyes in that capacity, and probably draw more eyes to Horace."

A flush spread across Tina's cheeks at the way Roxanne's eyes burned into her. "I thought you were straight." Tina glanced between Roxanne and Horace.

"I am whatever I need to be," Roxanne said.

"But what about protection, armor?" Tina said.

"Unfortunately not an option for those of us who must dress scantily. For us, it will be evening gowns only. The advantage is that we will be perceived as minimal threats."

Suddenly Roxanne flung her datapad at Tina's nose. With lightning reflexes, Tina's hand flashed up and caught it on edge. A split second later, she was across the cabin and shoving Roxanne flat against the seat, datapad raised like a cleaver.

Roxanne held up her hands. "Forgive me. It was a test."

Tina bit her lip, scowling, and edged back to the seat beside Bunny. "That wasn't very nice."

With fluid grace and core strength, Roxanne righted herself. "Until this is over, I am the nicest person you are likely to meet."

In that movement, Horace saw real physical training in Roxanne, much like Vincent's. Perhaps all gangsters thought it wise to train for combat. Horace wondered again what stories her scars told, and how many more scars were invisible.

Outside the windows, the airport dissolved into familiar shreds of encroaching desert. But they were not headed for the Strip yet. On either side of them, a dusty, decrepit expanse of trailer parks lay staked out in the desert to die.

"Say," he said, "where we going?"

"To see my surgeon," Roxanne said. "You did not think we could do this in a hospital, did you?"

"Does he have running water?" Horace said.

It was not among the trailer parks that the limousine eased to a stop, but before the front gate of a chain-link fence surrounding a storage facility. Hundreds of storage cells lay behind endless rows of orange, steel garage doors. Tumbleweeds and dust filtered down these man-made arroyos. The gate creaked open, and the hover-drive kicked up storms of grit as the car slid through the opening.

Tina said, "You're going to be cutting on my *face* in an environment like this?"

Roxanne said, "We do what we must. If we are compromised by a single camera with a tapped feed, we'll all be dead and this will all be for nothing."

Tina's face scrunched, and she crossed her arms tight.

Bunny's eyes fixed on Roxanne. "This is not just a storage facility." Roxanne just tilted her head in acknowledgment of Bunny's perception.

The limousine stopped outside a larger building with a flaking sign that read *CLIMATE CONTROLLED STORAGE*, waited for a towering garage door to scroll open, and eased inside. The closing door sealed them into a cavernous, concrete garage. Signs in six languages covered the walls with protocols on how to use the storage units.

The air in here was comfortably cool and dry, with only lingering traces of the dust that followed them inside. A sleek, red sports car, gleaming with fresh polish, sat nearby. The metallic ticking of its cooling power plant echoed in the yawning space.

Roxanne led them to a heavy steel door in a cinder-block wall, passed her wrist near a reader, and opened the door. More long hallways of narrow steel doors, painted orange like those outside. The air here was cooler still and smelled of industrial cleaners.

Up a freight elevator to the third floor, down another long hallway into a remote corner, and finally before a door identical to all the others, Roxanne waved her wrist past another reader, and the door slid upward with a rattling clank.

Inside was a cell, perhaps four meters by eight. Plastic sheeting swathed the walls and floor. Air scrubbers hummed somewhere nearby. A surgical station occupied the center of the chamber, beside which stood a tall, pale man and a short, plump, dark-skinned woman, both dressed in scrubs. The man was arranging instruments on a tray, the woman working the holographic interface to the regenestation that occupied most of the far wall.

"Doctor," Roxanne said.

The short woman approached, her gaze climbing Horace with growing amazement. "Ma'am," she said.

Roxanne introduced Doctor Athena Gilchrist as "one of the best reconstructive surgeons no one has ever heard of."

The doctor grinned at her. "We go back a ways, don't we, ma'am?"

Bunny's eyes fluttered for a moment until her awareness returned to the moment with a crinkled brow. "Good shielding," she said to Roxanne. "Good netsec, too."

"Nut sack?" Tina said.

"Netsec," Bunny said, rolling her eyes. "Network security. I can't get anything in or out of here."

"And neither can anyone else," Roxanne said. "As I said, precautions. Now, shall we get down to business?"

"Of course," said the doctor. "Who's first?"

"This one," Roxanne said, gesturing to Tina. "We have things to do later."

Tina swallowed hard and blanched.

The doctor said, "Don't worry, little girl—" Tina's face twisted at that, "—I am, in fact, an actual surgeon." She gestured to the man behind her. "This tall drink of milk is my nurse. I graduated from Harvard Medical School, and I've done something like two thousand procedures like this. I help Roxy from time to time, when the cause suits me."

"That many people need to run from their face?" Tina said.

"That's the world we live in," the doctor said. "Now, come on. We're on a strict timetable."

In the harsh fluorescence, Tina's eyes glimmered with controlled fear.

"It'll be all right, kid," Horace said. "We'll still like you if your nose falls off."

When Horace woke up that afternoon, the tall, pale nurse reconfigured the operating platform into a reclining chair. He was cold, clothed now in only a sterile gown.

Horace's face felt thick and wrong. His nose looked swollen, like he'd just been walloped with a two-by-four. He grimaced and worked his lips—at least they felt normal. Trying to raise his hands, he found them clasped within thick, padded straps. His eyes watered at the sensation of something in them.

"One moment," said the nurse as he unbuckled the straps.

Horace touched the tender flesh of his face.

The nurse held up a mirror and showed Horace a stranger, a man so profoundly changed that he checked to see if the mirror was real.

"Good work, right?" said the nurse.

"That is one ugly motherfucker." No trace of any incision remained. His brows were heavier, his nose thicker, wider, even appearing to have been broken a few times, his cheekbones bulkier. "What happened to my baby-blues?"

"Brown contact lenses. Check this out." The nurse pressed a button on his datapad.

Horace jerked in surprise as:

HELLO, MR. HARKNESS

appeared in stereoscopic 3-D in big red letters, hovering before him as if floating on air. "These are Heads-Up-Display lenses. Ms. Sukova requested them."

"Might come in handy." Horace eased himself out of the chair, still feeling his face. "Where is everybody? How's Tina?"

"Her operation went splendidly. I believe Ms. Sukova said something about taking her shopping. A car is waiting for you downstairs."

Horace scrutinized himself in the mirror from a variety of angles. It was a strange sensation, looking out from another man's skin. His tattoos had been covered with synth-skin.

He stood and took a couple of steps, suddenly conscious that his entire body felt *wrong*. His shoulders felt hunched, his arms hanging in unfamiliar ways, his legs bowed. Some normally resting muscles felt oddly tight. "Whoa!"

"That's the chip feeding into your motor cortex. Posture and gait are like fingerprints to a sophisticated recognition system. Right now, you don't even walk like yourself. It mostly works on automatic movements, like walking—"

"Will I be able to fight?"

"Certainly. Your muscle memory is still there. The chip works mainly in low-intensity situations."

Smooth blue text appeared in his HUD.

HORACE, THIS IS BUNNY. ARE YOU UP AND AROUND?

"Yes."

GOOD, GET DRESSED AND COME OUT TO THE CAR. WE NEED TO TALK.

Bunny was leaning against the limo in the cavernous entry garage, arms crossed, chewing on her lip when Horace emerged from behind the steel door to the storage bays. The lights in the garage were dimmed to just a meager few banks of fluorescence.

"Where's Roxanne and Tina?" he asked.

"Shopping. They took the Ferrari." She appraised him for a long moment. "Not bad. I mean, your face is really well known, but the change is profound."

"And I walk like a caveman now."

"Not much change there."

"Funny. What's up?"

She gestured with her head toward a steel fire door and led him outside. The sun approached the horizon, and the day's heat still rippled the air in every direction. The dusty, windswept alleys of the storage facility somehow gave him an unpleasant tingle. Too many this, too much that, endless chambers full of stuff its owners were unwilling to ditch or recycle but were also unwilling to jettison. A limbo for too many people's excess junk.

And a cover for illicit dealings.

Bunny pointed to the downtown skyline in the distance. "See that?"

He squinted. "See what? I'm on the verge of needing bifocals to take a piss."

"Those gnats swarming around downtown."

"You mean drones?"

"Yeah, hundreds of them. Media drones, police drones, corporate surveillance drones, and even some bigger ones that look suspiciously like our friends from Buffalo. I've been popping outside occasionally trying to get a lay of the land, contact some friends, and the networks are log-jammed with drone communication traffic."

"I've never noticed this before."

"Well, drones are so commonplace that people don't even think about them, except for the conspiracy-nutjob-crazies. Sometimes you have to step back and pay attention."

"So what does it mean?"

"How the heck should I know? Aside from the fact that we need to keep our heads down. You remember when I said I wasn't sure I wanted to be your friend?"

"Yeah."

"I'm sure now. I don't." Her voice quavered with barely restrained fear.

"I don't blame you."

He encircled her with one arm, pulled her against his side, but she wormed away.

"No, really," she said. "I'm not doing this for you." Anger found its way into her voice. "In fact, I didn't want to come at all. But Miss Sukova is...very persuasive."

"What deal did she make with you?"

"She said she would help me get my kids back. With my lock off, I can free them, protect them."

"That would be great." Somehow this made him feel better, less guilty at accepting her help. Bunny was here because she had a dog in the fight.

"The best." She let out a long shuddering breath. "Now, leave me alone for a while."

CHAPTER TWENTY-EIGHT

Roxanne had booked them an ostentatious hotel room at Caesar's to rest and prepare. Horace hadn't been able to afford even a cot under the stairs here in over a decade, must less this marble-tiled, diamond-encrusted suite that would have made the asshole of every tin-pot CEO in South America clench with envy. Shame that he wouldn't get to catch any sleep here.

But what the hell? If this was to be his last night on earth, might as well drown in the luxury of the moment.

After a long, hot shower, he stared at his new face through the fog in the bathroom mirror. With the contact lenses, he didn't even look like a distant relative. The contact lenses were uncomfortable, unnatural. He kept half-expecting messages to pop up in his vision like thirty-meter billboards; it felt like an invisible leash tying him to Roxanne's hand.

A chill trickled down his arms, and he flexed his hard, meaty hands and forearms. A strange feeling to look like someone else, someone who had never been born, this massive, thick-armed bull-ape, faster than a speeding right hook, hairier than a locomotive, able to leap tall curbs in a single bound.

The box on his chest beaded with moisture. The single dose of Go Juice remaining might well be his last hurrah.

And if he died tomorrow, would his body ever be identified? Would word ever get out that Horace Harkness had met the Darkness once and for all? Or would he just be one of millions of unsolved disappearances pickled in a drum of vodka somewhere?

Wrapped in a towel fluffier than an angora sheep, he stepped into his bedroom, toes luxuriating in the thick pile carpet, in time for a knock on the door.

He cracked the door and surveyed the knockout woman looking up at him with her cat-green eyes. Brilliant auburn hair gleamed and tumbled over lithe white shoulders and a ruby-red mini-dress that fit her like a sheer silk stocking.

"I didn't order a hooker," he said.

"Fuck you, Gonad the Barbarian," she said. "Why do you always have to treat me like a sexual object?"

She had already been incredibly fluid and graceful, but now her movements incorporated a profound sensuality that Horace found difficult to tear his eyes away from. She moved like Roxanne now, and had gone from bombshell to nuclear warhead.

"Why do you always show up when I'm mostly naked?" He stepped away from the door and let it swing open.

"A deep-seated compulsion toward explosive nausea. You look different."

"So do you. I like redheads. On second thought, maybe I did order a hooker."

The smooth roundness of her cheeks had been sharpened with higher cheekbones and a chin cleft. Her button nose had been lengthened, her lips thickened. The full-sleeve tattoos covering both arms were now concealed by synth-skin. "That's 'million-dollar escort' to you. Double that because you're uglier than ever."

"And worth every penny."

She blushed.

He let the sentiment linger between them for a moment, then said, "Did you and Roxy have a pleasant shopping trip?"

"If by pleasant, you mean ogled by every swinging dick within a two-mile radius and forced to shop at the swankiest boutiques on the planet, the kind that charge more to sniff their leather than I make in a year."

He turned away from the door and moved toward the duffel bag that contained his meager supply of clothing. Facing away from her, he doffed the towel, snatched up a pair of underwear and stepped into them. "It's a good thing you like the attention."

He smirked at the gasp of outrage behind him. "Why you always gotta bust my chops?" she asked.

"Like to dish it out but can't take it?"

Her voice grew nearer. "Seriously, they served us Dom Perignon while we sat there in our underwear—well, *I* had underwear."

"Nice visual." He pulled his pants on to conceal the bulge that swelled at the thought of half-naked Tina and Roxanne sipping champagne together.

"You're hopeless." Something tinged her voice that wasn't playful banter, but a deeper, harsher judgment.

"No, just unashamed. Got something you want to say?" He zipped up and faced her. The sensational luxury of the silk trousers caressing his legs made him appreciate Roxanne's choice of tailors.

His challenge pushed her back on her heels for a moment, and her new mouth worked some words around before they came out. "You did all this," she said, "went to all this trouble, practically destroyed your life, destroyed *my* life, Bunny's, Trask's, and everybody else's for this *stripper* you're supposedly sweet on. And now while she's in a coma—also on account of you—you're off fucking somebody else?"

"I'm not fucking her at this moment."

"You know what I mean!"

"And you have no idea what *I* mean."

"Then enlighten me, Don Juan de Asshole!"

"You got your head in all kinds of books. I'll bet you even read romance novels. A bunch of naïve, romantic bullshit."

"This is not about my choice of reading." She crossed her arms.

"No, it's about the fact that you don't know a business transaction when you see one. Roxanne is using me. I'm using her."

"Methinks thou doth protest too much."

"I have no idea what you just said, and you have *no idea where I've been, what I've done!*" The swell of emotion, a wave, a lifetime of blood and sex and pain like a ragged exposed nerve, the kind of pain that had to be embraced like its own kind of twisted lover, surprised him. "You got no right to judge me."

She stepped back from him, wary but unafraid.

He took a deep breath and steadied his voice. In that moment, he was struck by how young she was, how inexperienced. A few years ago, before he had dropped almost completely off the map, he'd been bedding pit girls younger than she was. So why did she seem so much more innocent and naive? "When was the last time you got laid?"

"None of your business!"

"Exactly."

She paced and stewed at this for a few moments.

"My whole life," he said, "I've been nothing but a piece of meat. So is she, and she knows it, too. I've seen Lilly put raw vagina in the faces of a hundred different guys so she can pay her rent. Unlike most people, I *own* it. So call me a little jaded."

"So goddamn jaded that you went off and fucked somebody while the woman you supposedly love—"

"I never said I loved her. I ask myself all the time if I really know what that amounts to. Does anybody ever? Suppose I do? What of it?"

She flailed clenched fists. "Then what the *fuck* are you even doing this for!"

He took a deep breath, let it out, took another, and started slowly, his voice soft. "Every time I walk into the pit, it might be a friend I'm facing, somebody I drank with, joked with, trained with, chased pussy with. And my job is to kill him, and his job is to kill me. And sometimes he doesn't come back. And for doing what I do, I get a huge payoff and women dropping from the trees. Feelings cause trouble."

He clutched the box on his chest. "Lilly is only the second woman who lights my fire all the way to the ground. But even if by some miracle we survive all this, I'm fifteen years older than she is, and the last time I saw her, she punched me in the face. How long you think that's gonna last? The one and only closest thing I've had to a relationship disappeared with my son inside her. That poster you've got on your wall is more than I have of her."

"Must have been your sparkling personality." Her words slashed across his face.

He looked at her for a long moment as the guilt welled up in his throat. Then he turned away so she couldn't see what his face was about to do.

Her voice softened. "Over the line?"

He swallowed hard and sat on the bed, let his voice go quiet. "The clock is ticking before they shut her off. You and me and Roxanne and Bunny, we could all be hacked to little bits by this time tomorrow. I've been a walking dead man for twenty-eight fucking years. I care about who I care about, and I do what I do, and that's all there is."

He felt her eyes on him for a long time.

"Look," he said, "kid—"

"Call me kid one more time, and I'll eat your balls for breakfast."

"Fine. 'Overconfident kid.' You think I'm some big romantic teddy bear. You think it's all so simple. You think there's a happily ever after. I'm sorry I don't subscribe to your little chivalrous, romantic notions about whose penis should go where. Truth is, I'd fuck Trask if it got me within range of Mogilevich."

"There's a disturbing visual..."

"There's no such thing as happily ever after, so all I got is happily right now." The words kept rolling out of him, surprising him in their volume and earnestness. "Heard a man say once that every love story ever told ends in heartbreak and tragedy, and I can vouch for that. There's about fourteen million 'ifs' between *now* and Lilly and me riding off into the sunset, and every one of them has a toe-tag with our names hanging from it."

Out in the common area of the suite, the doorbell rang with a warm vibrato.

Horace headed for the outer door, forcing Tina to step aside. In the foyer, he touched the intercom pad. "Yeah, who is it?"

A bored male voice replied, "Delivery for Ms. Roxanne Smith."

"Delivery from who?"

"Harmony Tech Industries."

"Leave it out there and shove off."

"Jesus, man, you gotta sign for it!"

"I said, fuck off!"

"Look, dickhead. My goggles can read your biosignature from here. You're a big sonofabitch, what, 170 centimeters? If I had nefarious deeds planned, I would have shot you through the door. Now open up. This is my last run tonight."

Horace opened the door, reached out, snatched a fistful of the man's jacket, and yanked him off his feet and into the room.

The man yelped and stumbled, but Tina caught him in a wristlock that cranked his yelp into a squeal. "Fuck! They don't pay me enough for this shit!"

In the hallway outside was a robotic cart laden with blockish aluminum cases. A red light flashed on the front of the cart, and a flat, electronic voice said, "Release him or security will be notified."

"Yeah!" the delivery man said. "Ow!" The name embroidered on his jacket read *Mitul.*

Horace sighed. "Fine. Let him go."

Tina released him, grinned, and kissed him on the cheek.

Mitul shrugged away from Tina and straightened his jacket. "The fuck is wrong with you people?" He wore a baseball cap and dark metallic goggles that wrapped around his head. Without question, such headwear would incorporate full netlink feeds.

A moment of panic sliced through Horace until he remembered that he was not Hammer Harkness anymore.

After a moment to further compose himself, Mitul gestured to the robot. "Come in, Mippy."

The cart hummed through the door and stopped in the foyer, the red light on its console still flashing.

"Stand down, Mippy," Mitul said.

The red light turned amber.

Mitul snatched a datapad from the top of the load and handed it to Horace. "Index fingerprint in the blue box."

Horace had not yet attached the prosthetic fingertip. Tina stepped in before his hesitation became too glaring, took the datapad, applied her fingertip, and handed it back.

Mitul waited for the screen to flash green and accept her ID. When it did, he glanced at her. "Thank you, Ms. Welch. Mippy, unload."

The robot's payload platform hummed with hydraulics and servos. Fifteen seconds later, the heavy-looking cases had been deposited on the floor.

"And a good night to you, Ms. Welch. And you, dickhead." Mitul pulled his cap tighter onto his head and stalked out. In the hallway, he said, "Mippy, come."

The robot followed him like a puppy.

Horace shut the door.

Tina fixed him with a simmering glare. "Mitul was an astute judge of character."

"Duly noted."

The cases contained, gently nestled in black, feather-soft foam, the kind of hardware that even Horace found difficult to wrap his mind around. Some of it was slathered in warning labels and blood-red tape that read "WARNING: DANGEROUS!" and big, black skull-and-crossbones.

The armor grabbed his attention first. Conceptually similar to his pit fighter armor, this military-grade combat armor would cover him from toe to skull. It resembled dark gray rubber, almost like a wet suit, but with a more cloth-like feel and a number of stiff but bendable plates encasing the abdomen, back, shoulders, thighs, and shins. A battery pack about two centimeters deep was spread just under the shoulder blades.

While Tina pored over the manuals, Horace dug into the cases like they were boxes of Christmas toys and Halloween candy. Knowing how dangerous the electro-fiber dagger had been, he touched nothing without first identifying what it was. However, he did try on the armor immediately. It fit him like a smooth, silky glove, reasonably comfortable to wear under clothes. The chest plate was uncomfortably tight over the box on his chest, but there was nothing to be done about it. The weight of the battery pack felt thick on his back, hugging his ribcage just under his shoulder blades.

As Tina read the manuals, sitting cross-legged on the floor in workout pants, she cackled in almost diabolical glee. Over and over, she said, "Oh, my god, you won't believe this shit!"

After he had finished zipping and buckling the armor into place, she stepped up to him and punched him in the kidney, hard, a blow that would have doubled him over—except that the armor instantly hardened under her blow. The armor's fibers had contracted and hardened instantaneously.

She stepped back, shaking out her hand. "Ow. So, yeah, it's reactive armor. The fibers are like muscle fibers that contract when it senses an incoming projectile or blow. The battery pack is recharged continually by movement and bio-electricity. You could wear it for weeks without a break."

He grinned. "Good thing the aft end is easily ventilated."

Her face scrunched up, and she sighed. "Dude humor."

He grabbed his crotch and grinned wider. "There's even a codpiece, little sister." The armor's crotch comprised a rigid cup similar to what athletes wore, hinged for easy access.

Tina grabbed a poker from the fireplace, approached him, and swung at his crotch, hard. With a meaty *thwack*, he felt the distinct impact of the blow, but the force of it was dissipated over his entire pelvis and the poker formed a *U*. "The manual says it's effective against bullets, flechettes, and some types of rail gun ammunition, with limited protection against vibro- and electro-fiber weapons."

"I can live with that."

Her face screwed tighter again. "And I'll be walking around in there practically naked."

"You can still back out."

"You need me."

"I don't need anybody."

"A lie, and you know it."

She was right, and he indeed knew it. But pride that went all the way to the bone squirmed and chafed at the notion. Since leaving Las Vegas, he'd been depending on the goodwill of strangers. He couldn't help thinking soon he would have to pay the piper.

"Fine," he said.

"What did you say?"

"I said, fine. Don't push it."

"Fine," she said. "Next toy is an electro-fiber sword. Camouflaged to look like a small flashlight. That baby is mine."

"Pray, share with the class."

She opened a box and several layers of packaging to reveal a palm-sized flashlight with a flat black casing. She pointed it carefully away from herself and thumbed the button. With an electric snap, a thin, gray blade sprang forth, about as long as her arm. As she twisted it and flicked it in her hand, the blade disappeared when viewed on edge.

Her brows rose in appreciation. "Light as a feather." The bent poker was leaning against one of the metal shipping cases. A deft flick of her wrist, a metallic clink, and the poker fell into two pieces, neatly bisected. Her grin spread like a sunrise. "Holy shit!"

"Yeah, and you could even take off your own leg with it."

"Stuff it, Grandpa. I've done more training with a sword than even you have."

"What's next on Santa's naughty list? Any vibro-cleavers in there?"

"Hah! Check this out." She handed him two black bracers that looked like leather. They integrated perfectly with the forearms of the armor. "Neuro-sensors in the cuff. In the right bracer, flex your fingers just so and you have electro-fiber blades. Won't show up on a metal detector or scanner."

"I'll have to make sure not to flex when I'm picking my nose."

"Gah! Must you?"

"Yeah, sometimes. You know, when they're crusty and stuck in the hair."

She mimed a retch.

"You have delicate sensibilities for a ninja. Would you like me to test your bath water for you? Fluff your pillow?"

"Fuck you, Jeeves. I'm still a female. If we degenerate into poop humor, you can read this yourself."

"Is there anything long range in there? Plasma cannon in a compact? Mini-nuke in a netlink?" He set about fixing the bracers to his wrists.

"Which brings us to your left bracer. A one-shot, electro-fiber *shuriken,* with a range of twenty meters. Good lord, this lady has a fetish for hardware."

He almost said, *She does indeed like her wares hard*, but in light of his earlier conversation with Tina, he refrained.

She apparently sensed him holding back and fixed him with a look not of disdain, but of thoughtful realization.

"What now?" he said.

"You're acting pretty saucy tonight, even for you."

"You feel that? That's being alive, little sister. I feel this way before every match."

She nodded. "I do feel it. Samurai used to train for a state of mind where they already believed themselves dead. Every day after that was borrowed time, on loan from their lord. Ninja had that, too, but they were a little more pragmatic about it."

He recognized his own speech to the fighters to let go of their fear of death. He and Tina had come to the same crossroads of philosophy by wildly different paths.

"When I was living on the street..."

"After your dad died."

Her eyes flicked toward him once, then she picked up the electrofiber sword again and focused her gaze there. "The days I got away with the craziest, most outlandish, most brazen shit were those days when I did it because there was nothing else for me to do. My life was already over. It's a fine line between this kind of freedom and sheer, suicidal despair. There's an old Zen saying, 'While you yet live, become a dead person. Then, do as you like.' God, the crazy shit I did."

"So just don't try to seduce me before Roxanne gets here. I'm spent." He gave her his best deadpan face.

She just stared at him for a moment.

She was either going to be really pissed at him for that one, or...

An irrepressible snicker bubbled out of her that cascaded into a full guffaw. "Ah, Horace. Ah, the humanity!"

CHAPTER TWENTY-NINE

Horace The Hammer Harkness did not reside in the mirror anymore. As he applied the prosthetic tip to his finger, he could even fool a basic fingerprint and DNA scan now. With his identity concealed, he felt secure enough to amble out onto the balcony, feeling like a silverback gorilla walking upright, such was the bodily disorientation. He gazed down over the Strip, that bejeweled explosion of extravagance and decadence that defied the cold desert night with gaudy promises, manufactured excitement, and illusions of life. In the distance, the great domed hulk of the Coliseum blazed its spotlights toward the stars. A world of time and distance existed between this moment and his night in the Coliseum a week ago.

Tonight, there would be no spots, no showmanship, no audience, no pumping up the crowd and giving them what they came for—at least not of a kind in his experience—nothing to expect except raw, untamed, unplanned combat and death. On second thought, perhaps it was all showmanship—roles to play, deceptions to maintain until the proper moment, but only for a small, specialized audience. With a thought of the impressive supply of hardware back inside, there would indeed be spots.

The synth-skin made his flesh tingle as it tried to bond to wounds that weren't there, or maybe it was the fact that his blood felt full of quicksilver. A painkiller had dulled the pounding beat of all the wounds of the last week—gunshots, laser wounds, contusions, lacerations, and deep, throbbing bruises.

He paced and paced, took a swig straight from the crystal decanter of Courvoisier on the bar, his brain spinning through a litany of unhelpful thoughts. His heart could blow a gasket half a second before putting a blade into Yvgeny Mogilevich's neck.

Bunny emerged from her room. "Roxanne is on the way." Her voice fluttered, and she wrung her hands like they were sodden dish rags.

Clothed now in a new suit of nondescript dark gray with armor underneath, Horace stood over her and saw the awe, longing, and fear seeping from every pore in her face.

"Any words of encouragement, Mr. He-Man?" she said.

"Who are you today, Bunny or the White Rabbit?"

"It's been a long time since anybody called me White Rabbit. White Rabbit's running legs are still amputated, just bloody stumps."

"Rabbits got some nasty teeth."

"Maybe my metaphor is backward. I can run, but with the lock on, I can't fight."

"Knowing that you're gonna be out there watching over us almost makes me think we have a hope. You saved us from that drone."

"I did do that. If the lock doesn't come off in time, I'll still do what I can do. But what I'm afraid of is that Mogilevich's place will be a big netsec dead zone like Roxanne's storage facility. That once you go in, you'll be cut off, and I'll be stuck in the parking lot, blind and deaf. And that if it does go all sideways, I won't see them coming to put a bullet in my head."

"If I die, you can have all my stuff."

A snicker cracked the brittle fear in her face. "Gee, thanks. Whatever shall I do with a matchbox that big?"

"Charge admission. 'The final remains of a once-great star!' Someone somewhere will remember me."

"I'll remember you."

The air in the car vibrated with pent-up emotion as Horace shut the door behind him and eased into the seat beside Roxanne. If anything, she looked more beautiful in a tantalizing burgundy evening gown, a velvety confection that set his memory afire. But there was no time to think about that anymore.

Roxanne's eyes burned with a firm resolve as she went through a checklist of preparations. She gave Bunny the destination, and Bunny took her place in the driver's seat. Tina settled herself across from them, a knot of barely controlled tension, squirming in her designer couture gown.

He adjusted himself, trying to settle into the armor. Without it, the silk suit would have felt like warm butter against his skin, but with the extra thickness of the stiff plates and battery pack, it felt like flimsy film wrapping an oddly-angled stone.

As the limousine picked up speed, the lights of the Strip slid past, painting Horace and the women with great splashes of brilliant color, then grew sparser until nothing but desert night surrounded the car. The crumbling remains of Highway 95 stretched out before them, but its roughness could not penetrate their cushion of air.

Roxanne checked a small flashlight that looked remarkably like the one in Tina's clutch purse. "Mogilevich had a palace built on Bonanza Peak. It's become quite a housing development over the last thirty years. Las Vegas' highest rollers have houses up there. The views are breathtaking."

"Didn't that used to be a national park or something? Protected land?" Horace said.

"When was the last time you visited a national park, Horace?"

"When I was a kid, I guess. Parents took me to Yellowstone. Never been the camping type, except for those times I had to sleep in my school bus."

Roxanne shrugged. "'For the people' was an idea promulgated by environmental crazies and communists such as Theodore Roosevelt and Woodrow Wilson. Or so the oligarchs would have people believe, every time they seize another chunk of once-protected land for themselves."

Northwest of the city, the limousine turned southwest off the highway and headed toward a snow-dusted, moon-silvered peak skirted in the black foam of pine forest. Along the highway lay endless kilometers of rocks and sand, cacti and mesquite and Joshua trees, a hellish inferno during the day, but tonight a placid, diamond-dusted plain surrounded by distant mountains. Even in the climate-controlled limousine, the scents of the desert filtered inside, dust and desert flowers, the earth as it cooled, and as the mountain drew nearer in the video monitor, dewy pines.

"We've picked up a couple of drones," Bunny said over the intercom.

Horace tensed.

"Military types," Bunny said. "Cousins to our friends from Buffalo."

"Does this happen every time?" he said.

Roxanne straightened in her seat. "No. Those drones cost fortunes. Mogilevich's resources seem to have expanded over the last couple of years."

Tina's grin simmered with malice. "Or maybe we've made him nervous by still being alive."

Bunny's voice came back to them. "Transponder codes, sent.... Green light to approach."

Horace let out the breath he hadn't realized he'd been holding.

Tina slapped him half-playfully on the thigh. "What happened to being okay with the walking dead man thing?"

"A drone missile from out of nowhere is not the same as facing down someone in the pit," he said. "When you can see their eyes, smell their sweat, and know whether they're gonna stand against you or fold."

"Point taken," Tina said.

On the video screen at the front of the limousine's cabin, enhanced to be as bright as day, they were passing through patches of strip mall, tourist shops, and retail outlets that had beaten back the natural landscape on the way up the mountain. Thickening pine forest had been chopped away from the road to make room for fast-food drive-thrus, clothing stores, restaurants, the forest relegated to distant clumps of dark-green foam. He tried to envision what this mountain, this rocky ripple in the fabric of the desert plains, might have looked like in its natural state, but he could not.

The lights of other cars were visible before and behind, a train of stained, tarnished affluence congregating at the behest of the biggest, meanest, richest dog in the junkyard.

The road wound and switched back, twisting to ever greater heights. Horace's ears registered the steadily changing elevation.

"How many people attend shindigs like this?" he said.

Roxanne poured herself a glass of merlot from the bar. "Last year, thirty-three invitees, plus guests and bodyguards. Everyone is very well-behaved, although there is always a certain amount of primate posturing and chest-thumping."

Tina said, "I think us dames should just do away with the Y-chromosome altogether. Wouldn't the world be a much nicer place?"

Roxanne leaned forward and raised her glass with a brilliant smile. "I *completely* agree, Ambrosia."

"Right, we're getting into character now," Tina said, straightening her evening gown.

Half an hour later, the limo pulled up to a massive, wrought-iron gate with an adjacent guard shack.

Two men wearing battle armor and helmets, carrying carbine-like weapons of a type Horace had never seen, stepped out of the shack, one approaching the driver's window, the other approaching the passenger compartment. One of them knocked on the rear passenger window.

Roxanne opened it, and the guard leaned down, peering pointedly at each of the occupants. Roxanne offered their names and gave him a generous view of cleavage and inner thigh until he grunted and waved them on.

As the car moved up the long, winding drive, Bunny came over the intercom, gasping almost in panic. "That guard wanted to look at my face! I could have been made!" They hadn't changed Bunny's face because she was not supposed to be visible to anyone. Most limos were handled by autonomous AIs. Drivers were redundant.

"They've never done that before," Roxanne said.

Bunny said, "I almost wet myself!"

"So what did you do?" Tina said.

"I let my Jimmy talk to him, my artificial person. Since the windows are one-way only, he couldn't see me. Jimmy powwowed with his security computer and told him the car is AI-controlled. And those guns they're carrying? Those are military-elite grade. Caseless depleted-uranium slug-throwers. You could shoot through a bunker wall with those. Retail price is—"

"I don't even want to know!" Horace said, suddenly feeling as if his armor would be as useful as tinfoil. He fixed Roxanne with a steady gaze. "So we can assume most of the guards are packing."

"A reasonable assumption," Roxanne said, meeting his gaze with cool steadiness.

"*Those* guns."

"Perhaps."

"And we don't have any."

"Horace, I—"

"Why would anyone agree to come to an event like this?"

"It's a way for Mogilevich to display his magnanimity. We are all now under his hospitality and protection. And we are not required to relinquish our own weapons until we exit the car. You can bet every one of these vehicles is a floating arsenal."

"But if anyone steps out of line, he can snuff them with no consequences."

"Like worms underfoot, yes."

"If, like you said, this is the way he keeps his enemies close, why doesn't he just kill us all?"

"If he were to kill his guests as you suggest, he would launch an open war with *everyone*. This world is an ever-shifting battlefield of alliances and betrayals. There is a great deal of squabbling at the edges of our respective empires, but we all make each other a great deal of money. If he turned everyone against him, even Yvgeny Mogilevich would not last long."

"You got a roster that tells who's playing for who?"

She smiled faintly.

He flinched as a display of text appeared in his vision beside Roxanne:

NAME: ROXANNE SUKOVA
ESTIMATED WORTH: $118 BILLION
PRIMARY FINANCIAL INTERESTS: LABOR, LAW ENFORCEMENT, HYDROGEN, FUSION RESEARCH
MARITAL STATUS: DIVORCED TWICE
CHILDREN: UNKNOWN
KNOWN ASSOCIATES: CONFIDENTIAL
EDUCATION: B.A. IN ENGLISH LITERATURE (OXFORD), LAW DEGREE (PRINCETON)
PRIVATE LIFE: CONFIDENTIAL
OTHER: BLACK BELTS IN JUJITSU AND AIKIDO.

"Blink twice to clear the message," she said.

He did so, and the second blink wiped his vision clean.

He glanced at Tina and a new display popped up:

NAME: AMBROSIA WELCH
ESTIMATED WORTH: $7 MILLION

OCCUPATION: ASPIRING ACTRESS, SINGER
SEXUAL PREFERENCE: LESBIAN
MARITAL STATUS: SINGLE
CHILDREN: NONE
EDUCATION: B.F.A. IN THEATER (MONSANTO UNIVERSITY)
PRIVATE LIFE: KNOWN RELATIONSHIPS WITH TWO POPULAR SINGERS
CRIMINAL RECORD: TEN YEARS PROBATION FOR TECH TRAFFICKING, AWAITING TRIAL ON LEWD CONDUCT CHARGES IN NORTH CAROLINA

"Well, aren't you interesting, Ms. Welch," he said with a grin.

"The contacts work similarly to netlinked glasses," Roxanne said, "but Bunny oversees the data feed."

He flinched again as a white, fluffy, long-eared shape charged out of the distance into his vision and coalesced into a rabid leporine figure with razor-sharp, bloody teeth and blazing red eyes, going for his throat. His hands went up to grab it, but it disappeared in a puff of pixel smoke.

And then an avatar of Bunny appeared in his vision and waved at him with an impish smile.

"Jesus Christ," he said after a long breath. "You want to see me go berserk, Bunny, do that again."

Roxanne smiled, an enigmatic twist of her lips.

Here at an elevation of almost three thousand meters, the stars sweeping their slow arcs above the desert shone sharper, brighter, the moon and Milky Way so bright and clear they looked almost within reach. The drive twisted upward on an even steeper slope toward a glow shining behind pine tree lines, a glow so bright it eradicated the spectacle of night.

"This place is built like a military base," Bunny said. "Surveillance everywhere. Infrared, motion sensors, 3-D imaging. If a gnat winked at you anywhere on these grounds, someone would know it."

"What about armaments?" Roxanne said.

"No weapon emplacements that I can detect. For firepower, it looks like drones and guards only."

"I hope we don't have to shoot our way out," Horace said. "We haven't exactly discussed how we're getting out of here."

Red text flashed in his vision from Roxanne: THAT PLAN IS STILL UNDER DEVELOPMENT.

"Got it," Horace said. That kind of suicide mission he could deal with. In the pit, as in war, no battle plan survived contact with the opponent, even when spots had been discussed in advance.

"Just remember this," she said. "Once we get out of this car, say *nothing* that will blow your cover, inside or outside the house. I do not know this for certain, but it is extremely likely that eavesdropping bots will be assigned to all the guests. I believe the entirety of his house is covered in hidden microphones sensitive enough to catch your slightest whisper and cameras that can read your lips."

"Got it," Horace and Tina said together.

The drive flattened and spread until it emerged into a broad artificial platform extending like a shelf of steel and concrete from the side of the mountain. Lights delineated the perimeter of the platform, and the shelf extended from the front of one of the strangest structures Horace had ever seen, a palace of sweeping domes and curving lines, an architectural vision from the dreams of someone who did not believe in straight lines. A great geodesic dome in the center emerged from undulations of polished stainless steel and silvered concrete like a crystal bottle from the sea. The entire dome glowed from within.

The snow-dusted summit of Bonanza Peak loomed beyond the house, rising perhaps another half kilometer against the sky.

The limo eased to a halt, its drive spooling down, and formed the last of a caravan of vehicles that circled the artificial platform, which dropped off sharply into the pine forest dozens of meters below and overlooked the sprawling skirt of forest that receded into stippled desert plain far beyond.

"Bunny," Roxanne said, "any indication that your lock has been lifted?"

"No. Nothing. And if it ever is, believe me, I'll know. The guy just has to key in a code."

"If we survive this, I'll see her parole officer sacked." Roxanne gathered her dress and clutch purse, a note of trepidation seeping into her voice.

"And I was right," Bunny said. "That entire structure is EM-shielded. All signals travel in and out through two firewalled repeaters. Once you're inside, I won't be able to see you. You'll have to come outside to talk to me, or I'll have to come in. And if I get out of the car, I'll be made within thirty seconds by facial recognition packages on the cameras." She sighed. "Maybe we should have changed my face after all. Your netlinks might work inside in walkie-talkie mode, but only with each other. Good thing I brought tea and a crossword puzzle."

Tina said, "Isn't it cheating to do a crossword puzzle with an AI in your brain?" She tried to sound flip, but an underlying quaver threatened to crack her voice.

Bunny said, "It sure is."

Roxanne put a hand that only trembled a little on the door latch. "Time to go."

CHAPTER THIRTY

More limousines and expensive cars were pulling in behind Roxanne's as Horace and the two women crossed the platform toward the entrance of the structure—he hesitated to call it a house, or even a mansion. It was a fascinating monstrosity, the intricacy of the exterior lines, the windows, the domed skylights, the balconies, all interspersed with swatches of solar-electric skin.

Other figures in suits and evening gowns disappeared ahead of them into the brightly-lit entrance, flanked on both sides by men almost as brawny as Horace. They were not overtly carrying weapons, but then, neither was he.

Just inside the door was erected a full security station, manned by three more large men in grim, gray suits. The guards had blockish Slavic heads, beady-eyed and crew-cut.

Roxanne led the way, striding up to the checkpoint like a queen breezing into her court. Two scanner pillars awaited them to walk between, plus a chrome pedestal with a finger-shaped indentation. Roxanne pressed her finger into the indentation, then passed through the pillars. One of the guards took her firmly by the arms, raised them to the sides, and frisked her in ways that would have gotten him throat-punched anywhere else.

When Tina repeated the process, the guard blithely ignoring Tina's—Ambrosia's—scathing glare, a twinge of protectiveness shot through Horace. He wanted to take those fingers and make the guy eat them with splintered teeth.

To distract himself, he surveyed the expansive foyer. As cold, shining silver, and crystal as the exterior was, the interior was warm, polished-wood, and mirror-smooth marble. The walls were gleaming expanses of intricately-carved wood in baroque style, the floors inlaid with gold leaf and mosaics of ancient Russian czars. Chandeliers the size of dinner tables, grand, inverted ziggurats of gold and sparkling crystal, filled the space with light. A sweeping staircase of red velvet and gold spiraled upward. In the shadow of the staircase was a hallway through heavy double doors leading deeper into the house. In the next room, servers circulated through a crowd of guests and bodyguards.

Horace stepped up to the pedestal and placed his synth-skin finger in the slot. A quiet hiss told him that the sample had been taken from the stored blood reservoir. The light in the slot turned green, and he walked through the scanners.

The guard grunted. "Weapons?"

"I'm clean," Horace said, holding open his suit jacket.

The guard eyed him for a long moment, then patted him down, immediately noticing the extra thickness and strange lines under Horace's suit. He paid special attention to the armpits, shins, and belt line, where weapons were most often concealed.

On the outside, Horace placidly allowed it. On the inside, anger spurred his heart quicker and formed a lump of sour heat in his stomach. He could crush this caveman's skull with one blow, and the guy wouldn't even know what hit him.

Apparently satisfied, the guard waved him on. Roxanne took Tina by the hand and led her toward the party just ahead.

As they breezed into the room, eyes swiveled toward the two women like x-ray searchlights. Immediately the wolves began to circle, and the other females in the room, perhaps a dozen altogether, hung back with arms crossed and eyes narrowed.

In his vision, halos of information appeared around the guests' heads, color-coded by alliance and probability of threat. If he focused on an individual for a length of time, the information would zoom closer for easier reading. And as he read, he could discern possible patterns of alliance and threat in the guests, those most closely allied with Mogilevich, those on the periphery, and those who were "enemies kept closer."

Only a handful were outright gangsters. Others were prominent executives, heads of state from South America and Eastern Europe, famous professional athletes, a porn star, and one that disturbed Horace most of all, a recruiter from Death Match Unlimited, Darryl Stone.

Horace had fallen so far from the major leagues for so long—an entirely new generation of corporate managers and fighters populated the company now—that he'd never met the man. He only knew him by face and reputation. Darryl Stone was young, part of the league's New Breed who had been publicly vocal about making sure the Old Guard was put out to pasture. The public wanted to see vicious young killers, not doddering old bruisers.

As the wolves circled toward Roxanne and Tina, Horace interposed himself and warned them away with a harsh glare. For some, however, even that was not enough. A short man with a nose like a pock-marked eggplant and a white bristle of hair encircling a shiny pate shouldered past Horace with a glare of annoyance.

"My dear Roxanne," the man said, taking her hand and kissing her fingers.

Roxanne smiled faintly. "A pleasure to see you again, Senator O'Connell."

"Please, you must call me Richard."

Over the heads of the conversation, Horace locked gazes with Senator O'Connell's bodyguard, a slight, hard-eyed man with the wiry build of ex-military or mercenary.

"Richard, allow me to introduce my companion, Ambrosia Welch. Perhaps you've heard of her. She was recently on Broadway."

The little big man turned his smile full onto Roxanne's auburn-haired companion. "Alas, I can't say that I have, but I would certainly like to." He took her hand and brushed her knuckles with his lips. "You're an actress, then."

"Yup."

"What have you done?"

"Like Roxy—Roxanne was saying, I was on Broadway. The biggest one was *A Midsummer Night's Wet Dream*."

The senator cleared his throat. "That sounds splendid, my dear. But don't you think it a pity that the once great symbol of culture in our country has degenerated to sex plays and performance art?"

"I can't say I have an opinion on that, Richard. I'm just a struggling actress trying to make a living."

"I'm sure that you have a splendid future ahead of you. Just splendid." He grinned wider. "Have you ever been to an event like this before, my dear?"

"I haven't."

"Then you're in for a treat. Here is where we see what men are truly made of." His eel-colored eyes glittered.

"I'm looking forward to it, Richard."

"Please, you must both join me at my table! We shall toast, and you shall indulge a smitten old man."

"If I didn't know better, Richard," Roxanne said, "I would think you are trying to steal my date."

"Oh, not steal. Share perhaps?" He kept his voice playful, but there was no mistaking the lascivious tinge to his tone.

Tina wrapped her arm around Roxanne's shapely waist. "Oh, I *never* share, sir."

The senator chuckled gamely. "Nevertheless, you must join me. Come, I'll spare you having to make niceties with people who don't deserve your time." He maneuvered himself to Roxanne's side and guided her toward a set of French doors leading deeper into the house.

Text flashed in Horace's vision:

> MOGILEVICH AND O'CONNELL HAVE BEEN IN BED TOGETHER FOR TEN YEARS.
>
> HIS TABLE IS LIKELY TO BE MUCH NEARER MOGILEVICH THAN THE ONE WE'VE BEEN ASSIGNED.

Horace kept his mouth shut and blinked the message away. Would he really be able to get close enough to Mogilevich for a decapitation or a skull-crushing Thunder Hammer? Would it really be that easy? And even if it were, what about Lilly's kids? Were they dead already?

God almighty, his mouth was dry. He took up a glass of champagne from a passing tray.

> DON'T. GIVE THE GLASS TO ME.

He diverted the glass' path from his mouth toward Roxanne's hand, and she took it with a grateful nod.

> IT IS BAD FORM FOR A BODYGUARD TO DRINK AT AN EVENT LIKE THIS, UNPROFESSIONAL ENOUGH TO BLOW YOUR COVER. YOUR JOB IS TO BE AS INVISIBLE AS POSSIBLE.

He wished this silent form of communication was two-way so he could tell her to go fuck herself. For half a second, he'd felt like a slave, like the Roman gladiators of old.

Senator O'Connell was regaling Tina with tales of his artistic patronage and how he just *adored* theater people. Why, he had been a theater major for a while in college. He had played Pocket in *King Lear,* the original version, his sophomore year at DuPont University. Tina effervesced with enthusiasm about Shakespeare, but that *King Leer* wasn't her favorite of the plays, she was more into *Her Twelfth Knight* and *Lady Macbeth's Lover*. The old man listened politely as they entered the great space under the central geodesic dome.

Around the perimeter of the huge circular chamber was a spectacular collection of antique cars. Horace wasn't a car expert, but he knew 1930s Rolls Royces when he saw them, along with Bugattis, Ferraris, Model T and Model A Fords, 1960s muscle cars, Porsches, Lamborghinis, Mercedes Roadsters, a DeLorean, a Duesenberg Coupe, even a hundred-year-old Batmobile from one of the old films. Dozens of cars, all gleaming with high polish.

The senator noticed Horace's interest and said to Roxanne, "Your large friend seems to have an interest in cars. What about you, ladies?"

"Oh, I *love* cars!" Tina said.

"An indulgent luxury from a less civilized time," Roxanne said.

"Come now, Roxanne, surely you have a few of your own indulgences," the senator said.

"I do."

"Mind sharing what they are?"

She laughed and touched his shoulder. "Oh, Richard. My indulgences are not for public consumption."

The wattle of flesh around his collar reddened as he laughed with her.

"That's my job!" Tina said.

The redness deepened and crept higher. He cleared his throat and stopped before a hundred-and-eighty-year-old automobile. "My dear ladies, this is a Bugatti Royale Coupe, from sometime in the 1930s, I don't precisely remember the year. Twelve-liter internal combustion engine. As perfect an automobile as was ever designed. Perfect lines, perfect curves, meant for men of exacting tastes. Much like you, my dear Miss Welch."

"You flatter me, Richie," Tina said, "but I'm not meant for men at all." She grabbed Roxanne and laid a brief but sensuous kiss across her lips. "I'm all double-X, all the time."

His smile turned brittle and cracked. "I'm sure you are."

Roxanne gently pushed Tina away with an indulgent smile. "I admire your enthusiasm, Ambrosia, but let's not give everyone a show."

"Are you sure, Roxy? I mean, Richie here has been so nice, and I'm sure he'd *love* a show." Tina threw her arm around his neck and kissed him on the cheek, leaving a smear of scarlet lipstick.

The redness in his neck crept up through the fringe of white bristle toward his bald pate. "Oh, indeed, I love shows, but let us table that topic for now. The night is young! My table is over here...."

In the center of the dome, surrounded by tables draped in white tablecloths and overstuffed chairs designed in a century long gone, was an old-style, square boxing ring, complete with canvas floor, ropes, and turnbuckles.

When they reached the table, Roxanne and Tina sat down with the senator, and text flashed before Horace's eyes.

> **STAND BACK A DISTANCE. BODYGUARDS DO NOT SIT WITH GUESTS. BESIDES, YOU WOULD BE AT A DISADVANTAGE THAT WAY. JUST HANG BACK AND BE INVISIBLE AS A MOUNTAIN IN THE DISTANCE.**

Other guests began filtering into the chamber.

Near the table, Horace stood with his hands clasped in front of him, reading the information of the incoming guests, committing faces and data to memory as best he could.

And then a dancing rabbit from Hell exploded into his vision with a silent *poof!* of pixels.

Bunny's elated shriek raked into his earpiece. "Oh golly! It's happened! I'm free! The son-of-a-biscuit let me go! I just sliced through the repeater system and found you!"

A surge of elation shot through him like a jolt of electricity.

"Oh my gosh I can't believe it! The White Rabbit is back! Let's go kick their naughty little behinds! Let's... Oh. Oh, something's wrong. Something.... I... Oh..."

CHAPTER THIRTY-ONE

Before Horace could open his mouth, Roxanne turned to him with perfect aplomb. "Frankie, I left my netlink in the limousine. Would you be a dear and go get it? I'm sure Ambrosia and I will be fine for two minutes, and I simply *must* show the good senator photos of my new yacht. Richard, perhaps you'll be so kind as to join us next week for a cruise to Havana?"

Horace nodded and walked back out toward the entrance as fast as nonchalance would allow. His departure was noted, but unchallenged.

Outside in the cold night air, he trotted toward the car. After so much activity on his feet over the last several days, his knees felt full of lava gravel and sent jolts of pain with every step. The platform was packed full of cars and limousines, both wheeled and hover-equipped.

He reached the side of their limousine and found the doors locked, the windows closed and darkened, even the windshield. He may as well have been looking at the dense carapace of a black beetle.

"Roxanne," he said into his netlink. "Can you hear me? Car's locked."

No reply.

He knocked on the window. "Hey, open up!" With no response, he rapped harder.

Unless Bunny opened the doors, there was no way he would get in there. The entire thing was armored. It would take heavy machinery for him to open a door unless the car allowed it.

"Bunny!" he whispered into his netlink. "Are you all right?"

No reply.

He rapped on the window while trying to peer through. He thought he could see Bunny's shape slumped over the steering yoke. There was no apparent damage to the vehicle, no holes in the glass or anything indicating she had been harmed from the outside.

Having no way to break into this armored car without drawing attention, he walked with as smooth and even a gait as he could manage back inside, within the shell of the building's electromagnetic shielding.

The guards motioned him to pass through the scanner again, frisked him again.

"Can't get enough, can you, brother," he said to the guard with a hand under his crotch.

The guard grunted with a mirthless half smile and waved him on.

"By the way, there's a toxic gas cannon up my ass, if you're feeling saucy."

"Quit while you are ahead, fuckhole," the guard growled in a thick Russian accent.

He hovered in an empty corner of the grand entry hall and muttered into his microphone. "Ms. Sukova, I can't get your netlink. The car is locked."

A moment's pause, then in a singsong lilt, "I'll be right there."

A minute later, she confronted him in the foyer with a withering glare and a sneer of disdain meant for the guards to see. "I cannot believe you were so stupid, Frankie."

The guards stared with narrowed eyes, curious and alert now from this unknown drama.

Roxanne pulled Horace outside and approached the car at an easy walk. The door locks clicked. Horace opened the door for her, and then followed her inside and shut the door.

"Bunny, are you there?" Horace called.

The bulkhead between passengers and driver slid downward, revealing the back of Bunny's head, slumped and askew, her face slack and sagging against the control yoke. Horace jammed his thick torso through the opening and touched her. "Bunny." Shook her shoulder. "Bunny!"

He felt for a pulse at her throat and found it hammering along like a rabbit's warning thump. Her eyes were half-lidded, fluttering. "She's alive, but out of it. Some kind of seizure maybe."

"Drag her into the back."

After releasing the safety straps, he cupped her under both arms as gently as he could and dragged her into the rear. They arranged Bunny on a seat and Roxanne prepared a tumbler of ice water. Bunny's face was strained, tight, her eye movements oscillating under half-closed lids at an impossible frequency.

She tipped a trickle of ice water between Bunny's lips.

Bunny choked and gasped and her arms began to flail, but her eyes did not open. A hoarse, ululating cry ripped from her throat, a cry of fear and confusion.

"What the fuck's going on?" Horace said, grabbing for her wrists, pinning them together.

Roxanne sat on her legs, holding them down while they squirmed under her. Water sloshed from the tumbler. Then he dashed the water into Bunny's face.

Another ragged gasp and the thrashing ceased. Bunny blinked, opened her eyes, glanced at them, licked her lips, her chin and eyebrows dripping.

"Uh," she said, "What are you guys doing?"

"You were having some kind of seizure," Roxanne said. "What do you remember?"

"Why am I all wet?" Her head sagged back, and her eyes began to flutter again. "I'm late! I'm late! For a very important date! No time to say hello, goodbye! I'm late! I'm late! I'm late!"

"Bunny, no!" Horace shook her.

Her gaze snapped back into focus, and her teeth chattered, but not from cold. "What? It's just too much! Too..."

"Stay with us, sister."

Her behavior was that of someone sedated into incoherence, except that the muscles of her face, instead of hanging slack, were twitching, tightening spasmodically into a succession of rictus masks.

"What the hell is wrong with her?" he said.

"Something to do with unlocking her AI, perhaps. It does remind me of the adjustment period of my own implants, but greatly amplified. Her brain is having trouble processing the deluge of information. It's like having a whole new sense group turned on, or in the case of a cyberpath, several sense groups, like turning on the lights in a house that has been dark for years."

"Can you see anything with your own implants?"

"I'm not a slicer. I don't have those kinds of capabilities."

"I hope she doesn't blow a few million synapses. How long is she gonna be like this?"

"Unknown. But we must get back inside. The bouts are going to begin soon, and Tina cannot entertain the senator forever."

"We can't just leave her like this."

"You stay here, try to keep her in the here and now. I have plenty of enemies inside, but no one is going to attempt to assassinate me. At least for now." She slid toward the door, then paused, her gaze holding on him for a long moment. Then she came to him, cupped his cheek, and kissed him on the mouth, long and warm and moist.

Then she was gone, and Horace was left with a twitching, spasming, muttering cyberpath. "Oh, my fur and whiskers! I'm late, I'm late, I'm late!" Another face-full of water roused Bunny again.

"Stop that!" she sputtered.

"Then stay with me."

"I can't tell I'm leaving! Oh, my gosh, I'm scared! It wasn't like this before!"

"If it's been twenty years, your brain isn't the same anymore. Mine sure as hell isn't. Talk to me. Stay with me."

"It's like Jimmy is bouncing around inside my brain. All the trillions of little tasks I wished he could do before but couldn't, he's trying to do all at once now. It's like I'm in a fog of static, but all the bits of static have meaning and purpose, and I can't grab any of them, and when I got the implants it wasn't like this—I could learn it all little by little, ease into it; now it's like being thrown into a hyperfighter when all you've ever driven is a tricycle..."

"You can do it, Bunny. You've done it before. This is who you used to be."

"I'm scared I won't be able to handle it, turn the throttle down; I won't be able to help you, I won't be able to get us out of here..."

"You've already done more than you had to. You are a superhero."

"Don't give me that. I'm just a girl from Paducah."

"And I'm a small-town kid from Nebraska. Everybody comes from somewhere. Try to focus on my voice. Just right here. There's a whole world out there and it stops at your skull. Just be Bunny for a few minutes. Just breathe."

She took a deep breath and relaxed against his lap. Her breathing slowed, and he could no longer feel the pulse surging through her wrists. He laid her hands on her chest.

"Tell me about Nebraska," she said.

So he did. He told her about the small town he grew up in, a town that had begun as a farming community in the nineteenth century, but by the time he was born had long since entered its death spiral, as there were no farmers around anymore except the indentured servants of a few megacorps. Except for picking fruit and vegetables, nearly all farm work was done with great robotic machines that ran on artificial intelligence and GPS, and the rest was done by migrant, labor-class workers. The megacorps owned most of the land, waiting on a few stubborn old holdouts to die so they could seize the rest, the children long since having gone off to the cities to try to make a living. From this, a big lunkhead with more muscles than brains, with the kind of physical stature that inspired either abject fear or the kind of amazement reserved for circus freaks, headed to the city like almost everyone he knew, wandered into a mixed martial arts gym, and the rest was history.

The boxing ring inside Mogilevich's house had scratched the surface of many of those memories. His first bouts had been in such rings, thick with the smells of sweat and muscle ointment, styptic powder and blood, leather and canvas, long before the genetic enhancements had turned his hands into hammers.

The first time he ever got into the ring, felt that rush of the clash, the strife, the victory that came when every breath was a string of razor blades in his lungs, when his arms had been reduced to slabs of limp steak, he knew it was what he was put on this planet to do. He won more than he lost, but he did lose a few, and all of those gave him lessons for next time.

"Why fighting?" Bunny murmured, dream-like, clinging to real-time consciousness as if it were a life-preserver. "Why not something nice like a brush salesman? My first boyfriend was a brush salesman."

He laughed at that. "Some of us are just born in the wrong century."

The protrusions of her implants were hard against his fingers. "Some centuries are just born wrong."

Then she sat up, blinking her eyes, rubbing them, chewing her lips, clutching the sides of her head and working at it as if it were a cross-threaded bolt.

He watched her warily for signs of another seizure.

"I'm getting Jimmy under control.... He's at least listening to me now.... I can't do any slicing yet, but the worst is over. I hope."

"Don't scare me like that again or I'll have to kick your ass."

"Is that any way to talk to a lady?"

"Ass kicking is pretty much my only skill."

With what looked like incredible effort, she composed herself and looked into his eyes. "Then go back inside and do it." Her gaze flicked from his eyes to his mouth three times, and then she clasped her hands between her thighs and looked away. "I'll be here when you come back out."

CHAPTER THIRTY-TWO

Horace refrained from bantering with the guards when he went back inside this time. The gathering room beyond the foyer had cleared out, so he snatched a couple handfuls of hors d'oeuvres left on platters and crammed them into his mouth.

As he paused to chew and swallow before heading back to the fight room, the empty room let him notice the artwork that festooned the carved, fluted hardwood walls: Renaissance paintings that looked worth more than entire counties where he came from, with a tastefulness that surprised him. He was no art expert, but he recognized greatness when he saw it. He didn't know what he had been expecting from Mogilevich's taste—velvet paintings of pin-up girls and dogs playing poker maybe—but here was a trove of priceless art.

A round of applause from the automobile gallery drew him away from the display and into the larger room beyond. The tables were filled now with the august guests and the eye candy they brought along to nibble. The air was redolent with scents of cigar smoke, clove cigarettes, car wax, and cologne worth its weight in gold.

Horace glided silently around the perimeter toward the table where Roxanne sat with Tina and the senator. He took his place there, catching the women's eyes, and stood sentinel with his hands clasped before him, emulating all the other bodyguards he had ever seen.

The senator looked somewhat less jovial now. Tina's altered face, more difficult to read than ever, registered tension and a trace of worry. What had happened while Horace was gone? Roxanne was leaning close to the senator, giving him plenty of generous looks, coaxing him back into a pleasant mood.

Tina caught Horace's eye again and swallowed hard, but kept quiet.

All the tables were occupied except one, two tables from where Horace stood. The lights around the chamber dimmed except for those directly above the ring. The hubbub of conversation diminished. Heads bobbed closer and spoke quieter.

From a door on the opposite side of the gallery, three figures emerged, and glowing red halos—targeting reticles—appeared around them in his HUD vision.

Flanked by two bodyguards, Yvgeny Mogilevich strode toward the ring with the gait and bearing of a man half his age. The mob boss smiled and nodded to his guests, pointedly shaking a few hands as he passed between the tables, pointedly ignoring a few others.

As he approached, Horace immediately recognized the father of the man he had killed in a limousine just over a week ago. His hair was white, combed back from a prominent widow's peak. Flinty eyes, buried in leathery wrinkles, scanned the crowd, brushing over Horace for a moment. Mogilevich's features were blunt, stolid, square-chinned, with a wide mouth and strangely thick lips, a face that might have been ruggedly handsome had there been a microgram of humanity in it. Nevertheless, there was still a magnetism about him.

His dark gray tuxedo bore the cut of a hundred years ago. Diamond-and-pearl cuff links glittered at his wrists. A silk handkerchief that matched his glimmering necktie was tucked precisely in his breast pocket. He climbed the steps to the ring and grabbed the ropes to duck between them, fingers glimmering with encrustations of gold and gems like barnacles.

Horace's blood turned to dry ice at the sight of Joey Luca at Mogilevich's side. Joey Luca, the former pit fighter he'd killed in the back of Dmitri's limousine. The heart injector felt like a brick against his chest, constricting his breathing. If there was anyone in the room most likely to recognize "Hammer" Harkness, it was Joey Luca.

Mogilevich stepped to the center of the ring. "Welcome, all, to my little event!" His voice was cordial, scratchy, filled with powerful inner strength, and amplified to fill the cavernous space. It was the same voice that had spoken the words "*I'm going to fuck you. And I'm going to keep fucking you until I can't fuck anymore.*"

Applause rippled around the tables.

"I am not a man of words—"

"You are a man of action!" came a voice from the tables, to a smattering of laughter.

Mogilevich smiled at this. "Indeed. So let us begin!"

A dozen waiters emerged in a column from one of the doors, each carrying what looked like an elaborately decorated egg the size of a human head. As the waiters dispersed among the tables, Horace saw each of the eggs was unique and breathtakingly beautiful, a masterpiece of porcelain and jewels, gold and silver filigree. He suddenly felt as if the Royal Crown Jewels of England were passing through the crowd. The eggs looked old and yet timeless, exquisite works of art the value of which he could not even imagine. The waiters paused at each table, opened the eggs like clamshells, and withdrew crystal glasses of clear liquid, distributing these to the guests. Roxanne, Tina, and the senator all received one.

Mogilevich received his glass last and raised it. "But before we begin, a toast! *Vashe zdorovie*!"

Bunny's voice shot with panic into Horace's earbud. "Don't drink it!"

"*Vashe zdorovie*!" replied the guests raising their glasses.

Mogilevich turned toward Roxanne and Tina with an ingratiating smile. "And because we are graced with the presence of such stunning beauties, *za milyh dam*."

Bunny kept talking. "I'm suddenly picking up dozens of new signals. They've got to be coming from the vodka."

Mogilevich raised his glass to the other six women in the audience, and everybody drank. Tina and Roxanne raised their glasses and appeared to drink, but Horace's vantage point let him see that they did not even touch the liquid to their lips.

Bunny continued, "Probably location transmitters, small enough to swallow unnoticed. Good way to keep tabs on everyone."

Red text from Roxanne appeared in his vision:

GOOD TO HAVE YOU BACK, BUNNY. HOW DID YOU SEE THIS?

Bunny's voice was coherent but still shaky, and there was a strange, electronic distortion in her words. "I'm tied into your implants, Ms.

Sukova, straight into your visual cortex. I hope you don't mind. And by the way, everything we're transmitting is now encrypted and passing through the house repeaters. It's designed to look like random burst noise. Hopefully the entities monitoring the signals won't notice for a while. And even if they do, it'll take them time to decrypt it."

Mogilevich was speaking, "—rules are simple. Two men enter the ring. One man leaves. No weapons. Unlimited three-minute rounds. Victors receive a million dollars, and the attention of our friends from Death Match Unlimited." He gestured toward Darryl Stone, who sat at ringside with a tall, buxom supermodel beside him.

Horace suppressed a snarl of disgust. In his day, there was no way Death Match Unlimited would have slipped between the sheets so blatantly with someone like Mogilevich.

Bunny continued, "I'm working on a couple of other things, too, but I have only one access point into the house systems, through this repeater. It's like trying to build a ship in a bottle or a mainframe through a keyhole."

With a flourish, the host said, "Now, I give you tonight's master of ceremonies." With that he climbed down from the ring and circled toward his table, the second table away from where Roxanne and Tina sat.

And into the ring stepped Colin Ross, the Scottish singer, actor, and international playboy whose professional, financial, and sexual exploits made metric tonnes of grist for the tabloid mill and billions of dollars for the entertainment industry. He had gotten his start in an Edinburgh face club. Dressed in a perfectly-tailored tuxedo, black hair perfectly coiffed, face tanned and devilishly handsome with a physique worthy of Michelangelo, Ross climbed into the ring and waved to the guests. Hoots, whistles, applause greeted him.

A look of beatific amazement bloomed on Tina's face at the sight of him.

Waiters again circulated through the crowd with gilded cards, which appeared to be the bout card for the evening, and distributed them to all the guests. Money began changing hands as wagering commenced amidst boisterous conversation.

This felt wrong, all of it. Ten men were going to die tonight, with no hope of resurrection, unless Horace acted, and thousands more over the course of Mogilevich's life if he failed, including Lilly and her children, Roxanne, Tina, Bunny, and probably Trask, too, for the sake of cleanup. His hand itched so powerfully to walk up behind Mogilevich and put an electro-fiber blade in the back of the gangster's skull that he had to be careful not to deploy the weapon in his bracer accidentally.

Ross' deep voice and cultured Scottish burr greeted the guests. "In case you don't know who I am, I'm Colin Ross, of stage and screen, raconteur, entrepreneur, and a few other French words."

Applause filled the gallery.

Roxanne was still chatting quietly with the senator, touching his thigh, leaning in close. The senator was beginning to warm up again under her deft ministrations.

Tina announced, "Apologies, but I must visit the little girls' room before the excitement starts. Excuse me."

She stood and flowed free of the table, chair, and senator, coming toward Horace. "Sonofabitch slid his hand up my crotch!" she hissed, her voice a razor of anger. "Practically stuck his finger in there! This is one of those days I wish my coochie had teeth!" Then she breezed away toward one of the doors the waiters used.

In Horace's vision, the map of a floor plan appeared, indicating the location of a toilet, and a green dot indicating Tina's presence moving toward it.

Colin Ross warmed up the guests with an amusing anecdote about three days on the Mediterranean on his yacht with six Lithuanian models.

Opposite where Horace stood, a pair of elevator doors opened and two guards emerged with one of the fighters between them. The guards were not there to protect the fighter; they were there to keep him from running. The terror on the man's face was plain, his spindly naked legs and torso sheened with fear-sweat. He wore boxing shorts, boots, and padded half-gloves that exposed his fingers. His skin was pale, his flesh flaccid, shoulders narrow and slumped, with a freckled nose too big for his face, his hair shaved clean. He looked more like an accountant than a fighter.

Ross read from a card, "Our first bout of the evening will be in the featherweight division. In the red corner, weighing in at 57.1 kilos, an artificial intelligence designer from San Jose, California, Jacob Goldman!"

To polite applause, Goldman was practically tossed bodily into the ring by the two guards. He gathered himself and stood upon trembling knees in boxing shorts pulled up almost to his breastbone.

The elevator doors opened again, and another man emerged, this one with a well-muscled body and the quickness and grace of a trained fighter, maybe *Muay Thai,* judging by the way he moved. With no guards, he brought himself to ringside with the confidence of surety. He was prepared to be Goldman's executioner. He climbed into the ring, beaming with confidence in his impending triumph, arms raised to the crowd, circling.

"In the blue corner! Hailing from Las Vegas, Nevada, weighing in at 57.1 kilos, with a professional record of twelve wins—six by knock-out—and one loss, Julian Mendoza!"

Another swell of disgust in Horace's breast at this caricature, this travesty of an honorable sport.

Cowering in one corner, Goldman looked frantic, practically vibrating, on the verge of hysterical mania. Mendoza might have trouble catching this guy. Then again, maybe it was wise never to underestimate one's opponent, especially when cornered.

What was in it for Mendoza to kill a man? A murderous compulsion? Just the money? Proving himself capable of cold-blooded murder for the attention of corporate executives and a shortcut to stardom? If he could kill a shlub like Goldman, he certainly wouldn't flinch from killing an opponent in the pit.

With a sudden scream of terror and rage, Goldman threw himself at Mendoza, slamming him into Ross, and all three fell down in a flailing heap. Ross scrambled to extricate himself, eyes bulging as he flung himself between the ropes and crashed into some ringside chairs, knocking them flying, clattering. Guards rushed to help him to his feet.

Darryl Stone hurriedly rang the bell to start Round One.

Meanwhile, Goldman had descended into a frenzy of shrieking and then Mendoza was screaming too. Blood spattered. Something wet and pulpy landed on the mat. Blood streamed from Mendoza's eye socket, slicked Goldman's fingers. Utter animal madness filled Goldman's eyes as he fell upon Mendoza like a rabid chihuahua.

The crowd roared and clapped.

Mendoza blindly tried to ward him away, but Goldman grabbed him around the neck and bit his face. Mendoza's screams rose into a shriek. Goldman's teeth snapped and tore and ripped away, and then he spat Mendoza's nose onto the mat. Gagging and choking on the spewing blood, Mendoza fell, and Goldman followed him down. Somehow the skinny man got behind him, fumbled with his legs until they were wrapped around Mendoza's waist, locked his arms around his neck, and squeezed for all he was worth.

The dozens of eyes around Horace gleamed, transfixed at the bloodshed, as the onlookers sipped their drinks and nibbled rare beef tenderloin canapes and caviar-topped quail eggs.

Mendoza flailed weakly, clawing at the arm squeezing the consciousness from him. His face was a ravaged mask of blood and torn flesh, his eye socket a red ruin. His struggles weakened. Goldman continued squeezing for all he was worth, screaming through clenched teeth, spittle flying, eyes wild and bulging-white.

Mendoza's arms finally went slack. Gasping, Goldman held on for another half a minute, as if he had to convince his arms to relinquish their hold. Finally he rolled Mendoza's body off him and scrambled to his feet, wheezing like a bellows. For a moment, he stood over the motionless body, drenched in blood, looking out over the audience, his face a mask of shock and revulsion and burgeoning elation. Then he put his boot on Mendoza's Adam's apple and stomped.

The muffled *crack* of cartilage brought the dome to utter silence for several heartbeats.

And then Mogilevich stood and began to clap, slowly, loudly, a grim mask barely covering the disappointment on his lips.

The crowd picked up the applause and carried it louder, cheering this poor geek who had managed victory against all odds. If a slow bloody execution for Goldman had been Mogilevich's intention, what happened ultimately to those who beat the odds? Was the mafiya czar good to his word?

A trembling smile of relief twitched at the corner of Goldman's mouth, and then he vomited.

Men came and helped Goldman from the ring, dragged Mendoza

away on a gurney, and another group came and mopped up the deluge of blood and piss and vomit on the canvas.

Fistfuls of cash changed hands, winners celebrating and losers cursing. Waiters circulated among the crowd, refilling glasses and replacing plates.

Colin Ross re-entered the ring, having collected most of his aplomb. "Well," he said, dabbing a napkin at a cut on his forehead, "I guess this isn't your typical night at ringside."

CHAPTER THIRTY-THREE

As the cleanup continued, Tina sashayed back to her place at the table, her face freshly beaming. The senator's two bodyguards, standing near Horace, turned their heads behind their sunglasses, fixed upon her, their expressions implacable.

"Well, that was quick!" Tina said to her table companions regarding the cleanup in the ring. "What'd I miss?"

"Some of the most extreme savagery I have ever seen," the senator said. "And proof that even the meekest of men can rise to do extraordinary things if they pull themselves up by their bootstraps."

"Wow, sorry I missed it!" she said, winking at him.

Meanwhile, the next bout commenced, an increase in weight class, and it proved to be much more conventional as two trained fighters clashed with all the ferocity they could muster. After what had happened in the first fight, they entered the ring intensely wary of each other. There would be no more such surprise victories tonight. Through a succession of increasingly bloody rounds, they gradually pummeled each other's faces into hamburger, drenched in sweat and blood.

Meanwhile, in between rounds, Roxanne introduced "Ambrosia" to Mogilevich. Horace shadowed them in the background, attempting to use the proximity to assess the gangster's security detail: three guards, bulky suits with bulges in the wrong places bespoke armor and weapons concealed underneath, hands gloved in black material resembling the gauntlets that had come with Horace's armor, but which he had chosen not to wear. He felt his own hands were weapon enough, and the gauntlets might have attracted extra unwanted attention.

Bunny's voice came into his ear, "His guards are wearing battle armor similar to yours, with full biometric telemetry feeding to somewhere. Trying to find out where. Trying to find out if there's a central AI or biologicals watching all this. Their armor also has some independent subsystems I can't crack. Also sifting for the serial numbers so I can get a make on it. Might be custom."

"Let us drink, Yvgeny!" Roxanne was saying. She raised a tumbler of amber liquid. An exquisite, silver-chased decanter of cognac sat on the table nearby. "A toast! To another year of success!"

Mogilevich's simmering eyes drank her in, savoring the perfect suppleness of her flesh as he raised his glass and drank the cognac as well. When they stood together, there was no mistaking the genetic relationship. Would his reaction be any different if he knew she was his flesh and blood? There was no question that this was a man who drew power to him, a magnet for men who craved such power. Roxanne had clearly inherited it from him.

Meanwhile another round of fighting rang in and rang out again, with neither fighter holding a clear advantage.

The waiter returned with a serving tray bearing prismatic crystal shot glasses and a bottle almost as elaborate as that of the cognac. Shots were poured, distributed, and tossed back.

Tina said, "Gosh, you're a swell host," then moved closer, intending to kiss Mogilevich on the cheek. Before she could touch him, one of the bodyguards interposed his arm, like the bough of a stout tree, and halted her in midstep.

"Oops!" she laughed, with a sparkling smile.

Roxanne made a wager with Mogilevich—of a staggering sum—on the current bout, then both women returned to their table with the senator.

Four more rounds passed, five, six. The men in the ring fought themselves into exhausted, battered piles, but they kept at it, coming out after every bell with fists and feet flying, at least for a few seconds until exhaustion overtook them again. The man with the deepest well of strength would live.

The senator kept attempting to ply the women with drink, which they accepted dutifully, but did not drink more than a dab to their lips.

And then, in the twelfth round, with the fighters' eyes swollen shut, the mat littered with teeth and spattered with blood, their hands pulverized into insensate lumps, one of the fighters managed to slip a hard spear-hand past an oncoming blow and bury his fingertips in his adversary's throat. The fighter flung himself into the split-second of advantage, swept his arms around the other's head, and cranked for all he was worth. A muffled *crunch*, and it was over.

The victor let the corpse fall to the mat and then collapsed to his knees.

When Ross returned to the ring, he said, "Let's hear it for Seamus Rodriguez! Holy Christ, that made *me* tired! Must be the altitude."

Fresh applause accompanied the victorious fighter back into the depths of the house.

Roxanne returned to Mogilevich, looking properly dismayed at having lost her bet. They passed readers over their wrists to transfer the invisible fortunes between invisible accounts, and celebrated with another round of shots.

Clearly not wishing to be outdone, other guests came to pay their respects to Mogilevich with toasts and wagers, gifts and tributes. Velvet boxes of pure-gold cuff links, solid-diamond watches, polished hardwood boxes of the world's most expensive cigars, vintages, and distillations accumulated on the table.

An anxiousness arose in Horace's body, a tension he found difficult to suppress. There were eight more men to die, and still he had not found his opening. He squeezed the tension into his clasped hands, flexing the chitinous plates of his fingers and knuckles until they ached.

Ross' voice rose again, "And now for our third bout of the evening! This one in the welterweight class. In the red corner, weighing in at 65.4 kilos, with a South American Federation record of sixteen victories—ten by submission—and four losses, a fourth-degree black belt in Brazilian *jujitsu*, Armando Carvalho-Silva!"

From the elevator emerged a young, swarthy man, a wiry knot of muscle and sinew, who jogged to the ring and went through the rituals of confidence and crowd-respect, bowing repeatedly, bowing to Mogilevich, crossing himself, kissing the golden crucifix around his neck.

Across the room, the elevator opened up again, and a man walked painfully toward the ring as if every step brought a wince of agony. His craggy face was shadowed by bruises and contusions.

"And now, fighting from the blue corner, weighing in at 65.9 kilos, a first-degree black belt in taekwondo, a brown belt in Brazilian *jujitsu*, the 2055 Arkansas Golden Gloves Boxing Champion, Jack McTierney!"

The name struck Horace like a sledgehammer to the sternum. Jack stepped into the spotlight of the ring, his face grim, his movements slow and ginger. Cuts, bruises, and circular burns covered his naked torso. His graying brown hair, usually slicked back into a forty-weight pompadour and accompanied by a jaunty grin, was now frizzed in disarray around a swollen, haggard face.

Jack's name almost jumped out of Horace's mouth.

He didn't know how many seconds of recognition must have shown on his face before he realized he was about to blow his cover, so he shut it down. Trying to conceal his reaction with a coughing fit, he turned away and struggled to compose himself.

At the sight of Jack's already damaged condition, the audience began laughing and muttering among themselves. Jack paid them little attention, just squared himself to face the young, muscular Brazilian who was going to be coming at him in less than a minute. The resolve and determination formed a clear foundation to the pain and weariness on his face.

Jack turned to Mogilevich and spat a wad of bloody spittle, then faced his opponent again.

The audience booed.

Horace's body started to vibrate with burgeoning rage. The only way to save Jack would be to act now. Right now. Jack had enough martial training to hold his own against his opponent, at least until youth and conditioning wore him down. Horace and Jack had known each other for so long, Horace was no longer certain he remembered how they met. If he didn't act right now, do something, the number of living people he could call "friend" would dwindle even further. It was one thing to throw yourself into the teeth of death, another to watch your friends thrown in for no fault beyond their unfortunate circumstance of association.

And he couldn't even open his mouth without danger of blowing his cover. He could not cheer his friend to victory. He could not react in any way. If he attacked here, right now, he would fail—the security around Mogilevich was too tight—and Jack would still be dead, and so would Bunny, Roxanne, and Tina.

With a ringing clang, the bout began. The Brazilian came forward, and Jack assumed a calm, ready stance. With a flurry of kicks, Carvalho-Silva came on, kicks that Jack blocked and batted down, but they were just feints to allow the Brazilian, undoubtedly an experienced grappler proficient in the bone-breaking art of on-the-ground fighting, to dive in close for a grab at Jack's legs. Jack fought back with a firm center of gravity and hammer-blows to his opponent's ears.

A quick twist, a flung leg, and they both fell to the mat, a straining knot of muscle. Jack's breath already sounded ragged and strained. Arms and legs slithered for advantage, wrenching, bulging. Jack was no slouch in the fitness department—he looked pretty goddamn salty for a middle-aged man—but he was already thoroughly tenderized. Horace had last spoken with him three days before. How long had Mogilevich's goons been working him over?

But then, echoing the savagery of the first bout, Jack clamped his teeth onto his opponent's ear. A howl of pain erupted from the Brazilian. Jack snarled and tore like a dog at a hunk of meat. The ear ripped free. Jack spat it out, and then landed several sharp blows against the ragged hole, spattering blood over his fist and face.

Then it was Jack's turn to cry out in pain as the Brazilian managed a joint lock, the kind of lock that, enacted at full force, turned a wrist into a shredded lump of gristle, tendon, and splintered metacarpal. The crunch echoed through the dome, and Horace's heart dropped into his bowels.

NOT YET! appeared in red block letters in his vision, and he found Roxanne's gaze fixed squarely upon him. **SAVE YOUR RAGE. OUR TIME WILL COME. I SWEAR IT.**

When he blinked the words away, he was blinking away wetness too. He met her gaze and let the steady depths of her eyes cool the fury that threatened to hurl him into immediate, disastrous folly.

The fighters kicked away from each other and scrambled to their feet. Blood dripped from the compound fracture of Jack's dangling left wrist. The Brazilian cupped a bloody hand over the gaping wound on the side of his head.

Never taking his eyes from his opponent, Jack knelt, picked up the ear with a nasty grin, and flung it at his opponent's chest.

With a roar, the Brazilian launched himself forward again, but this time ran into a solid front snap-kick straight to the solar plexus, which not only stopped him but doubled him over with a tremendous outrush of breath. Staggering back, his eyes blazed with pain and fresh ferocity, tempered with a new respect for his gray-haired adversary and a flicker of calculation.

The bell rang to end the round, and the fighters backed away from each other into their corners, where real trainers applied styptic ointments to the bleeding wounds. The Brazilian's ear was put on ice. Around Jack's ruined wrist, the trainer wrapped great wads of tape as thick as a cast. The tape would keep the wrist from flopping, but the hand was now useless, a liability. Both of the men were breathing now in ragged gasps, like exhausted dogs.

Round Two brought them together again, warily at first, then the Brazilian came in again for the grapple. They clinched, struggled, fell to the mat.

Every fiber of Horace's muscles yearned to charge the ring and drag Jack out of there, and Roxanne seemed to sense this.

IT IS TIME TO SHARE THE PLAN WITH YOU.

CHAPTER THIRTY-FOUR

After reading Roxanne's plan in his HUD, a calmness and sense of purpose seeped through the vibration in his torso, grounding him.

Now, for Jack's sake, all he could do was hope for a miracle.

The two fighters in the ring circled each other, trading blows and kicks. With cruel precision and purpose, the Brazilian aimed many of his shots at Jack's splintered wrist. One of the first things fighters of every stripe learned was to exploit any weakness. A cut above the eye, an injured knee, any point where pain could be amplified. Constant, grinding pain sapped the strength and the will, and the first fighter to run out of those always lost.

Jack did his best to protect the wrist, but he still needed that arm to block and grapple. He did his own hammering at the Brazilian's wound, but his body had already been so brutalized before the bout that he could put little strength or quickness into the blows. Pain hampered him at every turn.

Horace could not help glancing at Mogilevich and the guards to see if anyone had noticed his discomfiture. He felt like a bad poker player who had just missed the draw on a straight flush, squealed with disappointment, laid his balls on the table to be hammered flat, and then hoped no one noticed.

Another round bell rang, and again Horace could breathe. The fighters returned to their corners, gasping, sagging, trembling with exhaustion and pain.

The minute until Round Three ticked by with agonizing slowness. Every second was a razor across bone. Horace couldn't take his eyes off

Jack, wishing Jack knew Horace was here, that he wasn't alone. It was a lonely goddamn thing to die, and no one in the world knew it better than Horace. Even with tens of thousands of fans screaming his name, he had been utterly alone every single time the lights went out.

The bell rang, and the Brazilian charged like a bull, slamming Jack into the turnbuckle before the ring man could get completely out of the ring. Apparently Carvalho-Silva had spent the last round saving his strength for one great assault. Jack flung elbows at his opponent's neck and head, but the Brazilian went low, hooking an arm under Jack's crotch, and executing a fluid judo throw that landed Jack on his back with the Brazilian atop him. A twist, a whirl, and suddenly Jack's injured arm was jerked into an armbar, the wrist clutched against the Brazilian's chest, the elbow bent backward against the Brazilian's pelvis.

Jack screamed.

A phantom pain shot through Horace's arm from wrist to shoulder, the arm to which Andre the Titan had done exactly the same thing in '62.

A sound like a wet tree limb snapping echoed through the space.

Jack's body went limp, probably passing out from the pain.

The Brazilian levered himself up to kneel at Jack's head.

Jack's arms lay spread-eagled and slack.

The Brazilian drove the heel of his hand hard under the point of Jack's nose. There was a wet pop of cartilage. Jack's chin jerked upward once and then his head fell to the side, eyes half-open, and his feet began to twitch.

Horace's legs turned to water and his eyes misted. Even after a life fraught with so much death, so often *real*, it could still affect him. Amid the applause and approbation for the victor, he fell into another coughing fit to clear the lump from his throat and conceal the snot about to drip.

The audience gave a standing ovation.

Colin Ross stepped into the ring and began speaking, but Horace could not focus on what he was saying. The audience resumed circulating.

Mogilevich straightened his suit and said something to his security. He took a step from the table but was blocked by a guest bringing him another gift. Roxanne's eyes flashed, and she leaped up.

GO NOW!

Horace left the table, heading for the dome exit that led toward the toilets. Spreading smiles and congratulations, Roxanne and Tina wove through tables and guests to Mogilevich's side.

With each step past those priceless cars, past those sparklesilk suits, those embodiments of power and money, across the parquet floor toward that distant door, the cold water in his legs began to heat, and by the time he reached the door, the heat was sizzling, turning his hands into incipient Thunder Hammers.

A glance over his shoulder told him that Roxanne had been successful in delaying Mogilevich long enough for Horace to leave the gallery so that his absence was as innocuous as possible.

Even mobsters would hold a piss for two beautiful women. Horace would be waiting for Mogilevich in the toilet. When he came out, if he came out, Tina and Roxanne would be already in the car. Tina's job was to make sure Roxanne got out alive. Horace would be alone to fight his way out. It was the only way Roxanne could make good on her promises to all of them. To save Lilly and her children, Roxanne had to live. Horace did not.

Beyond the door was a hallway that curved with the contour of the house's outer wall. The walls were of pale teak, masterfully carved into intricate reliefs of pastoral scenes from an idyllic Russia, where peasantry toiled in contentment and livestock frolicked to the slaughter. A few paces down the hallway was a toilet, door hanging ajar, unoccupied.

"That's the one," Bunny's voice said in his ear.

He stepped into the most palatial shitter he had ever encountered. Every surface was marble, gold, or chrome. The feet of the porcelain commode were those of golden lions, the flush handles on the commode as well as the gleaming urinal also solid gold lion paws. The vanity was gleaming chrome and alabaster, the mirror surrounded by sparkling pinpoints of light. The toilet was surrounded by an enclosed wooden stall, with every surface either immaculately polished or intricately carved.

The air was redolent with sandalwood incense. He didn't know whether he should take a shit or meditate. Perhaps he would drop a long brown python down Mogilevich's neck after ripping off his head.

He slipped into the toilet stall and shut the door.

The moments began to tick by, each one kicking his thoughts to a higher gear. Should he hide behind the door? He was a master tactician of the pit, not the poo-poo room. And all three of Mogilevich's bodyguards would be with him. Maybe one of them would even hold the old man's dick and shake it for him. Should he go for Mogilevich first? That would be suicide if he didn't take out the bodyguards first. Once he took out the security, Mogilevich would be his to deal with. However, there was no question that Mogilevich was armed. Most likely, he would be a nasty customer all by his lonesome.

The door opened, and a shadow moved across the ceiling.

A thick voice said, "Somebody in here?"

Horace made noises like he was zipping up and grunted, then opened the stall door. There stood Joey Luca.

Horace ignored him and went to the sink to wash his hands.

Luca's eyes burrowed into him, flickering between recognition and confusion. Horace gave him a disdainful glance, dried his hands on a feather-soft towel, and stepped into the hallway, where Mogilevich waited between the two bodyguards.

Mogilevich entered without a glance at Horace. Before the door closed, Luca's reflection was following Horace with that look.

Horace paused near the bodyguards outside and reached for his breast pocket. "Say, fellas, either of you got a light?"

Before either of them could speak or act, his right arm swept up and he triggered the electro-fiber blade in his bracer. There was a tiny, electrical snap as it flicked out, thirty centimeters of gray mono-fiber extending past Horace's knuckles, and sliced one man from Adam's apple to temple. Horace's left hand lashed out and caught the second man by the throat.

Trained to be instantaneously alert, the second guard almost knocked Horace's grip aside, but The Hammer's massive, hardened paw reached halfway around the guard's neck, slammed it against the wall, and clamped as tight as a vise, choking off all breath. The man's gauntlet came up with another electric *snap*.

The armor of Horace's forearm seized tight, iron-hard, to stop the points of four blades that suddenly thrust out from the guard's gauntleted knuckles.

Then the familiar, warm flow of pain and blood told him the blades had penetrated his armor. How deep, he didn't have time to discern. The man's other hand gripped Horace's wrist and began to twist with an inexorable power that must have been augmented by the armor. But Horace's free arm swept toward the man, who did not see the oncoming blade until it was too late. It took him through the face and skull and frontal lobe, and his body went limp as a rag doll.

Horace let it drop, jerked his forearm free of the four blades—his pinky and ring fingers went numb—and charged through the bathroom door. He crashed straight into Joey Luca, who was coming to investigate the scuffle.

Horace grabbed the barrel of the slug-thrower that was already free of its holster. A burst exploded with deafening strobes of muzzle-flash from the auto-pistol. Bullets strafed across Horace's legs, ripping massive holes in his swanky suit, feeling like a succession of distinct but painless bumps. His legs seemed to slow and thicken for a split second before the armor released him to move again.

Recognition blossomed in Luca's face with a healthy dose of incredulous horror. "Hammer!"

"Hiya, Joey." Horace wrenched the barrel aside and it went off again, spraying connect-the-dots pockmarks up the gorgeous marble wall. The pressure of reinforcements coming any moment bore down on the back of his neck.

Luca jerked hard on the pistol, pulling Horace off balance and directly into an iron-hard punch to the nose. Horace staggered back for a moment, blinking away tears. Blood poured down over his lip.

"Code ten!" Luca yelled.

And then the lights went out.

The room fell into dimness, illuminated only by two small night-lights.

Luca tapped his ear in confusion, as if expecting to hear something that did not come.

Mogilevich burst from the stall, a chrome slab of pistol in his hand bearing upon Horace's face. Horace threw up an arm and ducked. The slugs raked across the arm where his face had been, the armor pulsing its protection against the barrage, but Horace felt a thump on the crown of his head, as if a nun had just whacked him with a ruler.

In the confines of the restroom, there was no time to think. He kicked Luca as hard as he could straight in the belly, driving him back into Mogilevich, whose next pistol burst tore through the ceiling and rained alabaster grit onto their heads. They both staggered off balance and Horace lunged with his blade. It went deep into Luca's belly. Luca made a guttural noise, and his armor, sensing the continuing intrusion, seized the blade and held it tight. Luca went down onto his back, knocking Mogilevich into the wall. Horace yanked hard to draw back for another blow, but only lifted Luca half off the floor. The blade would not come out.

Mogilevich slammed his hand against the solid-gold light fixture, and a section of marble wall fell inward. The gangster darted into the opening. Horace raised his left hand and fired the electro-fiber shuriken at Mogilevich's back before it disappeared into the opening, which whispered shut immediately behind him.

Luca curled around Horace's blade like a pinned insect. Horace could not pull away, so he fell upon Luca with his free fist, his first blow glancing from the side of Luca's cheek. Luca's free arm clawed at Horace's face. As Horace drew his arm back for another blow, tingling weakness made his arm feel as if it weighed two tons, like he had just spent a solid hour at the speed bag. His lungs felt full of broken glass.

With all the strength he could muster, he slammed his stone-hard fist again toward Luca's face, this time squarely in the teeth. The back of Luca's head slammed into the floor with a loud *crack*, and his eyes went glassy, the arm clutching for purchase at Horace's eyes falling slack for an instant.

In the moment of freedom, Horace took a deep breath, gathered his strength again, and raised his fist for a one-handed Thunder Hammer. Like a sledge it came down on Luca's forehead and burst his skull like a watermelon.

Every breath a ragged gasp, he hovered over Luca's body, trying to catch his breath for just a moment. His heart labored, struggled, tripped, and stumbled. The tattoos on his hands shone through their synth-skin covering. Any second now, more guards would converge upon the sound of gunfire.

He jerked on the blade again, but Luca's armor refused to relinquish its grip. All he could do was release the bracer and leave it.

He slammed the light fixture as he had seen Mogilevich do. The wall opened again, and there beyond lay a narrow passage dimly lit by red emergency lights.

The sound of oncoming heavy feet in the corridor filtered through the door.

He lurched through the opening and it whispered shut behind him.

CHAPTER THIRTY-FIVE

The passage crawled between walls, a narrow space filled with cobwebs and dust and the smell of rodents. Thirty feet from the bathroom, a mechanism built into the wooden studs revealed the backside of another hidden door.

Roxanne's voice came into his ear. "Did you get him?"

"Bastard ducked into a hidey-hole," he said. "Time to play whack-a-mole. Where are you?" He touched the wetness trickling down the back of his head, sticky in his stubbled hair, from the crease a bullet had made across his pate.

"In the car, but Tina ran back inside."

"Goddammit!"

Bunny's voice chimed in. "I can make their security chase their tails for a little while longer—oh, chase 'em! Chase 'em! Chase, chase chase!—but not much longer. Right now, they're combing the house for the boss, but Jimmy is sending false messages through their comm systems—hold it! I got him. The Bad Guy is in his office, going through his desk."

The crazed tinge in Bunny's voice did not fill Horace with confidence. Remembering how she looked just minutes ago, he wondered what she could she turn into. "Where?"

"Third floor."

"How do I get there?"

"How should I know? You're invisible to me. I recommend stairs. Kinda got my hands full..."

An explosion ripped through the structure somewhere and sent a deep shudder through the house. Dust rained down onto his head.

"There, that should keep them busy for a while. The White Rabbit is back, you doody heads!"

"What the hell did you just do?" he said.

"Had one of the drones launch a missile at the house. It was a very pretty explosion. Fire tulips!"

"You sliced a drone?"

"Yes, but it was very stubborn. I might not be able to hold it."

"Holy shit, make sure I *never* get on your bad side," Horace said.

"I would not recommend it, Mr. Potty Mouth. Now, don't talk to me. In the middle of a dogfight. Ruff-ruff!"

Filtering through the structure of the house came the distant whine of turbines and the ripping thunder of a mini-gun.

Roxanne's voice came through, "Horace, I'm looking at the blueprints of the house. Like Bunny said, the secret passages are *not* in the plans, but from the toilet, I can guess your position. Keep going and you should reach the elevator shaft."

Another fifty feet down the curving passageway, bathed in scarlet glow, he came to the end of the passageway and another door. He pressed a red button beside the door, and it opened into the dimly-lit column of the elevator shaft. Five meters below lay the naked, natural stone of the mountainside, upon which the house's foundations had been built. Twelve meters above hung the bottom of the elevator car. Two meters to his left was the service ladder.

Swinging himself onto the rungs of the service ladder, he began to ascend.

"Tina!" he called into his microphone. "Where are you?"

No reply.

"Talk to me, sister."

Still nothing.

The service ladder took him up the shaft, the steel and concrete enclosure eerily quiet, to the top of the elevator car. Pulling open the service hatch, he found the car empty and squeezed himself down through the opening.

"Bunny," he said, "I'm in the third-floor elevator. Where's his bedroom?"

A floor plan flashed into his HUD, with flashing dots to indicate Horace's and Mogilevich's locations. Then the floor plan shifted to transparent lines of varying opacity, indicating walls and hallways beyond what he could see, with a trail of animated yellow arrows on the floor indicating the direction he should go.

First, however, he tore off his suit and tie. There would be no obstruction to his movements, no veneer of civilization over his actions, and the black armor would provide better camouflage in darkness. Under the synth-skin, his tattoos shone through like a flashlight through clenched fingers. In his reflection in the polished stainless steel of the elevator walls, he resembled a disembodied head glowing like a jellyfish.

Opening the elevator doors revealed a hallway just as opulent as the rest of the house but swathed in dimness. The only light came from a door that was ajar at the far end, through which shone the glaring white of a shifting floodlight.

The yellow arrows on the floor pointed straight at that doorway.

Six doors, three on each side of the hallway, any one of which guards with guns could pour out of at any moment, lay between him and his target.

The dark, lush carpet was so thick and soft it was like walking on feather down, and it muffled his footsteps perfectly. The blaze of a floodlight came and went through the crack in the far door.

His ears sharpened to hypersensitivity, but there was no sound in the far chamber. The paintings on the walls of czars and czarinas seemed to watch him as he crept past, the eyes of ages past.

Then an electronic voice, impossibly deep and sonorous and menacing, emanating from hidden speakers, immersed Horace in ripples of sound from every direction. "Feed your head, children."

And then the music started.

A trickle of guitar riff. Backed by a repeating, wordless chorus of male voices singing an ominous crescendo.

"THUN-DER!"

The pounding bass of "Thunderstruck" ripped through the house at concert volume, pumping its strength into Horace's very bones.

His lips peeled back into a grin of feral glee, and he thought he heard a growl from the room beyond. "What the fuck!"

Horace paused with a hand on the door.

"THUN-DER!"

"Where the fuck is that coming from?" the voice said.

"THUN-DER!"

A voice emanated from what sounded like a walkie-talkie, a steady, comforting voice. "Unknown, Master. Regrettably, the audio is one of my systems that have been sliced. I am attempting to regain control."

"THUN-DER!"

"Do it! Or I pull your fucking plug! Total erasure!"

The music rose, and rose, and rose. The drums pounded like artillery.

A hoarse guttural cry of animal frustration tore from Mogilevich's throat.

Horace counted the seconds, waiting for his moment.

The music rose, then exploded with his cue. *"THUN-DER!"*

He charged through the door.

Across a broad expanse of antique, hardwood desk, Mogilevich stood, hand in a drawer, eyes bulging impossibly white in the darkness, mouth gaping. Behind him an enormous paned window reached to the ceiling with the floodlight from a drone sweeping back and forth through the glass. His hand snatched at something silver on the desktop.

The roar of seventy-thousand fans screaming Horace's name coursed through his mind like lightning.

The barrel of Mogilevich's pistol snapped up to face him.

"THUN-DER!"

The energy of crowds long gone washed over him again, and every hurt and sadness he had ever felt in his life disappeared in the tumult. He became a thing of steel and pistons and neon-blue.

In the window, streaks of tracers from the drones raked the stars, silken threads of phosphorescent slugs stitching the tapestry of sky.

Roaring like a bull, he dove across the desk, reaching for the gun and Mogilevich's throat.

Muzzle-flash painted spots in his eyes, and something ripped through his ear, turned the armor on his shoulder and arm into a hardened plate, but one hand closed around warm metal and flesh, and the other hand snatched a clump of suit.

His weight piled into Mogilevich and bore them both onto the floor.

Mogilevich's rings slammed into Horace's cheek with the effect of a baby's touch.

Like taking a toy from a toddler, Horace ripped the gun free and flung it away.

He gathered a knee under him, jerked Mogilevich off the floor by the snatch of suit, and slammed him into it again with all his strength. One of Mogilevich's ribs cracked. The jacket fell away, revealing a shirt soaked with blood. Horace's shuriken must not have missed after all.

"Where are the kids, fucker?" Horace roared in his face.

Then a second door across the room burst open. Dark figures charged into the room, laser lines and dots scanning the bookcases and shelves of jars. He slammed the mob boss down again, and the body underneath his fist felt softer somehow.

Laser dots homed in.

The chatter of submachine gun fire filled the room with light and noise, exploding across the hardwood desk and ricocheting from Horace's back.

With a roar, he seized Mogilevich with both hands and flung him through the air toward the guards.

Another spattering of gunfire at the spinning body, cries of "Hold your fire!"

The gangster's body piled into the two front guards, bearing them into the two behind. Two guards went down with him in a tangle of arms and guns, two staggered back.

Horace snatched up the chair knocked flat by his earlier lunge and flung it at the standing guards, then launched himself after it. The chair knocked down one of them, but the last guard brought up a fat, stubby weapon with a barrel the size of Horace's thumb and a massive drum of a magazine. A fully automatic barrage of shotgun blasts hammered into his chest.

Even under the armor, his Go Juice injector shattered under the onslaught. The heat of the muzzle blasts singed his face and hair. The entire torso of his armor seized taut, and the successive concussions not only knocked the breath out of him, the armor seized his ribs and diaphragm so tightly his lungs could not draw a breath.

The pounding impacts flung him backward. Another burst followed him as he tumbled, a thunderous roar that turned his hearing into nothing but a quiet ringing. Something hard swatted his right hand. He crashed into a leather easy chair, tumbled it over backward into shelves full of clear jars. What felt like a baseball bat slammed into his unprotected ankle.

Glass exploded under the barrage. Great heavy jars and shards of glass and isopropyl alcohol and gobbets of preserved tissue rained down onto his face, one jar crashing into his forehead with a painful thud, but it didn't shatter. His eye caught a close-up glimpse of the contents—a matched pair of oblong, biological globules with shreds of attached tissue—before the pain in his hand squeezed his eyes shut and the jar tumbled away.

When he opened them again, chunks of chewed steak dangled from his right wrist. He smelled blood. His blood. The entire forearm of his armor turned hard and tight, cinching off the spurting blood like a tourniquet.

A half-crazed absurdity jammed between infinitesimal moments of thought—What a useful feature! He would have to keep this armor for his next match!

The shotgun barrage ceased, and the sound of a massive magazine being reloaded replaced it, along with cursing, groaning, clattering.

Mogilevich coughed and gasped, "Blow his fucking head off!"

Footsteps crossed the room.

Horace shrugged away jars of testicles, struggling to right himself, struggling to breathe.

Laser dots danced through the jars, converging on his face. Two shapes loomed over him.

Then he caught a distinct *whish*ing sound, a round thump, a spurt and splatter. The laser dots swung away.

A burst of sound and sparks and smoke halted the figures.

A gurgle of pain from across the room.

He sucked in a great gasping breath and heaved himself upright. Agony lanced up from his ankle. His foot swung askew from the gruesome trench cut through it by a shotgun slug. The opposite half of the room filled with acrid, swirling smoke.

One of the guards sensed his approach and spun to face him—just in time to catch Horace's left roundhouse in the temple. Something crunched.

From out of the smoke between the pounding beats of music, sliding through the guitar riffs, emerged pale arms, a silken gown, and eyes as fierce as a leopard's. Tina seized one of the guns and with a deft twist wrenched it from a guard's hands and then she clubbed him in the face with it. She flung it at another guard, who paused to fend it away, only to have her sweep his feet from under him. He landed on his back with a terrific crash, heels in the air, and then Tina's fist slammed his front teeth into the back of his throat.

Then Horace caught the distinctive *snick* of an old-style switchblade from somewhere in the smoke beyond her.

"Tina!" he roared. "Behind you!"

Frozen in a moment of indecision between two targets, the guard before him spun back. Horace stepped in, captured the man's weapon arm in his left armpit and snapped the elbow with a hard wrench. In the middle of the man's scream of pain, Horace's headbutt slammed into his nose. Horace let him collapse and then crushed his skull with one last hard fist.

A glimpse of Mogilevich's gray-white widow's peak and savage eyes emerged from the roiling smoke, an arm wrapping around Tina's neck from behind. She instantly delivered a sharp elbow to the rear, driving a grunt from her attacker, but it wasn't enough. Tina convulsed. Horace heard the unmistakable sound of a blade stabbing into flesh, over and over like a sewing machine needle, the burble of lungs filling with fluid. Mogilevich dragged her back into the smoke, out of sight.

"Tina!"

Throwing himself into the smoke, dragging his injured foot and gritting his teeth against the agony in his ankle, his arms found only emptiness, blindness. His feet kicked a head lying free on the carpet, stumbling deeper into smoke, tripping over a limb, a submachine gun.

The chorus of "Thunderstruck's" guitar riffs tore the air like bullets. And through it, he caught the sound of footsteps stumbling away.

He waved his arms trying to dispel the smoke.

The face of a guard emerged from the smoke, and Horace cocked his arm to strike it down, but it hung from the doorjamb, nailed there by the electro-fiber blade through the eye socket, leaving the body to dangle there like a discarded doll.

"Tina!"

Bellowing through the smoke, limping on his ruined ankle, he found himself in a conservatory with a ceiling over-arched by a section of the great glass dome. A snow-white grand piano lay bathed in the light of stars and flickering tracers. Lush greenery obscured the room's limits. Across a floor of an intricate black-and-white mosaic, a dark, wet trail spattered, smeared by the prints of feet both bare and shod. As he followed, his own blood merged with the trail.

He followed the trail into the next room, a museum of sorts, filled with marble busts, wall-sized oil paintings, and glass cases containing ancient hand weapons, swords and daggers, sabers and double-edged broadswords, many of them encrusted with jewels, hilted in gold, ancient Slavic styles that resembled Nordic blades. Some of them wore their age as pocks in the steel, inevitable rust-spots carefully polished away.

Smashing one of the cases open with his elbow, he snatched a broad-bladed sword with a thick, gold-chased pommel. His massive hand made it look almost like a dagger. Its beauty made it a work of art, but it was still as proficient in the art of killing as the day it was forged a thousand years ago. It had a good balance and heft, and the edges were sharp enough.

Then he noticed the blood trails diverged. One trail went through a door into the next room, and the other...

Tina lay against the wall beside a display case of Chinese swords, a hand across her midsection, a dark pool spreading under her. Her eyes were closed. Her lips were wet.

He knelt beside her. Her eyes flashed open and a tiny stiletto slashed toward his face, but too encumbered by blood loss to endanger him.

Catching her wrist easily, he said, "Easy there, killer."

"Thought I could get him..." Her voice was a wet gasp.

He eased her forward to look at the wounds in her back. Multiple stab wounds, little wet mouths drooled crimson, licking at the perforations in her dress. "We're gonna get you out of here. Hang in there, darlin'."

"That'd be great..."

"You die on me, and you're gonna get the spanking of your life."

"Fuck you..." She said a name, too, but her breath trailed off to sibilance.

"Bunny," he said, his voice choking.

"There's a helo on the pad behind the house," Bunny said, "Ten minutes to a regenestation hospital from here."

"Can you fly it?"

"I'm offended that you even ask that question. Jimmy can fly anything."

"You and Roxanne okay?"

"We've had some close calls, but we're holding our own. Some of the guests have decided to re-enact the Gunfight at the OK Corral."

The faint crackle of gunfire sounded through his earbud.

Bunny said, "He's in the next room, hiding behind the bar."

"Guards?"

"None on the third floor."

"Thunderstruck" rose to a powerful final crescendo.

"By the way," he said, "Thanks for the soundtrack."

"It's Hammer Time."

He gathered himself, levered himself to standing, hefted the ancient Slavic blade, and dragged his foot behind him.

The next room was a well-stocked bar. Mirrored shelves glittered with glass bottles and crystal decanters, a walk-in wine cellar, the kind of place for a man who loved the finest of wines and liquors. The scent of cigar smoke lingered on the air. A bar about three meters long, a polished hardwood slab, before the shelves of scores of bottles. A trail of bloody shoe-prints circled behind the bar.

An idea brushed his mind as Horace surveyed the bottles behind the bar.

Bunny's voice in his ear, "I can't tell if he's armed. He's out of sight of the cameras."

The rest of the room was filled with low tables and antique chairs. Clamping the sword under his useless right arm, he snatched up a chair by the left hand and flung it straight at the wall of glass bottles and mirrors behind the bar. With a tremendous crash, shattered glass and bottles and liquor and splintered chair rained down behind the bar.

A cry of surprise and pain was Horace's reward. The room filled with the scent of vodka, whiskey, cognac, brandy, liquors with the highest alcohol content. From the low table next to him beside the ashtray, he snatched up an antique Zippo lighter, flicked it open, and thumbed the striker wheel. Flame.

He tossed the flame over the bar in an approximation of the cry's source. The flame arced down and disappeared. A flicker of blue and orange, then a *whoosh*.

Mogilevich screamed.

Horace waited.

Blue alcohol fire rose up behind the bar.

A figure stumbled upright, howling in panic, a torch of blue flame, flailing and slapping at itself in a vain attempt to extinguish them.

Horace caught the smell of burning hair.

He met Mogilevich at the end of the bar with his sword, driving the blade through the Russian's chest and out between his flaming shoulder blades.

"I guess you won't be fucking anyone anymore," he said.

And then, just to be sure, he chopped off Yvgeny Mogilevich's burning head and left it in his lap.

CHAPTER THIRTY-SIX

Cradling Tina's body in his arms, Horace followed the yellow lines in his HUD toward a back stairwell leading to the helipad. He couldn't run. He could barely walk.

Bunny giggled. "You're late, you're late, for a very important date!"

A tremendous impact and explosion echoed across the entire mountainside, making the walls and decor shudder.

"What the fuck was that?" he shouted.

"A drone, a drone, and now there's only one alone," Bunny sang.

"Was it your drone?" The last thing he wanted to share the sky with was an operational, hostile drone. After several moments of no reply, he said, "Bunny?"

Still no reply.

"Roxanne, are you there? Has Bunny gone bye-bye down the rabbit hole?"

Roxanne's voice, "Unknown. Did you get him?"

"He's as dead as Dmitri. And so is Tina unless we get her to a hospital."

The audible shudder of emotion almost choked off her words. "We're in the car. As soon as you're airborne, pick us up."

"No, thirty seconds can mean her life. Hospital first."

The pause and her tone bespoke annoyance at being countermanded, but she said, "Very well. We will attempt to descend the mountain by the road. What about Lilly's children?"

A stab of worry. "I didn't get that."

"We shall see what our new slicer can uncover in that regard. If we can keep her on the rails."

"Oh, guards! Oh, *guards!*" Bunny's weirdly enhanced voice sang over the house audio system. "The bad guys are hiding behind the cars in the gallery!" Then she came through Horace's earbud. "I'm keeping them busy. Engines hot and waiting."

Every step was a bone-grinding agony in Horace's wounded foot, but he carried Tina onward. His breath heaved. His heart tripped and spun, tripped and spun. Every step took twenty minutes. Her eyes would not open. He could not tell if she was breathing. She was still warm to the sensation of his one good hand.

Then they were at the side of the helo, a double-rotored speed-demon favored by the filthy rich. The cabin was so small that he had to prop up Tina in the front seat, strap her in, and then throw himself in the rear, cursing with frustration. He filled two seats. Before he could finish strapping himself in, the aircraft lurched skyward, leaving his stomach and scrotum on the helipad.

Below lay the stony sweep of the mountainside. The road down the mountain glimmered with headlights. Others were still clustered at the house's front entrance. On the parking platform, the strobe of weapons fire spattered back and forth.

"I see a firefight out front," he said.

Roxanne said, "Apparently there are some vendettas being discharged. We are moving downhill."

"Keep your heads down. We'll be back as soon as we can."

As the helo banked toward the glittering carpet of Las Vegas, Horace spotted two flaming wrecks lying off the road, one deep in the trees, the other on its roof near a sharp curve. Perhaps a kilometer off, a stream of liquid tracer fire rained down on several of the fleeing limousines from the military drone.

"I love spreading cheer and good will to people who so desperately deserve it," Bunny said. "Now buckle up and fly right."

The jeweled grid of Las Vegas swept under them with astonishing speed. Tina's head sagged against her shoulder, unmoving. He checked for a pulse at her throat but could find nothing.

Sadness streamed down his face until the next helipad rose out of the sparkling carpet to meet them. The carpet melded into white, then faded into black.

"Sir, we have to get you to a regenestation. You've lost a lot of blood."

"No, her first." He was lying half on the helipad tarmac, half in the helo, half-conscious, his good leg tangled in the harness of the rear seats.

"We've already got your friend regenerating."

"She okay?"

Four people were lifting him onto a gurney. "Too soon to say." An oxygen mask clapped over his face.

"I gotta find out about a friend. Buffalo, in the hospital. Coma. Gonna pull the plug." He was moving under bright hallway lights now.

"Jesus, what kind of suit is this?" someone said. "How do we get it off?"

"They can't pull the plug!" he said.

"Calm down, sir."

A prick and a hiss under the flopping meat of his ravaged ear. Suddenly he felt better, sleepy.

"Okay..."

Roxanne's voice was a husky whisper in his ear. "Horace, it's me. Can you hear me?"

He tried to lick dry lips, but accomplished little. "Yeah."

"You did it!" she whispered. "You big, beautiful son of a bitch! You did it!"

Warm fingers touched his cheek.

"Lilly."

"I am good to my word. She's in regeneration now, just like you and Tina."

A warm hand filled his good one. "The kids?"

"Bunny sliced Mogilevich's communication records like they were cream cheese. Buffalo PD has the kids in protective custody."

"You're the Goddess of Love and Mercy, whoever the hell that one is. Tina would know."

"And you are my warrior king."

"Hammer Time."

"So how come you didn't terrorize the whole hospital for *me*?" Tina asked.

"It didn't come up," Horace said.

"I wish someone would terrorize a hospital for me."

"You're a strange kid."

He waited for the inevitable profanity coupled with a literary reference he wouldn't get, but no such came.

Their beds occupied the same room, separated by a flowered curtain.

He said, "But if it makes you feel better, I would have."

Both of them were hooked to numerous tubes filled with regenite infusions.

He would be lying here for approximately a week while his hand and foot reconstructed themselves. Roxanne had paid for the process to grow him a new heart. It would be ready in two months, just in time for the holidays. If he took it easy, he might last that long.

Tina would be here for a couple of days while her internal organs healed the perforations from the switchblade. Her punctured large intestine would have turned her septic without the regenites to clean it all up.

For hours already they had drifted in and out of consciousness on the soporific effects of sedatives and hormones, trading banter. Horace vaguely remembered Roxanne and Bunny stepping inside. At one point, he woke up with a white rose resting on his chest, and no one seemed to know where it had come from.

Nurses came and went. Regenetechs came and went. Doctors came and went.

By the second day, he could remain cognizant for longer periods. Only the outline of his Go Juice injector remained on his flesh. Aches seeped through the nerve blockers on his arm and leg, even though all sensation and control otherwise had halted at his forearm and calf. His hand and foot were encased in regenegel baths that required utter immobility. Such procedures were nothing new to him, but that did not stave off the boredom of being bedridden, utterly immobile, for so long.

By the third day, Tina was up and around and dying to keep Horace abreast of the news. The consequences of what they had done were rippling across the world like a tsunami. The media was spinning itself into a whizzing frenzy. Some called Mogilevich an international power broker, a business tycoon, a respected philanthropist; others called him a criminal mastermind, gangland kingpin, corrupter of vulnerable politicians. Some news outlets were calling it "Bloodbath on Bonanza Peak."

The stories got wilder with each telling. Several powerful "businessmen" and their guests had been killed or injured. A military-grade drone had apparently gone rogue and attacked a number of vehicles. Yvgeny Mogilevich had been assassinated by persons unknown, likely a gangland hit.

Once Tina got on a roll, nothing would shut her the hell up; but it amused him, so he just smiled.

What about all Mogilevich's records? His communication and financial records alone could bring down great swaths of the global power structure. What about all that amazing *stuff* in his house, the art, the cars? Were his surviving lieutenants fighting over it like a pack of dogs? Would any of his other illegitimate children emerge to claim it?

Tina told him of another news story—she really had been chewing up the newsnets—about a rash of gruesome assassinations among the obscenely wealthy. And Bunny—don't even get her started about Bunny. She had mostly stabilized "somewhere out in La-La Land," as Tina put it. Bunny and Roxanne had been busy, and shadowy PR front organizations were busy spinning like information turbines.

"Bunny's data," he said.

"You got it." It had been coming out in clumps and drabs, dribbled all over the net, from no central source. The most damning of stuff. Public officials in collusion with the worst gangster kings. Dirty deals by the thousands. Corporate espionage that threatened to spark a rash of new wars. Slavery operations exposed, implicating dozens of the world's largest megacorps. Much of the information was twenty years old, but as soon as people started digging, they would find that many of the situations had had twenty years of secrecy to ferment, to fester.

Colin Ross had been killed in a mysterious car accident. His press people were releasing no details except to suggest that his limousine was attacked by a malfunctioning weaponized drone. The public outcry and grief were exploding all over the world. Intense public condemnation from activist groups had this morning spurred several megacorps to launch a study into the use of weaponized drones on domestic soil.

Word was spreading across the net of Regenecorp's collusion in fudging regeneration odds. The company denied everything, but its stock was still tumbling days later, and many were saying it was going to crash through the floor into the sub-basement. Corporative executives, those still alive, were being sacked. Board members had gone into hiding. Death Match Unlimited and all the minor leagues announced a moratorium on the fights, distanced themselves from Regenecorp, and swore that henceforth all regenerations would be overseen by neutral third parties.

Horace and Tina had been returned to their normal appearance, the implants removed. "By the way," he said to Tina, "I like you better now that you're back to the way you were. I can't say 'normal.'"

"Me, too."

"I didn't like the hooker look. It's better that you're less pretty."

"Oh. My. God. If you weren't an invalid, I'd beat you until no one could recognize you."

A soft knock came from the door.

Big, brown eyes in an elfin face peeked in, glimmering with concern. Horace's heart leaped, and a huge grin split his face. There Lilly was in all her beauty, even absent cosmetics, her hair a bit mussed. She was dressed in a t-shirt for another musical he hadn't heard of and a fashionable skirt.

"Hey," she said, a little timidly. "Is this a good time?"

His grin stretched even wider. "Absolutely."

Tina stood up. "That's my cue." She headed for the door, but two smaller figures crowded in around Lilly, one a kinky-haired, swarthy boy of thirteen, the other a pigtailed, carrot-topped girl of seven or eight.

The boy took one look at Tina and his gaze remained fixed. It was as if Horace could see the boy's hormones leap to a boil in real time.

Lilly put a hand on Tina's arm. "How are you?"

"On the mend. The question for the bruiser here..." Tina thumbed toward Horace, "...as well as everybody else is, how are *you*?"

"Same," Lilly said. She touched the spot near her collar bone where a tungsten *shuriken* had passed clean through. "On the mend. A little shaky still."

Tina started, "I'll just let you two—"

"Thank you," Lilly said. "For everything you did for us." The weight of gratitude in her carefully controlled voice left Tina speechless. "I hear you saved that bruiser's behind, too."

Horace would hardly have believed it, but Tina's cheeks flushed. She couldn't meet Lilly's eye.

"Aw, shucks," Tina finally said, scuffing the tile with her hospital-issue grippy socks. "T'weren't nuthin." Then she smiled back at Horace. "Anyway, you guys play nice." She took her leave.

The door closed behind Tina, and Lilly stood across the room for a long moment, squeezing her children close to her. Lilly and Horace held each other's gazes for another long moment.

Then she ran across the room and threw her arms around his neck. "Oh, my god! It's good to see your mug!" She held her composure for a second, then broke down in sobs.

Small arms came up to comfort her, a little carrot-topped head. The boy crossed the room more slowly, a look of wonder on his face. His dark eyes were bright and inquisitive.

Lilly cleared her throat. "Horace, I want to introduce you to my angels. Jimmy, Cassie, this is the man who saved us."

The little girl's eyes were big and green, with a spattering of freckles across her nose. She was, without doubt, one of the most beautiful children Horace had ever seen. "Hi!" she said, staring at Horace as if she had just seen a mountain get up and move.

"This is Jimmy," Lilly said.

"Hello, sir," Jimmy said. "Thank you for what you did. We were really scared."

"You're welcome, Jimmy," Horace said, trying to clear a hoarseness in his throat. Did the kid know it was all Horace's fault in the first place?

"I didn't believe Mom when she said she knew you," Jimmy said. "Sorry, Mom."

"You should listen to your mom more often," Lilly said, chucking him on the shoulder playfully. "Okay, rug-runners, go back out to the lobby with Grandma for a minute. I gotta talk to Horace."

The children chorused a "Bye!" and then reluctantly shuffled out.

"So what happens now?" she said.

"I guess we'll see."

She sniffled and wiped her nose.

He reached up and touched her face with his good left hand. His right hand was still enclosed in its bubble of regenegel. In a few more days, he would have a fully functional right hand as smooth as a baby's butt. It would take a few weeks to rehab to rebuild its strength.

He pulled her close and kissed her, and tenderness opened up between them like a new rose.

Something was coming loose in him that he was not ready for her to see, for anybody to see, an explosion of joy and sorrow preparing to crash like a calving glacier.

"Look, darlin', I, uh, got to, uh, do some business. Could use a little privacy, you know?" He pretended to raise himself out of bed.

"Okay," she said. Then she kissed him again, squeezed his hand, and departed.

As soon as the door closed behind her, he released a long, shuddering breath, and wept.

CHAPTER THIRTY-SEVEN

The six of them sat around the table in Campanello's: Horace The Hammer Harkness, Norman Trask, Tina O'Shea, Lilly Roberts, Vincent Caniglia, and Gaston The Freak Rousseau. He had, of course, invited Roxanne, but she had bigger fish-heads to fry. Bunny was staying with her eldest daughter and getting to know her two grand-children while trying to save the world.

In her previous incarnation, The White Rabbit had been a thorn in the side of some powerful people. Now, however, with the funding of Roxanne's empire behind her, directing her, she might well become a formidable global player. If she could avoid both prison and assassination.

Horace's chest was smooth again, except for the neat, vertical scar stretching from the juncture of his collarbones to his solar plexus. His head and face were freshly shaved. His new heart was humming along like clockwork for the first time in more years than he cared to consider. Its strength made him feel like he was back in the glory days—at least until he got up, moved, and all the old injuries took hold of his joints and muscles.

Another thing the heart had given him was a future to think about. He had never been much for thinking about the future. He tended to operate on instinct, living in the now, and since his heart had gone to hell, he could hardly manage to look past the end of a given day. So the last couple of weeks since he had gotten out of the hospital were a new experience for him. Planning something that someone else hadn't planned for him, building something from nothing, thinking about a future, and having someone he wanted to see in that future, were ideas so alien to him they made him queasy with worry. Then again, what did he have to fear? He had died twenty-seven times, and he had cheated it far more times than that.

Leaning back in his chair, wearing a new, tailored suit, and his once-bald pate now sporting a fresh growth of hair, Trask lit a cigar.

Vincent sat there with a cool, anticipatory grin, his sparklesilk suit glittering in the light of the candles, his eyes flicking from each of his companions to the next.

Gaston regarded each of them with an expression of cautious curiosity, having only just been introduced to Trask and Vincent. He had shaved his mohawk and trimmed his beard, appearing now to be much more conventional, almost respectable.

Tina wore a tailored business suit and dark-frame glasses that made her look like a hip librarian. It had taken some cajoling on Horace's part to convince Tina that her skills would be absolutely invaluable to training fighters who could win consistently, but she had come around.

Lilly sat beside Horace wearing a glamorous dress of her own design, a watery cascade of silvery-blue fabric. She had spent a week on the dress. Every time Horace went to her apartment to see her, she had excitedly showed him her progress. Then they made love with the enthusiasm of teenagers but the experience of seasoned adults. Today, she had been nervous to the point of nausea on the way to this meeting, but Horace had assured her that she would do fine, that the costume designer of a new pit fighting stable, one that would travel to every corner of the globe, was just as important as the three trainers, the promoter, and the money man.

Horace steepled his fingers with exaggerated pomposity. "So, ladies and gentlemen, perhaps you're wondering why I called all of you here tonight...."

About the Author

Freelance writer, novelist, award-winning screenwriter, editor, poker player, poet, biker, roustabout, Travis Heermann is a graduate of the Odyssey Writing Workshop, a member of the Authors Guild, an Active member of SFWA and the HWA, and the author of The *Ronin Trilogy*, *Rogues of the Black Fury*, and co-author of *Death Wind*. His short fiction appears in anthologies and magazines such as *Apex Magazine, Alembical*, the *Fiction River* anthology series, and Cemetery Dance's *Shivers VII,* and others. As a freelance writer, he has contributed to such game properties as *Firefly Roleplaying Game, Legend of Five Rings, EVE Online*, and *BattleTech*.

He enjoys cycling, collecting martial arts styles and belts, torturing young minds with otherworldly ideas, and monsters of every flavor, especially those with a soft, creamy center. He has three long-cherished dreams: a produced screenplay, a NYT best-seller, and a seat in the World Series of Poker.

Contributors

This publication would not be possible without the generous support of these amazing people. Thank you, all!

Bob Applegate
Mistina Bates-Picciano
Ian Brazee-Cannon
Rachel Brewer
Richard Chang
Jim Cox
The Creative Fund
Iain E. Davis
Jhaydun Dinan
N.B. Dodge
J.T. Evans
Nathaniel Finney
Thomas A. Fowler
Robert Fraass
David M. French
L.K. Feuerstein
Holly Hammond
Leigh
Sheila Hartney
Cody Heermann
Dorothy Heermann
Erica Hildebrand
Jeff Howe
Mark Innerebner
Lena Johnson
JwL
Richard B. Karsh
Carolyn & Chaz Kemp
Sam Knight
Tanith Korravai
Ty Larson
Matthew Lorono
Mario Lurig
Peter J. Mancini
Ann Myers
William Miskovetz
Franklin E. Powers, Jr.
Dan Read
Diann T. Read
Jon Reaper
Simon Roberts-Thomson
Brian Sanchez-Fishback
Keith Schuler
Kristie Seybert
Joshua Seybert
Kyle Simonsen
Jeffrey Stackhouse
Surly Stevicus
Gregory Tausch
Patricia Vandewege
Christopher Vogler
Amber Welch
Annie Zweizig